Ephemeral
Tomorrows

Book VI of The Quietus of Fate

By Brian C. Kershner

ISBN: 1-942082-12-6
ISBN-13: 978-1-942082-12-5

Acknowledgements

The Quietus of Fate series has taken a great many twists and turns over its life, and continues to surprise me with every chapter I write. A great many of the characters take interesting personal journeys, and challenge me to tell their stories with the gravity they deserve while at the same time not dwelling or reveling in them. It is important for me to treat every triumph and tragedy with reverence, while not letting things linger for too long.

I guess you could call that a pet peeve of mine. In literature and media of all kinds, there are times when scenes over-stay their welcome or become farces of themselves by hammering home a point that needed no elaboration beyond its essence. Death scenes are the first to come to mind. As it has become evident by now, there are no characters who are off-limits to meet their end, and while not all deaths are on-screen, the ones that are must have a purpose. The worst sin I could commit as a writer is to sully that purpose with a ham-fisted attempt to craft a hundred-line long death soliloquy. For example, I agonized for weeks over every single word of a particular death scene at the end of Future's Thorns. Yet at the same time, there were characters who spoke the least whose deaths reverberate the loudest.

There are still passages in these books that tug at me, stay with me, and bring tears to my eyes. Some of those passages I even have difficulty reading to this day. But powerful emotions like pain, loss, hate, and sorrow must be experienced, embraced, and dealt with. Writing can be a cathartic process, but then so can experiencing those emotions through the eyes of characters in the media that we consume. It is said that a picture is worth a thousand words, but if the words that I have written can help someone to come to terms with something they are feeling through the experiences of my characters, then those words transcend value.

B.K.

Table of Contents

From the ashes of a Dragon a Phoenix shall arise,
And a Ram will be blinded by the Light of Providence,
Shadows will be consumed in the flames of Pride,
While a hero battles a future of vice and decadence.

Laws of antiquity shall show the way to Tomorrow,
Men and Beasts shall tremble as the mirror shatters,
Light and Shadow shall become one in sorrow,
And hatred ephemeral shall rend the world to tatters.

The future is not yet written,
The past never truly dead,
The present favors the driven,
Time is how legends are bred.

-   Aralias Imstra
Prophecies of the Coromor

Prologue

Hearts Don't Lie

Creator's Calendar Year 1205; Light Reality

Bryn and Sabrina stood face to face for a very long time, just looking at one another without saying anything. Lissa began to grow more uncomfortable with each second that passed, suddenly clearing her throat as loudly as she could manage. Wolf could see Sabrina jump at the sound, but Bryn's look was more of amusement than discomfort. Without a word, Bryn took Sabrina's hand and motioned for the rest of the group to follow. Suddenly, as though thinking better of whatever she had planned, Bryn turned back and began to speak.

"Some of the things that will be said are not for those with tender or needlessly worried ears. I think that this wonderful girl and the man Wolf should come with me. Everyone else will be led to one of the dining rooms and fed. I know it is a bit early for a meal, but it will at least keep you entertained for a time."

Lissa stepped forward and scowled. She didn't like the idea of leaving both Sabrina and Wolf in the clutches of a member of the phasia, especially Bryn. There was something about the woman that Lissa didn't trust, and though she could not put her finger on it, she was sure that sooner or later it would come to her. Gwillim too took several steps forward, but did not keep his protests silent.

"Lady Bryn, I know it has been quite a few years, but do you remember me?"

Bryn released Sabrina's hand and looked at the older man for a moment and then smiled.

"You are that delightfully young and naïve Gwillim who fought as part of Korrd's army while he was in Brea, aren't you?"

Gwillim nodded.

"You seem to have aged well. Better than the others heroes of the Light," Bryn continued putting her hands on her shapely hips. "You do look more like your father now, and that is good. Though I think you would have been more handsome if you would have looked like Gwydeon."

Gwillim balked at the comment, and then when he heard Bryn laugh, he knew that she was merely toying with him. While it had not been common knowledge that Korrd Ranthall was Gwillim's father, those who did know had nearly forgotten the fact after Gwillim became so entrenched in the Rice family. Even the fact that Gwillim referred to Nathaniel as his brother helped to dull the memory. It wasn't until Gwillim had met Wolf that the recollection began to strike him, and now Bryn was flaunting the knowledge in his face.

"Don't be upset," Bryn said coolly. "I was only joking. Though, you may wish that you were not a member of the Ranthall family when this is all over. Now, go and enjoy the food. There will be time for stories and filling in of details later. Now though, there are family matters that must be attended to."

A soldier from the Army of the Fox appeared and motioned for the group to follow. Lissa lingered for a moment, but as she watched Bryn lead Wolf and Sabrina to another room, she reluctantly turned and followed the soldier to the dining room. Deep in her heart, she wondered what she was worried about; Bryn, or the fact that Wolf and Sabrina would be alone together.

* * * * * * * * * * *

Bryn led Sabrina and Wolf through one of the many doors in the throne room and into a dimly lit hall. After a quick look around, Bryn pressed her hand to a panel in the wall. After a moment, Wolf could feel the flows of the Blaze being pressed through the wall, as if they were extensions of Bryn's fingers looking for a switch. The flow of power disappeared, and a portion of the wall opened like a door. Looking at Sabrina's face, Wolf could see a knowing twinkle in her eye, as if she had known the secret passage had been there all along. The part of Sabrina that was Aerith Seth was making itself more prevalent inside Sabrina the more time she spent with Bryn, and Wolf began to fear whether or not she would be able to pull herself back from the memories if things went badly. Bryn smiled to both of them and then entered the smaller room.

When Wolf first looked into the room, he had to rub his eyes to make sure that he was really seeing what was in front of him. Bookshelves lined every wall of the room, except for a small section in the far wall of the room where the golden headboard of a large bed was pressed flush with the stone. Throughout the room there were objects of art; statues, paintings, sculptures, and half-finished sketches. Many of them seemed to resemble Bryn, with one brightly painted nude representation of the phase drawing most of Wolf's attention. The painting itself was not hung, but rather sat upright against one of the bookshelves next to a statue that seemed to have been carved from pure jade. Sabrina stepped into the room first, looking at the pieces as though she had seen them all before, and was surprised that they still existed. She moved from statue to statue, running her hand over some, and simply looking at others. When she came to the jade statue, which was also a representation of Bryn, Sabrina stopped, moved around to the back of the smooth object and ran her hand over the middle of the form's back.

"The mark's still here," Sabrina said absently.

Bryn smiled and joined Sabrina behind the jade statue. Curious, Wolf joined them and saw what Sabrina had been talking about. In the portion of the statue that had been carved into the shape of the small of Bryn's back, there was a mark that very much resembled an entry wound from a dagger.

"I remember when Grawn did this," Sabrina said looking back at Bryn. "He was so jealous of the fact that I could make all of these things for you that he resented you. He saw the beauty that he had in his hands and knew that he could not express the feelings that he had within him the same way that I could through painting and sculpture."

Bryn giggled. When the sound of the childishly pleased laughter hit Wolf's ears, it was like an aphrodisiac. His thoughts immediately went to the beauty of both the phase Bryn and the woman Sabrina. Suddenly he realized for the first time how beautiful Sabrina was. She was perhaps even more beautiful and desirable than Lissa. Wolf shook himself away from the thoughts and tried to concentrate on the conversation at hand.

"Oh my poor dear," Bryn said stroking Sabrina's cheek. "How it is after all this time that you do not realize that Grawn could never express his feelings for me even before you came into my life. Our alliance is nothing more than that, an alliance, and while we have considered ourselves man and wife for all these lifetimes, there is no passion there. And while Grawn still fumes about our little trysts, I have not let him forget about his affairs with Ellis."

The two stood again, looking into one another's eyes. An uneasy feeling began to fill Wolf's stomach, and he cleared his throat loudly enough to be heard. Sabrina seemed shocked again at her proximity to Bryn and took a step away inciting another giggle from the phase. Again emotions tore through Wolf, and try as he might to fight them, he could not take his eyes off of Sabrina. The words of love she had spoken in Frontier floated through his mind, and unconsciously he began to wonder what would have happened if he would have let her stay with him that night. But there was another voice fighting to be heard in the back of his mind. It was the voice of the phase Basille, who was screaming that Bryn was not to be trusted and that she was doing everything in her power to make sure she had the upper hand in negotiations. Bryn turned to face Wolf and smiled.

"It appears that we are making the young Ranthall uncomfortable," she said looking dead into Wolf's eyes. "Funny how he is more squeamish than his father or his uncle."

Wolf balked at the comment and stood as firmly as he could.

"But perhaps the time for reminiscing is over, and we should come to the matter that has brought you to me in the first place."

Relieved, Wolf smiled, nodded, and moved to one of the chairs that sat against the bookshelves near the door to the private bedroom. Bryn sat on the edge of the bed, and while Sabrina looked for a moment as if she would join the phase there, instead she turned and took a seat near Wolf, but on the opposite side of the door. Looking at Bryn, Wolf could see that there was a bit of disappointment in her eyes, but the look quickly passed.

"So, what is this threat that you mentioned in the throne room?" Bryn asked.

"You were always one to get right to the point," Sabrina replied, "but at a time like this I am actually relieved. It seems that someone is using the teachings of the Moridon in the creation of a new army. They call themselves the Creator's Torch Society, and they are reforming themselves as a new incarnation of the Hand of the Light."

"I see," Bryn said, her finger lightly tracing her full lips. "And so it was the portion of the story about the Hand of the Light that made you think someone was using the name of Aerith Seth?"

"At first," Wolf answered. "One of the members of our group, Susanne, was a member of this Torch, but was expelled after their leader was killed by Erdric Yarrow."

Bryn nodded silently at the name.

"She told us," Wolf continued, "that the Torch had been studying all of teachings of the Moridon, especially Moridon magic, and were going to use that knowledge to carry on the task of the Hand to exterminate anyone who gave their allegiance to the Shadows. But this task is misguided certainly, and I cannot help but think that your brother Erdric has something to do with it."

Bryn sat silent for a moment, her finger still tracing her lips in thought. Finally, her hand dropped back down to her lap and the knowing smile returned to her lips.

"All of this is well and good my little Ranthall, but there are pieces of this puzzle that you are leaving out, and for good reason. Instead of dragging them out of you as Grawn or any of the other phasia would do, I am simply going to tell you what I know. For instance, I know that you have brought the *Coromor*, the *Chosen One*, and two of the *Erieal* into my kingdom. I also know that you, little Ranthall, have the powers of my former brother Basille within you, and that one of the members of your little company is also a child of a member of the phasia."

It was only the influence of Basille's powers that kept Wolf from being nervous. Thanks to the memories of the Blaze, Wolf knew that it was child's play for a member of the phasia as old as Bryn to see the lines of power from people who made no attempt to hide them. This was especially true when the powers were the type at Nathaniel's disposal. Sabrina had also been easy to pick out as the third generation's *Chosen One* because of Bryn's ties to Aerith Seth. It was then that Wolf began to see the truth of the meeting in the throne room. Grawn had not asked them to leave because he did not want to be bothered, it was because he knew that even with his powers combined with Bryn's, they stood no chance against the amount of power that stood before them. The Army of the Fox would have been no good to them, and even the Stone guards would not have lasted very long in the fight that would have raged between the *Coromor*, his follower and members of the phasia.

"I see you are catching on little Ranthall," Bryn teased.

The nickname was beginning to grate on Wolf the more he heard it.

"Why do you insist on calling me that?"

A spark of defiance shot through Wolf unlike any he had ever felt before. It was as though Basille was armoring him against any ridicule or insult.

"Forgive me, Wolf," Bryn replied. "After fighting alongside both your father and your uncle, I cannot see you as any more than a little boy, but then again, I suppose that is the price I pay for living for so long. But there are more important things here than a petty nickname. If you believed that the reformation of the Hand of the Light was orchestrated by Erdric, then why would you have come here asking about Aerith Seth and tempting the fury of Lord Grawn?"

"It was something that happened after," Sabrina answered. "Rael and Trece happened to show up in Aradon looking to gather information for Shau-ling."

"I know," Bryn said quickly.

"Oh, so you have recently returned from the Council?" Wolf chimed in.

Bryn nodded.

"That is another reason that I am indulging you. Rael and Trece gave their report to Shau-ling about your little group and their findings while in Aradon. So, this revelation about the Creator's Torch Society is not as much of a revelation as you might think. Also, Rael and Trece reported something strange outside of Aradon, and so they led me there to feel it for myself."

"A large cloud of power?" Sabrina asked.

Bryn nodded.

"That seemed to come from the powers of Aerith Seth?"

Bryn smiled.

"But were also coated with a huge power that defied description?" Wolf added.

For the first time, Bryn shook her head.

"I can see how you mortals would have viewed it that way. Even you, Wolf, though you have the powers of a member of the phasia at your disposal, you haven't had the lifetimes of experience using them to realize what it is you were seeing. That power that seemed to coat everything in the area came from Shau-ling himself, but had elements within it that I have never experienced. Normally all of our powers operate with certain forces in a constant state. Those forces are time and space. While we all use our powers to create primal forces out of space, the space itself still remains constant. What was different about this footprint of power was the fact that neither time nor space were not operating as a constant. They had been changed."

Wolf could see that Sabrina was lost by the description, and Wolf himself was barely following the stream of thought. As though suddenly realizing that she was not talking to another member of the phasia who understood the nature of power, she picked up two books from the table near the bed and held them up.

"To make it simpler for you, imagine that these two books represent Aradon from yesterday, and Aradon from today. They are both the same in form and design, except one is a little older than the other, and people are in different places. If I use my powers in Aradon, either yesterday or today, the only thing that happens is that people die, buildings burn, or any of a hundred other things. But the things that remain constant is the fact that Aradon is still the same size and shape, and it is still either yesterday or today. But with the powers we all felt in the wood, it was as though this had happened."

Bryn took one book, turned it on its edge, and laid it across the other.

"It was as though Shau-ling had taken a piece of Aradon from tomorrow or yesterday or even from another reality and put it were the same piece of Aradon already existed."

Wolf shook his head hard, the memories from the Blaze barely filling in the details to Bryn's simplistic description.

"But why would Shau-ling exert his power to replace a piece of the forest out in the middle of nowhere?" Wolf asked after a moment of thought.

"That is the part that I do not understand myself. But I do not think that the two incidents are connected. The aura of power from Aerith Seth was weaker and older, predating the power exerted by Shau-ling."

"So it was from Aerith Seth," Sabrina said picking up on Bryn's wording.

Bryn nodded.

"So now we have three separate mysteries," Wolf concluded. "Erdric and the Creator's Torch Society, someone using Aerith Seth's powers, and this cloud of Shau-ling's power outside of Aradon."

"If I were you," Bryn said as she stood and smoothed her dress, "I would concentrate my focus on the Creator's Torch Society and my brother Erdric's involvement. I think you will find that it hits you closer to home. Shau-ling is not a force that your little group is ready to face, let alone question his motives. And as far as the person using Aerith's powers, if I know Aerith half as well as I think I do, the person will find you long before you find him. For now though, we should join your companions for an early lunch, and then I shall convince Grawn to allow you all to stay here for the night. You can decide where you want to travel to in the morning. I may even be able to find out where the Torch is heading for you."

"We again thank you for your help Bryn," Wolf said rising from his chair, "and if there is any way that we can repay you for this assistance, let me know."

"If you find Aerith," Bryn said quickly, "tell him that I love him. And tell him that I am still waiting for him to keep his promise."

Sabrina smiled, and followed as Bryn led the pair out of the private bedroom toward the large dining room where the rest of the People of the Ram waited.

* * * * * * * * * * *

Evening had fallen on the Kingdom of Barer when Wolf finally made it back to his room. The afternoon lunch had stretched to late afternoon and then to an early dinner. Bards from around the world were in Barer and entertained throughout the meal, and for a time, the People of the Ram had forgotten their task in the unlikely company of two members of the phasia. Perhaps it was the fact that Bryn had been an ally of the Light in the last generation, or the fact that they knew they didn't stand a chance against the combined might of their guests, but Bryn was a gracious host, and Grawn kept his objections to a minimum. Mystery upon mystery were being stacked like wood to be thrown on the great fire that was the War between

Emries and Shau-ling, and Wolf wondered how many of them would actually be solved by the time they finally made it to Shau-ling's palace.

A yawn escaped from Wolf's lips, and he stretched his suddenly tired body before reaching down, taking hold of the hem of his shirt, and pulling it up over his head. Just then, there was a knock at the door, and before Wolf could answer it, the door opened, and Lissa stood smiling at him. Her curly red hair hung down loosely around her neck and shoulders, and in just a white shirt and simple black pants, she looked more beautiful than she ever had. Perhaps it was the wine that was distorting his eyesight, but she was more beautiful than even Bryn. There were no words spoken between the two, and Lissa closed the door behind her and within a matter of seconds found herself in Wolf's strong arms. Closing his eyes, Wolf leaned in to press his lips to Lissa's but in his mind, all he could imagine was holding Sabrina like that, his lips against hers, her body against his. While his eyes were open, all he could see and feel was Lissa, but in his mind, there was only Sabrina. Falling onto the bed, Wolf found himself with the incredible situation of making love to two women at the same time, one in form, and one in thought. Each touch and caress was echoed in his mind. As he stroked Lissa's long red curls, he could also feel the soft waves of Sabrina's thick brown hair. The sensations running through his body when the act of passion finally began were almost too much for him. He existed in both places at the same time, feeling Lissa's muscular and hard body moving against his, sweat coating both of them, but in his mind feeling the soft and silky skin of the princess, her delicate pink skin yielding to his stronger embrace. The sweat from Lissa's lips mixed into the taste of every kiss, while in his mind he could only taste the sweetness of Sabrina's mouth on his. When finally it was over, Wolf collapsed onto the soaked coverlet of his bed, exhausted emotionally, physically; body, and soul. He barely felt Lissa cuddle up against him and pull the cover over them before falling dead away into the peace of sleep. Never though did one question enter his mind, and never for a moment did he wonder why.

* * * * * * * * * * *

It was a few hours before dawn when Lissa woke. Wolf was still there beside her on his bed, and the private smile as he slept brought an inner pleasure to her. She knew that he was dreaming about her. As gently as possible, she separated herself from his sleeping form, and recovered her clothes from the floor and silently got dressed. Lissa hoped that she could find a servant so she could enjoy a warm bath before going back to sleep, but doubted the possibility. After finishing getting dressed, Lissa bent over Wolf's sleeping form, kissed him gently on the cheek and then walked back to the door. Upon opening it, she was greeted by the face of the barmaid from Frontier.

Felicia was quite shocked when the door opened right in front of her, and it was only the fact that Lissa's hand immediately went the girl's mouth that stifled the scream. Lissa had been shocked too, but wanted to make sure that Wolf was not awakened accidentally. After a moment, Lissa removed her hand from the girl's mouth, and pressed her finger to her lips. Felicia nodded and watched as Lissa closed the door. When Lissa finally turned back, Felicia spoke in a hushed voice.

"Isn't that Wolf's room?"

Lissa tried to conceal a blush, but finding it no use, she nodded.

"Lucky girl."

"What are you doing up?" Lissa asked trying to ignore the comment.

"I've always had trouble sleeping, so I was just going to take a walk. I could ask you what you are doing awake, but I don't think I would be sleeping much either if Wolf were sharing my bed."

Lissa could feel the crimson returning to her cheeks.

"I was actually looking for a servant to run a bath for me."

Felicia smiled.

"Oh, that's easy. There are bronze vessels in every room behind the curtain in the far wall. I'll go down to the kitchen and have a servant bring up some buckets of hot water for you. I was heading down there anyway for a cup of warm milk. It usually helps put me to sleep."

"Thank you Felicia," Lissa said smiling, "I owe you one."

As Lissa walked away, Felicia smiled slyly.

"You have no idea."

* * * * * * * * * * * *

Sabrina tossed and turned most of the night in her bed. The dreams that plagued her mind were like none that she had ever experienced in her life. Aerith Seth's memories of his times with Bryn were what disturbed her the most, the sexual part of their relationship keeping her from the peace of slumber. In the part of her mind that was still close to consciousness, Sabrina heard a sound. At first she ignored it, but when it came again, it was enough for her to pull herself away from the lecherous dream and rouse herself. The sound was a knock. As she threw back the sweat soaked covers the knock came again. Wrapping a robe around herself, the princess hurried to the door and opened it just enough to see through the crack. When Sabrina saw who was at the door, she opened it wider in shock.

Wolf Ranthall stood in the doorway, his hair in disarray, wearing only a pair of unfastened pants. Before Sabrina could say anything however, Wolf stepped into the room, took her in his arms and kissed her passionately. Sabrina had never felt anything like the warm of Wolf's body against hers, or the emotion that was conveyed in his kiss. Part of her wanted to protest, but her heart would not let her. The man that she loved, but thought she could never have, was here with his arms wrapped around her, kissing her passionately. No words were spoken when the kiss finally relented, because no words were needed. The look in Wolf's eyes was all that Sabrina needed to see. He wanted her, and she wanted him. The next moment, Wolf picked Sabrina up in his strong arms and carried her over to her bed.

* * * * * * * * * * * *

Lissa awoke again, this time fully rested. The bath had done wonders for relaxing her tired body, and as she stretched and craned her neck, her body did not groan or complain as it had after the restless night in Frontier. Quickly Lissa dressed and took a quick look out the window to see that the sun was only newly rising in the sky. Eager to get started on their trip, Lissa opened the door to her room, and heard another door open at the same time. For some reason, Lissa felt as though she did not want to be seen.

Peeking out through the cracked door, Lissa looked down the hall and saw that it was Sabrina's door that had opened, but she was not prepared for what she saw. Wolf stepped out of the newly opened door and silently closed it behind him before walking toward the far stairway that led down to the main receiving hall outside of Grawn and Bryn's throne room. Rage built up inside of Lissa, one unlike she had ever felt before. Angrily she strode down the long hall and forcefully opened the door to Sabrina's room, sending it slamming into the wall. Sabrina shot up in bed, reflexively covering herself with the sheet. When she saw who it was, Sabrina's expression changed from shock to anger.

"What the hell is wrong with you, Lissa?"

"Did you sleep well?" came Lissa disgusted reply.

"What?"

Lissa could feel the rage build even more looking at Sabrina. Suddenly she began to see every way that the princess could be perceived as better than Lissa. Sabrina was a princess, she had a real father and mother where Lissa had been abandoned, she had softer skin, a nicer complexion, and a richer wardrobe. Lissa was just a common girl and would never be a queen or have any power. No wonder Wolf wanted her.

"You couldn't just let me have him, could you?" Lissa accused. "I should have known when you told me in the forest that you wanted him that you would have done anything to get him. What did you tell him? What lies did you spread about me? Did you give him that 'pity me because my father doesn't love me' routine?"

By this time, Sabrina was up and the anger boiled within her. The argument that ensued was one that had been brewing for years, through neither one of them had realized it. In those few minutes, every grudge, every hidden gripe, and every jealousy hit the air in a stream of one way dialogue. Neither were capable of listening to what the other was saying, as they continued shouting at one another. It was the shouting that woke Wolf from his slumber in the adjacent room, and when he arrived at the door to the room, the two supposed sisters had drawn a crowd of both servants and members of the People of the Ram. Pushing past one of the servants, Wolf tried to make his way into the room to break up the argument, but Gwillim restrained him.

"I wouldn't do that."

Ignoring the warning, Wolf stepped quickly into the room and within a matter of seconds had stepped between the two women and pushed them apart. Both were silent for a moment because of who it was that had broken them apart.

"What's going on? I never thought I would hear the two of you fight like this."

Lissa turned away and folded her arms.

"And I never thought you would betray me."

Wolf took hold of Lissa's shoulders and turned her to face him.

"Lissa, how could I have betrayed you, especially after last night?"

Lissa slapped him.

"Don't talk to me about last night Wolf. I saw you coming out of Sabrina's room a few minutes ago. You just waited until I left your room last night and came here to be with her didn't you?"

Between the pain in Wolf's cheek from the stinging slap and the confusion in his mind Wolf could not answer. He was also not in any state of mind to avoid what would happen next. Sabrina spun Wolf around and slapped him on the other cheek.

"You were with her last night before you came to me?"

Sabrina stormed out of the room pushing past both Wolf and Lissa, but shot a dirty look back at the pair before shoving several servants and Gwillim out of her path.

"Lissa," Wolf said turning her back to face him, "I don't know what you're talking about. I wasn't in here a few minutes ago, and I don't know what Sabrina is talking about. You and I fell asleep together and I didn't wake up until just now when I heard the two of you screaming at each other. Now if we can all just calm down and talk about this, I'm sure we can sort it all out."

Lissa pulled away from Wolf's strong grasp and spoke, trying hard to hide the tears welling up in her eyes.

"How could you do this? I know what I saw Wolf. How could you?"

Lissa fled the room immediately after her words, her hands covering her face, trying in vain to stop the flow of tears. Wolf was left standing in the middle of the empty room, trying hard to figure out what had just happened, and how he could hurt two women in his sleep.

Chapter XXXIX

Treachery from Within

Creator's Calendar Year 1205; Dark Mirror

Ever since the fall of Scalla to the forces of the phase Draven, the people of that once quiet and prosperous town lived in fear. Jeresei and Kalbraks roamed the lands freely, and if any human crossed their path, then that human would never see another sunrise. Most likely the unlucky person would find themselves on a spit deep within the palace of Scalla, slowly roasting, their screams sounding like music to the sick and twisted captors. However, in Draven's mind the humans of Scalla still did serve a purpose other than main course for a Jeresei dinner table. Draven fully expected his throne room to be cleaned every day, and that his meals be served to him as they would be to any proper ruler. Naturally, he always had the servant who brought him his food taste it first to ensure that there was no poison added, and for the first few days, many servants dropped dead without Draven raising a hand. Finally the attempts on Draven's life deceased, but the ritual of tasting continued, and every once in a while a servant would die. That was the price for continued vigilance. Servants did not work at the palace of Scalla out of choice. Draven's threats on their homes and families did not leave much in the way of choosing. However, those that did work at the palace learned that there were many perks to being in close service to the phase. First was the fact that the Jeresei and Kalbraks were forbidden to prey on those who walked the halls of the palace. In the first few weeks of Draven's reign though, many lost their lives as they were descended upon from the shadows by the quick red-skinned beasts. Even after the mandate began to be enforced, the servants were wary of long shadows and dark corners. Besides the tasters, cooks, and those given the responsibility of cleaning, there was one other job that needed to be performed in the palace. This assignment was usually given to the youngest and swiftest of the servants, and that position was torch lighter.

Near dusk every night, a single servant went as quickly as possible through the palace lighting the many torches and lanterns in the palace. The last to be lit were the ones in the throne room and Draven's private chambers. It was like delaying the inevitable. Every slave who ended up with the position of torch lighter knew they would have a chance to be in the presence of Draven alone, and wanted to avoid it as much as possible. Several torch bearers had merely been in the wrong place at the wrong time when Draven lost his temper and used his granted abilities as a phase to strike down the unwitting slave. So, there was a measure of fear in the poor young boy as he slowly opened the door to the throne room and crept in as quietly as possible.

At first when the young boy looked around, he sighed with relief as neither Draven nor his monstrous host called the Dark Riders were present. Not allowing himself to get comfortable with the silence, the boy quickly moved around the room, lighting torches and lanterns, until he came up the dais to light the torches near the throne. At the bottom of the short choppy steps there was a smear of drying blood, and the table that had once stood near the throne had been crushed by falling debris. Looking up, the boy could see a huge hole that had been ripped in the ceiling. A new fear crept into the boy's heart, and he moved even faster lighting the remaining torches and lanterns before moving toward the door to Draven's private chambers. Half way to the door, the boy saw a blue light out of the corner of his eye, and immediately froze. Turning toward it, the boy watched the portal begin to open, and fear overwhelmed him. For a second he was unable to move, but finally dropped his steel-shafted torch and ran for the still open throne room door. He had only barely closed the door behind him when the portal finished forming and never saw the three forms that emerged.

The first form shot out of the portal like he had been flung from a catapult, and continued in a long high arch before finally landing on the far side of the room. Two daggers were in the man's hands a moment later, and the blades of the daggers radiated the pure power of the string of Earth. For a moment, nothing happened, and the man straightened and scratched his head with the hilt of his dagger. A blond girl emerged from the portal next, followed by another woman in a short red dress.

"It doesn't make any sense," Gideon said quickly turning to his female companions, "at least da Dark Riders should 'ave been here."

Bryn, ignoring her son moved over to the dais, kneeling quickly to examine the red smear on the floor and the large stain on the red carpet. Running her fingers over the drying blood, she scooped up some of it with the tips of her fingers and looked closely at it. The liquid was thick and still very red, despite the fact that it must have been several hours old.

"Phasia blood," Bryn said after a moment more of study. "And unless I miss my guess, it's Draven's."

Taya too had moved toward the dais, but to the other side of the throne.

"There are more blood stains over here, and then of course this nice big hole in the roof. It doesn't look like it was an architectural genius who made it either."

Bryn closed her eyes and opened herself up the Blaze. What greeted her was an amazing mass of power, the likes of which should not have been able to be contained by the feeble walls of the palace. Draven's use of the Blaze was clearly evident, as well as some of the power used by his Dark Riders. The fact that Nightwing's power was there also meant that for a time, Gwydeon Sandar had also been part of whatever had happened, but as she probed deeper, the line of power that had been part of Nightwing disappeared. That was when Bryn found the power that scared her the most. The power that Emries had given to his champions deserved respect from even the phasia, but it was nothing that the phasia feared because it was in part akin to their own, and therefore operated under certain rules. Every phase knew that there were things that the *Coromor, Chosen One,* and the *Erieal* could not do, just as the phasia themselves had things they could not do. One in particular was the inability to create life out of nothingness. That feat was even hardly possible for Emries and Shau-ling. They both needed a place to start from, and often that was the Blight, the formless mass on the edges of consciousness, where life is death and form is formlessness. However, the power that Bryn found staring back at her defied the understanding of even the ancient memories of the Blaze, and that was the power of the Creator. Finding the new and frightening power, Bryn's eyes snapped open, and she quickly realized that she was lying on the floor and Gideon was holding her.

"What's wrong Bryn?" he asked as soon as he saw that her eyes had opened. "Ye suddenly went white as a sheet and dropped ta the ground."

Bryn nodded her head silently and sighed.

"I'm fine," she said quickly, sitting up. "And please Gideon, stop using that damn accent."

That was all Gideon needed to know that Bryn was alright. Despite her protests, Gideon helped her to her feet and then made his way over to where Taya stood, examining the hole in the ceiling. It felt strange for them to be home again, and in a way, it didn't even feel like home any longer. Too much had happened to them in their time away, and in Gideon's heart, when Erika died, Scalla died with her. Bryn too was examining the room, but her mind was more interested in tracing the battle that had raged in the room. It was obvious that the strings of power that flooded the room were those of a battle, especially because of the amount of pure Blaze energy that had been channeled. However, unlike a battle that Zarsi or Saurn would fight, Draven's battles were much easier to track because of the way that he used the Blaze. Most of the phasia fell back on it like a last resort, using pure streams of the Blaze to level towers, decimate armies, or keep an opposing phase on the defensive. Others, like Saurn and Zarsi, wove a little bit of the Blaze into every attack, making even a stream of normal fire ten times deadlier. Draven took a different approach when using the Blaze, and took a page from his predecessor Basille's book.

Basille had never considered the Blaze a force that should be used as a direct offensive tool. It was more suited, in his mind, as a defensive measure and a force that could be used to enhance the powers that had already been granted by Shau-ling. So, Basille channeled the Blaze into himself, increasing the power and endurance of his muscles, accelerating his reflexes to the point that no mortal would be able to keep up if he ever truly exerted himself. Taron stumbled on this same ability, but his slow-witted and arrogant tendencies never allowed him to extend that knowledge to its fullest potential. Bryn, seeing what Basille had accomplished with his use of the Blaze turned it within herself also, but as that fighting had never been her forte, she instead increased her physical beauty, until she had surpassed Caris, sparking a new war between the two sisters. Draven had seen the wisdom of Basille and turned the Blaze internally also, making him faster and more agile than any other phase, save perhaps the twins Rael and Trece who seemed to have inherited several advantages from Kamen's string. So, in tracing a battle where Draven fought, a phase, or any other person who could see the residue of power, could see every movement that Draven made. For several minutes Bryn was lost in the battle that only her eyes saw. The duel that raged between Draven and what Bryn could only perceive as a god was impressive and frightening in its speed, skill, and lethality. She then could see the end of the battle and gasped loudly, prompting more responses from her family.

"Did you find something Bryn?" Taya asked quickly.

Bryn could only nod. Gideon and Taya were at her side a moment later, and were not able to see the flash of bright white light that flashed briefly through the slightly open door of Draven's private study.

"There was an incredible duel here between Draven and someone who wielded the Creator's power as though it was his own. Sometime during the battle Nightwing was destroyed, as was one of the Dark Riders. Then the battle raged even hotter. The two stalked each other for a long time, and then the pace increased until they moved so fast that I doubt the human eye could have perceived their movements."

Gideon winced. If Nightwing had been destroyed, then Gwydeon was lost.

"How did it end?" Gideon asked, not waiting for Bryn to continue.

"Draven lost."

The voice was familiar, and as Gideon spun toward the now open door to the adjoining chamber, he was relieved and elated to see Gwydeon standing proud and tall. It was only after Gideon had a moment to truly look at the man that he had grown to respect and call a friend, that confusion set it. Maybe it was the way that he held himself proudly, or maybe it was the confident look in his eyes. No, it was the wings.

* * * * * * * * * * *

Draven looked up at the form of Wrath and prepared to create a portal. The War for Ascension would continue briefly enough for him to destroy Rael and Trece, and then Draven would turn his sights back to those who wounded him so deeply. Gwydeon Sandar had nearly robbed him of his life, and only because he had not been thorough in destroying Vengeance, Draven still lived. The phase swore that the Brother of Angels would find his newly sprouted wings clipped long before Draven would allow himself to be put in such a position again. Suddenly Draven felt flows of power in the back of his mind. There were two portals forming. Once was centered near Vengeance, while the other was centered in the throne room of the palace. As the portal formed, Draven waited. He knew that the portal had been originated by one of his Dark Riders, and Draven felt the sly smile form on his face. Perhaps he would not have to trifle with the twins after all. The other portal bothered Draven a bit though. Every member of the Dark Riders had a very limited ability to create portals, and when they returned from completing their orders their portals could only go to one of two places. The first was the throne room of the place of Scalla, the other was to Draven himself, wherever he was. Draven could feel that the portal forming near him was of one of the Dark Riders, but the same was not true of the portal in the throne room. That portal had been made by a phase. Draven felt the smile on his face grow larger. Someone had thought they could sneak into the kingdom and take him out of the little war before he could launch an attack on anyone else. Draven wondered who it was. Surely, Jeroch was not brave or stupid enough for such a maneuver, but it was just like Grawn or Warron to try something so direct. Draven would have quite a surprise for the unfortunate phase after he finished hearing the report from his Dark Riders.

CHAPTER 39

The portal finished forming, and a moment later, Holocaust stepped through. Immediately Vengeance went to work, repairing the wounds that scarred the once flawless armor of the creature. Half of the floating skull was riddled with cracks that could not easily be fixed, even by the reality altering powers that Vengeance wielded.

"What happened?"

Holocaust had not been made with the ability to communicate with words or any other form of true language. However, because of its connection with Draven, Holocaust did have the power to transmit his thoughts and memories directly into the mind of his master. For the next few moments, the exact details from the battle against Logan Ranthall, Caris, Rael, and Trece played out in Draven's mind, and with every image that filled his mind, Draven's anger grew in intensity. The hatred for Logan Ranthall burned through him like a fire that could never be quenched, and even if Draven ripped the mortal apart with his bare hands, it would still not be enough. Even though Holocaust had not seen the end of the battle, Draven assumed that the Flame had been destroyed by the combined might of the four traitors, and since Shadow had not returned from the battle, it was safe also to assume that he too had been killed. Two of his Dark Riders were dead, and Draven would have his revenge soon enough. However, there was time enough for that later. One of his brothers from the Council had stupidly encroached on the sovereignty of his kingdom, and Draven would begin to take his measure of revenge on the foolish soul.

* * * * * * * * * * *

Bryn took several steps back when she saw the man Gwydeon Sandar enter the room. She had been with the group who had called themselves the People of the Dragon once upon a time, and Gwydeon had been one of the most prominent members of that group. It was, in fact, Gwydeon who had put the final nail in Bryn's coffin through his collaboration with Emries. Gwydeon had tied her to the side of the Light in the previous generation, and part of her would never forgive him for that. When she learned upon her rebirth that Gwydeon had survived the final battle with Shau-ling, and had been the instrumental force in defeating Jeroch, something within her ran cold. A mortal had made it all the way to Shau-ling's throne room and lived, and he had not shown the touch from Emries or Shau-ling's influence at all. The only corruption on him was the love in his heart for that woman Midarin Rice. While Bryn was sure Midarin was a charming woman in the privacy of a bedroom, she could not see the formerly exiled princes as a match for the caliber of hero that Gwydeon Sandar was. For all intents and purposes, Gwydeon Sandar was everything that Aerith Seth had once been, but without the aid of powers. Now though Gwydeon had gone through several transformations, and not just due to his advancing age. In fact, as Bryn looked at the man, his appearance was the same as it had been the first day that he left Aradon, tagging along with his friends who had been tapped by Emries to save the world. The creature that had been named Nightwing had touched Gwydeon, that much was certain, every member of the phasia who paid attention to the battle at Brea knew that fact to be true. But however long the man had spent beneath the metal shell, none of the power still hung on him. The power that did inhabit him now was what made Bryn step back. It was the same signature of power that she had felt when probing the area and watching the battle that Draven had fought. Somehow, Gwydeon had been imbued with the powers of the Creator. However, Gwydeon was not alone. After stepping through the doorway, making sure his wings cleared the narrow doorway, a young woman entered carrying a sword that Bryn instantly recognized as the Sword of the Ram. Draven had doted over its abilities and that he would use it to strike down the phasia with little or no regard for them, and now it was in the hands of this little girl. Obviously, the sword was the trophy that Gwydeon chose to keep from the battle, though Bryn would have been happier if Gwydeon would have taken Draven's head.

"You don't need to be afraid of me Bryn," Gwydeon said looking at the phase, "I have no reason to harm you. Besides, if Gideon is here with you, I am sure it is by choice."

Gideon shook off the confusion and walked quickly over to his old friend. They embraced a moment later, with Gideon trying to carefully place his hands to avoid contact with the bright white wings. As soon as the two stepped away from one another, Gideon hesitated and then spoke.

"When we heard 'bout Brea, we thought ye were dead," Gideon said in his thick accent which brought an aggravated stare from Bryn. "Den da whole Nightwing t'ing came out, and thanks ta Bryn here, Taya and me were able ta put together da pieces and figure out it was you da whole time."

Gwydeon's blank expression prompted Gideon to continue.

"Give me a little bit more credit den dat, Gwydeon. Ye were very careful in da way da troops attacked, usin' portals ta move da Stone inta position, and den keepin' da Jeresei from guttin' everyt'ing in sight. Not only dat," Gideon continued, "but ye also called a retreat when ye could 'ave destroyed da entire place."

"And you were merciful in your duels against Midarin and Pike," Taya added.

Gwydeon looked past Gideon at the young blond woman.

"You look more like your mother every year," he said quickly.

The girl blushed slightly, taken off-guard by the comment. Gwydeon laughed and scratched his head.

"You're probably wondering about the wings."

Gideon nodded, trying not to look to eager for an explanation. The girl, which Gideon immediately recognized as Sabrina Binosear, also seemed to take interest in the explanation that was coming.

"Well," Gwydeon began, "you already know that I was made into Nightwing by Draven. How that happened I don't want to explain right now, but it's really not important. I'll just say that it was the only choice I had at the time and leave it at that. I did Draven's bidding, and I brought Sabrina to him, but there was more that I needed to know. Draven is a phase, and even when they are carrying out their own plans, they are still the creation of Shau-ling, so I went to see him. Pike, for all his courage would not let Sabrina go without him, and so, I had to take Pike with me. I couldn't let him go one on one with Draven, so I took him with me to see Shau-ling."

Gideon swallowed hard. As if sensing Gideon's fear, Gwydeon smiled.

"It's not as bad as you might think. Shau-ling acted as though he had been waiting on us. Naturally, it took Pike a few minutes to listen to reason and understand that if Shau-ling had wanted him dead, he would have been crushed in the matter of a few seconds. But you know Pike, he's a hot head, and even twenty years under an island isn't enough to cool him off."

Gideon smiled and nodded, leaving the questions about Pike's return from the dead for another time.

"Shau-ling then explained that our world was sick, and that it was man that was the cause of the sickness. Shau-ling had taken the fight to the mortals through his phasia, but in the process, they lost their way. Emries too had lost his way, and began to fight for his people, the mortals as though he were the Creator. Both Shau-ling and Emries had sinned in pride, and through the actions of one phase, Basille, the fate of the world may well had been sealed."

"The breach," Bryn commented, everything suddenly dawning on her.

Gwydeon nodded.

"Would someone fill in the mere mortals," Taya said putting her hands on her hips and glaring at the rest of the assembled group.

"The breach," Bryn said trying to keep her tone from being condescending, "is the term that the phasia have given to the division of worlds that the Creator has made. Because of Basille's actions in the last generation after his death, another world was created, a world where some things have happened differently."

"Bryn is very astute, as that I am sure Shau-ling had kept this hidden from his children so far," Gwydeon countered. "It is only because of her connection with the past, and the fact that she was one of the original phasia that she is able to even perceive the breach. In the beginning her feelings would have been only that, feelings. However, as they began to happen more frequently, the feeling that something was wrong with this world became more prevalent."

"And," Bryn continued, "I had to know why I was feeling the way I did. So, Ellis and I did some extensive searching, which took us back to the

Blight. The Blight was reduced to nearly half its size, and within the Blight we could feel the breach. It is only now beginning to come together in my mind thanks to being this close to Gwydeon and now hearing the words that were spoken by Shau-ling."

Gideon sat down on the dais and looked up at his friend.

"So, dere's a whole other world. And t'ings are different dere?"

"Because of the knowledge that the Creator has given me," Gwydeon started, and then suddenly stopped. "Oh, I hadn't gotten to that part yet. Well, anyway, I came back here after my meeting with Shau-ling to fight Draven, and the Creator freed me from my bonds as Nightwing and gave me real wings and some of His power. Now I have knowledge from the other world, and I understand better what is going on. In the other world, the phasia have not conquered everything, and the forces of the *Coromor* have a chance to prosper. But this is not just a coincidence. The Creator is tired of this war between Emries and Shau-ling and wants an end put to it once and for all. So, if Emries' forces are right, they should be able to conquer whether they have the advantage or not, the same for Shau-ling's forces."

"And if neither are right?" Taya asked.

"Then the Creator will sentence this world to fire and start over somewhere else."

Everyone in the room was silent for several moments until Gideon stood up, drew one of his daggers, and a moment of thought slashed the flesh on his palm.

"Then we have to figure out which side is right and make sure that they win," Gideon said, speaking in his proud clear voice, suddenly serious. "I swear it with my own blood that I will not let this world die if I have one breath left to stop it from happening."

Suddenly a portal formed in the center of the room. Bryn had been so distracted by Gwydeon's new powers that she had ignored the flares of power in the back of her mind. Draven and his pets Holocaust and Vengeance emerged the next second, each armed and ready for a right. A thunderous wind battered the walls of the palace moments later as the huge form of the beast Wrath descended through the hole in the ceiling and stood eager to fight and kill all who opposed his master.

"I don't think you will have much breathing left to do when I send you to meet your darling wife," Draven prodded. "And you, little girl," he said pointing at Sabrina, "belong to me."

Gwydeon's wings extended slightly, and in the next moment, the bright crystalline blade was in his hands. The Brother of Angels stepped in front of Sabrina and held up the slightly blood colored blade of his sword and pointed it directly at the heart of his nemesis.

"I killed you once," Gwydeon's voice boomed, "and I'll kill you again."

Draven laughed.

"No chance of that. I have other matters to attend to...like making sure the forces of the Shadow in the other world prevail."

The portal that formed under Draven's feet the next moment signaled the attack of the Dark Riders. Holocaust loosed a stream of liquid fire that sent Gideon and Taya diving out of the way, while streams of lightning were blocked by a wall of earth that Bryn created with the barest amount of time to spare. Gwydeon did not move, but wrapped his wings around himself. The flame hit the snow white feathers of the wings and not even a single feather was damaged by the flame. When the flames finally dissipated, Gwydeon retracted his wings and launched into action, taking the fight to Wrath, the largest, and conceivably most dangerous of the Dark Riders.

"Take out Vengeance," Gwydeon called as he flew quickly across the room and locked blades with the monster. "She's the key."

Gideon's dagger hit the air the next moment, but a streak of lightning hit the blade, and the next moment it had reappeared, impaling the hand that Gideon had used to throw it. Holocaust let another volley of fire flow from its extended hands, but this time Taya was ready for it. She encased herself in a bubble of air and floated above the attack, while at the same time, creating a massive gust that blew the attack back on the Dark Rider.

Vengeance's powers came into play the next moment, warping reality so that the space occupied by Taya's wind did not exist for the flame, and the molten liquid ended just before the prevailing winds and reappeared on the back side of the gust, causing Gideon again to leap clear. Bryn took the momentary distraction as an opportunity and turned her powers loose on Vengeance. Though still weakened from her fight with Ellis, Bryn created a pillar of Blaze fire around Vengeance, burning her inside out. Gideon could still see the sparks leaping from Vengeance's blade, and before she could exert her power to save herself, Gideon hurled another dagger, knocking the blade out of the white-skinned woman's hand, letting her continue to burn. Sabrina leapt into action also, dodging the winds and liquid fire, recovering the lightning sword from where it lay near the pillar of Blaze. She laid it quickly the ground and drove the point of the Sword of the Ram through the pulsing lightning blade, shattering it. After a moment, the sparks stopped hitting the air, and the hilt lay on the ground, lifeless. When the pillar of Blaze flame finally receded, Vengeance was no more.

As Gwydeon locked blades with Wrath, the differences in his new powers became evident. No longer did Wrath enjoy the advantage of strength, and Gwydeon stood square opposite Wrath, the large creature pushing downward with all the weight that it could manage. Gwydeon disengaged his sword the next moment, stepping into the monster, inside his reach, and then streaking upward, slashing with the crystalline blade from stomach to neck. Wrath however was quick to react to the tactic, batting at Gwydeon with its oversized hand, knocking him sideways. It took only a few seconds for Gwydeon to right himself, his wings catching the violently changing breezes in the throne room. For several tense seconds, Gwydeon waited, expecting Wrath to quickly regenerate the wounds and launch skyward after Gwydeon. But watching the gigantic beast, it no longer laughed at the closing of its wounds, and winced in pain as one nail found the exposed tissue and for the first time felt true pain. Draven had said that no mortal blade could wound Wrath, but now that Gwydeon was the Brother of Angels, that rule no longer applied. Bolstered by a new sense of confidence, Gwydeon charged, using his enhanced speed to dodge through all of Wrath's attempts to strike, each stroke leaving long slashes on the creature's arms, legs, and chest. Finally, Gwydeon saw an opening and sped forward with all his speed and might, and slashed hard at

Wrath's neck. Gwydeon touched down at the foot of the beast, watching and waiting for something to happen. Finally it rocked backward, falling into one of the walls of the throne room, blasting it outward, and sending the severed head rolling back through the room.

Holocaust watched the death of both Wrath and Vengeance, and for a moment toyed with the idea of fleeing as its master Draven had, but its decision was made for it the next moment, when Bryn began to hurl stream after stream of fire in its direction. Gideon and Taya kept up the pressure, with Gideon making the ground heave and shake under the Dark Rider's feet, and Taya sending precise gusts of wind to hit Holocaust square in the chest, keeping him off balance. Holocaust had stopped trying to attack, and was merely trying to dodge Bryn's strike and keep its balance when suddenly the tip of a sword emerged through its armor. Because of its nature, Holocaust was unable to feel pain, but when the sword suddenly withdrew, there was emptiness. Holocaust's power was gone, and when the Sword of the Ram crashed down on the floating skull, crushing it, the Dark Ride was no more. Sabrina admired her first kill for a moment, the powers of the *Chosen One* filling her, when Gwydeon returned from his duel and put his arm around her.

"Well, Draven is obviously planning something," Gideon said as he extracted the dagger from his palm and carefully wrapped the wound.

"And that means it can't be good," Taya added.

Gwydeon was about to chime in when he noticed that Bryn was looking around as though trying to figure out something. A pained expression crossed her face.

"What is it?" Gwydeon asked.

"Someone's coming," Bryn answered. "And whoever it is has company."

Neutrality

The land outside the town of Frontier was not to be traveled lightly, no matter the power that a person held. In generations past, it had been contested by several armies, all of which had been under the command of the phasia. Jeroch and Saurn in particular coveted this land because of its proximity to Marcwell, but no one was able to hold an advantage for long, due to the Army of the Fox, under the command of Bryn Aplee and later, Aerith Seth. So, when the green portal opened on a knoll just outside the town of Frontier, Evan had a strange sense of home fill him. The part of Evan that was still linked to the memories of Aerith Seth could remember many days staying in the quiet town, escaping the rigors of leading the Army of the Fox, but more often escaping the jealous temper of Grawn. It wasn't that Aerith was afraid of Grawn, it was more that Aerith was afraid that he would kill Grawn. Meredith took Evan's hand the next moment, and the two stood looking down until suddenly a flash of memory struck him. Slowly, Evan turned and scanned the horizon. While he didn't know exactly what he was looking for, he knew there was something out there. Finally, his eyes found a small cottage hidden in the shelter of a rock outcropping on the edge of a forest. Evan felt a smile come to his lips and holding Meredith's hand tightly he began walking. It took only a few minutes for the two to reach the cabin, and while Meredith thought it was strange for Evan to be leading her to the private place, many things had become strange with Evan since his inheritance of Aerith Seth's power. One of the things that she noticed almost immediately was his renewed sense of pride and confidence.

Meredith had not known Evan prior to her joining the Enforcers, but his reputation as a kind and gentle ruler had preceded him. Meredith had made her name as an archer in the service of Midarin Rice and the kingdom of Brea as part of the Order of the Sword. However, she began to grow restless and the courtly life in Brea, while pleasant, was also stifling. The other part of being an archer in Brea was the constant comparison to Midarin and her exploits as a member of the People of the Dragon. Before long, Meredith was the best archer in the ranks of the Order, and Meredith constantly found herself referred to as the younger Midarin. When Pike Rhuiden came to Brea, looking for recruits for his Enforcers, Meredith was the first to sign on. She wanted to make a name for herself and no longer be in the shadow of the heroine Midarin Rice. But Meredith would soon find that making a name for herself would not be easy.

When she first arrived at the training facilities in Kandor, she was looked on as an outsider, and had to earn the respect of those who had already become full members of the Enforcers. In the months of hard training and instruction that would follow, many of the new recruits fell by the wayside. Pike drove everyone to be the absolute best that they could be, and would accept nothing less. He had served with powerful men and women in the last war, but Pike was a realist and knew that with the exception of Gwydeon Sandar and Midarin Rice, everyone in the People of the Dragon could have been better. Pike's ambition was to build a group who was better and more prepared for the war to come than the People of the Dragon had ever been. Meredith was ready to quit and go back to Brea six months into her training. It was all too much for her. In the morning she was awake before sunrise, dressed quickly, and then was out for morning sword practice taught by Turok Korven. Turok was a student of Arathorn Geoffry and Aryx Terian, both sword masters and founding members of the Lion's Mane. Since Gwydeon Sandar was no longer alive, Pike once said, Turok was the next best teacher. Sword practice lasted two hours, and then the Enforcer trainees would break for a quick breakfast and then would have bow practice for an hour and then the first of several classes.

Instruction in the Enforcer training was normally headed by Pike, as that he had the most knowledge, but sometimes others would come in from neighboring kingdoms. On several occasions, Midarin Rice came to speak, as did Jerrard Mystic and his wife Erika. They covered everything from the battle tactics of the forces of the Shadow, to personalities of the known phasia, to the nature of the powers they would face. Everything that could be taught about the war that was about to be fought was given to the Enforcers in large pieces, and the rule was the more a person knew, the better chance they had to survive. But there was a point when everything became too much for Meredith. She was excelling in everything that she did, but because she was so insistent on doing everything for herself, she had very few friends, and loneliness and sorrow began to creep into her heart. That was when Evan Sinn found her.

Evan was placed in charge of all the matters of the court of Kandor while Pike focused on recruiting and training the Enforcers. However, the pressure on Evan had doubled since the Enforcer training began. Though he was already a member of the Enforcers in name, Evan was determined to shoulder as much burden as the rest of the group, and wanted to be accepted as a warrior as much as a leader. So, between the diplomatic meetings, arranging of treaties, and other matters of court, Evan would be out in the training fields with the rest of the Enforcers, working as hard, if not harder. For Meredith, Evan was an inspiration, showing her exactly what it was to be an Enforcer, showing her that even though he was already a member of the Enforcers, he still wanted to be the best. Before long, Meredith began to see Evan as more than just an inspiration, and they began to spend as much time together as possible. In fact, it was Evan that relayed the message from Pike that Meredith had been granted her position within the core group of the Enforcers, the elite of the elite. After that, the romantic aspect of their relationship grew.

In the privacy of his chambers, Evan was not at all the same man he was when running the court of Kandor or training to be a member of the Enforcers. Evan was a quiet and reserved man, a poet and a writer. Through his heart flowed romantic sentiments unlike Meredith had ever heard in her life. Many nights the two would simply lie together, Meredith secure in Evan's strong arms as he stroked her hair and whispered his words of love and devotion into her ear as she slipped into peaceful and contented slumber. While in public Evan would never question the decision or tactics of his lord Pike Rhuiden, in private, Meredith had heard Evan rage about the lack of wisdom that some of Pike's decisions showed. Evan always followed orders, even orders that he knew were wrong, and at times they cost more than just the loss of lives, but also loss of dignity. The war with the neighboring kingdom of Askronilka being the most prevalent. Pike had been in the Mercenary City on a recruiting mission with Rachel and Elizabeth, when suddenly accusations began to fly. The lord of Askronilka accused Pike of robbing his daughter of her maidenhood and thus spoiling any chance that she had for a proper marriage. Pike or course refuted the charges and swore that he was a married man and devoted to his wife. Recollection suddenly hit Meredith. Pike had said nothing, it was Rachel and Elizabeth that voiced their objections. Evan had told Meredith that Pike had indeed slept with the lord's daughter, and while he treated the accusation as though it were beneath even his notice, inside he must have known that he was in the wrong. However, in the days that followed the incident, the lord of Askronilka continued to hurl his insults and accusations, and eventually began to mass the troops of his land for a battle. Pike was ready for a fight and when the Enforcers took the fields outside of Kandor and waited for the charge of the army from the Mercenary City, Evan knew that what they were doing was wrong. Yet, everyone fought, and many died, Enforcers and mercenaries alike. Meredith wondered if that incident grated deeper on Evan now that he knew the truth of it. Or perhaps it was that Evan already knew that Pike had lied about the affair. She knew that there was much more to the man that she loved than he had been able to reveal to her in their time together. But, she hoped that there would be more time for the two of them to grow and learn everything that could be learned about one another.

When the two lovers reached the door to the quiet cottage, Evan hesitated before taking hold of the handle and gently pushing on the door. For a moment nothing happened, and then Meredith watched as the polished silver handle began to glow and then beat with a rhythm much like that of a heart. The heartbeat faded a moment later, and the door slowly swung open to reveal the interior of the cottage. Meredith immediately began to smile upon entering the cottage, a sense of peace and warmth filling her. The place was unlike anything she had ever seen in her life. The interior of the cottage was bright and warm, the walls painted in a cream color, but dominated by tapestries and paintings. The wall closest to the rock outcropping that served as a shelter from the elements had a portion cut out to reveal a small waterfall, that babbled quietly, oblivious to the visitors. A bed sat near the small waterfall, the thick down comforter pulled back to reveal red silk sheets with lace pillows strewn around the bed in a pattern that someone must have thought suited them. There was a wardrobe that stood in the corner opposite the waterfall, and as Meredith stopped to examine it, she noticed several sets of both men's and women's clothing, many black shirts and many more scandalous red dresses. Meredith picked one that she thought was the most decadent and draped it in front of her turning to face Evan.

"Do you think this suits me?"

For a minute, Evan just stared, his mind flashing to several places at once. Seconds later his memories flashed back to another time, and he saw Bryn's beautiful naked body sauntering across the room to that same wardrobe, holding a dress in the same fashion and teasing the man who watched her. This had been the place that Bryn and Aerith met to have their sexual trysts, but it was more than that. They could escape here together, be at peace, and be content in the love that they shared. For a long time, Evan had questioned whether or not a phase could feel any emotions at all, but with Aerith's memories as his ally, he could feel the genuine love that the two had shared in their time together.

"The dress is right, but the hair is wrong."

Evan spun reaching for the sword on his hip as he heard the stranger's voice from the doorway. It was merely a reflex before his mind processed the timber of the voice. Meredith dropped the dress and drew her blade, but Evan's motion the next moment forced her to return it to its sheath. Aerith Seth had returned to the only place that had ever truly felt like home to him, but it did not feel right without the woman who had made it home. With a few proud steps, Aerith crossed the room, bent down and recovered the short dress from the floor and held it up to the blond woman who looked up at him with wonder in her eyes. Some of the look was confusion, while more of it was a growing understanding of exactly who she was looking at. Before Evan could speak and foil the mystery of the new arrival's identity. Aerith held the dress back up to Meredith's body, and regarding it for a moment smiled and nodded.

"I suppose it will do, though I think white would be more your color."

A moment later the dress was no longer red, but a pure and shimmering white. Evan chuckled to himself watching Meredith blush, and then watched as the redness in her cheeks deepened when she found that the dress went from being clutched in Aerith's hand, to wrapped around her body. The white fabric clung to every curve as though it had been sewn onto her form, and Evan had never seen Meredith look more beautiful then she had at that moment. Aerith took a step back and looked at the blond woman for a moment before reaching toward her and freeing her hair from the piece of fabric that held it back in a tail. The shimmering golden tress of hair feel about her shoulders, and she looked more angelic, an innocent air surrounding her.

"There," Aerith commented smiling, "from a warrior to a princess in a matter of seconds."

Meredith's mouth opened, but no words came out. There was nothing that she could say that could express the feelings that ran through her. It was a combination of embarrassment, pride, joy, and confusion. Evan rescued her from the silence.

"Meredith Heron, I'd like you to meet the first *Chosen One*, Aerith Seth."

Aerith took a long slow bow, and when he stood straight again, a wide smile graced his face.

"Please Evan," Aerith said taking Meredith's hand and kissing it lightly. "Can't you see that the poor girl is overwhelmed? The title was a little much."

At that moment, Meredith realized that Aerith was mocking her, and she withdrew her hand from his. The reaction was met with a laugh from the ancient visitor.

"She has a spark to her," Aerith said moving to the bed and sitting quickly. "That's good. Docile women were alright for the men in Emries' line, but I always liked them with more of a fire and toughness. Arin Ranthall had Victoria Rhuiden. She was a proud and strong woman, and a natural warrior. For a while I didn't think that Elwyne Tamerlane would turn out to be as tough as she was, but after watching her take the torture and question at the hands of Shau-ling himself, I had to change my opinion. And now Evan, you have Meredith. All in all, I think I've done pretty well for myself."

It was Evan's turn to laugh.

"You certainly still have a few tricks left in you Aerith," Evan said finally, "but I assume you aren't here just to embarrass Meredith."

The blond woman shot a look of defiance at Evan, which drew another laugh from Aerith. Sensing her discomfort, Aerith snapped his fingers, and Meredith again stood in her black shirt and breeches, the white dress neatly hanging back in the wardrobe.

"Careful Evan," the ancient man said after a moment, "it is not wise to make a woman like Meredith angry. Though I doubt her temper is as severe as Bryn's, it is still not a fire that I would stoke if you can avoid it. But, you're right, there is another purpose for my visit."

Evan took a seat at the table near the door and waited for the explanation. Meredith continued to stand where she was, taking a few seconds to pull her hair back again and tie it back.

"While you have been playing tag with Wolf Ranthall and the rest of his group, I've been doing a little snooping of my own, though it wasn't my intention. I had a few good-byes that I wanted to say before I passed on from this world, but unfortunately, it's never that easy."

"What do you mean?" Meredith asked.

"Well, being the being of neutrality that I am, many who don't want to follow either Shau-ling or Emries, use my name to champion whatever cause they are fighting for. Of course they completely have forgotten about the Creator and only use his name when they have no other option. Well, it seems that it had happened again, but instead of being some little group out in the middle of nowhere, it's this group called the Creator's Torch Society."

Evan chimed in immediately.

"The same lead that Wolf and the others are chasing."

Aerith nodded.

"Right. Only he's barking up the wrong tree here in Brea. Bryn's not going to give him any more than she wants him to know, but I think that she'll point him in the right direction anyway. See, the Torch, through using my name, has fashioned themselves as a modern version of the Hand of the Light, and unfortunately their new leader is no Aralias Imstra. Maybe the name will ring a bell, Duncan Rhuiden."

Evan's blood ran cold. Duncan Rhuiden, while a prince of the noblest kingdom in the world, was also a cold and heartless bastard to everyone who stood in his way. From the day he was old enough to understand what it was that he would become once he took the throne in Marcwell, that knowledge and greed for power made him more vicious. Everyone was a pawn in his little game, and he would use anyone that he could so long as it got him closer to the throne. Many got the impression from Pike that it would not be an easy transition of power, and many more thought that Pike would never relinquish the throne to his perverse son. That was when Duncan started jumping at shadows, thinking that Pike and Cairyn had assassins waiting around every corner, ready to end his life and line of ascension. Evan was ready to comment, but Aerith continued.

"Now Duncan has gotten it in his head that if Pike isn't going to give the throne of Marcwell to him, than he is going to use the Torch to take it by force. I was in Trelon when the good son told his mother that he was going to take Marcwell and then he was going to come back and take Trelon even if it meant putting his sword through his mother's heart. Of course, he said it much better than that, but I like to get right to the point. Well, as much as a bastard as Duncan has always been, I never thought that he would be stupid enough to move this recklessly. The direct approach was never his style, and he never wanted to get his own hands dirty."

"Someone else is pulling his strings?" Meredith asked.

Aerith smiled.

"Beautiful and smart," Aerith said looking at Evan. "It's a good combination isn't it?"

Before Evan could comment, Aerith turned his attention back to Meredith and continued speaking.

"I also thought that he was being controlled by someone else, and because of the vindictive and arrogant nature of his new attitude, my first thought went to one place and one place only."

"The phasia," all three said together.

"Well, I couldn't just go off and do anything about Duncan without proof. Now, I wasn't about to get Duncan face to face and force the truth out of him, because I'd end up killing him. So I went to the next best source of information, the one guy who knows everything about the phasia, Shau-ling."

Evan didn't believe what he was hearing.

"You actually went to see Shau-ling?"

"Well, not the Shau-ling of this world. Remember Evan," Aerith said calmly as though he were teaching a dim-witted student, "there are two different realities now, and both Shau-ling and Emries exist in each reality. That means I can too. So I went to see Shau-ling and called in a favor. As always though, Shau-ling is very smart. He knows that he can't interfere in this reality without handing the whole war over to Emries, so without coming out and telling me, he told me that while it's not a member of the phasia directly, it's a child of one of the phasia."

"Michael," Meredith said quickly.

Evan nodded, everything falling together in his mind. Aerith sat silently waiting for his compatriots to fill him in, but when the information didn't come immediately, Aerith spoke up.

"Alright," he said a bit annoyed, "I did a lot of the leg work that the two of you are supposed to be doing, so I expect that if you know something, you fill me in. I'm the one who's going to die here, so I'm the one who needs the answers."

Meredith walked across to where Evan sat and rested her hand lightly on his shoulder.

"When we were in Aradon with Wolf and the others, we heard them talking to a woman, Susanne Praen who used to be a member of the Torch."

"Thanks to your powers," Evan continued, "we were able to hear everything that went on in the house, and I could also pull from Sabrina all of the information that she had, that way we could get all the information and not risk discovery."

"Good work," Aerith said inwardly pleased at the resourcefulness of his charge, "so, what did you find out from this Praen woman?"

"She was a valued member of the Torch, and one of their best," Meredith said quickly, "but she was seduced by a member of the phasia, Erdric Yarrow, the same man who killed their leader Dei. When the new leader Seraphina Masile took over, the Torch became more militant and started learning the Moridon magic to take the fight to the forces of the Shadow. Susanne found out shortly after that she was pregnant, and while the group wanted to expel her for treachery against the cause, Seraphina kept her within the group. Her intention was to raise the child to use as a weapon against the phasia and all the other creatures that served Shau-ling."

"Use a creature of Shadow to fight the Shadow," Aerith said shaking his head.

"Exactly," Evan continued. "When the child was born, it was a boy, and they named him Michael. So, if a child of the phasia is the one that's leading Duncan around by the nose, it's a pretty safe bet that it's Michael that's doing it."

Aerith took a moment to reflect.

"But he's not acting alone," Aerith said finally. "While a child of the phasia has power, and probably power enough to pull the wool over the eyes of someone as driven as Duncan, for the entire Torch to fall for it means that there is a greater force at work. That kind of manipulation is something that Erdric would love to be involved in, and if he is there, there is a good chance that Aldridge is there too. Those two vultures love to cause trouble for the Binosear family, and if they can get there hooks into one, that's all the better. That way they can say they succeeded where Jeroch has always failed."

"Did Duncan say where the Torch was going?" Meredith asked.

"To deal with Pike," Aerith answered.

Evan did some quick figuring in his head.

"If the battle kept going the way it was when we left Lakestone that means that the Enforcers ought to be making their way back to Scalla."

"If they aren't there already," Meredith commented.

Aerith scratched his chin and looked toward the door, his thoughts immediately going to his estranged granddaughter.

"I got the impression from the way that Duncan acted that while the Hand was under his control, they weren't there with him in Trelon. I think that he sent them on to Scalla and used this Michael character to create a portal to get him in and out of Trelon to throw us off the trail. Unless I miss my guess, I think that Pike and Jerrard are in for a lot of company and a nice little war."

Evan shook his head.

"So, where do we go now? Do we sit here and wait on Wolf and the others to meet with Bryn, or do we go to Scalla and keep an eye on Pike?"

Aerith took a deep breath and sighed.

"I will take care of Bryn. The kind of things that she could do to Wolf and his friends are not things that the two of you would be able to perceive or prevent. Maybe she'll listen to me long enough to get those kids out of harm's way and back on the right path. If I'm lucky I'll get in and out without Grawn even knowing I'm there."

"Then what do we do?" Meredith asked, echoing Evan's question.

"I want the two of you to go back to Aradon," Aerith answered. "I told Cairyn to go back there to be safe. For some reason, I get the impression that Duncan wouldn't hesitate to take Cairyn out of the picture if he had a chance. So, I want you two to make sure that she gets there and gets settled in. Besides, I have a feeling that once you get there, you will find something that is well worth your trip."

Evan nodded, and though he didn't agree with the errand that Aerith was sending them on when their friends were in trouble, he would do it because if there was anyone who knew what was best, it was Aerith. Being a creature of neutrality meant that you could not fight for either side, or allow your emotions to get in the way of what was the true path. Chances were that if Evan and Meredith were in Scalla, they would be tempted to help the Enforcers and would break the rules. Evan pulled a red stone from his pocket and opened the portal quickly, before he and Meredith disappeared through. As the portal closed, Aerith lay back on the soft feather bed with its warm down comforter and rested his head on one of the lace pillows. Part of him could feel Bryn's body cuddled up against him and the soft warmth of her breath as it passed over his body. He would get to see her again after all, and as he listened to the quiet murmur of the waterfall, Aerith closed his eyes and allowed himself to drop into a peaceful sleep with dreams of the only woman he had ever really loved.

Absolute Power

Creator's Calendar Year 1205; Dark Mirror

The Order of the Sword stood silently as they watch the last of the Jeresei break and run under the onslaught of the monstrous creature called Stone. Gwydeon and Midarin had told them stories of the destructive power of the huge creatures, and for a time, they were the most feared adversary that a phase could bring to bear. Many of the Stone warriors had assaulted the walls of Brea, and they had always been pulled away when the rest of the phase's army retreated. Only on a handful of occasions had one of them been toppled, and when it did happen, the event usually caused the retreat of the forces of the Shadow. There was a great respect for the power of the Stone, a respect that was held by both the Light and the Shadow. Not allowing the Order to become lax with their confusion and wonder, the generals ordered their men to secure the courtyard and to prepare for an assault. There was always the chance for another army to descend on Sador and try to take them while they were vulnerable. Midarin Rice on the other hand had no such worries in her mind, but rather turned her attention to the new ally for the forces of the Light and approached the seated Stone warrior, with Rachel Core in tow.

Part of Midarin had been wounded when she learned that her friend Stone had to be killed in the previous lifetime. Though it had been the key to their victory against Shau-ling, she still did not like it. But now it seemed that she was getting another chance. There was another part of Midarin however that had begun to worry. The Stone were powerful adversaries to be feared, and as long as there was a mystery as to the motives of the huge creature, there would still be fear in Midarin's heart. As the two mortals approached, the Stone sat up straight and locked its eyes on the leading form. Midarin stopped just short of the massive feet and spoke.

"Thank you for helping us."

The Stone shifted and let the rumbling voice hit the air.

"W...E...L...C...O...M...E./.F...R...I...E...N...D./.M...I...D...A ...R...I...N./.S...T...O...N...E./.M...A...K...E./.F...R...I...E...N... D./.M...I...D...A...R...I...N./.H...A...P...P...Y.?.

Midarin smiled.

"Yes, you made me very happy helping us defeat the Jeresei and Shadowwalkers."

"G...O...O...D..."

Rachel tugged at the sleeve of Midarin's shirt, trying to prompt her to ask the millions of questions that Rachel herself had deep in the back of her mind. Midarin on the other hand was trying to exercise caution and not push the volatile creature too hard.

"Can I ask you a question Stone?" Midarin asked softly.

"Y...E...S..."

"How do you know who I am?"

The Stone rumbled for a moment, as though its thoughts had a sound. For several seconds the rumbling changed pitches and ranges from the low and barely audible to the higher range that made the hairs on the back of Midarin's neck stand straight up.

"F...R...I...E...N...D./.M...I...D...A...R...I...N./.M...E...T./.S... T...O...N...E./.W...I...T...H./.F...R...I...E...N...D./.G...W...Y...D ...E...O...N./.A...N...D./.L...O...R...D./.L...O...G...A...N./.I...N./ .C...A...V...E./.D...U...R...I...N...G./.S...T...O...R...M..."

Midarin nodded. It was almost twenty years ago when the People of the Dragon took shelter in that huge cave to find shelter from a storm. It took only a few minutes for them to realize that they had walked into an ambush that introduced them to the twin phasia Rael and Trece. It was because of that battle that Logan first held the powers of the Blaze and was able to sway Stone over to their side.

"T...H...E...N./L...O...R...D./L...O...G...A...N./T...O...O...K./S...T...O...N...E./T...O./B...R...E...A./T...O./H...E...L...P./.F...I...G...H...T./L...O...R...D./S...A...U...R...N./A...N...D./F...I...N...D./F...R...I...E...N...D./K...O...R...R...D..."

Images flowed through Midarin's mind of the battle with the Light Keepers in the streets of the Brea, and sneaking into the dungeon with Gwydeon and Arin Domae in an attempt to rescue Gideon from Saurn. Later Korrd joined the force and that was when everyone learned the truth about the Ranthall family and that Korrd was actually the *Coromor*. Bryn also joined the group at that point, and from there everything began to spiral out of control as the collision course between Korrd and Shau-ling had reached its point of no return. Something was nagging at Midarin though. It was the way that Stone kept referring to Logan as Lord Logan rather than Friend Logan. Stone called Saurn, Lord Saurn, and Saurn was a phase. Perhaps it was because in the collective Stone memory, Logan was considered like a phase because he once held the Blaze.

"I...N./R...U...I...N...S./O...F./S...C...A...L...L...A./S...T...O...N...E./W...A...T...C...H...E...D./F...R...I...E...N...D./M...I...D...A...R...I...N./D...I...E./B...E...C...A...U...S...E./O...F./L...A...D...Y./B...R...Y...N./S...O./S...T...O...N...E./A...T...T...A...C...K...E...D..."

Later Gwydeon had told Midarin that the idea to make Stone attack Bryn was to keep Shau-ling from knowing what the group would do next. Stone was a Bonded creature, and because of that he was a liability. Gwydeon, with Emries help, bought time for the third generation of the prophecies by sacrificing Stone and forcing Bryn to work for the forces of the Light for at least a short time.

"F...R...I...E...N...D./.K...O...R...R...D./.T...H...E...N./.S...H
...A...T...T...E...R...E...D./.S...T...O...N...E./.W...H...E...N./.S...
T...O...N...E./.W...O...K...E./.U...P./.T...H...E...R...E./.W...E...R
...E./.M...O...R...E./.S...T...O...N...E./.A...N...D./.S...T...O...N
...E./.R...E...T...U...R...N...E...D./.T...O./.M...A...S...T...E...R...
"

Suddenly it all dawned on Midarin. Stone had explained in the last war that the Stone were creatures that did not reproduce, but Shau-ling would take an old Stone and shatter it into a hundred pieces, and then each piece would become another Stone. Midarin wondered if it really took Shau-ling's power to create the new Stone, of if it merely took Shau-ling to break the Stone. Apparently, instead of killing Stone, Korrd had merely broken him to the point of creating many more. For Stone if would be just as though his master had done the same thing, except that since this Stone had broken the Bond by working for the forces of the Light and killing a member of the phasia, perhaps he still felt the pull to do what was right. If that was true, the other Stone made from the breaking should have felt the same way.

"S...T...O...N...E./.C...O...M...E./.T...O./.S...A...D...O...R./.F
...O...R./.L...O...R...D./.Z...A...R...S...I./.A...N...D./.T...O...L...
D./.T...O./.K...I...L...L./.H...U...M...A...N...S./.B...U...T./.S...A...
W./.F...R...I...E...N...D./.M...I...D...A...R...I...N./.A...N...D./.W
...A...N...T...E...D./.T...O./.H...E...L...P..."

Rachel shook her head, trying hard to follow the story, but there were too many gaps.

"How long was it before you came here to Sador?"

Stone stared blankly at Rachel.

"It's no use Rachel," Midarin commented. "Stone don't understand the concept of time. They simply follow orders. It would be like asking a mountain how old it is. It doesn't know anything accept the fact that the sun and moon have passed over them many times."

Stone nodded its head in long strokes, taking the meaning that Midarin was trying to convey. Stone had learned much in the presence of humans and had learned to see many new things. It also had learned to tell the difference between Jeresei of one clan from another by their leaders and the way that they acted. It was a very different world from the one that Shauling had presented to Stone in the beginning.

"F...R...I...E...N...D./.M...I...D...A...R...I...N./.D...I...F...F...
E...R...E...N...T./.F...R...O...M./.F...R...I...E...N...D./.R...A...C
...H...E...L./.D...I...F...F...E...R...E...N...T./.B...U...T./.S...A...M
...E..."

Midarin smiled a secret smile and tried hard not to blush. Stone had remembered everything that he had been taught in those few minutes late in the night after the battle of the cave when Midarin first told Gwydeon that she was pregnant.

"What does that mean?" Rachel asked, puzzled.

Midarin laughed.

"It means that we have nothing to fear from our friend Stone here. He is what he says he is, and we'll leave it at that."

Rachel shrugged and was about to make a comment when Evan Sinn ran up and flashed a quick salute.

"Lady Midarin, our spies have found that a battle has taken place in the palace of Sador, and it seems that Lord Nathaniel has made his way to the throne room to battle the phase Zarsi. We don't know if Lord Logan is still with him or not, for none of our spies dared to enter the throne room."

Midarin nodded and drew her sword.

"Stone, help my men get this place ready in case more Jeresei and Shadowwalkers show up. And if you feel any portals coming this way, tell this man, Evan, as soon as you feel them."

"Y...E...S./.F...R...I...E...N...D./.M...I...D...A...R...I...N..."

Evan saluted again at the order and went off to help his men to secure the area, and Midarin and Rachel sprinted off toward the inner halls of the palace of Sador. Midarin had no idea what to expect when she got there, but somewhere deep inside of her, she knew that something had gone horribly wrong.

* * * * * * * * * * *

Midarin and Rachel arrived at the doors to the throne room, uncomfortable with the scene that lay before them. Throughout the room were scattered broken pieces of painted glass, and blood stains littered the floor everywhere the pair looked. It was obvious that some sort of battle had taken place here, but before either could examine, or question further, the doors to the throne room opened. Revealed by the opened doors was the crumpled body of the phase Zarsi and the boy Nathaniel perched on the throne with his legs draped over one of the arms. The throne room was in tatters, remains of tapestries and paintings still smoldering on the walls. Debris littered the room, mostly from the huge holes in the walls and ceiling of the room, and as Midarin and Rachel stood looking in disbelief of the scene, several chunks of rock fell from above, crashing to the ground.

"Ah," the boy said after a moment, "mother, Rachel, so good of you to join me in my victory."

There was something different about the boy's voice. Midarin found it hard even to believe that it was her son there before her. The arrogant tone in his voice was the new and disturbing quality, something that he certainly had not learned from his father, Gwydeon.

"We've taken Sador," Midarin said slowly, "but there were many losses."

The boy scoffed at the mention of casualties, and swung his legs from the arm of the throne, letting them fully rest on the floor. Sitting up straight, Nathaniel looked down on the two women, and from the look in the boy's eyes, Midarin could tell that Nathaniel thought he was humoring them.

"I have taken Sador, mother," the boy responded. "When Zarsi fell to my blade, his servants lost the will to fight, that is why they broke so quickly and easily. Had you merely waited before charging the walls, the bloodshed would have been much less."

Fury began to boil within Rachel.

CHAPTER 39

"You know better than that Nathaniel," Midarin said keeping her voice calm.

"Nathan," the boy corrected.

Midarin took a step back as if struck. The condescending attitude of the boy was unlike anything that Midarin had ever seen in him, it almost reminded her of how Logan had acted while he was under the control of the phase Caris.

"The Jeresei and Shadowwalkers would have continued fighting and probably would have inflicted far more casualties had it not been for the Stone turning to our side," Midarin continued trying to ignore her tormented thoughts.

"Which also wouldn't have been possible without my victory."

Arrogance oozed from every word, and the boy's pride seemed to glow brighter as he impressed himself more with the deeds he imagined accomplishing.

"You're wrong Nathaniel," Rachel challenged, putting emphasis on the name. "It was Queen Midarin who pulled the Stone to our side, and it was her leadership that held us together through the charge and the ambush. It was her through all of this. So you killed a member of the phasia, so what? Your mortal father killed more of them with his blade and no powers than you will with all of your powers as the *Coromor*."

Nathan rose from the throne the next moment, and extended his hand. Rachel could feel the invisible grip tighten around her throat, constricting quickly and cutting off the air to her lungs. In a moment the pain would begin, the burning hunger of her lungs for the sweet air. Midarin watched in horror as Rachel was lifted from the floor, the invisible forces of Wind suspending her from her neck, further increasing the suffocating pressure.

"My name," Nathan said, with all the venom he could manage, "is Nathan Sandar. If you forget it again, I will crush you like the insignificant bug you are. My father was a great man, and he killed the weak as he was destined to. I also have a destiny, and I will not be told how I am to fulfill it by the likes of you. Not even you, mother, can imagine the greatness that you see before you and the future that I will build with the powers at my disposal. Shau-ling will fall at my feet, but not before the rest of his phasia are taught the lesson that they have needed for centuries. I shall break all of them as I have broken Zarsi. I shall make them beg for their lives and they will all submit to me, Nathan Sandar, the Lord Ram, the chosen of the great god Emries."

A maniacal laugh tore from Nathan's throat, filling the room with the insane sound. Rachel gasped for breath, no sound escaping from her tortured throat. A heartbeat later, Rachel fell to the ground, her loud gasp echoing through the room. Nathan looked down at the open door, shock painted on his face, but that look turned quickly to rage when the four forms appeared in the doorway. Logan Ranthall still lived, and he had used his powers to free Rachel from her suspended position. The people with the former hero infuriated Nathan and confused Midarin. The twins Rael and Trece were well known to Midarin from their many raids on the Kingdom of Brae, and Caris was known best for her attempted seduction of Logan in Frontier.

"Perhaps I can save you a bit of a trip Nathan," Logan said pulling the Dragon Sword from the scabbard at his side and bringing it to bear. "There are four members of the phasia standing right here in front of you. And just to make it fair, we'll even go one at a time."

Nathan laughed again, the laugh more like the cackle of the insane than of a mentally stable person.

"This is bad comedy, Logan. You, a member of the phasia? Next you'll tell me that my father is a god."

Logan took several steps forward.

"Your father was a great man to be sure, and his place in the Heavens will be granted to him soon enough, but right now, this is about us. I want another shot at you, considering you left me for dead out in the mud."

Nathan shook his head.

"Poor Logan. Don't you know that this world doesn't need you anymore? Your time is past. The People of the Dragon are dead. You've done your part to ensure that the power passed into my hands and now it's time for you to just curl up and die peacefully. If you refuse, you know that you will face pain and suffering unlike anything you could ever imagine. Death would be a pleasant release."

"I've already died once today," Logan said finally, pulling his body into a fighting stance, "I don't intend to have a repeat performance."

The crystalline sword of Order formed quickly in Nathan's hand as he launched himself from the dais and landed mere inches from Logan. When the two blades met, sparks filled the air, and the two combatants took several steps back from one another, sizing up the other man. Nathan could tell in the first strike that something was different about Logan. There was more power flowing through the man's veins, and even his posture showed more confidence and pride. Before Nathan could charge again, Midarin stepped between the two men.

"There's no time for this," she said forcefully. "We have to work together if we are going to win this war. Now Logan, I don't know why you are traveling with three members of the phasia, but I'm sure you have a good reason. If the two of you could get your heads on straight and think like the heroes you are, then maybe we can sort through this without anyone having to die."

Nathan glared at Logan and then channeled a simple flow of wind to knock the older woman out of his path before he struck. Thanks to Logan's increased reflexes, he was able to get the blade of the Dragon Sword up in time to block the strike.

"There will be no peaceful end to this," Nathan spat with fury, "as long as Logan stands with the phasia, he is my enemy."

"You have no idea how right you are," Logan answered, filling himself with Blaze energy and pushing back against the boy's strike.

The two men separated again, but the break in the action lasted only moments before the two flung themselves at each other again. Strike after strike connected with only empty air or the ring of steel as the two men traveled speeds the human body was never designed for. Midarin was unable to follow the contest, seeing only the flash of the blade when they connected with one another. Finally, the two emerged after a huge flash, their backs to one another, Logan panting and looking back over his shoulder at the boy. Nathan turned, a huge gash opened across his chest, the red viscous liquid flowing freely from the gaping wound. The boy chuckled as he ran his finger through the wound, collecting blood on the tip, and then pressing it to his lips, tasting it. The sly grin grew on the boy's face as the wound closed while Logan looked on. Midarin had picked herself up from where she had been thrown, stepping again between the powerful men.

"Enough!"

Nathan lifted the blade of his sword.

"Move, mother," Nathan said coldly, "I wouldn't want you to get in the way and find yourself impaled on my blade."

Midarin stood firm, letting the threat wash over her.

"So be it."

Nathan charged forward, all regard for the life of his mother gone. Rachel screamed something unintelligible and knocked Midarin out of the way, taking the brunt of the boy's blow. When Midarin looked back, to her horror she saw Rachel with the blade of the sword of Order thrust through her chest, the blood-soaked blade erupting from her back. The frown on Nathan's face might have been for the fact that he had killed Rachel, or for the fact that he wished that it had been Midarin slowly dying on his sword. Midarin could not tell for sure. However, as Nathan stepped back, Rachel slumped to the ground, her breathing labored, and life quickly slipping away.

"Too bad," Nathan said letting the Sword of Order disappear from his hand. "I warned you puny mortals not to interfere, and now look what has happened. Well, while it was fun playing with you Logan, I am afraid that there are bigger fish that deserve my attention now. But have no fear little dears, I shall get back to all of you soon enough, and you will rue the day that you stood against the Ram."

CHAPTER 39

The portal formed the next moment, and when Nathan stepped through, the last thing anyone heard from him was the same cackling laughter. Logan slipped the Dragon Sword back into the scabbard at his side and moved quickly over to the fallen form of the girl Rachel. She had fought bravely during the rescue attempt of Cairyn and Sabrina, and Logan was genuinely sorry that she had gotten involved. Midarin sat next to Rachel, the girl's head resting in Midarin's lap. After an examination of the wound, Logan sighed and shook his head. Caris also had probed the wound silently, and the extent of the injuries was more than even a member of the phasia could mend.

"There's nothing I can do, Midarin," Logan said quietly. "The power of the sword that Nathan had is acting like a poison and eating her from the inside out. The strike touched her heart, and while I can't mend the damage, I can dull the pain so at least she can die in peace."

Midarin nodded, trying to hold back the tears. Logan silently sent the flows of Water and Wind into Rachel's body, numbing the fires within her, granting her a few moments of peace before the end. Logan walked away from the two women, a weight descending on his heart. Midarin watched as Caris put her arm around Logan and the four arrivals began talking in hushed voices.

"Midarin?" Rachel said in a weak voice.

"I'm here Rachel," Midarin said taking hold of the woman's hand and smoothing her hair back with the other.

"Thank you for letting me lead the archers."

Midarin let an uneasy laugh escape her lips as the first tears began to fall.

"I'll say hello to my sister for you...I'm sure she's proud of Queen Eagle-Eye, the fighting princess."

It was then that the recollection hit Midarin. Before she had been banished from Brea, an emissary from the Kingdom of Trelon had come to pay a visit to Brea congratulating the King and Queen on the upcoming marriage of their daughter. Midarin had been out practicing the bow with one of the men from the army when a strange blond haired girl approached and watched for several minutes. The girl held a baby in her arms, and as Midarin shot arrow after arrow into the center of the target, the baby gurgled its approval. When Midarin had finished, the blond girl waited.

"I guess they should call you eagle-eyes" the girl had said, *"don't worry if they talk about you, they say the same thing about me and my sword."*

The girl's name was Eldar, and the little baby in her arms was her step-sister, Rachel. How Rachel had remembered all this time that she had seen Midarin on that day, and Eldar had given her that nickname. Midarin also couldn't believe that she hadn't remembered it before, especially being so close to Eldar for those few days during the war. But things were different then, and the memories from her days as a princess were what she was trying hardest to avoid.

Midarin smiled down at Rachel as she closed her eyes for the last time and faded away into the peaceful embrace of death. For a long time Midarin sat, Rachel's hand limp in her grasp, her body finally still. Wiping her face, Midarin stood and picked up the bow and quiver that lay discarded by Rachel's body. When Logan turned back to his old ally, she was restringing her fallen friend's bow, a new look of determination falling over her tortured features. Midarin finished quickly and stood tall, her shoulder pulled back staring at the assemblage of phasia and her former comrade in arms.

"I suppose you want an explanation," Logan said turned to face Midarin.

Midarin shook her head.

"As I said before, you have your reasons for being with members of the phasia. It's no secret that I have my own vendetta against Rael and Trece for damage that they caused to my kingdom, but I'm willing to forget that for now. As for Caris, she may have a problem with me, but I don't care about her. All I know is that the boy that killed Rachel was not my son, and was certainly not Gwydeon's gentle child. The only explanation I want is why he's become what he is now, and what I can do to get revenge for Rachel."

Logan nodded.

CHAPTER 39

"Then you should come with us to Scalla," he said quickly. "Your answers will be found there. All I can tell you now is that your son is sick, and that Emries has poisoned his mind with an evil that defies description. Nathan thinks that he is doing what is right by hunting down the phasia and then killing Shau-ling. But the real enemy is not on the side of the Shadows. Emries has been the sickness in this world all along, and it is up to us to make sure that his plans never come to fruition. Nathan will probably strike at Draven next, since he is the most visible of the phasia. So we'll head to Scalla and try to end the boy's threat there. We have to stop Nathan any way that we can, even if it means killing him."

Midarin nodded.

"I was ready to kill you once Logan," came the woman's cold reply, "thanks to Caris having her hooks into you, and if I have to, I'll bury an arrow deep into my own son's heart if it will keep this world from falling deeper into the Shadows."

Chapter XL

Raven's Wing

Creator's Calendar Year 1205; Light Reality

Two days of preparations had passed quickly, and over the ramparts of the palace of Scalla, troops from the Raven's Wing could see the mass of soldiers approaching, obviously ready for a battle. As the men looked on though, the approaching force halted at the top of a wide hill several hundred yards from the city and waited. Horn calls went up from the approaching ranks, and then banners hit the air in the front ranks. The banners were familiar to say the least, a springing lion on a field of white. It was the banner of the Lion, the most celebrated Lord of Marcwell, Cedric Binosear. When the calls rang out through the courtyard of the palace of Scalla for the Raven's Wing to form, many of the soldiers felt as though they did not want to answer. Standing against a phantom army was one thing, an army flying the banners of Marcwell was something else entirely. But, regardless of trepidation, the Raven's Wing formed and readied to march.

Pike Rhuiden's anger boiled as he watched the banners of Marcwell rise in the opposing ranks. He knew that Duncan was arrogant, be he never in his wildest dreams could have imagined that the boy would have resorted to these tactics. Duncan believed he was the rightful heir to the throne of Marcwell. While Pike may have made a deal with Cairyn for the line of succession to move to Duncan on his twenty-first birthday, he was not about to hand the kingdom over to a maniac who cared little who won the war between the Light and the Shadow. In many ways, Duncan was as bad as a member of the phasia, not caring about the world around him, so long as his little private world revolved solely around him and his schemes. The self-importance of the boy Pike once called his son ate at his insides.

As Pike climbed down from the wall, he was greeted by the faces of the men and women he had grown to love and respect more than his own family. But the confidence they once had in their leader had been stripped away by the debacle in Lakestone. Pike knew that Zak and Valin would follow him to the end of the world no matter what happened. They each had their personal vendettas to call in against the phasia, and as long as Pike gave them the opportunity to be in combat with the forces of the Shadow, his methods were never going to be called into question. Turok was a loyal man, but he had the advantage of having followed some of the greatest warriors of all time in Arathorn Geoffry, Cedric Binosear, and Aryx Terian. As a member of the Lion's Mane, Turok had been one of the best, and his loyalty to the cause could never be questioned. But one thing he had learned in his service with the Mane, was the fact that there was a right way and a wrong way to do things. History taught that a reckless man, while he may eventually accomplish his goals, those that follow him usually end up in the grave. A wise leader protects his followers, sometimes even more than himself, for the good of the cause. Turok was beginning to see Pike for what many had always said he was; a greedy man, whose only goal was to get revenge for his loss. Ren also would follow Pike, but men with a strong sense of duty like Ren would never be heroes because they could never fight the way that the phasia fought. Pike remembered Gwydeon and how selfless he was at the end of the quest, but he also remembered the bitter and angry Gwydeon that had conspired with Emries in the forest outside of Scalla to ensure the quest would be victorious. That was the one quality that Ren could never have. He was too honest and too straightforward. Rachel was a different nightmare altogether. In many ways, Rachel reminded Pike of both Eldar and Midarin, displaying the combination of their best qualities. Rachel was fiercely loyal, passionate about doing what was right for the forces of the Light, a strong warrior, a staunch ally who was not afraid to speak her mind, and a true and caring friend. Pike knew that he had betrayed Rachel in the way that he dealt with Elizabeth's death. However, Pike had to bury away the pain and put up the strong front to keep the memories and old wounds from destroying him from the inside.

Jerrard and his family had been Pike's allies for years, dating back to the final battle with Shau-ling and the ugly events that led up to it. In this war, Jerrard had the most to gain, and the most to lose. His father had been murdered by his own kind, and while his blood was the same as those he fought against, he fought with the same intensity that any other warrior of the Light had. If Jerrard's children had half the tenacity of their father, Pike was sure they would be worthy additions to the cause. While Pike had no love lost for Aryx Terian, he also could not help but respect the man. He had been through battles and wars that Pike had only heard stories about, and through his vigilance and loyalty to the man he called lord, Aryx had been one of the staunchest devotees of the Way of the Light. When the others from Lord Cedric's group hid in the palace in Marcwell, Aryx came and fought alongside Logan and the People of the Dragon, and now he was back in the fold for a third time, refusing to be passed by. Midarin Rice was a member of the People of the Dragon, and that would never be taken from her. She and Pike were the only members left alive after Elwyne's death, and even through Jerrard was there at the end, he had been Korrd's ally and had not been through hell like the rest of the group. Together they had shared more than Pike even wanted to think about, and if there was going to be a war, Pike knew that he could count on Midarin to be right there beside him every step of the way.

"Turok," Pike said turning to the grim man, "arrange to have Celina moved inside the palace so she's safe. I don't think they'll be able to get into the courtyard, but I'd like to keep the wounded as far away from the battle lines as possible."

Turok seemed to cheer up a little at the command, and went quickly to carry out the order.

"I hate to bring this war down on your head Jerrard, but I can use all the help I can get."

"Anything for an old friend," Jerrard said drawing his sword. "Erika and Taya will help here in the courtyard, coordinating the care of the wounded and making sure that all supplies continue flowing to the regiments. Storm and I will join the Enforcers to lead the units and take the fight to this new threat."

"I'll take lead of the archers," Midarin said confidently, "but when the fighting starts I'll be right there with you."

Pike nodded and turned to the remaining members of the Enforcers.

"I know you all have just been through hell in Lakestone, and I would be lying if I said it was going to get better from here on in. It's only going to get worse, but you know as well as I do that this is what you all signed on for. This is what we have been training for, the defense of the way of the Light. I know we will be fighting against my son, but this new Hand or Torch or whatever they call themselves are as much a threat as the phasia."

"To your throne maybe," Rachel scoffed.

"Pike may have selfish motivations," Aryx chimed in, "but he is right about the threat that these people pose. They have been duped into perverting the noble cause and powers of the Moridon, and when banded together they would be more powerful than any army of Jeresei or Kalbraks. There is a reason that it took a member of the phasia the power of Saurn to stop the first Hand of the Light. It will take all of the prowess of all of the warriors in this army as well as in the Enforcers to even put up much of a resistance to their mystical weaponry."

Pike took a deep breath and twirled *Fury* in his hands.

"Then let's get ready, cause I'll be damned if I'm dying today."

＊ ＊ ＊ ＊ ＊ ＊ ＊ ＊ ＊ ＊ ＊

When Wolf finally made the quick journey downstairs to the receiving hall, there was a palpable tension filling the air. Lissa and Sabrina, while trying their best to ignore each other, still took the opportunity to exchange evil stares. When they both saw Wolf enter the room however, all of their venom was directed at him. Lissa took a step toward the young man, but Gwillim headed her off, taking her by the wrist and pulling her away. Bryn stood by, quietly amused at the entire scene, and especially pleased knowing that she had absolutely nothing to do with it. Wolf noticed also that Felicia was with the group as well, carrying a pack as though she were prepared to travel.

"Good of you to join us, Wolf," Bryn said quickly, trying to head off some of the aggression that floated through the room. "I was afraid that you were going to portal off somewhere after the fight I heard about upstairs."

"That you had nothing to do with, I'm sure," Wolf countered, relying more on his own instants than the thoughts being directed at him by Basille.

"No, no," she said smiling. "In fact, I knew nothing at all about it until Felicia filled me in on the details this morning, which brings me to an item of business. Felicia wants to reenter my service, but I am afraid that I don't need any more servants. So, if you wouldn't mind her tagging along, at least for a little while longer until you reach your next destination."

"Absolutely not," Sabrina interjected. "The places we are going are no place for innocents, and the only reason she came this far in the first place because lover-boy over there wasn't thinking with the right part of his anatomy."

Wolf fumed and was about to hurl an insult of his own when Nathaniel cut them off.

"That's quite enough!" The boy's voice was filled with power. "I don't know what happened last night, and I don't care. But if the three of you are going to allow this to interfere with our quest, then you all might as well go home. Sabrina, we need you, and Lissa we need you. Wolf, while it would be nice to have you with us, if you are going to be a disruption, then I would rather you go back to Aradon and keep the people there safe."

Bryn tried to contain the pleasure inside her at the infighting.

"This is not the time or the place for this Nathaniel," Wolf responded.

"I think it is," Nathaniel countered. "It's only out of respect for Sabrina and Lissa that I don't drag this all out of you right now and put an end to it. But I know that Sabrina and Lissa are both deeply wounded by what has occurred and I for one have more respect for their feelings than that. But if you leave me no other option, I will make sure that the truth is known."

Wolf stood defiantly and stared at Nathaniel. The inner hatred of the *Coromor* began to fill Wolf for the first time, and he began to understand why the phasia fought so hard to end the life of the petty creature. Instinctively, Wolf let the powers of the Blaze fill him. Nathaniel saw the flows of power enter the boy and let the powers of the *Coromor* rush into his body. In that next instant, everyone in the room with power clutched hard to the primal strings within them and prepared. No one knew what had triggered the stand-off, but it was now as though a spark had been loosed in a room full of powder kegs, and if it bounced the wrong way, the whole room would explode. Jared had watched the scene a bit detached until he felt something familiar in his heart and mind. He could feel the flows of power in the room, from both members of the *Erieal*, the *Coromor*, the *Chosen One*, Wolf and himself. Bryn had wisely kept herself from touching the Blaze, fearing that doing so would ignite a battle she would be unable to escape from before being struck down. The girl Liette also was filled with power, but looked uncomfortable without her sword in hand. Her power was unlike anything that Jared had ever felt, and seemed to be coming from outside of her, rather than from a string of power that flowed through her. Liette wasn't the only one still wishing they had their weapons, but it was evident that if a battle were sparked in the next few moments, only powers would be the deciding factor, not steel. Susanne, though unable to feel the power around her, knew that something had occurred and that she was in a very precarious position there in the center of what could be the battlefield. But as Jared searched deeper into the power in the room, he felt another presence. It was that of a full member of the phasia, and it wasn't Grawn, Bryn, or Wolf. The power was there, like a faint memory in the deepest recesses of Jared's mind. Finally, he found it. The power was that of his mother Caris, and when he traced the power, it led to one place.

What happened the next few moments in the receiving hall of the Palace of Barer could have been remembered as the greatest battle that never happened. No bard would hear the story, and no history of the third war against the Shadow would ever record it. It was even doubtful that any involved would ever speak of it again. Jared, already filled with the powers of the Blaze lashed out, sending two bolts of lightning soaring from the tip of his scepter into the unsuspecting body of the former barmaid Felicia. The girl cried out in pain and slumped to the ground. Everyone in the room was shocked and unable to act for the next few moments, and before either Nathaniel or Wolf could lash out at the man they thought was an ally, they saw the body of the girl begin to move. No longer did she have the guise of the pretty blond barmaid, but instead her facial features had changed to a more refined and adult beauty, and the blond color retreated from the strands of hair, replaced by a dark brown. Wolf recognized the woman as the phase Caris immediately and channeled all of his power over the Blaze at the reviving form. Nathaniel too loosed an assault, and in a matter of seconds, Caris had been vaporized, only her cries of pain echoing through the room for the next few seconds remained. Everyone slowly released their powers, the desire to strike one another down receding. Lissa for one had a hard time letting go of the string of Fire, her need to kill Sabrina and Wolf screaming in the back of her mind loudly and then suddenly falling silent forever. Wolf turned his attention to Bryn, who threw her hands up, a worried expression leaping to her perfect face.

"I didn't know it was Caris," she said without being asked. "She has always had the ability to use her transformation powers without touching the Blaze. If you search the memories that Basille and the Blaze have given you, then you'll know it's true."

Wolf didn't have to search the memories, he already knew that Bryn was telling the truth.

"That explains a lot," Wolf said finally. "Sabrina, did you come to my room in Frontier late in the night?"

Sabrina look of shock answered the question fully enough.

"I didn't think so. Then Caris was the one who has been toying with our thoughts, trying to pit us against one another."

"It still doesn't explain last night," Lissa responded angrily.

"Unless Caris took Wolf's form to be with me," Sabrina said, repulsion filling her.

"Caris doesn't take male form," Bryn answered. "She feels it's beneath her."

"Then someone else did," Wolf commented. "I swear on everything I hold dear that I was not in Sabrina's room any time last night, and slept until I was awoken by their fight."

Nathaniel turned to Sabrina and looked her square in the eyes.

"Could you have imagined it?"

Sabrina looked up at Wolf and then back at Nathaniel before shaking her head.

"I saw Wolf walk out of Sabrina's room," Lissa insisted, "and then walk down stairs to the receiving hall."

Gwillim chimed in before Wolf had a chance to speak.

"That's impossible," he said his hand on Lissa's shoulder, "I heard Sabrina's door open when you kicked it in, and I ran out immediately. When Wolf came to break up your fight, he came out of his room. If he walked downstairs as you said he did, then he would not have been able to run back upstairs and then sneak back into his room without my seeing him."

"And if he would have used a portal, we all would have felt it," Nathaniel added. "Even with the ability that Basille had to split his portals to hide the destination, the use of the power is unmistakable."

"And," Bryn added, "my servants reported to me that no member of your group had been down here when I arrived to greet you moments ago. The first person I saw was Sabrina in tears and then Lissa."

"Then someone else is behind this," Susanne interjected. "I don't pretend to understand what happened, but I do know that if Wolf could not have been there, then Wolf wasn't there. So that means we have to look for another option."

"Like what?" Lissa asked, her anger ranging higher, still unabated.

"There are other members of the phasia who can change their form," Susanne answered, disgust filling her voice. "I know that from experience."

"Erdric," Nathaniel added quickly.

"She's right," Bryn said nodding. "Caris and Erdric had a lot in common, and for some reason Erdric tried to emulate everything that Caris did. It served him well in infiltrating Marcwell on several occasions."

"And if we find the Torch," Sabrina said trying to ignore the fact that she may have been seduced by a member of the phasia, "then we find Erdric."

"Because Michael is leading them," Susanne finished.

Wolf finally made his way to the bottom of the stairs and walked slowly up to Bryn.

"I believe that you had nothing to do with Caris and her little game, but if I find out otherwise, you better believe that I will come back here and repay you for it."

Bryn let the threat pass over her.

"I think that your talents would be better suited taking care of my brother Erdric and his little followers. This Creator's Torch Society was massing just a few days march from Scalla, and unless my spies are wrong, they should be there sometime this morning."

"Then we need to help Pike and the Enforcers, because he would have gone to Scalla after Lakestone," Liette said, contributing to the conversation.

Wolf nodded, keeping his back to the little girl.

"Remember what I said," Wolf's voice was low and full of power.

Bryn watched as the boy turned and joined the rest of his group. Perhaps Bryn had been wrong in her initial opinion of Wolf. He was very much like Logan and Korrd. He had the same temper and fierce loyalty, and Caris had also proved that he was as gullible as the rest of the Ranthall men as well. Perhaps that was why Emries had marked that line. He had always preferred followers that didn't question orders. As the group left, Bryn smiled and turned only to be faced by a man she thought she would never see again.

"Been a long time, Bryn," Aerith said smiling, "I need a favor."

* * * * * * * * * * *

Wolf knew the group would be uneasy for a while, and he was not surprised to see Lissa waiting for him as he walked out through the portcullis of the palace of Sador. She had recovered her sword from the detachment of the Army of the Fox that guarded the palace and it hung from the scabbard on her belt. What did surprise Wolf was the fact that Sabrina stood with Lissa, both with serious looks in their eyes. There was some hesitation within Wolf, and he did not know whether or not he wanted to approach the two women, but silently resolved that it was better to confront the situation than to hide from it.

"Wolf," Lissa said calmly, "we just wanted to tell you that we believe everything that you said back there, and we're both sorry that we didn't listen to you before."

"And," Sabrina continued, "neither of us would be surprised if you wanted to keep your distance from us and just focus on what we have to do."

"Don't think that there is any pressure," Lissa added, "to choose between us or anything. I think you know how we both feel, but after all this, we don't want to fight about you or over you."

Wolf nodded and smiled.

"I'm glad I don't have to choose," he said trying to lighten the mood, "because it would be impossible. Let's just do what we need to do, and the rest will take care of itself."

Sabrina forced a smile, and turned to rejoin the rest of the group. Lissa lingered for a moment and then wrapped her arms around Wolf and held him tightly before giving him a light kiss on the cheek. Wolf was a bit uncomfortable for a moment, and then tried to put the events of the morning out of his mind and focus on the task at hand. There had been a moment when the People of the Ram seemed ready to rip each other apart, and looking into the eyes of the girl Liette, Wolf felt as though she still had the desire.

"If you're done putting your love lives ahead of the prophecies, maybe we can get started?"

Gwillim groaned.

"Liette, I thought we had solved all of this back in Frontier."

"We did," Liette answered, "and I still think Wolf is a traitor. Now I think that Jared is in it with him. Besides how could he have felt Caris if Nathaniel and the rest of you couldn't?"

"Because she's my mother," Jared answered harshly. "And no matter what she was doing to disguise her powers, she and I still share that bond that she could never sever no matter how much she didn't want me. I felt her potential powers, not her active powers as Nathaniel and the rest of you do. It's something that the phasia don't even think about hiding because only members of their immediate families could feel it. Since most of the phasia don't have children, that's never a threat. I'm sure it was just an oversight for Caris."

"A convenient oversight," Liette countered.

Jared drew his sword and rounded on Liette, but Nathaniel cut him off.

"Do we have to go through this again? We aren't going to let a member of the phasia beat us. Caris poisoned our minds and showed us just how vulnerable we are. Unless we are a hell of a lot more careful from here on in, a phase like Jeroch or Saurn will pick us off without even thinking about it. And don't forget that Rane, Cash, and Grimm have their own scores to settle with us, and I know they'll try to collect on those debts before too long. So, the last thing we need is to be at each other's throats and doing the phasia a favor. So if you have these thoughts and these doubts, keep them to yourselves and just do what you are supposed to."

Everyone gave their affirmative.

"Good," Nathaniel continued. "Now, we know the Torch is heading for Scalla, so we're going to portal into the courtyard. Jerrard should feel it immediately, so there will probably be guards all around us when we come out. Just keep your hands away from your weapons and pray we don't walk out in the middle of a warzone."

Without any prompting, Wolf closed his eyes and channeled the powers of the Blaze into a single point of empty air. It took only a few seconds for the portal to form, and when it had finished, the People of the Ram stepped through, meeting their new fate on the other side. Wolf stepped through last, and the portal closed behind him. A few moments later, a woman appeared where the portal had been. Her green dress clung to her body, regal and tawdry at the same time. Caris brushed her hair back and let a chuckle flow though her carefully guarded expression.

"As though it would be that easy, Jared," she said into the air. "You are every bit the fool that your father was, but perhaps you will be useful to me before too long."

* * * * * * * * * * *

Bryn stood looking at the man who stood before her, a thousand questions racing through her mind, and a thousand more emotions plaguing her heart. It had been too many years since her eyes had rested on Aerith's face, and she didn't know whether to kiss him or slap him. Because of the confrontation with Wolf Ranthall, she chose the latter. Aerith smiled, even as the flesh of his face stung from the impact of Bryn's open hand.

"A favor?" she said incredulous. "You haven't come to see me in all of these years, through all of these hardships, and now you come here to ask me for a favor?"

Aerith laughed, watching Bryn trying to be angry. He knew her better than any man or woman who had ever associated with her, even Grawn and Ellis. Aerith knew that Bryn was happy to see him, but didn't want to let him know.

"I love you too," Aerith commented.

Bryn raised her hand as though to slap him again, but instead took hold his shoulders and pulled Aerith toward her, pressing her lips to his in a hard kiss. The kiss broke off quickly, and Bryn pressed the side of her face to Aerith's strong chest, holding him tightly.

"Please tell me you're staying this time."

Aerith stayed silent. Bryn sighed and looked back up into the man's eyes.

"I can't Bryn, but I will keep my promise to you, that much I swear. But there is still too much to do, and too many loose ends that need to be tied up."

Bryn nodded her head and sighed.

"What do you need?"

Aerith swallowed hard.

"I know Wolf and the others are on their way to Scalla to fight the Torch, but they have no idea what they are getting in to. The fight there is just going to be a diversion to throw Pike and the Enforcers off the track and give Duncan the opportunity he needs to seize Marcwell. No matter what happens, we can't allow Erdric to get his claws into Marcwell, otherwise no one is safe, and he will lead his new army right here to exterminate you and Grawn."

Bryn nodded. Aerith was right. Erdric had dreamed of ruling Marcwell almost as long as Jeroch had. Once he had that seat of power, he would consider himself apart from Shau-ling's commands and at the head of the Council. Thanks to his little army, Erdric would be able to ignore Shau-ling's mandate and do everything in his power to make sure that no other phase had a chance to take his prize. Because Barer was so close to Marcwell, the Torch would surely be battering down the walls, looking to keep the charade of being the Hand of the Light reborn up as long as possible.

"I'll mobilize the Army of the Fox and send them to Marcwell. In fact, Grawn and I will command them ourselves."

Aerith kissed Bryn on the forehead and pulled her tightly to him.

"Thank you Bryn," he said softly. "I swear I will come back for you when this is all over."

Before she realized what was happening, Bryn felt the form of Aerith Seth disappear, and found herself holding nothing. Her heart felt as though it would break, but she summoned up all of her courage and strode toward the throne room to begin the preparations for war.

* * * * * * * * * * *

Pike looked on as the force on the hill began to advance. Their march was slow and deliberate, as though they were waiting for something. The Raven's Wing had assembled outside the walls of the palace, catapults and archers ready to loose their deadly volley into the ranks of the approaching Torch. Out of the corner of his eye, Pike could see Jerrard tense and begin to look around. Suddenly he motioned with his hand and a portal appeared. Confused, Storm followed his father through, and Pike dove through also, just before the portal closed. When Pike tumbled out the other side, Jerrard stood holding his black bladed sword, an ominous green aura cloaking it. Storm too held his sword ready to combat whatever invisible enemies his father was waiting for. In the next moment, Pike would realize what Jerrard had felt, as a portal appeared in the very center of the courtyard.

Midarin had been watching everything from the walkway suspended from the top of the inner wall of the courtyard where the Raven's Wing's archers were placed. When the portal appeared, she drew back the bowstring of her trusty bow and aimed with deadly precision, waiting for whatever emerged. When she saw the familiar red armor and the gruff appearance of the man who stepped through, she sighed deeply and made her way to the nearest ladder.

Gwillim held his hands up immediately upon seeing Jerrard and Storm armed. The older of the two laughed as soon as he saw his old friend and returned his sword to the scabbard, crossing the distance and extending his hand. Gwillim met Jerrard half way, but instead of shaking his ally's hand, pulled him into his arms, hugging him tightly and then releasing him.

Jerrard didn't say anything as he watched the rest of the group emerge from the portal, the last one filling Jerrard's heart with hope.

"It's good to see you again, Gwillim," Jerrard said finally. "Only next time could you pick a mode of transportation that won't scare the hell out of me?"

Gwillim laughed.

"I thought that is how you people with phasia blood preferred to travel? What would your father think?"

Jerrard joined Gwillim in laughing at the old private joke and then greeted each of the new arrivals that he knew. When he came to the last three members of the group, Gwillim was quick to assist Jerrard with introductions.

"This beautiful young woman is Susanne Praen, a former member of the Creator's Torch Society," Gwillim started.

"Good," Storm chimed in. "Any knowledge that she has will be imperative now that they are at our walls."

"And these two men are Jared Vale' and Wolf Ranthall."

Jerrard waited for a moment, looking into the boy's eyes before extending his hand to Wolf.

"I've been waiting a long time to shake your hand Wolf, I'm terribly sorry about your mother, and I wish I could have been there to pay my respects."

Wolf smiled and nodded. Pike stood close, regarding the three new members to the group, but turned to his daughter and gripped *Fury* tightly.

"Sabrina, you take Lissa and Liette to the front lines and help Turok keep the Raven's Wing together for the charge. Gwillim, you stick with Nathaniel and Midarin, keep the archers on target and them off guard. Susanne, if you could stick with me, I'll need all the information you can manage to give me about the tactics of your former group. Jared and Wolf,

I don't know what you can do, but I'm sure you'd be great in the charge with the rest. Welcome to the Enforcers lads."

Pike extended his hand, but Wolf stood firm.

"No offense Pike," he said sternly, "but I'm here to help Nathaniel, not to join your little army. There's a member of the phasia and his kid leading the army you're about to fight, and in case you didn't know it yet, your son is with them, ready to carve you up and take Marcwell for his own."

"Why you little . . ."

Before Pike could continue, cheers came up from the ranks of the Raven's Wing.

"What's happening?" Jerrard yelled up to the suspended walkway.

"The Torch is withdrawing," a soldier called back.

"It was a trick," Nathaniel said the next moment.

"They wanted us to be here so that Duncan could attack . . ." Sabrina started.

"Marcwell," Pike finished.

Unexpected Challenges

Creator's Calendar Year 1205; Dark Mirror

The burned out and desolate city of Sarmeel stood as one of the few remaining testaments to an age long past. Sarmeel had not seen a human inhabitant within its walls since long before Aralias Imstra gave the world the prophecies of the *Coromor*. In fact, the only people who had managed to survive a confrontation with the feral city had been the People of the Dragon. However, their visit had been marked by further devastation of the remaining buildings thanks in large part to a massive tidal wave that had been summoned by Pike Rhuiden in defense of his friends. However, deep beneath the surface of the city, a secret kingdom had been slowly building over the years.

Since his forceful expulsion from the kingdom of Askronilka by Ellis several generations past, Farax had called the desolate town his home. No other member of the phasia cared about the ruins, and so no one would come looking for him, thus disturbing his many experiments. For many years, Farax had been considered one of the greatest of the phasia when it came to creating new monsters for the forces of the Shadows. He was constantly tinkering with the designs that Shau-ling had created, adding little improvements over the centuries. Several of the clans of the Jeresei were his personal triumphs, giving them the ability to change the patterns of weather around them by imbuing them with a minute ability to channel the Blaze. While Shau-ling had been upset at this modification originally, it later became a standard ability in the later generations. Of course, Shau-ling had taken credit for every bit of the ingenuity that Farax had shown in researching and creating the new Jeresei. There had naturally been failures to the process, Jeresei that were horribly deformed after using their power, or simply burst into flames at random. But that was in the past, and a few lives were so little a cost. Even if he would kill tens of thousands in his experiments, it would not matter, there would always be more.

There was always a fine line between success and failure when changing that which a god had made. The secret of the Jeresei was well kept from Emries and the rest of the forces of the Light, a secret that Shau-ling himself only had the barest knowledge of. When Farax first began his experimentation on the Jeresei, they were an off-shoot of the Kalbrak race. Dim-witted and slow, that incarnation of the Jeresei were terrible servants and only marginal warriors. But when inspiration struck Farax, he knew that if Shau-ling would allow his experiment to occur, he could create the greatest fighting weapon that the Shadows had ever seen. They would be one step down from the phasia in power, and would make any army who stood against them run with fear. With Shau-ling's begrudging permission, Farax set out to search for the perfect testing grounds, and came upon the city of Sarmeel. It was a thriving community with hundreds of people, oblivious to the fate that would befall them. Farax had created a chemical that was laced with a tiny fraction of Blaze energy, with special combinations of the flows of wind and water. The chemical was placed into the city's water supply, and over the next few days, the powers of the chemical took effect and began to change the inhabitants of Sarmeel.

The change started simply enough, and innocuously enough that no one would have thought that anything was out of the ordinary. It started with the lowering of tolerance for the failings of others. The slightest mistake or misspoken word often incited an argument, and as the chemical took hold further on the inhabitants, the aggression level rose and these arguments led to bloodshed. Before long, the humans began to take on more animalistic tendencies, like a craving for raw flesh, a greater desire to hunt and kill weaker species, a fear of what they didn't understand, and a pack mentality.

Eventually these mental changes gave way to physical changes, as the powers of the Blaze began to alter the humans and turn them into the beasts that would eventually be named Jeresei. Once Shau-ling saw the promise that these now creature showed, he ordered Farax to use his chemical on some of the straggling tribes of men high in the mountains and across the great sea in the vast desert that lay there. In a matter of years, thousands of mortals had been changed into Jeresei, their only allegiance to Shau-ling and any who wielded authority in his name. They eventually replaced the Kalbraks as Shau-ling's favorite servants, until Jeroch developed the creatures call Shadowwalkers. Though Jeroch always took credit for mutating the humans into usable creatures with the help of his mysterious Black Tower, it was truly Farax who was the genius.

Farax knew in his heart that the Jeresei were better warriors, but because Jeroch had created the winged beasts, he knew that Shau-ling would give them every advantage possible. While Shau-ling had groused at Farax using a small bit of the Blaze to convert human to Jeresei, he did not hesitate to give the Shadowwalkers the ability to channel the pure power of the Blaze in their flaming breath. How Farax hated Jeroch for the slight. But Farax had returned to his underground kingdom of Sarmeel with new focus. He would create the perfect servants for Shau-ling. It took him nearly two hundred years, but finally he had molded the creatures into killing machines. In Farax's mind, his new creations were perfect. They felt no pain, had the strength of a Stone, had a very limited pull on the Blaze for their attacks, and could kill their foe even after their own death. The name of the beasts had been an after-thought. He called the little monsters Snags.

The Snags had several abilities that made them unique from the rest of the fodder at Shau-ling's disposal. First and foremost was the fact that as the Snags grew older, they evolved. At first, they were little fist sized balls of fur. To an unsuspecting person, they would merely sit and purr, like a kitten. However, once touched, the ball would open to reveal a mass of sharp teeth. The jaws of a Snag had every bit of strength that a Stone could put behind a single punch, and if necessary, a Snag could bite through a sword, armor, or even a wall of solid rock. After a few years of growth, a Snag developed a tail. It was actually Farax's design for the tail of Snag that gave Shau-ling the idea for the tail given to Nightwing. The only difference was the fact that the entire length of a Snag's tail was sharpened. The only substance that the tail of a Snag couldn't cut through was the indestructible stone Berionite. Also at this age, the Snag's had the ability to move by bouncing. A Snag could bounce the length of several mortal strides, or the same distance straight up. The final stage of the evolution of the Snag granted them some measure of intelligence, and the ability to touch the Blaze. Unfortunately, Farax was not granted the latitude with his use of the Blaze that Jeroch had, but Farax did find a way to make due. The only way that the Snags could channel the Blaze was to use their tails as a conduit, thus making their tails an even more formidable weapon. Any wound inflicted by a Blaze enhanced tail of a Snag could not be healed by any normal methods, and the person would find themselves dead within a matter of hours, depending on the depth and severity of the wound. Also the Snags had the ability to channel the Blaze into themselves, augmenting their speed and agility, allowing them to move at speeds near the limit of mortal comprehension. They were truly elegant weapons.

However, Farax had been shocked when Shau-ling had not seen the beauty of the beasts he had created. To Shau-ling, the Snags were toys in comparison to the Jeresei and the Shadowwalkers. But, Shau-ling did consent to keep one of the more advanced Snags, a Black Snag, in his Hall of Terrors. It had been little concession for all the work that Farax had put into crafting the creatures, but it did not stop him from continuing to use them as the security for his underground kingdom. Farax had been very pleased when Logan Ranthall and his little group had entered Sarmeel. The Snags had been powerful enough to wound several of their group, but before the remaining Snags could hunt them down and finish the job, Shau-ling's Jeresei showed up and ruined the trap. The tidal wave that hit the town would set Farax's work back several months, and would not pick up again until his rebirth into the third generation. However, when Farax did return, he found that hundreds of his Snags still existed, and they had evolved even further during his absence. Several of the Black Snags had become more intelligent, sharing a form of telepathic communication but on a purely animalistic level. There were no words or any true language, but there were feelings and instincts that flowed from one to another that could dictate a tactic that would be used. Farax had loosed some of the evolved Snags on the twin towns of Rana and Rama, just to see what they were capable of. Farax was shocked and marveled as he watched the Snags pick their targets, focusing on those who were strongest and the heaviest threat, disabling them by gnawing off their sword arm, or cutting out their eyes, and then leaving the wounded creature to move onto the next most dangerous opponent. Part of Farax wanted to parade these advanced Snags in front of his master, but he had better uses for them. Eventually he would take his little army up against the *Coromor* and his followers and let the Snags tear them apart.

As he sat as his workbench, pouring over the notes of his creation and the growth of the Snags, Farax felt a familiar twinge in the back of his mind. A portal had formed somewhere inside the city, and tracing the line of power back, Farax could tell that it had come from the kingdom of Sador. That kingdom had been in the control of Zarsi for many generations, but Zarsi knew that Sarmeel was Farax's home and would not dare portal in so close, especially if he was coming to challenge Farax in the War for Ascension. Besides, Zarsi knew that every bit of Farax's kingdom lay below ground. This intruder must have vanquished Zarsi and was looking to add another member of the phasia to his list. Smiling to himself, Farax used a tiny trickle of the Blaze to open the cages deep beneath the workshop to loose the Snags. Whoever the visitor was, he was in for a very rude reception.

* * * * * * * * * * *

Nathan Sandar let the portal close behind him quickly before Logan or any of his phasia brethren could follow. They had been foolish to stand against him in Sador, and had even converted his mother to their cause. Nathan heard the voices in the back of his head telling him that he couldn't trust anyone, that he was alone. The voices had served him well so far, keeping him one step ahead of Logan Ranthall in both of their duels, and helping him to find the hidden string of power deeply hidden within the string of Order that gave him the power to change time. Zarsi's attack with the full power of the Blaze would have destroyed Nathan and ended the life of the third *Coromor*. But thanks to his new powers over the flows of time itself, Nathan had been able to skip through time and reappear in the same spot after the Blaze had receded enough to be safe. However, he did not want to press his advantage. Taking on one member of the phasia had tested him more fully than Nathan thought possible, but to go against four at the same time was suicide. It was a pity that Rachel had to die the way she did, but she was just a mortal after all, and the mortals were created to serve the gods. Nathan knew that he was the living embodiment of a god and that all mortals should be thankful to lay down their lives to protect him. But the time for such thoughts were too much of a trifle for Nathan to worry about. Draven was the target that his sights were firmly set upon.

For some reason, Draven kept to the haunts of his predecessor Basille, taking control of the kingdom of Scalla. Unfortunately for anyone who tried to assault Scalla, there was no real place to hide when approaching. Every bit of land around Scalla was flat and barren. There were no forests to hide in, no mountain ranges, nothing except those damn wide rolling hills. Because of this, there were no decent places to portal into that Draven wouldn't have been able to pick up on. Also, Nathan did not have a lot of spare time to aim his portal or think much about the destination because of Logan and his new allies. So, Sarmeel was as good a place as any to start. With the mines of Quea to the South, the twin towns of Rana and Rama to the east, and Illimar to the north, Sarmeel was the perfect ground to strike at several of the phasia all at once. Scalla though was the most dangerous because of Draven, and Nathan had a large score to settle because of Gwillim. His mother and father had tried hard to shield him as much as possible from the war, because his role had been so important, but now that he had been awakened to the full potential of his powers, he would not be held back any longer. Laughing quietly to himself, Nathan began walking through Sarmeel toward the plains of Scalla.

As he walked, Nathan began to get the feeling that he was being watched. Every crack in every piece of rock seemed to follow his every step and movement. Out of the corner of his eye, the boy caught a faint hint of movement, but as his head turned to follow it, there was nothing there. As he turned back, he saw a small ball of white fur laying on the ground. There was a soft purring sound coming from somewhere deep inside it that was strangely soothing. For a moment, Nathan didn't know what to make of the strange object, but as he glanced to his left, he saw several more of the balls of fur, some white and others gray, laying on the ground a few strides away. Nathan swore to himself that the fur balls had not been there moments earlier, and when he looked back to the original object, he noticed that where there was once one of the things, there were now ten to fifteen. Fear beginning to creep into him, Nathan looked around and realized that he was surrounded by the balls of fur.

The objects now made no effort to disguise their movements, bouncing out from the cracks and crevices of the ruined buildings, filling in the blank spaces in the perimeter around the human. In a matter of moments they had formed a perfect circle around Nathan, a full stride away from him. The next few balls of fur that emerged were much different from the rest. They appeared to be larger, and all of them had a dark black fur. It also occurred to Nathan that the purring of the larger black balls of fur was a much lower pitch. While the little balls sounded like young kittens, the black balls of fur sounded like old fat cats that did little else but lay in a sunbeam. The outer perimeter of the sea of white and gray fur was sealed with black, a border between Nathan and the rest of the city of Sarmeel. Before he knew what had happened, the balls of fur had stopped purring, all except the black ones. The white and gray balls then began to bounce, slowly at first, only a few inches off the ground, and then finally they bounded as high as Nathan's eye level. Watching the bouncing balls, Nathan found himself lost in the rhythmic motion of the gray and white waves, the low sound of the purring lulling him to sleep. Nathan was so mesmerized by the movement that he did not see the black balls around the perimeter of the bouncing mass open to reveal bright eyes and rows of razor sharp teeth. Nathan's attention was not broken from the rhythmic mass until a gleam of light caught his eye. One of the bouncing gray balls had produced a tail that glowed like the sharpened metal on the edge of a knife when it catches the light at the right angle. Before he knew what was happening, Nathan saw that all of the balls had produced tails, and the purring had stopped. All hell broke loose the next second.

Several of the balls of fur leapt at Nathan, sending him scrambling to the ground. However, the creatures had been faster than Nathan had anticipated. Pain struck the boy as he hit the ground, the feel of warm blood soaking his shirt and clinging to two long wounds that ran down his back. Nathan rolled on his side, channeled a small bit of his power to heal the gaping wounds, and he saw the new threats bouncing across the area where he lay, their tails flashing in the light, ready to inflict more damage on his body. The *Coromor* channeled a strong flow of wind, scattering the balls of fur and giving Nathan the opportunity to get back to his feet and face his opponents. The creatures obviously had underestimated their opponent, taking him for just another mortal, and they changed their tactics. Instead of leaping at him one at a time, the bouncing mob came in waves, several tails flailing at him from several directions, landing blows almost as fast as his powers could heal the damage. Finally, Nathan encased himself in a shield of Wind and began to channel bolts of fire into the bouncing balls. Several of them exploded one right after the other, but while the shield of wind protected Nathan from the slashing tails and the biting teeth, the smoking green blood that erupted from the detonated forms penetrated the swirling winds, burning Nathan's skin. Suddenly he realized that he had not woven his shield tight enough, but remedied that with the slightest thought. Even through the tiny creatures could not get through his defenses and were being picked off one after another, they continued to batter against the whirling winds. Nathan was not ready for what happened next.

The black balls had been sitting silently, watching the action until the shield of wind had been erected. As if it sensed what had happened, one of the black creatures leapt into the air and spun fast on it vertical axis, sending its tail whirling with an impossible amount of speed. As soon as the blade of the tail contacted the shield of wind, the flows were cut, and Nathan had barely enough time to react before the spinning creature cut him in half as well. Cursing himself, Nathan leapt clear of the mass of creatures and formed the shield around himself again, fortifying it with the flows of Earth and Fire. Now as the little creatures collided with the shield, they burst into flames, sending more of their acidic blood splattering through the air. It took only a dozen or so frying before the assaults stopped. It was a tenuous stalemate. Nathan had used much of his powers against Logan, Zarsi, and then in the creation of the two shields without a chance to rest and refocus. Unlike the Blaze, there was a limit to how much power the *Coromor* could call on in a short period of time.

"How do you like my little pets?" a high pitched voice said from behind Nathan.

The boy whirled around, still maintaining a firm hold on the shield that surrounded him and locked his eyes on the man before him. Farax would never be considered the most handsome of the phasia, from his beady eyes, hunched posture and oily skin and hair, he resembled his namesake the Vulture a little too well.

"They have your personality."

Farax laughed an annoying cackle that made Nathan's ears ring.

"My Snags are perfect little boy, or should I call you little Ram?"

Nathan scowled.

"How much more power do you have left, *Coromor*? You look tired. I'll bet that if I shatter that little shield of yours that my Snags would tear you apart and have a nice dinner. Then I could go back to Shau-ling and tell him that I killed the *Coromor* not Draven, and then I would be the favorite in the War for Ascension."

Nathan laughed, trying to hide the discomfort of his powers beginning to fail him.

"This is bad comedy Farax," the boy jibed. "I could call down a flow of lava that would melt all of you in a single stroke and not even break a sweat."

Farax laughed again.

"Then do it," the phase challenged. "If you could have eliminated my Snags so easily you would have done it by now little *Coromor*. You're as good as dead."

Nathan knew that he didn't have much time left. If he didn't release the powers that were sustaining the shield soon, he wouldn't be able to fight a Jeresei, let alone a Snag or Farax. Trying to look as though it were a planned occurrence, Nathan slowly let the flows unravel and dissipate into the air, but kept hold of a minor bit of fire, letting a ball of flame float over his palm.

"Why let you little creatures here do your dirty work for you? Why not take the opportunity to get the kill yourself? Then there would be no one in the Council who would question your worth."

Nathan could feel his powers slowly return, and he needed only a few more minutes to be back at full strength. Farax only had to take the bait and talk too much like all the other phasia, and he would play right into Nathan's hands.

"Do I look like Taron to you little boy?" Farax countered. "It doesn't matter how you die, so long as you die."

Nathan saw that his plan had backfired, and it was only by sheer luck that he ducked out of the way as the bolt of power erupted from Farax's hand. The phase leapt into the air the next moment, letting the flows of wind suspend him. Nathan rolled across the ground, feeling the loose rocks and debris rake against the new-mended skin on his back. The Snags sensed and opportunity to strike and launched themselves at the tired boy, diving down on him in waves of motion and fury. Nathan had been able to recover the use of some of his abilities as the *Coromor*, and retaliated with streams of fire that flew from his fingers, catching several of the Snags, sending acidic blood into the air until it fell like rain. Several drops hit the boy, stinking his flesh and burning deep beneath his skin. As Nathan made it back to his feet, he channeled the flows of water into his skin, flushing the acid from his body, easing some of the pain that racked him. Farax was not content to let his Snags have all the fun however, sending streams of wind across the area, keeping the boy off-balance. Several times the strong gusts pushed the *Coromor* into the attacks of the Snags, rewarding the boy with several long and ugly cuts. Blood flowed down the boy's body, his exhausted powers unable to keep up. The Snags had surrounded the boy again, but he was on his knees channeling his powers into a shield once again. Having learned their lesson, the Snags kept their distance from the shield, waiting for their lord and master Farax to descend from his perch and give them the opportunity to finish off the poor intruder who had dared to defile their home with his presence.

"So, you thought that you would make easy prey of the great Lord Vulture," Farax cackled. "Now you see what a fool you are."

Nathan smiled. He was beginning to recharge his powers again, but did not dare channel any of the power to healing his wounds. As long as Farax thought that boy was beaten, Nathan had a chance, but if Farax did the intelligent thing and finished Nathan off now, there was nothing that the boy could do to stop it for happening.

"What's so funny boy?"

"I didn't even know you were here," Nathan said meekly, mixing as much truth into his story to make it believable. "I was going after Draven, and this seemed the safest place to launch my attack."

Farax didn't know whether to laugh or be outraged.

"To tell the truth, I wasn't even worried about you," Nathan said pressing his only advantage. "Logan killed you so easily in the last generation that I didn't even think you were going to be much of a challenge."

Rage filled Farax, and he filled himself with the Blaze. Nathan felt the power surge up within Farax and waited for his chance to strike. He would get only one shot, and if he missed the Snags would tear him apart and Shau-ling would have a much easier road to dominating the world.

"Now you know that your fate was indeed sealed by the great Farax Soar, the Lord Vulture of the Brotherhood of Phasia, puny mortal. I shall end your life as Logan Ranthall ended mine in the previous lifetime, a monument to failure."

Farax's blast of Wind and Earth sped toward Nathan the next moment, the cue for Nathan to take his one last chance. Releasing all of his powers in a focused burst, Nathan channeled an flow of Wind into the shape of a long solid arch, and when Farax's attack hit the wall of wind, it sped down the trail the current created, taking it right back toward its creator. Farax, not expecting the boy to have anything left to defend himself with was unable to avoid the attack, and as the bolt of earth and wind struck, Farax felt his body go numb and his skin began to crackle and ache. He couldn't move his joints and in a matter of seconds, he could not drag breath in and out of his lungs. The flows of earth had entered him, turning him to stone. But the battle was not over for Nathan. He released the shield of fire, wind, and earth, sending it back toward the Snags. It was a large enough distraction that he could use the last trickle of power within him to open a portal and fall through before the Snags leapt again, this time only finding air with their glowing tails.

Marcwell

The cheering from the ranks of the Raven's Wing continued for a few more moments as the withdrawal of the Creator's Torch Society concluded. What the members of Raven's Wing didn't know was that the attack had been a carefully planned feint designed to keep key pieces in the game out of the way so the larger force could strike where it would hurt the most, the Kingdom of Marcwell. Though Marcwell was not defenseless by any means, the greatest portion of Marcwell's army had been redeployed across the countryside trying to prevent the force of the Shadow from gaining a foothold. As Pike stood in the courtyard, listening to the cheers and waiting for his Enforcers to report back to him, his blood burned with fury that was focused in a hundred places at once. The boy Wolf Ranthall was acting as though he were the third *Coromor* of the prophecies and that Pike didn't even matter. Then there was his own son Duncan, vying for Pike's rightful throne with a force behind him. Unless Pike acted quickly, Marcwell would be under siege, and not even the Enforcers would be able to do anything about it. The detachment of the Lion's Mane that remained in the city would function well enough, but they were too small in number to handle a prolonged assault. Without the reserves from the Order of the Sword, who would not arrive in Marcwell for another week at the earliest, the proud kingdom would fall and soon have a pretender on the throne.

Inwardly cursing himself for being caught by surprise, Pike turned to his old ally Jerrard and extended his hand.

"Marcwell doesn't have a chance against the kind of force that Galen and Aryx describe. Midarin only sent the detachment from the Order of the Sword three days ago, and their march won't put them in Marcwell for another week, probably more because their commanders won't push. I need to borrow the Raven's Wing to defend Marcwell. I figure between you, Nathaniel, and Sabrina, you ought to be able to open a portal big enough to get us all there."

Jerrard nodded. Marcwell was an important piece of the puzzle. For years, it had stood as the shining beacon in the falling shadows, and even though it had fallen under siege in the last generation, Pike's ascendance to the throne had wiped that from most people's memories. If Marcwell were to fall by force of arms in this generation, many would begin to lose hope and fear the armies of the Shadow that were beginning to mass around the world. A people who are afraid are easier to rule, a lesson taught by the phasia for centuries.

"My army as well as myself are at your full disposal, old friend," Jerrard said extending his hand and shaking Pike's firmly. "But a portal that big is going to take some time to prepare for."

Nathaniel turned away from where Jerrard and Pike began talking about deployment and the best battle plans for the terrain and walked over to Wolf. Through the whole conversation Wolf had kept his opinions silent, and as Nathaniel approached he felt his lips curl into a sly smile. He knew what the boy was thinking.

"It was a mistake to come here," Nathaniel said as soon as he was sure he was out of Pike's earshot.

Jerrard, Storm, Aryx, Pike, most of the Enforcers, and Liette were wrapped in their conversation, hammering out the final details of what would be their glorious assault. Gwillim had followed Nathaniel, and Lissa and Sabrina were very close to Wolf, each for their own reasons.

"Pike's wrong," Wolf responded. "This wasn't some feint or some guarantee that Pike would stay here while Duncan was away starting his assault."

"Then what was it?" Sabrina asked, trying to be on the same page as their unquestioned leader.

"A trap," Gwillim responded, seeing the truth of the situation. "Duncan knows the kind of power that Jerrard has at his disposal, and so he knows it would be easy for Pike to get back to Marcwell quickly."

"And that's what Duncan is counting on," Lissa finished. "Taking Marcwell wouldn't be enough so long as the rightful king was still roaming the countryside fighting the good fight, he would still be seen as the Lord of Marcwell, no matter who was sitting on the throne."

"So he would have to get Pike back to Marcwell," Jared chimed in, "so that he could kill two birds with one stone."

Sabrina silently nodded.

"But he couldn't have known that you all would be here," Susanne added. "I doubt a single phase, or a child of one of the phasia could create a portal big enough to move whole armies. And the last the Torch could have known of us would have been when we were in Barer, and that is only if Erdric is on friendly terms with Grawn and Bryn, which I get the impression is not the case."

"And Rane didn't strike me as the kind who was willing to share too much information with her siblings, unless it was to try and trap us," Lissa commented. "But she couldn't have followed us into Bryn's kingdom without her knowing about it."

"And Caris is dead," Jared said proudly. "So that is one member of the phasia that won't be sharing too much information about our whereabouts."

"For some reason," Sabrina said shaking her head, "I don't think it would make much of a difference if the entire Raven's Wing showed up in Marcwell or not. Duncan wants Pike, and I get the feeling that Pike wants that showdown to happen as much if not more. Whoever wins that battle will be the Lord of Marcwell, and the Raven's Wing, the Torch, and the Enforcers will have to deal with that. Because as long as there is a person on the throne who has a tie to the Binosear bloodline, then that person is the rightful lord."

"And if both are killed?" Wolf asked.

There was something in Wolf's tone that disturbed Sabrina. Maybe it was the part of him that was phasia, or maybe it was the intonation he put on the word both. In Sabrina's mind, she could see Wolf waiting until the duel between Duncan and Pike was over and then killing the victor with a quick blast of Blaze fire. Or maybe he would challenge both, using the prestige of the Ranthall name to create a new line of succession.

"There is no clear line of ascension after Duncan," Sabrina said. "If Duncan has an heir, it would fall to that child as long as it was a boy. If it was a girl, or if the child was too young to rule, it would fall to myself for safe keeping until the child came of age. However, if I were married, the line could fall to my husband."

There was a knot that formed in the pit of Wolf's stomach. Then it was as though a light had been shown in a dark room, and possibilities flowed through Wolf's suddenly awakened mind. Schemes that had been hidden from his view were suddenly so clear.

"Nathaniel, you and Gwillim work with Pike, and keep up the façade that we are going to cooperate. Jared, Sabrina, Lissa, I need you for a little plan just in case this is a trap."

"What about me Wolf," Susanne asked the warrior in her coming to the surface. "I know I'm kind of an outsider here, but if I can help, I will."

Wolf smiled.

"I didn't mean to leave you out Susanne. Pike seemed to think of you as a valuable source of information, so let's play up to that."

A shiver of repulsion passed over Susanne's features.

"If I have to."

"Do you have a problem with working with Pike?" Lissa asked.

"No," she said quickly, "but there was something about the way he was looking at me that made me really uncomfortable."

Sabrina and Lissa both kept silent.

"It was probably the outfit," Jared mumbled.

Susanne either ignored or didn't hear the comment and join Gwillim and Nathaniel as they made their way to the rather animated war council. When they were gone, Sabrina turned to Wolf.

"So what is this that you need our help for?"

Wolf looked past Sabrina for a moment and made sure that Nathaniel was locked in conversation before he began speaking. When he did so, Wolf made sure to keep his voice low.

"I know this is going to sound crazy, but I am starting to see a pattern form in all of the weird things that are going on. Everything right now has been revolving around Marcwell in some form or another. We all know that everyone thinks it's the key to the war, but for some reason I think there has to be something more to it. Marcwell, as we all know, is about to be in the center of a civil war between Pike and Duncan, but those who have made the happenings in the palace their business have probably seen this coming for a long time."

"Wolf's right," Lissa added. "Duncan has been spouting off at the mouth for a long time that Pike would never willingly give up the throne and how he would probably have to fight for it."

"And then he would say that Pike and mother had assassins waiting to kill him so that he would never sit on the throne, and that every member of the Enforcers had standing orders to kill Duncan if they were ever alone with him," Sabrina commented.

"But nothing really tipped me until Sabrina was talking about the lines of succession," Wolf continued. "If both Pike and Duncan were killed in the battle, the role of protecting the kingdom would fall to Sabrina if there was no capable heir, or to her husband if she were married."

"And?" Sabrina asked.

"Doesn't it seem like there are a lot of people who are trying to force a relationship between you and I?" Wolf asked looking right in her eyes.

Suddenly everything clicked in Sabrina's mind. Caris had visited Wolf's room disguised as Sabrina to try and lure Wolf away from Lissa, and then that other member of the phasia seduced her in Wolf's form, trying to further the relationship. If Sabrina and Wolf did fall for one other, that would put the kingdom in Wolf's hands, a Ranthall's hands, and in stable condition for the remainder of the war. That was the part that didn't fit. Why would the phasia want the most visible kingdom in the entire world in stable condition when they were trying to pull it apart? The only possible angle that could be there was if the phasia were hoping to use the string of power that Basille had given Wolf to pull him back to the side of the Shadows. As if Jared read her mind, he began to question Wolf.

"But why would a phase want to put you on the throne?"

"Did I say a phase wanted to put me on the throne?"

No one spoke and waited for Wolf to clarify. All of them had wild theories running through their heads, and millions more questions. But Wolf put them all to rest.

"There was a reason that I didn't include Gwillim or Nathaniel in this conversation. I didn't include Gwillim because of his close attachment to Nathaniel and the possibility that he would make his thoughts too visible, and Nathaniel because of the part of him that is tied to Emries."

Sabrina and Lissa both wanted to question, but Wolf cut them off.

"Jared's right in thinking that there is no reason a member of the phasia would want to put me on the throne of Marcwell. It would make the kingdom stable again simply because I'm a Ranthall. The phasia have been trying to tear that kingdom to shreds for lifetimes now, but it became a more legitimate goal after Cedric and his cause. While Erdric is following the true methods of the phasia by causing unrest and most likely a civil war with Duncan, his plan isn't to put anyone but himself on the throne. Once that is done, Erdric can use the Torch to exterminate the other members of the phasia and then attack Shau-ling, keeping their private little war going."

"Then what was Caris trying to do by taking Sabrina's form in Frontier?" Jared asked.

"Exactly what I said she was trying to do when we were in Barer. She was toying with our minds and trying to pit us against one another. Somehow, she found out that Sabrina had some feelings for me, and then used that to make me begin questioning my feelings for Lissa. If something began to happen between Sabrina and myself, Lissa would feel betrayed and jealous, and may be manipulated to cause Sabrina harm."

Lissa kept silent, but knew deep down that if Caris had indeed pushed deep into her and ignited the anger that she was desperately trying to keep at bay, standing there confronted with the woman that she called sister, then Lissa could have been motivated to kill Sabrina.

"And with me out of the way," Sabrina said, "there would be no *Coromor* in the next generation, and so the prophecies would have one less opportunity in the next generation. The phasia could focus all their energy on hunting down the next generation's *Chosen One* and then be free to do as they pleased with no fear of the loss of their master."

"But someone else had other plans," Wolf continued. "And used Caris's interference to keep Sabrina in the loop as well. If Caris had merely worked on me, when I confronted Sabrina with the things that she had said, there would have been no relationship, just anger, frustration, and pain. It would accomplish the goal of making us all jaded and turn us against one another. If we don't fight together, we are easier to pick off."

"But by seducing Sabrina in your form," Jared commented, "there would be a chance that there would be genuine love between the two of you, and a marriage."

"Thus keeping the throne of Marcwell in the hands of forces of the Light," Wolf finished.

Lissa frowned. There were pieces of the explanation that weren't making sense.

"But who would want that?" She asked quickly. "And not only that, who would have the power to walk in and out of a phasia controlled palace, take Wolf's shape, seduce Sabrina, and get out before anyone could do anything about it?"

"Emries," Sabrina answered without thinking.

Wolf could only nod.

"That's why you didn't want Nathaniel or Gwillim here," Jared said putting the pieces together, "because if he knew what you suspected, so would Emries."

"I still don't understand why?" Lissa repeated.

"Neither do I," Wolf answered, "and that is the part that bothers me. Emries has his own agenda, and is resorting to tactics that I would say more suited the phasia than the first *Coromor*. If Emries was concerned about Caris' interference, he could have alerted us rather than furthering her influence by taking the course of action that he did."

Sabrina breathed a sigh of relief, spared the repetition of the ordeal. But Wolf's words had sparked something else within Sabrina, a recognition of the whirling of plans within plans, and the thoughts and emotions of a man who should have been long dead. Somewhere Sabrina knew that Aerith Seth was letting curses hit the air as he was putting the same pieces together that Wolf had. Aerith had never trusted Emries, and now Sabrina could feel that mistrust and hate flowing through her veins mixing with her own disgust for what the so-called god had done to her.

"So from now on," Wolf continued, "we're going to have to watch our steps and keep our eyes open. Emries is going to pop his head out again to try and further whatever plans that he has tried to set in motion, and since he may not do everything directly, we'll have to keep an eye on Nathaniel. For now, we'll keep this between the four of us. If anyone asks, we were talking about Bryn and Caris and whether or not they were working together. Because the four of us who were the ones personally involved, we wanted to keep this private."

Everyone nodded.

"Jared," Wolf said turning to the young man. "Get with Nathaniel and start making preparations for the portal. If possible keep my name from being mentioned in connection to powers of any kind. The less Pike knows about what I can do the better. Make sure that Nathaniel, Gwillim, and Susanne know that as well."

Jared nodded and started to walk away.

"Oh one more thing," Lissa said taking hold of Jared's arm. "Keep an eye on Susanne, and don't ever let her be alone with Pike."

The look on Jared's face was one of puzzlement, but then took the comment at face value and walked away. Sabrina, Wolf, and Lissa stood together for a moment, the uneasy silence flowing between them. Wolf was the one to break the silence.

"We've been through too much to let things like what happened this morning come between us. There's going to be plenty of time for us to figure out how we feel or what we want, but the thing that we all have to remember is from this point forward we each know exactly where the others stand. I am not going to make a choice. Sabrina, I have become very fond of you, and I've very fond of Lissa as well. Lissa, I know you understand that I haven't betrayed you, but I want you to know that I wouldn't give my attention to someone else without talking to you first. My mother raised me better than that. So, in the future we have to be able to talk to one another about what we feel and how we think so that no one is tricked. We got caught this time because we kept secrets from one another."

Sabrina and Lissa both nodded. Sabrina then leaned in and kissed Wolf lightly on the cheek.

"I don't know exactly what it is I feel, Wolf," the princess said softly, "especially after what happened in Barer. Most of it still hasn't had time to sink in. Part of me still loves you and wishes to be with you, but those are feelings that I have never had about anyone before so I don't know how I'm supposed to act, especially since I know about your relationship with Lissa. Plus, I don't know how much of it is real and how much of it is because of what Caris and Emries have done. We don't know how long Caris has been haunting our steps or interfering. It's hard enough to see you with her, but because she's my best friend and pretty much my sister, it's that much tougher. But, I want what is best for all of us, even if it means that I have to be content just loving you."

"I don't know how much trust I have left," Lissa said crossing her arms, "and my heart wanted to die after I saw what I thought was you leaving her room. Even though I know it wasn't you, part of me wonders if you wish it would have been. I've never felt this way about anyone either, though I thought I did once. But I was betrayed then too. Part of me wants to believe that this is my second chance. I'll just have to be content hating the ones who did this to us."

All three fell silent again, dealing with the words in their own way. It was only when the scout burst through the courtyard, sprinting at full speed that the three left their emotional torment and joined the other members of the People of the Ram and the Enforcers.

"Lord Jerrard, a message from the border guards on the borders to the lands of Alimidar."

Jerrard broke from conversation with Pike and Storm.

"Report."

"A large force of troops has massed and is marching on the Kingdom of Scalla. By the time this message has made it here, the troops have most likely already crossed the border on their way here. The army is flying the Banner of the Wolf, and the Banner of the Leopard in its ranks."

"Caris and Ellis," Aryx mumbled.

"But the man at the vanguard of the force fits the description of the phase Jeroch according to our scouts."

Jerrard's blood ran cold. If Jeroch had massed the armies of two of his siblings and was on their way to Scalla, then he intended to level Basille's former kingdom. Jerrard knew that there would be repercussions for not allying himself with the Brotherhood of Phasia, but he did not imagine that they would be this severe. After dismissing the scout, Jerrard turned back to Pike, a wide frown on his face.

"I'm sorry old friend, but with this new threat, I cannot lend you the services of the Raven's Wing. I will need every man to defend my lands."

Pike wanted to argue for a moment. The kingdom of Marcwell would be far more important for the later acts of the war, but Pike was not willing to argue with his old ally. Sighing to himself he nodded and turned to face Nathaniel.

"Looks like we'll have to do this on our own," Pike said after a moment. "I'll admit we aren't going to have very good odds, but all I'll need is a clean shot at Duncan. He's the key to this, and if I kill him, the rest of his little group should fall by the wayside."

Sabrina was the first to challenge the assumption.

"Father, you can't be serious. Didn't you hear what Wolf said when we got here? Duncan and the entire Creator's Torch Society is being controlled by a member of the phasia and his son. The real enemy here is Erdric and Michael, not Duncan. Once that control is broken, Duncan may come back to his senses, and we might have a chance to turn the Torch back to their true purpose."

"Unfortunately, princess," Galen interjected, "I don't believe that the Torch will ever return to the purpose that they originally set out to accomplish now that they have begun to walk the path the Moridon chose to follow. It was a path that led to the group's demise. Just as the Moridon were when they began to serve Aralias Imstra and Aerith Seth, the Torch is now driven to eradicate every visage of the Shadow no matter where it lurks."

"But what Shadow lies in Marcwell?" Midarin asked.

"That," Galen responded, "is what only the Torch and their leadership can see. In the days of the Hand of the Light, many seemingly innocent kingdoms fell to the might at the command of Aralias Imstra, and every siege was proven right with the revelation of a hidden phase or pocket of Shadow influence. Whether that will be the case in the matter of Marcwell, no one can say. This Torch is not the Hand of the Light, no matter what they believe. But as long as they are driven by the quest to assist the *Coromor* and uphold the mantle of the god Emries, then nothing will stand in their way, and there will be no turning them from the path that will eventually lead to their destruction."

"And we saw what the misguided beliefs and fear can cause first hand when Saurn manipulated the Light Keepers in Brea during the last generation," Midarin added. "Fear and paranoia are weapons that the phasia know very well how to use."

Wolf frowned at the description from the blind man, more pieces falling into place. The Moridon were protecting the mantle of Emries, doing the job that the *Coromor* was destined to do before the *Coromor* was ever born. The Hand of the Light was the way for Emries to deliver Aerith Seth to his fate at Jeroch's hands and start the prophecies. The Moridon were used more completely than even the person who carried Emries' powers as the *Coromor*. Now that the Moridon were extinct, Emries found a new group to carry on the self-destructive traditions. The fact that Emries was leveraging members of the phasia for the pursuit was perverse poetic justice, just as it had been when Saurn and Jeroch started the prophecies by killing Aerith Seth.

"Then we have no choice," Pike commented. "Since the Torch will not come to their senses, we have no choice but to do everything in our power to protect Marcwell. The phase Erdric and his son will be our primary targets, but if Duncan does anything that threatens Sabrina, Nathaniel, or myself, don't hesitate to use whatever force is necessary to stop him."

All of the Enforcers nodded trying to ignore the implication. Pike turned back to Jerrard again.

"I wish I could stay and help you old friend, but I have to take care of Marcwell and the legacy that has been left to me."

CHAPTER 40

Jerrard nodded and then put his hand on Turok's shoulder.

"We'll take good care of Celina for you," he said calmly. "I'll make sure she gets to you as soon as she is able."

Turok exhaled slowly and nodded his thanks.

"My family and I will meet up with you in Marcwell when this latest threat has passed," Jerrard said finally. "Good journey my friends."

Midarin hugged Erika and Taya and then shook Jerrard's hand before turning her attention to Pike.

"If you have no objections," she said gripping her bow tightly, "Aryx and I would like to help you in Marcwell."

Pike smiled.

"I wouldn't have it any other way."

For the next few minutes, the Enforcers made their preparations for the quick journey to Marcwell. Finally when all had prepared their weapons for battle, Nathaniel, Jerrard, and Jared began to create portals for the journey. The Enforcers were the first to step through, followed by the People of the Ram. As the Enforcers were making their way through, Wolf took hold of Sabrina's arm and pulled her to the side. Thousands of thoughts were whirling through his head, and he had very little time to make sense of any of them. Basille was practically screaming in the back of his mind, the memories of the Blaze finding solutions to mysteries that had plagued the phase just before his Banishment.

"It's Aerith Seth all over again," Wolf said quickly.

Sabrina's confused look prompted Wolf to continue.

"Emries used the Hand of the Light to get Aerith Seth into position to sacrifice him so that the first *Coromor* could be born. Every lifetime Emries has helped to manipulate the bloodlines in order to ensure that the power passes down to the correct descendant to ensure his powers continue and that Shau-ling is destroyed. The prophecies say that after seven generations the *Coromor* shall live again to battle Shau-ling and save the world from the

Shadows. Cedric and Korrd thought that the prophecies meant that all the people who held the power of the *Coromor* would live again, but I think it just means that Emries will be born again and he will be the one to battle Shau-ling. Emries is manipulating the bloodlines so that after seven generations the body that he is born into has pure blood, untainted by the blood of the phasia. That is why he is trying to push the two of us together."

Sabrina was about to respond, but Wolf stopped her, looking up at the portals and then back at here.

"There's no time for more. Just know that Emries will try to tempt you. No matter what happens in Marcwell, be strong and keep your eyes open. With the powers at Emries' disposal, he could trick you in one of a thousand ways. Just remember, I was out of arrows."

Confusion struck Sabrina as Wolf pulled away and walked quickly over to Jerrard. Lissa took Sabrina by the arm and pulled her toward the portals.

"Come on," she said ignoring Sabrina's protests. "We have to go."

Jerrard saw Wolf coming over and extended his hand, but Wolf ignored it getting close enough to say several words into Jerrard's ear.

"I don't expect you to believe me, but Basille's string of power is part of me. He sent you to Illimar to save your life and used Erika to keep track of you. She would always visit her sick relative as an excuse to report back on you."

Jerrard's heart was in his throat, and all he could do was listen as Wolf continued.

"I wish I had time to explain more, but I don't. In the private study, Basille was working on charting the bloodlines for the generations. Basille was wrong. There is a book label bloodlines, it should have changed by now. See where it all leads. You'll understand soon enough. Be careful. Emries is not what everyone thought he was, and if we keep being led by the nose, this world is going to end."

Wolf turned away and ran for the portals.

CHAPTER 40

"Just find the book," he called out, ducking through the quickly closing portal.

Jerrard was left in a total state of confusion, the words of a dead friend's son rolling though his mind, and the army of a would-be uncle marching to destroy him.

People of the Dragon

Creator's Calendar Year 1205; Dark Mirror

As soon as Bryn felt the portal forming, she traced the powers that created it. The portal was definitely forged with the powers of the Blaze, but there were surges in the power that were unfamiliar. Bryn could tell from the size of the portal and the amount energy being employed that there were several people coming through the portal. After being alerted, Sabrina took refuge behind Gwydeon, who held his sword ready for combat. Gideon and Taya stood side by side, ready to use the powers at their disposal. Having already battled one of her own, Bryn did not relish the thought of being face to face with another member of the phasia, especially if it were going to be in combat. She had never had any ambition to lead the Council, but she would not hesitate to defend herself in a duel. The War for Ascension was the understood way of the phasia, and if it were Jeroch coming through the portal, ready to defend his position at the head of the Council, Bryn would fight, prepared to bear the target on her back were she to be victorious. As the portal opened, everyone in the remains of the throne room of Scalla tensed and nervously waited for the first person to emerge from the swirling blue mass. Gideon lowered his daggers as the first man stepped through, but Gwydeon did not lower his blade. Logan Ranthall was a sight for sore eyes, but something inside Gwydeon told him that it was not the same Logan that he had known for most of his life. When Midarin Rice stepped out second, some of Gwydeon's fears were allayed, but when he saw Caris, Rael, and Trece, the automatic defenses kicked back in, and he stood firm, ready for battle.

When Bryn saw Logan, the same elation that she had felt the first time they had met was no longer there. The part of him that had once been linked with Aerith Seth was no longer prominent within him, and a new, more familiar power inhabited that corner of his being. It was only when Bryn probed the corners of his mind where the fragments of Aerith Seth's memory had once been that she felt the fires of the Blaze burning her thoughts. The feelings coursing through her were like those felt when entering the guarded mind of a phase. Logan looked over at Bryn the next second, a knowing smile creeping onto his lips.

"Good to see you Bryn," he said, the Ranthall pride thickly laced in his words, "you look well. Much better than your counter-part Ellis I am sure."

Bryn scowled at the mock compliment. Not only was Logan showing the powers of a member of the phasia, he was also showing the attitude.

"Logan," Gideon said taking several steps forward, "it's good ta see ye old friend."

Gideon extended his hand, but Gwydeon intervened. He too had seen the change in Logan, and the new powers that inhabited him. However, unlike Bryn, Gwydeon had been able to determine the source of the new powers and did not like what he found. Logan had touched the Blaze, but it was not a chance or minute contact as it had been with Cedric. The man who had once called himself the Dragon was bathed in the aura of the Blaze the same as Caris, Rael, Trece, and Bryn. Logan was as much a member of the phasia as the others. It took only a second to swoop down from where he stood on the dais and block Gideon's path to where Logan stood. Gideon saw the quick flash of motion out of the corner of his eye a split-second before the winged form interjected. Instead of stopping, Gideon leapt back, hands going to his daggers. Gwydeon may have undergone some fantastic changes since the last time that Gideon had seen him, but he was still Gwydeon Sandar, the most noble and courageous hero of the War of the Dragon, and it was obvious that he sensed something was wrong.

"You have a lot of explaining to do, Logan," Gwydeon said still holding his sword firmly in front of him, ready for combat. "Because unless I've lost my mind in the last few minutes, I would venture to say that you've traded in your powers as the *Chosen One* for the powers of a phase. Or are your new friends just tagging along, hoping that you won't kill them?"

Logan frowned and his hand shot down to the hilt of the Dragon Sword that hung on his belt. Gwydeon was quicker, pushing the tip of his crystalline sword forward so that the point of the blade pushed into the flesh of Logan's exposed throat.

"I wouldn't do that Logan," Gwydeon said, all warmth gone from his voice, only to be replaced with frigid intensity, "I don't want to have to kill you."

Logan's hand drifted away from the hilt of his blade, but Bryn could feel the surge of power in the man at the same time. He was channeling the powers of the Blaze. Before Bryn could warn Gwydeon, the blade of Chaos burst from Logan's palm and raced forward. Gwydeon was faster however, his wings batting quickly, propelling him backward, while he brought the crystalline blade downward to block Logan's blow. The attack never came, but the two men stood squared off, combat ready, looks of determination etched on their faces. It was then that the only true mortal in the room stepped between the two men. Midarin Rice had more to lose from this confrontation than anyone, a husband and a friend, but when she locked eyes with Gwydeon, she could tell that he was not the same man that had left her in Brea only a few hours ago.

"That's enough," she said and then looked Gwydeon dead in the eyes, "both of you."

Logan released the string of Chaos, and let the black sword disappear from his hands. However, Gwydeon lingered and hesitated, but finally Midarin's cold hard stare made him relent. While Gwydeon may have lowered his blade, he did not return it to the scabbard, nor did he relax from his combat posture.

CHAPTER 40

"A lot of things have happened since you went to Trelon, Gwydeon," Midarin said quickly, "and I understand less of them than I want to. But right now, we are all on the same side, fighting for what is right. The only problem is that most of us don't know what right is anymore."

"Midarin," Bryn said turning her attention to Gwydeon, "for once is showing her astute side. What Logan has or hasn't done concerning the Blaze is immaterial now. We all have a stake in this war, and while some of us have a purely selfish interest in how it all turns out, you mortals have far more to lose than any of the phasia."

Midarin nodded, taking the compliment for what it was.

"Gwydeon, look at me. You know me. We've been through too much together to break down at a time like this. Just listen to what Logan has to say, and if you don't believe him and you think he's lying because he's touched the Blaze, I won't stop the two of you from fighting. But please, listen to him, you owe me that much."

Gwydeon sighed, nodded, and then sheathed his sword.

"I'll listen."

Logan tried hard to hide the smile that began to curl his lips. Gwydeon was a bright man, not only that, he was a powerful ally. However, if the words that Logan spoke were not enough to make Gwydeon see the truth and see the war for what it was, then he did not relish the fact of making Gwydeon an enemy. As soon as he had locked eyes on Gwydeon, the Blaze had told him what the other man had become. While there was more than enough power between Caris, Rael, Trece, and himself to battle and vanquish the extension of the Creator, how many would survive that battle was a serious question.

"Gwydeon," Logan began, "I've never lied to you. While you and I didn't see eye to eye on a lot of things, we have helped each other through tough times. I was there when Gabrielle died, I was there when Emries tempted you there on the Mount Tantis. I was even there when we thought Jeroch had finished you off for good in the Hall of Terrors. You were there for me when Elwyne was kidnapped, then again when she was killed by Cedric. You helped me through it all. What I'm going to tell you won't be easy to accept, but once you start to put all the pieces together, you'll see I'm right."

Gwydeon nodded.

"This goes way back, even farther than you and I can even fathom. It goes back to the beginning when Shau-ling and Emries were created."

Gwydeon waved his hand.

"I've heard that part," he said gruffly. "I heard it told from Shau-ling's own mouth, and later had it confirmed by the memories that the Creator has given me. Shau-ling was originally known as Halicon, and he and his brother Emries have been at war within one another long before this world even existed. Their battle simply escalated when Emries created humans on this world."

"When Emries tried to supplant the Creator as their patron and god," Logan added.

"To the point where he took the book of laws that the Creator had given him and presented it to humans as his laws, not the Creator's," Gwydeon continued. "At that point the Creator became so angry that he sent Halicon here to force Emries to admit his deceptions and return to the Heavens. In order to do that, Halicon remade himself as the embodiment of every nightmare that men ever had, molding himself into the creature that we call Shau-ling."

"But Shau-ling couldn't fight the battle alone," Bryn continued, her knowledge of the subject second to none, "and so he created his first phasia to act as his will upon the world. These beings would embody the most horrible and deplorable traits of the human race which became the phasia. At first there were only the six of us, Kamen, Jeroch, Grawn, Bryn, Ellis, and Aryx Terian. When Emries saw that his army was completely overmatched, instead of creating his own servants as Shau-ling had, he imbued powers over the primal elements into four of his most loyal generals. These four men became the *Erieal*."

Midarin and Sabrina seemed to be the only people shocked by the revelation, but as Bryn continued, they listened intently, trying to fill in the blanks.

"And so the battle raged between Emries, who by this time had become known by the men as the *Coromor*, and Shau-ling with the *Erieal* and the phasia as the major pieces in their little chess game. However, Emries' following grew stronger, but the forces of nature that Shau-ling had relied on so heavily were failing him, and the fight was slowly killing the world that he had in essence come to save. So, Shau-ling started killing innocents, through the phasia of course. Whole cities were burned to the ground. Men, women, and children, it didn't matter who we killed so long as the mortal population was ground into dust. But Emries saw what we were doing and tried to turn it against us. He marked bloodlines with power and cultivated them, trying to create the perfect humans to fight against us. But the war had raged for centuries by then. Emries had seen his powers lessened considerably by the Creator for his disobedience, and we beginning to fade. He knew that if he continued to fight on, he would lose, weakened to the point that he would be destroyed, and that his grander schemes could never come to fruition. That was when Grawn, Ellis, and I made our fatal mistake."

"Aerith Seth," Gideon added absently.

"Correct."

"I don't understand," Midarin said a moment later. "If Emries was weakening and dying, why would you help create the prophecies that would allow Shau-ling to be destroyed?"

"From a mortal prospective," Bryn answered, "I am sure that is how it looks. However, that is as far from the truth as possible. Unlike the younger phasia, we six of the original council never had the desire to usurp Shau-ling and take over his throne of power. We were dedicated to the destruction of Emries and to the eradication of the human race. Perhaps that is why Shau-ling welcomed us back into the Council in this generation. But we didn't know that Emries was weakening. We had noticed that he was reserving himself in battles, relying more on his soldiers and the *Erieal* than on his given powers. But we all thought that his dabbling in bloodlines was more important than petty victories and squabbles over plots of land. He was trying to create the perfect weapon, a creature of such power and awesome prowess that no member of the phasia could stand up to him. Even Shau-ling would be powerless to destroy this creature if Emries were successful in his manipulations. This boy, this weapon of infinite talent and destructive power was born, and became the man that you call Aerith Seth."

Gwydeon nodded, the words making sense in the jumbled mass of thoughts that clouded his mind. The Creator had given him knowledge that a human was not able to perceive, and little bits would become tangible for a moment and then disappear again like the finest grains of sand in a strong wind. But Bryn's words were mixing with the scattered thoughts, making the pieces of the larger puzzle that he could slowly connect together.

"By this time though a rebellion of sorts had started within the phasia. We all saw that the war was going nowhere. Shau-ling too saw that his troops had too much free will, too much of the human character flaws within them. He called us noble villains. So he imprisoned Kamen in the body of what you knew as the Flame, and then banished Aryx for eternity."

"Why?" Sabrina asked, walking closer to the group, joining the conversation.

"Because he was too noble," Bryn answered. "He could not stomach the killing of innocents, and so he was no longer useful as a soldier. So Shau-ling made him as mortal as he could, sentencing him to life amongst those that he cared for, giving him all the emotions that a normal human would have. But because the phasia were moderately eternal, meaning we could die but we would be reborn and did not age, Aryx never looked a day older though his centuries of life, which would eventually lead to pain and loss when he decided to marry. It was because of his second wife that Aryx stumbled across the boy Aerith Seth in an orphanage in Lakestone."

"By that time though," Caris added, "the Council had grown to ten. Kamen had become the Flame, but still held a seat on the Council. Warron, Saurn, Erdric, Farax, Aldridge, and myself rounded out the Council, but Bryn is right, we were more rebellious than the original phasia, and we wanted to rule the Council, knocking Jeroch off of his perch as the favorite of the phasia. That was when the War for Ascension truly started."

"Shau-ling was furious at the impudence of his new children," Bryn continued, "but did not exercise the power that was at his disposal to stop the war. Kingdoms still fell, and mortals still died, so the task of the phasia was being upheld. However, the Council was splintered when the prophecies came to light."

Gwydeon let his wings relax back and fold against his back. This was the part of the story that he had been waiting on. Much of the information that Caris and Bryn had given was common knowledge to those with power. However, the secret motivations that started the War of the Lion that led to the next two wars were the all-important pieces that no one but Grawn, Bryn, and Ellis could fill in.

"As I said before," Bryn responded, "Emries was weakening, but this was information that none of the ten members of the Council had. We learned that he had created his super being, the boy Aerith Seth. However, we didn't get to him first. He fell into the service of Aryx Terian and his wife in Lakestone. But Saurn was quick to contact Aryx after the wife died in the night and purchased the rights to the boy. Aerith was then sent to the mines of Quea."

"A simple way to dispatch him," Caris commented. "In those days if anyone lived more than two weeks in the mines, they were considered either lucky or touched by the Creator. Saurn had to be sure that this boy really was the perfect being that Emries had created through his bloodline manipulation. When the boy lived through the first year, we began to believe. When that year stretched to five, there was no doubt that the boy was Emries' *Chosen One*."

"Behind the scenes," Bryn said, "there were other schemes brewing. Grawn, Ellis, and myself knew that there was no way to simply kill the boy, so we began to study and search for a way to tempt Emries into failing. It was then that Ellis and I realized that the humans were growing weaker right along with their master. Each generation, the essence of power that filled them was a little less than it was in the previous generation, and so Ellis and I figured that Emries was looking for a way to destroy Shau-ling so he could use the powers of the Blaze to revitalize his little puppets. With the being Aerith Seth under his control, it looked as though Emries would succeed in his quest. So, with the help of Saurn, we pulled Aerith Seth into the ranks of my army where I took him for my lover and taught him exactly what I wanted him to know. He was the instrument of destruction of Shau-ling, but if taught properly, he could be whatever he wanted, good or evil. Emries was furious. He knew that he had lost his chance. So, Ellis and I leaked our plans to Aralias Imstra about the *Coromor* and the way for the darkness of Shau-ling to be destroyed forever."

"To those of us in the Council," Caris continued, "it was both the ultimate betrayal and the method for advancement. Jeroch was understandably confused because he did not know the amount of free-will that had been allowed to the original six phasia allowed for this depth of treachery. Shau-ling banished Grawn, Bryn, and Ellis immediately, replacing them with Zarsi, Taron, and Basille. Thanks to the banished ones, we learned that Shau-ling could be destroyed by the right combination of powers. So, we began to jockey for position in an attempt to make good on that. Zarsi was the first to try, and his battle with Shau-ling resulted in the scar that he is cursed with to this day."

"But what no one knew was that we were saving Shau-ling from Aerith Seth," Bryn concluded. "The only way for the prophecies to begin was through the death of a chosen hero, or the *Chosen One*, Aerith Seth. As much as it pained me, I released Aerith from my service and sent him to Aralias Imstra and the Hand of the Light as a return favor to Saurn. That way, Saurn could be the one to destroy the Hand of the Light and bring Aerith Seth to Shau-ling. But we were later to learn that Saurn tried to betray us by trying to convince Shau-ling that Aerith Seth's death would not be the best path because it would start the prophecies. He did not realize the danger, and so he spoke recklessly as always. Luckily, Jeroch took Aerith's head starting the prophecies, and now we have gone through two generations and are well into the third."

"The only part I don't understand," Gwydeon said thoughtfully, "is why you tempted Emries into the prophecies. Wouldn't it have been enough just to kill Aerith Seth and wait for the seven generations to pass, thus killing Emries and the mortals."

"If only it would have been that easy," Bryn answered. "Aerith Seth was protected, and immortal. Emries had to allow Aerith Seth to be killed, but he would only do that if he were convinced he could profit by it. But of course, the Creator dealt us a blow after that incident by decreeing that the *Chosen One* would continue to keep a balance between the forces of Light and Shadow. That was when we began to doubt whether or not Emries was truly behind Aerith Seth's appearance, or if he was a tool of the Creator, a foil perched between the two squabbling children."

Here Bryn paused, shaking her head, the irritation of how completely she had been deceived at the height of her hubris and pride plainly evident on her face.

"As to why we tempted Emries that is very simple. We believed that if we could embody the powers of our archenemy into a lowly human that it would be easy to kill him. However, Emries played tricks on us to ensure it wasn't that easy. Firstly, Emries hid the power from us, and we could not simply search for the *Coromor* with our powers unless his identity was revealed to us. We would have a general idea of where the power was, but as to whom to target, we were in the dark. The other trick was the fact that the *Chosen One* still had the power to destroy Shau-ling, and that the *Chosen One* had the power to give birth to the *Coromor* of the next generation. So, we not only had to hunt and kill the *Coromor* but also the *Chosen One* in order to fully negate the prophecies. And thanks to the willfulness and treachery of the younger phasia, that has proven impossible for two generations."

"And if the humans make it to the seventh generation?" Taya asked.

"Then Emries will be born into the body of a mortal with all of his godly powers at his disposal with no one powerful enough to stop him from succeeding in his goals and destroying Shau-ling. He will be free from the limitations imposed on him by the Creator, and would be unstoppable."

Gwydeon stayed silent. He knew the implications of what Bryn had just said, and the peril that the world would face if Emries were to conquer Shau-ling and take the Blaze as his source of power. Emries would bleed the world dry, and when nature began to die, Emries would turn his sights to another of the Creator's worlds and spread his selfish evil there, keeping the chain of destruction alive. Emries was the evil. However, as Shau-ling had said in the confines of his throne room, the humans are not to blame for the fact that they had been misguided. They were not evil, as Aryx had always contended, but the evil ways of their patron had caused them to follow the wrong path.

"So Draven is our ally?" Gideon asked, not believing his own words.

"Far from it," Gwydeon answered. "He says he wants to help the Shadow to win in both realities, but that is only so he can ascend to the lead of the Council and then overthrow Shau-ling. As Bryn said, the younger phasia lost their way, and do not understand what they are fighting for. Caris, Rael, and Trece have only begun to understand the consequences of their actions thus far, but I think it is too late for them to make any changes to their nature. The war is too far gone for that."

"And we have another threat to deal with that is more dangerous than Draven will ever be," Logan commented. "Nathaniel, who now refers to himself as Nathan, has gone mad. I'm sure that's due to our friend Emries. He killed Zarsi and Rachel, and would have put a hole in Midarin too if it hadn't been for the four of us showing when we did. He intimated that he was going after Draven, and so he will be coming here before too long. But as long as Emries is controlling his mind, he is a threat to every one of us."

"But we can't ignore Draven," Gwydeon countered. "If he is going to cross over to the other world and use his powers to tip the balance there, the results could be catastrophic. Our only course of action is to go after him and make sure that he doesn't succeed, no matter what that may be."

Logan grimaced. He knew that Gwydeon was right, and as much as he wanted another crack at Nathan and Emries, he knew that the trouble Draven could cause in the other reality could not be ignored.

"Ok, we stop Draven, then we come back for Nathan."

Gwydeon nodded, then turned toward Midarin.

"I can't take everyone," he said glumly, "my powers aren't that potent yet. I'll just take Logan with me, and hopefully we can stop Draven and make it back before Nathan shows up."

Midarin smiled a weak smile.

"Just hurry back this time."

Logan turned to Caris, Rael, and Trece and nodded.

"If Draven shows up, you all know what to do."

Caris nodded. Turning back toward Gwydeon, Logan regarded his old ally for a moment. Gwydeon had a familiar look in his eyes. It was the same burning intensity that Logan had seen when they fought together on the Island of Mist against Rael and then against Jeroch. Gwydeon could taste Draven's blood and he wanted nothing more than to drive his crystalline blade through the phase's heart one more time. However, with Vengeance out of the way, Draven would stay dead. Seconds later Logan stepped forward and Gwydeon's wings began to glow and pulse with brilliant white light. The light flared, and then the two heroes, one who had been embraced by the Creator and one who had embraced the limitless powers of the Blaze, disappeared.

"It's much more efficient than portals," Bryn said absently.

"And impossible to track," Caris added.

Midarin seemed uncomfortable with the proposition of being left with four members of the phasia. Gideon too was on edge, especially considering the last time he had seen Rael and Trece, they had been doing everything in their power to make sure that every member of the People of the Dragon died a painful death. However, the discomfort was ended as four bright lights appeared in the sky above the palace and shone down through the broken ceiling. Immediately all of the phasia turned their attention to the open sky, watching as the four whirling balls of colored energy floated down and hovered before each of them. Bryn looked at the swirling ball nervously. She had turned her back on her master and on one of her own, and now the summons had come. She was not ready to answer the call. Caris too felt hesitation in her heart. Ignoring Shau-ling's call to a Council was treason, punishable by banishment or death. However, because of her connection with Logan Ranthall, Caris was afraid to go back, even if it were to report everything that she had seen. Rael and Trece of course had no such qualms. Draven had attacked them first after all, and they had information about the *Coromor* and Gwydeon Sandar that Shau-ling would have found useful.

"Time to answer the call sisters," Rael said coldly, "master summons us."

"I'm staying to watch over Scalla and wait for Draven as Logan asked me," Caris responded, turning her back on the ball of energy.

"I'm staying too," Bryn added. "There is more to be found here, and I am not ready to face master with the news that I have to relay."

"You have done nothing wrong," Trece urged. "You have done everything to help defeat Emries and the *Coromor.*"

"You can return with a clear heart," Bryn said, choosing her words carefully. "So go, tell master everything that you have heard, and beware those that would strike you down for such news."

Rael and Trece looked at one another and then blades of energy appeared in their hands.

"To ignore the call is treason, and if you do not embrace the ball of energy and answer the summons, Trece and I will strike you down and justice will be served."

"Didn't you to listen to anything that Bryn said?" Taya exclaimed. "The whole world depends on what happens next. If you stand here and hack away at one another, there will be less people who know the truth and have the power to do something about it. Someone has to stay alive to report to Shau-ling, and someone has to live to take on Nathan and make sure he doesn't get to Shau-ling."

"Taya is right," Gideon added. "Didn't you two learn anything in the last generation? If you phasia would have worked together instead of being at each other's throats all the time, you would have beat us. But as long as you insist on this War of Ascension and these traditions of honor and obedience under penalty of death, Emries will defeat you."

Rael considered the argument for a moment, and then motioned for Trece to touch the ball of white energy that floated before her. There was a silent argument that raged for several moments, until Trece finally relented and touched the ball disappearing through the portal that formed.

"I shall tell master that you put up a valiant fight, but were unable to match our speed. Because of your wounds from the previous battles, you were not able to stand up to our combined power."

Bryn smiled and nodded.

"I could have been killed by worse," Caris answered.

Rael nodded, touched the ball of black energy and disappeared.

A Time to Mourn

Creator's Calendar Year 1205; Light Reality

A red portal appeared in the woods outside the sleepy country town of Aradon, only to be noticed by the birds that sat in the trees of Logan's Wood. As Evan Sinn stepped out of the portal he looked around and sighed deeply. From what Aerith had told them, Cairyn Binosear would be making her way to Aradon, but it was three days ride at a moderate pace, and Evan could not imagine the queen traveling any faster than that. There was no urgency for her, so long as she was out of the palace by the time Duncan's army descended on the walls. However, Evan knew that Trelon was a secondary consideration to Marcwell, and that was Duncan's true prize in this family war.

"Three days," Evan said into the silence of the woods as the woman he loved, Meredith Heron, emerged from the swirling red portal.

With a thought, Evan closed the portal and shoved the light red stone back into his pocket. There was more than enough time for Evan and Meredith to go to Scalla, check on the Enforcers, and then come back to Aradon to make sure that Cairyn was safe. Aerith hadn't said that they were supposed to go to Trelon and escort her along her path. If that were the plan, Evan could have easily waited for her in the woods and then used a portal to get her to Aradon. But if he were to do that, Evan would break one of Aerith Seth's prime rules. Evan did not know if he could trust Cairyn with his life, because there was a chance that she would leak the information about his powers to Pike. So, he could not reveal himself for what he was. But something that Aerith had said puzzled Evan. There was obviously another reason that they were supposed to be in Aradon, and Aerith had said it would be something well worth their time. It was then that Meredith tapped him on the shoulder and pointed to the old church on the hill. Two forms were emerging from the structure, and as Evan looked at the face of one, he recognized his friend Pike, but something was different about the man. He did not carry himself like the wounded old soldier that he was, and from the facial features that Evan could make out, he looked much younger. Then even noticed the blond woman at Pike's side. There was something familiar about the woman's features, perhaps it had been someone Pike had mentioned, no, it was more than that. Suddenly the image of the statue popped into Evan's mind, and he knew the truth. It was Eldar Merin. Too shocked to do anything else, Evan took several steps forward until he emerged from the undergrowth of Logan's Wood.

As soon as Pike and Eldar saw the form emerge, they reached for their weapons, but before Pike drew *Fury* from his belt he waited to see what the intentions of the strange man were. There was something familiar about his face, almost like he had seen it before, but he couldn't place where. Maybe if the man had a beard, or maybe and eye patch? The man held both of his hands up, showing the he was unarmed. The woman that emerged from the forest following him raised her hands also, and it took only a few steps before the two pairs were looking right at one another.

"I know you from somewhere," Pike said absently, "but I don't know from where."

"My name is Evan," Evan responded, "Evan Sinn."

Pike looked puzzled, trying to place the name. Evan searched his memory. Aerith had told him what his role had been in the other world, and he stretched his mind to remember.

"I was in the service of Gwydeon Sandar in the other world," Evan said, tipping his hand a little, "maybe that's where you saw me, Pike."

Eldar slightly drew her sword from the scabbard at her side, but a motion of Pike's hand stayed her strike. A coy smile curled onto his lips the next moment, and as he scratched the start of the beard on his chin, the smile moved into his eyes.

"Well now, Evan Sinn," Pike said, "for you to have the information that you have, you are obviously a lot more than the one armed, one eyed, general from the Order of the Sword that I remember. Maybe we should go somewhere and talk."

Evan nodded, burying Pike's description of his other self deep into the back of his mind.

"It wouldn't be wise to go into town," Meredith said, adding her voice to the conversation, "I don't think the townspeople would take too kindly to a young Pike, and a suddenly resurrected Eldar Merin."

Meredith too had made the connection, but not the same way as Evan. She had heard Lord Pike's drunken ramblings about the woman Eldar on the night he was trying to lure Meredith to his bed. He had talked about her golden hair, the fierce fire in her eyes, and her strong shapely body. It wasn't a far stretch to take the alcohol-induced words and apply them to the woman that stood before Meredith.

"Then the church," Eldar responded, her words edged with distrust.

Evan nodded his accent and tried not to let the fact that he was face to face with two people from the Dark Mirror, never mind the fact that one of them was supposed to be dead, and was about to sit down and talk with them.

* * * * * * * * * * *

As soon as Wolf stepped out of the portal, he thought he had stepped into hell. The Torch had already descended on Marcwell, and as Wolf looked around for those brief few seconds, he could see members of both the Lion's Mane and the new Hand of the Light lying dead in the courtyard outside the palace of Marcwell. The Enforcers had joined the fray immediately, slashing forward toward the doors of the place like a scythe through wheat. Members of the Torch dropped left and right, falling to the combined might of the Enforcers and their leader. Midarin and her children were also moving as a group, but not with the force and relentlessness of Pike and the Enforcers. Nathaniel was content to stay out of the battle as much as possible. Gwillim, Aryx, and Liette used all of their combat prowess to ensure that no one got close, and Midarin used her extended range to help fend off those who were stupid enough to attempt to bring battle to the family. Wolf's attention turned to Sabrina, who was standing behind Lissa and Susanne, using bits of her power to keep their enemies at bay. Wolf however was not content to stand by. Channeling all of his abilities through the gift of Basille's string, Wolf surrounded himself in an aura of Blaze energy and lifted himself above the battlefield. Most of the Creator's Torch Society and Lion's Mane stopped fighting and looked up at what they could only perceive as a phase. However, Wolf was not content with a distraction. He extended his hand to Sabrina and Nathaniel. Nathaniel immediately opened himself to the powers of the *Coromor* and joined Wolf in mid-air. Sabrina at first was reluctant to use her powers in such a way, but finally filled herself with the powers granted by the mantle of Aerith Seth and launched into the air.

"Behold, members of the Creator's Torch Society, I am Wolf Ranthall, the destroyer spoken of in your Prophecies of the Dragon. I am here among you with the third *Coromor* of the Prophecies, the Lord Ram, Nathaniel Sandar, and the woman who inherited the power of the man you fight in the memory of, Sabrina Binosear. She is the *Chosen One* of prophecy, the woman who will be the mother of the next generation's savior."

Sabrina tried not to blush at the description of her.

"The man that you follow into this needless war is Duncan Rhuiden, the man who claims he is the rightful heir to the throne of Marcwell. But was it not the first *Coromor* of the prophecies, Cedric Binosear who made Marcwell the shining pillar of hope that it is today? Was it not the second *Coromor* of the prophecies Logan Ranthall, my father, who was offered the throne after his triumph over Shau-ling in the last generation?"

A subtle mistruth. Though the second *Coromor* of the prophecies had actually been Logan's brother Korrd, all of the world had heard Logan's name proclaimed from the towers of Marcwell, and it was Logan that had returned from the Island of Mist a hero.

"Lord Pike was merely holding Marcwell in trust for the next generation of the prophecies, waiting for the day that the Ram would be proclaimed and take his rightful place as the ruler of Marcwell. So I say to you that you are following a pretender in this man Duncan, and that you abandon this war against those who would stand with you against the forces of the Shadow. Let the *Coromor* take his rightful place."

For a moment, nothing happened. Pike kept looking up at Wolf, anger etched deep into the lines of his face. Then, as though he caught on to Wolf's scheme, he held *Fury* aloft and cried out.

"Long live Nathaniel Sandar, *Coromor* of the Prophecies and rightful Lord of Marcwell!"

Suddenly the cry went up all around. Members of the Lion's Mane and the Creator's Torch Society cried out as one in support of Nathaniel. As Wolf, Sabrina, and Nathaniel descended from the heights above the courtyard, Wolf thought he saw a flutter of fiendish pride flow over the young boy's features, but his attention was quickly diverted by Pike and the Enforcers.

"You bought us some time, lad," Pike said, the memories of a similar show in Rana popping into his mind. "You're more like your father than I thought. Next thing you know you'll be having a banner stitched up and waived by every one of my Enforcers. But time is not enough. Duncan is already in the palace, and we have to deal with him now before it's too late."

Pike turned and called the Enforcers to follow. Nathaniel and the rest of the Rice family followed quickly behind, leaving Susanne, Lissa, and Sabrina standing with Wolf.

"Somehow I don't think that was a good idea," Sabrina said cleaning her dagger.

"Me either," Lissa added.

"I'll explain later," Wolf commented, "now all we have to do is keep Pike from killing Duncan, and I think we may actually have a chance of finding out who is pulling all of our strings and what Emries is actually after."

* * * * * * * * * * *

Jerrard Mystic stood in the courtyard of the palace of Scalla trying to shake the confusion from his mind. Storm had run to start readying the Raven's Wing for the true invasion, only this time it would not be the conjurers of the Creator's Torch Society, it would be at least one full member of the Brotherhood of Phasia, and his army. Erika saw the confusion in her husband's eyes and went to him. It took Jerrard several moments to realize that Erika was there holding his hand, and he could not get past the feeling that he was coming full circle. Everything had started for Jerrard when he joined the Lion's Mane in defense of Lord Cedric and was there fighting the army of Jeroch in the streets of the city of Lakestone. Perhaps Pike had been right all along. There was something more in Lakestone than just the ruins and the flooded streets. It had served as the original palace for Shau-ling, and the forces of the Shadow continued to use that as an initial base of operations for their assaults through the generations. It also could not be a coincidence that Basille chose to stay close to Lakestone, and the fact that he had the most complete knowledge of everyone and everything associated with the Blaze. It was the words of the boy Wolf Ranthall that had shocked Jerrard the most. No one but Jerrard, Erika, and Basille had known the nature of Jerrard's relationship with his father and how their meeting had come about. Jerrard had never told anyone, especially no one of the Ranthall family. Wolf had to have been telling the truth about inheriting Basille's string. If that were the case, more credence would be given to his words, and Jerrard would have to go back to Basille's study to find the answers. However, the matter at hand was Jeroch and his army. Scalla was not the place for that battle to occur, and for some reason, Jerrard's mind kept drifting back to Lakestone, as though some inner force was beckoning him there.

"What is it Jerrard?" Erika questioned lightly, holding his hand.

Taya and Storm by that time had returned back to their father's side.

"Storm, inform the Raven's Wing that we are marching for Lakestone. Let the enemy see us move. That should keep Jeroch off-balance and buy us a little time to get ready for him."

Storm wanted to question his father, but he dutifully nodded and ran to complete his task.

"Taya," Jerrard continued, not allowing time for questions that he had no answers for, "go into the place and make sure the Celina can travel. I'm not going to leave her here if I don't have to."

His daughter nodded and headed off, leaving Erika alone with her husband.

"Now are you going to tell me what's going on?

Jerrard squeeze his wife's hand and looked down at her, trying hard to force a smile.

"Maybe nothing," he said his gaze returning to the mass of troops, "maybe everything."

* * * * * * * * * * *

Upon entering the old church, Pike began to feel uncomfortable again. As the two pairs had been walking, they talked briefly, relating who they were and how they had come to be there. The man Evan Sinn had revealed himself as a messenger of Aerith Seth, the man who was the origin of the powers of the *Chosen One*, the very powers that Logan Ranthall had held that brought Pike into the war against Shau-ling in the first place. And now Pike found himself on the other side of the battle, fighting not against the phasia and the creatures he had once perceived as evil, but rather against the *Coromor* and its patron Emries, in an attempt to save the world from the wrath of the Creator.

"So," Evan said summing up the last few moments of conversation, "Shau-ling sent you here to get Wolf and take him back to the Dark Mirror reality so that he can fight this Draven character?"

Pike nodded.

"Essentially, yes. Shau-ling said that Wolf was the only one who could bring balance back to this world, and without him, there would be no way to stop the Creator from burning it all to nothingness and starting over somewhere else. All I need to do is find Wolf and find somehow to take him back. Though I don't have the foggiest idea of how to do that because I don't have any powers left."

"What about..." Meredith started.

Pike cut her off by raising his arm and showing where the scar that marked him as a member of the *Erieal*.

"I gave up my tie to Emries so that I could know the truth. After being in the Blaze for twenty years, according to Shau-ling, this world and the Blaze chose me."

"That makes sense," Meredith commented. "Humans are at the heart of this entire war. That is what Emries and Shau-ling have been fighting over all these years. Emries thought he was more powerful than the Creator and presented himself as the Creator to the first humans. They didn't know any better so they followed."

"And they used nature for their own whims," Eldar continued, nearly quoting the lessons that she had been taught by Shau-ling, "and slowly started to drain its life away. But not even Emries was wise enough to see that circumstance. All he wanted was a new fuel to keep his precious humans alive. And if he had to kill his own brother to do it, he gladly would."

"So," Evan said looking at Pike, "the Dark Mirror world chose you to defend it, and Shau-ling sent you here to bring back the only man who could put it all right."

Pike smiled.

"Welcome to the war Evan," he said holding back a laugh. "When I started in this it was easy. All we were supposed to do was find the Jeweled Dragon's Flame, take it to Cedric, collect whatever reward there was and go home. Yeah sure there was this part about battling Shau-ling, saving the world, and maybe dying in the process, but that didn't even figure in. Then the Shadowwalkers come and blow up Aradon, kill our friend David, and basically send us running for our lives."

"Through Dreamscape, the bar in Illimar, Sarmeel, the twin towns, Falke, Taren," Eldar started, "where I died, and then through the rest of the quest until they thought it was all going to be over. Pike ends up under the Island of Mist trapped within the Source of the Blaze, Logan goes nuts and hides in Aradon for fifteen years, Gwydeon and Midarin went back to Brea, and Gideon went to Scalla."

"Everyone else was killed," Pike continued, "and those of us that did live didn't have much of a life after the Hall of Terrors and the fight with Shauling. It was like whatever protection we had during the quest had been lifted, and only Gwydeon and Midarin seemed to be spared the worst of it."

"That was Emries' doing," Evan answered. "If Gwydeon and Midarin were spared the worst, that's because their son Nathaniel was the *Coromor* and Emries had to make sure that the person who carried his mantle would have a fighting chance. Emries didn't care about the rest of you. To him, you were just a means to an end. Once you outlived your usefulness to him, he tossed you away."

"You keep talking like that," Pike said gruffly, "and you're going to make me upset."

"There's time enough for stories later," Eldar interjected, "we have a mission to perform."

Evan stood and turned to Eldar, smiling.

"I don't think you need to go looking for Wolf," he said before taking a deep breath. "Something tells me he'll be here before too long. He was on his way to Barer when we left him. He was going to meet with Bryn Aplee of the phasia and try to get some information. If what Aerith told us is accurate, Bryn should point Wolf in the right direction, and that to me means Scalla. But I don't think that will last. There is something about this church and the book up there that you tell me just happens to contain the Creator's Laws. There's going to be something big that happens here, and it may be within the next day or two."

Silence returned to the church until Pike laughed and pulled *Fury* from his belt, laid it on the ground beside him, and sat back in one of the aged pews and looked over at Meredith.

"Looks like we have time for stories after all. I want to know everything that's happened over here since the first war ended."

Meredith sighed.

"Alright, Pike," she said looking first at Evan and then back at Pike, "but you're not gonna like it."

＊ ＊ ＊ ＊ ＊ ＊ ＊ ＊ ＊ ＊ ＊

As Pike stepped into the throne room of the palace of Marcwell, anger boiled up through him as he looked at the throne. There, seated with one leg propped up on an arm of the golden throne, was his son Duncan, and beside him stood two woman dressed in the battle uniform of the Creator's Torch Society and another man in similar garb. As soon as Duncan's eyes locked on his father, he raised his hands and clapped softly.

"Well done, Lord Pike," sarcasm dripped from every word, "I must say that I thought this little detachment of the Torch would be harder for you and the Enforcers to handle. But then I did not count on the resourcefulness of my little sister and of course Nathaniel."

Wolf could hear the groan of the wooden hilt of Pike's ax *Fury* as it twisted in the strong man's hands. Pike was ready to spill the blood of the infidel that called himself a Rhuiden, and Wolf was sure there would be little to no remorse to the act. Before Pike could speak, Duncan continued.

"Let me introduce you to your new daughter, father," Duncan said motioning toward the tall red-haired woman at his side. "This is my wife Bridgette Dalen. And before the thought crosses your mind father, you cannot have her."

Pike took a step forward, but Turok's strong hand restrained him.

"I just could not give up my taste for red-haired girls," Duncan taunted. "The younger the better in my experience."

Wolf could feel the hostility pour from Lissa. So, Duncan had been the man who she had loved and been betrayed by.

"My other two companions here are Seraphina Masile and Michael Yarrow, the senior generals of the Hand of the Light, and now the personal advisors of the Lord of Marcwell, me."

Instead of Pike chiming in, Lissa, Sabrina, and Susanne stepped forward at roughly the same times with weapons ready. Each had their own grudges to bear, and unlike Pike's they were not imagined slights.

"Where is your pitiful excuse for a father, Michael?" Susanne said looking around.

"He has no reason to trouble himself with the short-sighted arguments of mortals," the boy answered, his tone full of arrogance and spite, "and does not waste his time on insignificant worms like you. How it is that you were even chosen to be my mother is beyond me. Perhaps Erdric is capable of pity after all."

The next few seconds were a blur. Michael's rash words had incited the fires within Susanne, and not even the words of the Creator could have stopped her from sending her dagger hurtling toward the dais. The young half-phase was quick enough to dodge the attack, but only enough to pull Seraphina Masile into the blow. The woman's eyes went wide the last second, obviously surprised by her supposed ally's tactic. She began to bring her hand up to try to shield herself from the blow, but whatever tactic she had intended to employ was too little too late. The blade of the dagger pierced the woman through the heart, killing her instantly, and bringing a ripple of disbelief and shock through the few members of the Torch who were scattered through the throne room. Many charged out, behind the Enforcers to inform the others of their order that the woman who had brought them back from the brink of destruction after the death of Dei had been killed by the same traitor that had brought the phase Erdric into their midst in the beginning. The Enforcers sprang into action, guarding the entrance and exits, making sure that no members of the Torch could get in to try and take revenge for their fallen leader. Midarin had drawn her bow, and took careful aim at the heart of the boy Duncan Rhuiden and waited for the time and necessity to take the shot. Lissa however had begun moving up the dais with her sword drawn, ready for a fight.

"You see how easy it is to die, Duncan," Lissa said venting all the fury she could muster. "Now, get up, and defend yourself or I'll step out of the way and let Midarin take her shot. You know as well as I do that if she wanted to kill you, there would be nothing you could do to stop her, and not even your phasia handlers could do anything to stop it either."

Duncan laughed and slowly rose from his perch.

"I see you have been with Pike for too long, Lissa. It's a pity too, you were such a sweet girl. Perhaps the sweetest I have ever tasted."

Lissa spat at the arrogant prince.

"You've grown feisty as well," he said moving down the dais, but keeping his eye on both Lissa and Pike. "Maybe feisty enough that father here would have taken you to his bed."

The comment caught both Pike and Lissa off-guard.

"It's time the truth came to light father," Duncan said cruelly. "I know about all your little affairs, and while I know you and Lissa have not shared the same bed, I know that you and your little ally Midarin have had many torrid nights together."

Midarin lowered the point of her arrow, letting the bowstring grow slack in her hand. Pike did not react to the words, his built-in defiance of every rumor coming to the surface. But unlike the pervious accusations, not one member of the Enforcers came to Pike's defense. Part of that respect had been left behind in the bloody waters of Lakestone.

"If it were only an affair, dear father," Duncan said, venom thick with every word, "I might be content to merely applaud your conquests. Midarin is far better fair than some of the chambermaids and dignitary's daughters that you have plundered in the past."

Rachel turned back and looked at Pike. She had been with Pike in Askronilka when the first accusations came to light about Pike's infidelity, and she was quick to defend him. However, there was no defense to be offered this time, and Rachel knew that she had been wrong to defend Pike, and that the war fought and the lives lost had been for a lie.

"You weren't just content to have the would-be wife of your old friend, were you Pike?" Duncan said, the disguise of a vengeful son finally lifting. "You had a child with your old ally, trying to find a new heir to your throne here in Marcwell so that you could kill me, and hold onto the kingdom for a little longer."

Pike stood firm, neither challenging nor denying the accusations. He knew his reasons for going to the arms of his former ally. Originally, he had searched for comfort and for the loving embrace. But later, when he saw the kind of man that Duncan would become, he had hoped to have a son with Midarin, and then he could supplant Duncan and have a fit ruler sit on the throne after he was dead.

"If you wish to deny these charges, feel free."

Pike remained silent, and Midarin took several steps back, the full betrayal hitting her.

"And so you had a daughter. A pity that she cannot sit on the throne of Marcwell, otherwise you could have just turned it over to Sabrina and killed me anyway."

Aryx stepped forward and sheathed his sword.

"You are wrong Duncan," Aryx said proudly. "Liette is my daughter, not Pike's."

Everyone in the room was silent, shock floating through the room, mixed with flashes of anger from Pike and confusion from Liette. Sabrina and Lissa too were shocked, but part of Lissa always felt more akin to Liette than she ever had to Sabrina. Wolf was not shocked by the news, especially after looking the girl in the eyes for the first time when they had met in Logan's Wood. Though the girl's origins did not change much, they would likely cause problems later between Aryx and Pike, and Wolf was certain that the old grudge between Pike and Nightwing would resurface.

CHAPTER 40

"Well, despite all of that, Pike was not without another mistress. After he learned that Midarin had given birth to a daughter and that his plan had backfired, he looked for another woman with reputable name to sire a child for him. But there were no old heroines with names powerful enough to supplant the tradition of Binosear blood inheriting the throne. Perhaps there was one..."

Wolf could feel the rage grow inside of him. He knew where Duncan was leading, and he would not allow his mother's name to be slandered like a common whore.

"Lying bastard!" Wolf yelled charging forward.

Duncan sidestepped the charge and brought his sword to bear the next moment. The two men were locked in combat, striking at one another as fast as they could. As Sabrina watched however, she knew that the battle would not last long. Wolf had the advantage of power from Basille's string, and once his rage cleared and he began to think like the powerful man that he was, it would take only the barest thought to crush Duncan like a bug. However, out of the corner of Sabrina's eye, she saw Michael raise his hands and a beam of white energy shot from his extended fingers toward Wolf's unsuspecting form. Something snapped inside of Sabrina, and she leapt across the distance, the bolt catching her full in the chest, sending her sprawling to the ground, all life stolen from her fragile body. Wolf screamed something unintelligible and cradled the fallen girl in his arms. Duncan stepped away from the pair, the cruel smile back on his face.

"Pity," he said laughing. "Have fun with the Torch. If you happen to survive them, and each other, I'll be waiting for you in Aradon."

Michael added his laughter to Duncan's and after creating a portal, Duncan, Michael, and Bridgette disappeared. Wolf's attention was totally focused on Sabrina. He knew that she was dead and no power, no matter what source held it could bring her back. Only the Creator could create life, and only Emries and Shau-ling could breathe on the embers of life and bring a fallen warrior back from death. Nathaniel approached and put his hand on the patch of burned and mangled skin in the center of Sabrina's chest. As Wolf looked up, he saw the aura of energy around Nathaniel flare, and for a moment, Wolf thought he could see Emries form leaning over Nathaniel, guiding his actions. Seconds later, Sabrina coughed, her life restored by the patron Emries through his instrument. However, Wolf knew the reason, but he played at relief and love, clutching Sabrina to him and kissing her lightly. Taking a moment, he looked up at Lissa and quickly winked at her before turning all of his attention back to Sabrina. Lissa caught on, and quickly folded her arms, letting everyone who looked at her believe that she was upset. Wolf kept kissing Sabrina on the forehead, and then whispered to her just loud enough so Nathaniel could hear.

"I'm so glad I had that one arrow left in the forest. I just wished I could have saved you this time, but fortunately for us both, I didn't have to because Nathaniel was here."

Sabrina caught on, even in her weakened condition. Wolf's love and attention were a diversion, the code had tipped her. She reached up and wrapper her arms around Wolf, kissing him passionately on the lips. Wolf to his credit tried hard to hide his shock.

* * * * * * * * * * *

Jerrard and Erika exited a portal and found themselves back in the private study that Basille had spent much of his time in. It took Jerrard only a few minutes of searching before revealing the large book with a thick red cover and golden lettering. The simple title was bloodlines, and as he flipped through the book, pictures came alive showing long dead ancestors of men that had lived in Scalla during Basille's time. Halfway through the book, Jerrard saw a section titled Emries' Manipulations. This was what Jerrard had been looking for. As he sat down at Basille's desk and studied the book quickly, he noticed that several bloodlines were marked as special, and tracing was done back to their origination. Some of the names Jerrard recognized immediately. One was Ranthall, another Sandar, and another Rhuiden. The list went on and reasons stretched through hundreds of pages that Jerrard had no hopes of understanding. The final two pages of the book were a drawn out family tree of several families whose bloodlines intersected at some point or another. This is what Wolf had told him to search for. Jerrard saw what he was looking for immediately. Emries had been watching the Ranthall and Binosear lines, and if they were to join in this generation, meaning Wolf and Sabrina, then Emries' bloodline manipulations would eventually come to fruition in the seventh generation where he would be reborn as Emries Ranthall, fully empowered with the abilities of all of the ancestors that came before, and filled with all of the limitless potential of the human race. A god among men, and a conqueror ready to shake the Heavens.

Chapter XLI

The Broken Council

The Council chamber lay silent and cold, deep in the forgotten recesses of Shau-ling's palace. As far as every member of the phasia knew, there was no direct route from the interior of the palace into the Council chambers, and the only true way in was through a portal. However, though the phasia could create a portal that led to the Council, no member of the Brotherhood really knew where the Council actually was. It was as though it existed somewhere in a pocket of time and space away from the rest of the world. The eldest of the phasia, Jeroch included, at one time believed that the Council existed in the limitless potential of the Blight. However, after many years of searching through the churning mass of life-giving energy, Saurn had been unable to find anything that would have resembled the Council chambers. Yet, he continued his search throughout every lifetime. While the younger members of the phasia cared only that the Council was there to restore their power, the older members could not let the unsolved mystery simply lie and take everything at face value. Shau-ling had made them too inquisitive for that. But, no matter how they pried and how they searched, no clues would ever be revealed, and the Council chambers would remain as much a mystery as it ever had.

Many of these thoughts filled Jeroch's mind as he stepped through a portal right behind Shau-ling into the empty blackness of the Council. As soon as his foot hit the smooth black floor, Jeroch felt power rush back through his body, the likes of which could only be felt by drawing deeply on the powers of the Blaze. However, in the sanctity of the Council, a phase did not have to draw on the powers, but merely had to open their consciousness to the powers around them, letting the power fill, rejuvenate, and heal them. Shau-ling had said many times that the Council lay close to the Source of the Blaze, something that Jeroch had seen only once after the battle with Kamen in the previous generation. To all of the other phasia, the source of the Blaze was as much a mystery as the location of the Council. Shau-ling quickly traversed the span of the Council chambers, coming to the center circle. When he stopped in the confines of the etched shape, a dim white light appeared beneath his feet. It was barely enough light to give Jeroch a better look at the reptilian features of the creature that he called master, but somewhere deep within the pit of the phase's stomach, he felt a peace with Shau-ling at the heart of the Council. Jeroch watched as the remaining wounds from the battle with Saurn quickly knitted on Shau-ling's exposed flesh, and even his tattered robes seemed to heal themselves. Jeroch thought he saw a brief smile flash across Shau-ling's features just before lights began to appear in the chamber.

As Jeroch looked on, symbols appeared around the perimeter of the Council chambers one by one, in the order of the birth of the members of the phasia. The first was a formless mass lit in a dark black light. In the darkness of the chamber, the light was still visible, and Jeroch felt himself fill with pride that his symbol, the Shadow, was the first to appear within the chamber. The next to appear was the soft colorless light that revealed the symbol of the Shark. Jeroch smiled to himself, a private joke about Grawn losing his bite over the years springing to mind. Next was the red light under the symbol of the Fox, quickly followed by the blue light under the symbol of the Leopard. Jeroch sighed to himself, knowing that only four of the original phasia still existed, and three of them had only recently returned from disgrace. For so long Jeroch had been denied some of his own memories, the truth about the original members of the phasia, the holes in recollection and time that were the necessity of circumstance. Shau-ling could not have allowed any of his children to remember the member of the phasia that walked away, or what he would become later. It was only after Aryx Terian returned to the fold in the guise of Nightwing that Jeroch found those holes in his memory filled. He was unsure as to whether or not Shau-ling had also allowed Grawn, Bryn, and Ellis to recover their memories, but even without the truth as their ally, Jeroch's oldest siblings were a force to be reckoned with. Though as Jeroch thought about it, if he were in the same position as Grawn, Bryn, and Ellis had been in, and knew the things that they knew, he might have been inclined to do the same thing as they had, even though the thought made his stomach lurch. The symbols for the next group of phasia, the phasia that formed the first council after the split of Aryx Terian and Kamen, appeared next. First, appeared the green symbol of Warron the Boar, followed by the red lighted symbol of the striking Viper for Saurn, and the proud green form for the Lady Wolf Caris. Then came Erdric's blue Scorpion, the clear light under the soaring Vulture for Farax, and last the blue Badger for Aldridge. There was a brief pause before the next four lights appeared, signaling to Jeroch the transition between Councils. After the purge of Grawn, Bryn, and Ellis, Shau-ling added to the Council, and then found two more members added after Kamen's destruction. Zarsi's white Cobra brought a small grin to Shau-ling's face, the challenge once issued by the hasty young member of the Brotherhood was something that would never be forgotten by any phasia young or old. Jeroch scoffed at the red Jackal that appeared next, knowing it was a perfect symbol for the fool Taron. The next two symbols appeared at the same time, as the twins Rael and Trece, the Lord Panther and Lady Tiger were inseparable in all facets of life. As the last symbol appeared, Jeroch felt the hatred flow through him. Draven Batoe cawed as much as his namesake the Crow, and hopefully he would not answer the call to the Council, marking either his death or treachery.

Shau-ling hesitated a moment and took a long deep breath before turning his attention back to Jeroch. The phase could see the weariness in his master's eyes, the battle with Saurn having obviously taken its toll. Every exertion was a chore, and even close to the source of the Blaze, there was no comfort. The strain was eased to be sure, but Jeroch had the haunting suspicion that there was something else going on, and as Shau-ling sighed deeply again, Jeroch knew his worst fears may be close to coming to fruition.

"Shadow," Shau-ling said his slight hiss more noticeable in the quiet chamber, "take your place in the Council and I will send out the calls for the other members of the Brotherhood. There is much to discuss, and I am afraid to say that our altercation with Saurn may be tame in comparison to what awaits us now."

Jeroch wanted to ask some of the questions that rattled around in his mind. Why had Aerith Seth returned to save them from Saurn? Why was Shau-ling not able to dispatch Saurn easily? Why was the Council going to be more dangerous? But Jeroch kept the concerns to himself, stifling the questions and burying them deep down within himself. Shau-ling detested questions. That was part of the reason that some of the phasia were not looked upon as highly. Jeroch knew when to keep his mouth shut and listen. That was an art that some of the younger members of the brotherhood would never be able to learn.

"Yes Master."

Jeroch took a careful few steps across the Council chamber and stepped onto the lighted form that he had stood on through several lifetimes. Shau-ling turned again to face his first child as though to add something, but broke off seconds later, shutting his eyes and extending his hands toward the floor of the chamber. A low hum filled the room, and the lights under the unoccupied symbols began to pulsate. The pulsing of the lights sped up and the hum grew in intensity. When the hum finally relented, balls of light emerged from the symbols and hung motionless in midair. Shau-ling opened his eyes, looked at the colored globes and then motioned skyward with his hand, a motion that sent the lights streaking skyward to search the world for the wayward phasia.

"I wonder how many of the fools are still alive," Shau-ling mused.

Jeroch kept his council to himself. Inwardly Jeroch hoped that some of his more troublesome brothers had been exterminated by the forces of the Light. While there was never trust or comfort when dealing with other members of the phasia, there had always been those of the Brotherhood that Jeroch had never felt comfortable with because they were either too brash or too stupid. The first of the phasia to appear after the summons was one of those phasia, Taron.

"Greetings, Shadow," Taron said proudly, pulling his shoulders back, "I'm sure we're being brought here to be told that the war is over and that the forces of the Light have been defeated for good."

"Through no deed of your own of course," Jeroch countered. "But Master has a good reason for summoning us that is to be certain."

Erdric and Aldridge appeared at nearly the same time, and a few seconds later Warron appeared. Warron looked annoyed at the summons, but then Warron was always annoyed at something. However, since Basille's banishment, Jeroch had noticed that Warron had become much more withdrawn and brooding. It was almost as if he took the destruction of his longtime ally personally.

"I see that your friend Draven has not made his appearance yet," Warron said, locking his eyes and Jeroch.

"My personal hell has not yet come to an end, I'm afraid," Jeroch responded coldly. "Draven would live a thousand years just to spite me."

Warron laughed and looked at Taron.

"I suppose that you are my personal hell. It's too bad that Pike Rhuiden is dead. I rather enjoyed his dismantling of you in the last generation."

Taron fumed and was about to respond when Rael and Trece appeared.

"We may be the last," Rael said as he looked around the assemblage of his brethren. "Zarsi met his end in Sador at the hands of Nathaniel Sandar, and Trece and I killed Bryn and Caris."

Shau-ling cocked an eyebrow and looked at the twins with mild amusement.

"We had traveled to Scalla to finish our little battle with Draven only to find Bryn and Caris waiting for us there. Caris had earlier cost us our chance to finish Draven off, and so Rael and I took retribution," Trece continued.

Shau-ling laughed.

"You need not lie for your sisters," Shau-ling mused, "though it is quite wondrous to see four, or should I say five of my children working together."

Rael and Trece looked at each other and then back at Shau-ling.

"Ah," the reptilian man said scratching his chin, "I see that my little secret is coming out at last. Well, many things are about to change my dear children, and as Taron so bluntly put it, the war is indeed at an end, but not in the way that his stubborn mind perceives."

Jeroch chuckled to himself, wondering if Taron knew he had been insulted.

"My dear twins," Shau-ling started, "I know everything that has happened to my phasia in every lifetime, and I know their minds and their schemes more fully then they do. Only twice in my existence has a phase surprised me, the first was Basille and his recklessness after death, and the second was a few moments ago when Saurn tried in vain to kill me."

Warron smiled and nodded. He had known of Saurn's plan for some time but had refused to have any part in it. Having heard what Shau-ling had done to Kamen, Warron knew that two members of the phasia had little chance to topple the master, especially with Jeroch around. While few had respect for the first born, Warron had gained it over many begrudging centuries. Jeroch was no coward, as many of the younger phasia thought, and he was not one to be trifled with in open combat.

"I know that Bryn and Caris still live. I know that Zarsi met his end at the hands of Nathan Sandar," Shau-ling corrected, "the Ram and third *Coromor* of the prophecies. Farax also met his fate at the hands of the man who wears the name Sandar, while Grawn and Ellis met their ends at the hands of Bryn and her family Gideon and Taya Viruci. Bryn did not return home because of her guilt over the death of both Grawn and Ellis, and the hope that with all that has gone wrong that she will have some time to be with her family and perhaps find happiness with Aerith Seth. Caris did not return home because she believes that her heart has finally thawed from the cold block of ice that it has been from the day I forged her and that she has found what real love feels like."

CHAPTER 41

Erdric laughed.

"A whore finds love," he mocked, "with a priest I imagine."

"Worse," Shau-ling said, suddenly serious, "a saint. Logan Ranthall."

The name drew an immediate reaction from everyone but Rael and Trece. Even Jeroch found himself incited to rage by the name of the man who had helped seal Shau-ling's fate in the previous generation. Erdric and Taron shouted across the room to one another, arguing over who would be the first to get their hands on Logan. Warron was plotting the death of Caris in his violent and angry words, while Jeroch tried his best to hold his tongue and beat away the accusations from Aldridge who thought everything was a conspiracy against him.

"Silence!" Shau-ling bellowed. "It is fitting that the youngest of you are the only ones who have sense enough to keep their mouths shut. You damn fools have had your plots and your schemes, all this time thinking that you were too smart and above your master. You are more pathetic than the humans you were fighting against. Do you honestly think that I did not know what Grawn, Bryn, and Ellis were planning from the beginning when they gave the prophecies to Aralias Imstra? I did. But I could not allow their seeming treachery to go unpunished. They were banished for a time to throw Emries off the trail. I wanted him to believe that the prophecies were a way to destroy me, not the other way around."

Blank stares filled the room.

"You don't even know why you are fighting, do you?" Shau-ling asked, looking each one of his phasia dead in the eyes before letting his gaze move to the next.

Jeroch held Shau-ling's stare the longest. Jeroch had always had suspicions about the true nature of the war, and that somewhere along the way, sometime after Aryx left the phasia, that the Brotherhood had truly become the evil that mankind said they were. Shau-ling nodded in accent to Jeroch's unspoken thoughts and continued speaking.

"The phasia were created to help destroy Emries and his followers. Perhaps I have coddled you too much, and perhaps I am to blame for the path that you have followed. Somehow you have all lost your way, but I too feel that I have lost the purpose of this war. It took a mortal, or at least a man who was once mortal to make me realize what it is that we should be fighting for. The men and women that the world called the People of the Dragon have more right to call themselves phasia then you do, and Logan Ranthall has proven it."

Taron immediately stepped forward, his pride always more powerful than his brain.

"Lord Shau-ling, how can you say that Logan Ranthall, the man who was proclaimed as the Dragon by your enemy Cedric Binosear, is more of a phase than any of us? He followed Emries lead and did everything that he could to destroy us."

For once, Jeroch agreed with Taron, a frightening thought in the least. How a mortal, a puny pawn in Emries game could be considered on the level of the children of a living god was ludicrous.

"But he has touched the Blaze," Rael countered. "Logan Ranthall pulled on the Blaze so deeply that his mortal body died. I watched it myself. Trece and I both saw it happen. His heart now beats the same as ours. His blood knows the fire of the Blaze with every beat. He is a phase."

"Blaspheme!" Warron called out. "No mortal can use the Blaze to become one of us! I refuse to listen to such nonsense, and I will strike down anyone who champions this rubbish."

"I champion it," Shau-ling countered. "Do you dare strike me down, and die as all others have that have challenged me? Will you follow your friend Basille into the hell that is Banishment and deprive me of another willing servant in this fight for survival?"

Warron stood firm.

"You allowed Logan Ranthall to undergo his transformation?"

Shau-ling nodded.

"I assisted in it. Because of my connection with the Blaze, it would not have been possible had I not intervened. Logan may be a powerful and resourceful man, but even the Blaze is too much for him. It would have burn him alive had I not lent my assistance."

"It would have been worth it to be rid of such a nuisance," Warron replied. "Logan Ranthall does not deserve the honor to be called a member of the Brotherhood, and I will never accept him as such. If he ever sets foot in this Council, I will kill him."

Shau-ling clenched his fists and rounded on Warron.

"You dare threaten to spill blood here in the Council! I should strike you down here and now for your insolence."

Warron fell to his knees and pulled open the front of his shirt.

"Strike, father," Warron said proudly. "Show me the same mercy you showed Basille."

Shau-ling stood straight, looking down on his rebellious child. He needed warriors in this fight to reclaim the honor that the phasia once fought for, and killing those who did not understand was not a way to gain those warriors. He turned away from Warron the next moment and shook his head.

"I'm not going to kill you, Warron. I cannot blame you for your ignorance. You had not yet been created when we lost our way, so this is the only way you have ever known. This war was not supposed to be fought blindly, and it was not supposed to be fought like children squabbling in a sandbox. Once Bryn and Ellis had given the prophecies to Emries through Aralias Imstra, the window of opportunity opened. However, because the phasia were so splintered and because I had to hide the three away to keep the secret of their deeds, there was no way to break the phasia from the road I put them on. It was my error, and mine alone."

Warron stood, and launched forward, a long spike of diamond appearing in his hand.

"And this error seals your fate!"

Shau-ling spun quickly, bringing up his hand, the flows of power launching toward the phase before the thought of the action had time to process. The hidden string wove itself through the flows of Earth, Fire, Air, and Water, creating a pure white combination, adding slight touches of Chaos and Order. When the beam struck Warron's chest, he cried out in pain. The screams continued as the muscled body began to be eaten from the inside, out, piece by piece. Screams echoed through the Council chamber, all of the other phasia struck dumb by the sight. It wasn't until several moments after the final bits of Warron disappeared that the screams finally stopped. Shau-ling looked at Jeroch and the phase could see disbelief in his master's eyes. The remaining members of the Council had just watched one of their own be Banished by their master. Erdric and Aldridge turned on their maker immediately after, launching blasts of ice in rapid succession. Rael and Trece came to the defense of their master, forming a shield of Order around him, while Rael let disks of Chaos energy ripple across the chamber. Taron also turned on Shau-ling, enhancing his aura of power with his string of Fire and charging across the distance toward the shielded man. Jeroch intervened quickly, the blades of Order and Chaos forming in his hands. Taron ignored Jeroch at first, but quickly paid attention as both blades slashed at him simultaneously. Jumping back, Taron brought a fist downward, his aura stretching out toward Jeroch's face. The eldest of the phasia was quicker, spinning through the attack and burying both of his blades into the gut of his taller counterpart. Taron staggered back, blood pouring from the twin wounds. He tried to intensify his aura, but the damage was not merely done by the blades themselves. The powers of Chaos and Order were eating deeper into Taron, killing him from the inside. Because Taron never thought the powers to heal were important enough to notice, he choked on the blood that he began to cough up and collapsed to the ground.

Erdric and Aldridge scattered when the disks of Chaos energy flooded the area, but they were quick to reform and keep the blasts of ice rocketing at their younger siblings. Trece was content to keep her powers focused on protecting Shau-ling, but Rael's assault was direct and precise. Disks of power claimed Erdric in the chest, and before Aldridge could do anything to help his fallen friend, he found the points of two blades emerging from his chest. Jeroch retrieved his blades and lingered only a moment looking at Rael and Trece before letting the blades disappear. They had come to the defense of their master and creator, and for that Jeroch had no quarrel with the twins. Shau-ling looked at the three fallen forms and then shook his head. It was his recklessness again that had caused destruction, only this time it had been four of his own children that had met their ends because of it. Warron had been Banished, and he would never again live to see another sunrise. But unless Shau-ling was wrong, this world did not have many sunrises left, and the Creator would be giving no choice but to lay waste to that which He had made. For the first time since the inception of the Council, blood of a phase had been spilled on its pristine floor, and it marked a change.

"My children," Shau-ling said, dejection filling his voice, "what has happened here is a terrible thing, and must never be repeated. The Council was meant to be a place where the phasia could meet and plan their strikes against the forces of the Light, while at the same time healing their wounds. And yet on this day it was witness to the death of four of the phasia, one by my own hand. The creature Shau-ling no longer deserves to live, and so the phasia of old no longer deserve to live."

Jeroch for the first time had true fear in his heart.

"The Blaze is the force that gives us strength, gives us power, and makes us what we are. Yet, the Blaze is also the force and life of the world that we are fighting so bitterly for control over. I will no longer let the use of this sacred power destroy the very thing I was trying to protect. From this point forward, the phasia are freed of their bond, and the string that they carry will return to the fire. You are now pure creatures with pure hearts and pure souls. I grant you that which has been kept from you since the very beginning, and I make you more than you ever were. No longer will you be creatures with the ability to draw from the Blaze only through my allowance. Now you shall be as I am, free, a child of the Creator who willingly gave himself to the Blaze, as Logan Ranthall has. He has shown me that men and mortals are not the enemy, it is Emries and his perverted war that is the enemy."

Shau-ling raised his hand and a bright white light filled the room. Jeroch felt as though his insides were on fire, and the strings of Order and Chaos in the back of his mind began to pulse and shiver. In an instant, the strings were pulled away from him, and his connection with the Blaze was severed.

Rael and Trece watched as Jeroch fell to the ground, motionless and lifeless. Soon the pain hit each of them, the primal string in the back of their minds ripping away everything.

* * * * * * * * * * *

Bryn stood, idly chatting with Caris while Gideon and Taya surveyed the remains of the palace that they had once called home when the pain shot through her like a white hot needle. Inside her mind, the string of Fire burned to the brightest intensity, sending waves of heat through her, the air searing in her lungs, her blood boiling. With the last bit of air in her body, Bryn cried out in pain as she collapsed. Caris too felt pain rocketing through her. It was a dull throbbing at first, until the daggers plunged into her mind, the pain like a scythe ripping through her thoughts. When the primal sting of Earth was ripped away, Caris fell. Gideon and Taya were by the side of the fallen women seconds later, clutching them tightly. No breath escaped from either of the women's mouths, and there was no beat of a heart within their chests. As far as Gideon could tell, both women were dead.

* * * * * * * * * * *

Jeroch felt the pain in his head as he pulled to a sitting position, and then suddenly realized that something was wrong. Ever since the day that Shau-ling forged him, Jeroch could feel the fires of the Blaze burning just beyond his consciousness. Now though, that fire was gone, and the memories of the Blaze had also fled his fragile mind. He knew only that which he had physically experienced, and even then his memories previous to the present lifetime were very fuzzy. It was like someone had suddenly put blinders on his mind, and he could only know what any mortal would know. That was when he heard his own heartbeat. It was not the methodical heartbeat that had been a comforting constant throughout every battle and every war. Now it beat with an erratic rhythm, fast, choppy, hard. It beat so hard that Jeroch could feel it pounding against his ribcage, making his chest ache. Rael and Trece had recovered their senses too, instantly dismayed that for the first time since their birth, the only thoughts in their minds were their own.

"My children," Shau-ling said looking down, "you have been given the gift of mortality. You are now as human as the men and women that you have fought for generations."

Jeroch started to stand.

"Before you ask any questions, Jeroch," Shau-ling said quickly, "let me explain. As long as you possessed a part of me, the primal string within you, you were limited to being the servants of Shau-ling. Now I have taken that part away from you. You have a choice, a choice you should have been given in the beginning. Kamen made me see the danger of ultimate power, and Aryx taught me that the human, while easily misled from the true path, can walk it. So now you have the choice. You may live as Aryx did, a mortal for the rest of your days, or you may open yourselves to the Blaze, let it fill you and sooth you. It is not drawing on its power as you have all through your lives, but surrendering to it, becoming one with it. And in doing so, you become my children again."

Jeroch stood and looked Shau-ling straight in the eye.

"I am your first son," he said proudly, "and be it in Heaven or in Hell, I will follow you and be your most loyal son. I shall be with you father, to the very end and everything that follows."

Shau-ling nodded and turned then to the twins Rael and Trece.

"And my proud fine son and daughter?"

Rael and Trece looked at each other for another moment and then Rael turned to Shau-ling.

"The part of us that was Kamen always wondered what it would be like to be free. Trece and I saw what it was like with Gwydeon and Midarin, and the love that they shared. Part of me, and for the first time there is only a me, wants to find out what that is. While I want to be there for you at the end father, I can't let this slim opportunity that I have pass by."

Trece took Rael's hand and held it tightly.

"There is so much that humans have, and so much that we could never have. Now, we can have children, mortal children who will know right from wrong and the evils that we never really understood. Maybe that way, even if the Creator decides to destroy us all, we can still say we won, because we learned what the Creator always wanted us to know."

Shau-ling smiled and let a portal form.

"Then go, my proud children. Enjoy yourselves and the world that the Creator gave to us."

Rael and Trece stepped through the portal, and as Shau-ling turned to face Jeroch, the former phase noticed a change had come over his master. The reptilian edge to his features were gone, and his complexion darkened to a tanned skin tone. His features were very much like an old mortal, and his eyes showed a warmth that Jeroch had never thought possible.

"Come my son," he said the cold edge gone from his voice, "Shau-ling and the phasia are forever cast to the whim of time and memory, but from this day forward, Halicon returns."

Blurring the Lines

Creator's Calendar Year 1205; Light Reality

Pike had tried hard not to interrupt or let his discomfort show too much as Evan and Meredith related the story of the years following the War of the Dragon. Everything that they said made sense, considering what had happened in Shau-ling's palace on this side of reality. Gwydeon had died, Elwyne had survived, and everything turned out for the best for about everyone involved. Jerrard had lived to return to Erika and have two children. Logan and Elwyne lived together back in Aradon where they had a child before Logan either died or was killed. Midarin lived alone in Brea, creating her army in Gwydeon's memory, and Pike, well, the story of the Pike in the Light reality was the only portion that sat poorly in the pit of the Dark Mirror Pike's stomach. Lord Rhuiden as Pike was referred to in the Light reality had become a bitter, conniving and lusty old man who cared more about vengeance then doing what was right. Eldar actually had giggled at some of the portrayals of Pike as a man who sang with the bards, got stinking drunk and then seduced barmaids or servant girls for his amusement. Pike on the other hand found the same portrayals offensive and they made his heart ache.

"So," Pike said summing up, "in this reality, I'm a bastard who cheats on his wife, never sees his children, plans on killing his own son to keep his throne, is almost always drunk, and sleeps with anyone who looks at him the right way."

"Look on the bright side, Pike," Eldar commented, "you were always a bastard."

Meredith stifled a chuckle, and Evan had to turn his head to hide the bright smile. Just then, a bright white light flashed in the room, and Evan felt an enormous power, unlike anything he had ever felt before. Eldar and Pike too seemed nervous at the growing power. Only Meredith, who was still very mortal and untouched by the war, was oblivious to the presence. The light originated in the corner of the room, close to the stand where the Creator's Book of Laws stood uncovered. When the light receded, two men stood by the book, one standing proud and tall with the Dragon Sword hanging from his hip, while the other had . . . wings. Pike was the first to bound across the room, Eldar quickly following. There were no words spoken between the four, only quick embraces and looks of shock. Pike then turned and motioned for Evan and Meredith to approach, which they did with only a hint of caution.

"Evan Sinn, Meredith Heron," Pike started, "let me introduce you to Gwydeon Sandar and Logan Ranthall. Oh yeah, they are from my little reality."

Evan felt a twinge in the pit of his stomach. It was as though his could feel the separation between the realities beginning to shrink. The more the two realities interacted with each other, and interfered with the natural flow of events, the more the separation would begin to weaken, and the line between the dark and the light would begin to blur. The man with wings that Pike had introduced as Gwydeon Sandar took a step forward and looked Evan over carefully.

"You seem to have fared a lot better in this reality Evan," he said after a moment, "but I think you would look better with a beard."

"But the extra arm and no eye patch are an improvement," Logan added.

Evan cocked his head at the appraisals, and Meredith stepped forward running her hand across Evan's smooth cheek and chin.

"Maybe Gwydeon is right," she whispered into his ear, teasing him, "you would look better with a beard."

Evan chuckled and extended his hand to Logan.

"It's a pleasure to actually meet you, Lord Logan," Evan said quickly, "I did not get the privilege before you died in this reality."

Logan took the comment for what it was, and then a hope shot into his heart.

"Elwyne?"

Evan shook his head.

"I'm sorry Logan, she passed away a few days ago. But you do have a son on this side. His name is Wolf and from everything I have seen of him, he is a fine young man."

Logan smiled, pride filling him, but then turned his attention to Eldar.

"Part of me knew you would be here," he said softly, "and I'm sure you understand why."

Eldar nodded, but both Gwydeon's and Pike's blank looks prompted the blond woman to fill in the pieces of the puzzle.

"Shau-ling revived me with the use of the Blaze, and because of that I have some of the knowledge of the Blaze filling me. Shau-ling has ensured that any time the Blaze is used for extraordinary deeds, I can't help but know about them. Logan here has, with the help of Shau-ling, the Flame, and a couple members of the phasia, become a member of the Brotherhood of Phasia."

Pike looked Logan dead in the eyes, and then smiled.

"So," Pike said scratching the start of a beard on his chin, "do you have one of those cute titles? What are you, Lord Guppy? Lord Butterfly?"

Evan, Meredith, and Eldar all found the humor in the comments, and Logan was not unaffected by the jibe. He let a smile come to his lips briefly before shaking his head. Only Gwydeon's serious look was not fractured.

"Lord Phoenix," Logan said, "but that's not important now. We aren't here to be social."

"Let me guess," Pike said drawing *Fury* from the loop in his belt. "An old friend of ours is coming to this reality to cause some trouble?"

"Right," Logan said nodding.

"And who is this old friend?" Meredith asked.

"Draven," Gwydeon said coldly.

Pike scowled.

"And Draven would be?" Evan asked.

"The member of the phasia that has made life miserable for everyone, mortals and phasia alike, in the other reality," Logan answered.

"And he's coming here? Wonderful," Evan said shaking his head.

"Well, are we going to be the People of the Dragon again, or should we be the People of the Phoenix?" Pike asked, looking between his three old friends.

Logan laughed at the comment.

"Doesn't have the same ring to it, does it? I guess it's the People of the Dragon again. Only this time, we're fighting to protect Shau-ling, not destroy him."

* * * * * * * * * * *

As Wolf helped Sabrina up, trying to be as loving and concerned as possible to keep up the illusion for Nathaniel, Lissa tried her best to ignore everything, talking with Susanne, filling her in on everything with a hushed voice. Susanne kept the act up, acting as though she was consoling Lissa, while Lissa vented her imaginary fury on the tall blond. Pike's fury however was very real and very vehement. The Enforcers were doing their best to keep the doors to the throne room blockaded, but it was only a matter of time before the members of the Torch got through, trying to seek revenge for the death of their leader Seraphina Masile. Midarin had turned her attention back to Aryx and Gwillim, and the three old friends chatted quietly, trying to make sense of all the things that had gone on since arriving in Marcwell.

"Zak," Pike said, returning *Fury* to the loop on his belt. "I need to know our situation. Take Liette with you and get me a layout. I want to know exactly how big of a force we are dealing with, if there's any way that they can get to us. How much do they control, et cetera."

Zak nodded and smiled.

"You got it boss."

He sprinted off the next moment with Liette following quickly behind him. Turok, Ren, Valin, and Galen held the door, the pounding on the thick wood only relenting for a few moments before starting again, the sounds of battle flowing from the courtyard. Pike turned to Midarin, interrupting the private council.

"We can't stay here," Pike said coldly, "not in the middle of this war. Besides, I don't think Duncan will come back."

"He wants to hurt you, Pike," Midarin answered. "That much was clear when he started talking about your affairs. He wants to break you down from the inside and kill your heart before he tries to take your life."

"He can't hurt me," Pike responded, his jaw set firmly. "I have nothing left to take."

Rachel was there, staring at Pike, and when their eyes met, Pike felt the daggers from the woman's stare. She drew her sword and dropped it at her former lord's feet.

"I won't fight for you anymore, Pike," she said calmly. "I've defended you through too many lies and broken promises, and I won't do it anymore. I'm not a member of your Enforcers anymore."

Nathaniel stepped up, picking up the sword.

"It's not about the Enforcers, or Pike, or Marcwell anymore, Rachel," the boy said, the power of Emries still filling him. "This is about hunting down two members of the phasia and killing them. It's about fighting the war that needs to be fought, not the war that is being fought outside that door. We have to find and kill the phasia, and then find and kill Shau-ling. Everything else is trivial. So, if you won't fight for Pike, I ask you to fight for me as a member of the People of the Ram."

Rachel looked at the boy, back at Pike, and then at Nathaniel again.

"I fight long enough to find Taron and pay him back for Elizabeth. After that, I'm done. I'm not going to betray Elizabeth's memory by fighting for no reason."

Pike felt the barb dig deep into his heart.

Wolf kissed Sabrina lightly on the forehead and then pulled Jared into the quiet conversation. Rachel, Pike and Nathaniel continued their little parlay with Midarin and Gwillim, trying to figure out what to do next. Lissa went to join the conversation, and Susanne joined Wolf's trio.

"I think the act is working," Susanne said looking at Nathaniel and then at Lissa. "But I'll keep acting as the mediator just to keep Nathaniel off the trail."

"Good," Wolf said nodding. "That should buy us a little bit of time to find out what's going on. But I think that we need to worry about Duncan and his lackeys. He tipped his hand when he started taunting Pike with my mother."

Sabrina gave Wolf a puzzled look.

"My mother was the famous heroine that Duncan was referring to. It was just a taunt to get us riled up and start a confrontation. But looking back, I think it was more than that. Midarin is right, Duncan and the phasia are trying to hurt Pike. Pike is wrong though in thinking he has nothing left."

"Aradon," Sabrina said.

"Exactly," Wolf replied.

"Pike still has family there, doesn't he?" Jared asked.

"His mother and father," Wolf answered. "Erin, his mother, is the town healer and resident expert on just about everything, and Tam is the mayor of the village. It would be just like a member of the phasia to strike there."

By this time, Zak and Liette had returned from their mission. Also, the sounds of battle had stopped in the courtyard.

"Pike," Zak said, catching his breath, "the Lion's Mane has been defeated, but the Creator's Torch Society has had to turn their attention to something else."

"There's another army marching on Marcwell," Liette continued, "waiving a banner with the symbol of the Fox."

"Bryn," Aryx said quickly.

Pike growled and pulled *Fury* back into his hand.

"Surrounded and outnumbered," he said looking around the room.

"Pike," Wolf said stepping forward. "I think you are missing something."

"What could I be missing, boy?" Pike fumed. "Maybe if you weren't being so stubborn and bull-headed like your father, you would realize that this little war is bigger than you and whatever it is that you think you are doing."

"That's funny coming from you Pike," Rachel countered.

Pike turned toward Rachel, but found Midarin cutting him off.

"I think you should listen to what Wolf has to say."

Pike growled again, but turned back to the man who was the spitting image of his father.

"Bryn is here fighting for her own reasons, but I can't imagine that it is to destroy Marcwell. Though I think that she will serve to give us an opportunity to escape."

"Escape?" Pike asked. "Why would I want to leave my kingdom?"

"Marcwell is lost father," Sabrina said joining Wolf. "The battle is moving again, this time it is moving to Aradon."

The realization suddenly hit Pike.

"My parents..."

Wolf could see the concern in the eyes of the older man, the anger and sorrow in his heart suddenly parting and letting the man who lay beneath rise to the surface. Family was the one thing that he cared about, even if that didn't extend to his own wife. Turok moved away from the door and put his hand on Pike's shoulder.

"There is no honor here Pike," he said coldly, "and there is no victory either. Lord Cedric taught me to go where the fighting was, and never wait for it to find you. Make sure your family is alright, and let the Enforcers take care of the fighting. Let us go back to Scalla to help Jerrard."

Pike nodded absently, his worry overriding everything else.

"Thank you Pike."

Turok, Ren, Valin, and Zak waited until Wolf created a portal and then stepped through one at a time, heading for a confrontation with the army of Jeroch. Pike looked at Wolf and sighed.

"Well, if we're going to go, we better go now."

Wolf nodded to Jared, and the two created a portal and followed the rest of the group as they made their quick journey to Aradon. What was lost on the fleeing members of the Enforcers and the newly constituted People of the Ram was that one of the fallen bodies in the throne room had disappeared into nothingness. The body of Seraphina Masile was gone, and when members of the Creator's Torch Society broken into the throne room

CHAPTER 41

moments later, they were left with a puzzle that they would never be able to solve.

* * * * * * * * * * *

Logan stood looking around the old church of Aradon, a feeling of longing entering his heart. Part of him wanted so much to go home to the little farmhouse that he had lived in as a young man, just to see it one more time. Another part of him wanted to visit Elwyne's grave, pay his respects to the woman that he loved more than anything else in the world. But as he felt a twinge of power in the back of his mind, he knew that time for remembrance was at an end, and the time to fight was close at hand.

"There's a portal forming," Logan said to the rest of the group, "and its close. Best guess, I would have to say it's in the old Mithacarthian Woods at the bottom of the hill."

Evan looked at Logan for a moment, the name not registering with him. Then suddenly everything was clear.

"Logan's Wood," Evan said quickly. "It was renamed in your honor after you died in this reality."

Logan smiled weakly at the name, his distaste for the glorification of his name entering him.

"Logan's Wood then. It should be forming any time now."

There were nods all around, and the six warriors quickly exited the old church and made their way down the hill, following Logan's directions until they saw the blue glow appear in midair. Evan and Meredith stayed back, not wanting to get involved in any confrontation, but Logan, Gwydeon, Pike, and Eldar kept their weapons ready for a fight. When the portal opened, Gwydeon lowered his sword as he watched his wife, Midarin step through the portal quickly followed by several others. The only other people that Gwydeon recognized was the older, grizzled Pike, Gwillim, Sabrina, Nathaniel, and Aryx Terian. The Creator gave him the names of the others in the assemblage, but they did not matter as he saw the face of Midarin and his heart fluttered.

As Midarin stepped out of the portal, her heart nearly stopped. For so many years she had dreamed of seeing Gwydeon again, and there he stood in front of her with two other people that had been long dead. Eldar Merin looked exactly as she had the day that Taron had ended her life, and Logan Ranthall looked the same as he had the day he died. But it was Gwydeon that Midarin's eyes kept coming back to. His features were still handsome and strong, and as soon as she saw the wings, she realized that he had become what Emries had promised, the Brother of Angels. Midarin didn't even hesitate, but ran across the distance and locked her arms around the slightly taller man, clinging to him. Gwydeon held her tightly, feeling the love of the woman who was Midarin, but not the Midarin he had been with for the past twenty years. Gwillim was also taken aback by the appearance of the man that he would have gladly called father, and part of his heart was at peace as he watched Midarin smile in the warmth and strength of Gwydeon's embrace.

When Wolf finally emerged from the portal, his eyes locked on the older man who held the Dragon Sword aloft. Faint memories in the back of his mind, either Basille's or his own, told him that the man he looked at was his father, Logan Ranthall. There was a moment of uncertainty, but Sabrina pushed Wolf forward, and after stumbling a step forward, stood face to face with Logan. One corner of Logan's mouth raised into a sly smile as he regarded the boy.

"You look good Wolf," Logan said finally, "I guess I could have done a lot worse."

Wolf smiled.

"Mother always said, at least I didn't look exactly like you, then I would be unbearable."

The comment caught Logan in the depths of his heart, and he quickly reached out and pulled the boy into a tight embrace. While Logan may not have been the man who had been the father of the boy Wolf, he was going to make the most of the opportunity. However, all the meetings were not of joy and fulfillment. That much was clear by the look on Lord Rhuiden's face as he found himself face to face with not only a younger version of himself, but also a resurrected Eldar and seemingly resurrected Evan and Meredith.

"How?" was all that Lord Rhuiden could croak out.

Evan stepped forward and gave the brunt of the story.

"I can't explain everything Pike," Evan said calmly, "but I will say that things are not as they seem. There is another world, another reality apart from ours where the forces of the Shadow have an advantage. Gwydeon, Logan, Pike here, and Eldar come from that reality. They came here to help set everything right, and stop a disaster from befalling the entire world."

Liette pushed the older Pike out of the way and drew her sword.

"You're wrong, Evan. Because they are here, everything will go wrong. The balance between the two worlds is going to be thrown into chaos, and it will start to spin out of control. The two worlds will begin to merge and it will all be destroyed."

The girl suddenly had much more power in her voice, and a maturity that had not been there before. She suddenly turned to Wolf.

"It's all his fault," she accused. "It's because of Wolf that this whole imbalance was created, and he is the reason that the two worlds exist. If we kill him, then everything will return to normal, and we can concentrate on destroying Shau-ling."

"That's quite an accusation Liette," Meredith said, adding her voice, "and what proof do you have?"

"Basille gave his string of power to Wolf from the Other Side, creating the imbalance," Liette responded. "It's because of Wolf that this other Pike and that creature you call Eldar is here. They are servants of Shau-ling sent to bring Wolf back to help the forces of the Shadow prevail in the other reality, and then they will return here, join the phasia, and try to destroy us."

Eldar pointed the tip of her blade at the little girl.

"We were sent to retrieve Wolf, but because he is the key to saving both worlds from the fire of the Creator. We are supposed to find the truth, whatever it is."

"Emries is the enemy," the young Pike chimed in, "he needs to be stopped."

Lord Rhuiden stepped forward, *Fury* in hand and ready to strike.

"And you would try and stop him? Even if it meant killing the *Coromor*, right?"

The younger Pike stood toe to toe with his older counterpart.

"I don't care about Emries, and I don't care about the bloody *Coromor*. Look at yourself old man, look at what you've become. This isn't you, you aren't the guy who saved your friends from the Jeresei in Sarmeel, or the guy who stood by Logan when he proclaimed himself as the Dragon in Rana. Now you're just some washed up, bitter nobody. Where's the fire that you had when you were eye to eye with Emries on Mount Tantis, giving him what for over being led around by the nose?"

Lord Rhuiden took a step back, but the younger Pike grabbed him by the shoulders and got right in his face.

"Wake up! Quit thinking like a drunken fool, and start thinking like the hero that everyone thinks you are. This war isn't about Taron, or Eldar, or Cairyn, or Sabrina, or Nathaniel, or even Emries and Shau-ling. It's about finding out what is right and what is wrong, and making a choice to follow the right path. If you want to know the truth Pike, you'll find it, but if you want to be a blind old fool who would rather save his throne then the world, so be it."

Lord Rhuiden pulled away, his axe ready to strike the young upstart. Pike pulled his ax from the loop in his belt and readied for battle. The two mirror images faced off against one another, ready to strike the other down in defense of what they believed was right. It was then that laughter resonated in the air. Gwydeon knew the laugh immediately, and pulled away from Midarin's grasp, looking around for the source of the vile noise. Logan too found the familiar chords disturbing, and it only took a single skyward glance to find the twisting and flipping form spinning though the air before it landed several strides away. Draven always had a flair for entrances, and this was no exception.

"I see things don't change much, even here in the so-called Light reality," Draven said mockingly. "You mortals are always at each other's throats, making my job so much easier. But I just couldn't resist getting a good seat to watch Pike rip himself to pieces."

The young Pike turned to face Draven, fire in his eyes. He had wanted a piece of the phase ever since he had rescued Sabrina from the palace of Trelon. But before he could step to combat the phase, Lord Rhuiden charged, his ax slashing down hard at the unaware young man. Aryx was a step faster than his former ally, darting in the way of the strike and intercepting it with his blade.

"There is no honor in this Pike," Aryx chided.

Pike stepped back, separating the blade of his ax from Aryx's sword. After a moment, Pike raised his ax again and smiled.

"I've always wanted another crack at you Aryx," the older man said firmly. "Ever since we met one on one when you were Nightwing, I've wanted you. Now, I've got that chance."

"Father, don't," Sabrina cautioned. "Aryx isn't our enemy."

"Oh yes he is little girl," Draven poked. "Didn't you know that your precious Aryx was once a phase? Oh yes, he was one of Shau-ling's first little pets, and one of his proudest."

The fire in Lord Rhuiden's eyes grew brighter.

"Come, come Rhuiden," Draven chided, "strike!"

Aryx locked his eyes on Draven.

"After this, worm, you and I will cross swords."

"You'll have to get in line," Gwydeon said, his eyes never leaving the object of his fury. "If he survives me, he's got to answer Logan and then Pike.

"I'm touched," Draven said, clutching his hands to his heart.

Aryx's eyes met Lord Rhuiden's again, the hatred consuming the man he had at one time considered a friend and ally. Draven laughed as Aryx took a defensive position waiting for the strike to come that would mark the beginning of the battle between to former members of the *Erieal* and two men who were considered the greatest heroes in the battle against the forces of the Shadow. Logan watched the standoff with a sense of detachment, not caring about Aryx Terian, or the Pike Rhuiden of the Light reality. Aryx tensed, but seemed to relax a moment later, and Logan felt the cause, as the powers of the Blaze flared in the back of his mind, signaling the arrival of a portal. Gwydeon felt the portal form, but did not allow his eyes to leave Draven. Midarin had pulled herself back to herself, her bow poised and ready to strike not at the people emerging from the portal, but rather at the heart of the man who once was her lover, Pike Rhuiden.

Duncan, followed by Michael, Bridgette, Erdric, and Aldridge stepped from the portal, and all but Duncan wore evil smiles on their faces. The look on Duncan's face was one of determination, and it was focused on his father Pike Rhuiden. Logan found his eyes drifting to Aldridge, the phase that had been his first conquest in the previous generation.

"Back away Terian," Duncan said coldly, "the old man is mine."

Lord Rhuiden turned to his son and glared, his teeth clenched.

"Let's finish this, once and for all."

The War to End All Wars

Creator's Calendar Year 1205; Light Reality

Logan's Wood was filled with a tension that was almost palpable. Three sides of the same conflict were represented, and there were enough personal feuds and bad blood to fuel a thousand wars. Lord Rhuiden stood firm staring a hole through his son Duncan, the words of his counterpart from the other reality echoing in the back of his mind. There had been much power in those words, but hatred and fear were overriding logic, and all that Lord Rhuiden could do was stand transfixed, waiting for an opportunity to spill the blood of his own child with his infamous ax *Fury*. Gwydeon Sandar too had a grudge that he needed to put an end to, a hatred that transcended both time and space. Draven was the ultimate foil to the creature that Gwydeon had become, pure evil to Gwydeon's pure good. Their previous crossing of swords had nearly brought an end to Draven's role in this massive war, but an evil the magnitude of Draven's was not something that could be so easily erased from existence. But as the war between the Light and the Shadow had always been dominated by the wild cards, it was fitting that there were so many thrown into the confrontation in Logan's Wood. First and foremost of course were Evan Sinn and Meredith Heron, the representatives of Aerith Seth. But the stranger wildcards, like Liette Forer and Galen Pryde made the line between Light and Shadow seem that much thinner. If reality was truly becoming such a fragile and tenuous thing, then it was the actions of these rogue warriors that could shatter it all.

Lord Rhuiden took a step toward his son and waited. Every voice in his head was screaming for him to strike quickly, before anyone could ruin his chance at securing his throne and his kingdom. But Duncan was not standing idly, he had his sword drawn and ready for a fight. The young man wanted the throne that by all rights and agreements was his. Furthermore, the boy was not alone in the confrontation. His confederates were there waiting to add their blades to the assault, and all of them would be gladdened to see Lord Rhuiden dead and the throne of Marcwell in the hands of someone that they could manipulate and control to their own sick and twisted ends.

"Enough talk, father," the word sounding sickening to Duncan's ears, "strike, and prove the traitor that you are."

No one saw the separate flashes of light from the edges of the forest, but all were quick to notice the appearance of two new pieces to the game. The first was a nondescript man dressed in all white robes. His face was expressionless, and his gait was calm and even. Logan was the first to react to Emries' appearance, and hatred boiled in him unlike any he had ever felt. Now that Logan had embraced the powers of the Blaze and become a member of the phasia, the fires of anger burned hotter within him for the man who had been the eternal enemy of Shau-ling and the phasia. But despite the ancient rivalry, Logan had his own reasons to hate Emries, and those personal betrayals ran deeper than even the Blaze. The other arrival sparked many to react, but none stronger than Aryx Terian. He knew the powers of the metallic beast that floated before them, because he had once been encased underneath the metal shell. Lord Rhuiden too noticed the beast Nightwing, but his reaction was more of puzzlement than anger. The offer to meet with Shau-ling and the gift of Taron's life were still fresh in the back of his mind.

"My my my," Emries said approaching slowly. "Isn't this just a cozy little scene? Forces of good pitted against the forces of evil, personal betrayals, hatreds, and lies taking precedent over the true war between the Light and the Darkness. How touching."

"That's enough out of you, Emries," Logan said, holding the Dragon Sword poised for battle. "The more I hear you talk, the more you sound like Draven. You don't care about any of us, as long as you win the war. By any means necessary, right?"

"The Light will prevail," Emries said coldly almost rote, letting the pure crystalline blade of energy appear in his hand. "And you will not stand in my way Logan Ranthall, nor will any of these other pests who call themselves the People of the Dragon. Nathaniel Sandar and his loyal followers will do as they are meant to do, and will strike the final blow against Shau-ling to prolong the prophecies."

"Over my dead body," Logan replied.

"So be it."

All hell broke loose the next moment, a battle unlike any seen in any previous generation. Logan charged the god Emries, the Dragon Sword held high, until the blades collided in a flash of light, and the two edged into one another, trying to gain an advantage. Lord Rhuiden also took the opportunity to charge, *Fury* poised to secure the throne of Marcwell for his own and leave the bloody corpse of his son Duncan rotting on the battlefield. Father and son met, each mid-slash, but the boy was no match for the strength of the father, and sprawled to the ground. However, he made his way back to his feet quickly, hate propelling him. Personal vengeance had won out over logic, and all that would be left in the end was to pick up the pieces.

* * * * * * * * * * *

Pike surveyed the scene for a moment, and knew that the battle was going to grow ugly, especially with the presence of Emries and Draven. He had gone to the light reality to help save everyone, not to be involved in the middle of a fight, let alone one of this magnitude. He and Eldar had the responsibility to get Wolf out of harm's way, and he would do anything in his power to make sure that happened. After the talk with Evan Sinn and Meredith Heron, Pike was sure that Evan could use the powers granted to him by Aerith Seth to get Wolf to safety, but whether or not Wolf would go was another story. It was obvious he was headstrong and stubborn like his father, but hopefully there would be enough sensibility in the boy to override the Ranthall pride and Tamerlane stubbornness. He would have to understand the stakes, have to understand the cost indulging in emotional maelstroms. And for the irony of ironies, Pike would have to be the one to make him see reason.

* * * * * * * * * * *

Draven felt the power of the blow that rained down upon him. Gwydeon had wasted no time in charging the youngest member of the phasia when the battle between Ranthall and Emries began. Gwydeon wanted Draven dead, that much was obvious. Now that Draven did not have the cushion of the Dark Riders, he took the fight with the self-proclaimed Brother of Angels much more seriously. Again and again Gwydeon's sword rained down, but Draven was quick to parry with the makeshift sword made out of the flows of Chaos. It was not nearly as powerful as the Sword of the Ram that he had once had in his possession, but it would do in the meantime. Gwydeon was not playing, and the hatred in his eyes made him more powerful. Each strike had more force than the last, and Draven could feel that Gwydeon was getting stronger the longer the battle raged on, and it would only be a matter of time before the crystalline blade breached Draven's nearly perfect defense and ended the phase's life once again. Gwydeon thrust hard at Draven, but the phase was faster, spinning out of harm's way and bringing his sword to bear. While Draven may not have been a match for the hero in terms of strength, the years of utilizing Basille's techniques to increase his speed and agility were enough to give him a small quickness edge. Gwydeon did not hesitate and blocked the blow that would have pierced his heart, and countered with a broad downward slash. As fast as Draven was, without the crutch of the increased power from the Sword of the Ram, he was no match for the divine power of Gwydeon Sandar. The crystalline blade tore through the taut flesh of Draven's chest, leaving a long bloody trail. The phase winced in pain and then recoiled. Had Gwydeon pressed the advantage, Draven would have been dead.

"You are beaten coward," Gwydeon mocked, his sword poised for the final strike. "You cannot be allowed to interfere in this world and cause the kind of destruction that you have in my home."

"Strike then," Draven answered, "end it, if you can."

Gwydeon raised the sword high in the air and brought it crashing down.

* * * * * * * * * * *

Evan stood back watching as the duels raged on. Powers flashed and flared as often as steel, and as much as he wanted to intervene, use his powers to help the forces of the light and his friends, Evan knew that if he did, he would risk tipping the balance. Meredith also stood firmly, her bow in hand ready to strike at anyone that would threaten them. It was then that Pike and Eldar drew their attention.

"We have to get Wolf out of here," Pike said quickly. "He is the key to all this."

Evan looked across the battlefield and saw Wolf standing firm, watching Logan's duel with Emries. Wolf winced with every contact of the two blades, but knew that it was his father's fight and not to interfere. Lissa and Sabrina both stood close to Wolf, waiting for an opportunity to make their presence known. A spray of ice shot across the distance, separating the three young people, and as soon as Lissa got back to her feet, streams of fire launched across the distance toward Erdric and Aldridge.

"Do what you can," Evan answered, "I'll help with the portal to get you out of here."

* * * * * * * * * * *

Nightwing was obviously different from the creature it had been when Aryx was inside of it, that much was obvious by the way it moved in combat. The need for redemption had compelled Aryx to charge the metallic beast, and hatred for the part of him that had once been evil drove him to continue fighting. Though Aryx knew the truth about his connection to Shau-ling and the origins of his life, he looked back at that time and could not see his actions as evil, at least not until the end when his conscience forced him to walk away. However, his time as Nightwing was different. It was clouded in Shadow, clouded in evil, a creature only of death.

Nightwing was keeping up with the strong opponent, blocking every blow as if it knew where the blow was going to strike. That would have been a safe assumption considering that every bit of knowledge of tactics that were part of Aryx became part of Nightwing. Nightwing moved with a feline grace from block to parry, each time taking its own slash toward the defenses of the legendary Aryx Terian. Aryx, though no longer blessed with the powers that had once been at his disposal as a member of the phasia, did still retain the part of him that had once been part of Lord Cedric Binosear's *Erieal*. It took only a few moments to generate the anger within himself to touch the primal flows of power within him and to channel the fires into the blade of his sword. The springing lion on the blade of the sword glowed with a new intensity, and every slash of steel was followed by a ghostly trail of hot white flame. Nightwing took quick notice of the new tactic and drew on the powers that had been a gift from joining with the Blaze. With a quick motion, Nightwing discarded its blade and drew two of the bladed feathers from its wings. A thought later, the blades were charged with fire and ice, and Aryx smiled, knowing he would have his first challenge since his defeat at the hands of Arathorn Geoffry all those years ago. As Aryx thrust in again, the initial blow was blocked by Nightwing's flame blade, but though he was vulnerable, the sword of ice did not come crashing down as Aryx had expected. Suddenly the proud warrior realized that the creature was toying with him, using him and keeping him out of the fight with the members of the phasia where he truly belonged.

"You are more of a devil than I believed possible," Aryx said pulling away from the metallic monster and holding his sword in a guarding position. "I was able to resist your pull once, and I shall not let you pull the innocent soul within you into the hell that is reserved for the likes of the phasia."

"YOUR PRIDE AND ARROGANCE WERE YOUR UNDOING WHEN YOU WERE IN SHAU-LING'S SERVICE WHITE LIGHTNING, AND IT SHALL BE YOUR UNDOING AGAIN IF YOU DO NOT DEFEND YOURSELF TO THE LIMITS OF YOUR CAPABILITY. I DID NOT CHOOSE THIS BATTLE, BUT AS THAT I AM EMBROILED IN IT NOW, I WILL SETTLE OUR SCORE ONCE AND FOR ALL."

The twin blades came raining down the next moment, and it was all Aryx could do to block the strikes and stay one step ahead of the creature that was once an integral part of him on so many levels.

* * * * * * * * * * *

Erdric and Aldridge worked well together in most lifetimes and complimented each other in every way that counted. Their powers were very similar and their level of ability was almost identical, however it was their ambition that normally drove them down separate roads. However, when faced in situations when there was only one option, as there was in Logan's Wood, then they were a truly deadly combination. With their combined bursts of water and ice, the two phasia were keeping the team of Wolf, Lissa, and Sabrina off balance. However, as Wolf ducked through the blasts of energy, he could feel something within him that he could he could not explain. Ever since Draven had appeared in the clearing, Wolf felt as though he had two trains of thought running through his mind. He could feel the sickeningly evil thoughts of the phase slinking on the edge of his consciousness, the memories of deplorable acts turning his stomach. However as Lissa and Sabrina sent streams of fire back at the phasia, Wolf found a new stream of thoughts entering his mind from the man Draven, a plot both evil and flawless. There would only be a few moments for Wolf to be able to intervene, and as Lissa popped up again to send a stream of fire toward Aldridge, Wolf sprinted from his hiding place toward the duel between the Brother of Angels and the self-proclaimed King of the Devils. As he crossed the distance he did not see Pike out of the corner of his eye. A hand took hold of him and jerked him to the ground in the nick of time as another beam of ice passed through the air where his head had been only a moment earlier. Though grateful to be alive, Wolf fought away from Pike's strong grip and forced himself to his feet. As he saw the act play out in front of him, all he could do was shout.

"Midarin! Get down!"

* * * * * * * * * * *

Susanne felt the anger and hatred boil within her as she made the long slow walk across the field of battle toward her son. Fire and ice flew around her, mixed with the flashes of light from the incredible duels between Logan and Emries and Draven and Gwydeon. However, nothing could dissuade Susanne from her goal. The child had been perverted as the instrument of his warped father and had become the opposite of everything she had come to embrace from the teachings of the Torch. More than anyone else could ever realize, Michael was an abomination, and Susanne would sooner die than see the boy draw breath any longer. The boy however was not passive and would not allow the woman who had given birth to him to simply take that life away. He held his sword aloft, ready for a fight, and that is what was coming for him. Susanne charged in quickly, her dagger poised for the strike. Michael's attempt at a parry was no match for the older woman's speed and experience. She dove under his block, and the point of her blade sped toward his black heart. Though momentarily shocked, the boy exercised some of the power that was within him to speed up his reflexes and sidestep the attack. The blade did strike flesh however, a long jagged gash was ripped in Michael's side by the point of the dagger, sending a plume of blood splattering in all direction. The sight of blood drove Susanne further down her vengeful path and invigorated her. Even with his accelerated reflexes, the boy was no match for the superior training and tenacity of the older woman, and it took only a handful of passes for Susanne's dagger to find the soft flesh of Michael's chest and bury the point deep in his heart. When the blow was finally struck, it was as though time stopped for the two. Even with the explosions and flashes of power that erupted around them, all either of them could hear was the beat of Michael's heart. The boy looked down to see the hilt of the dagger protruding from his chest and the victorious look on the woman's face. For the last few seconds, they could hear only the steady beat of Michael's heart as it slowly wound down to nothing, and it beat one last time. Even then Michael still looked down, blinked his eyes once, and then collapsed, all life fleeing from him in the steady trickle of blood that oozed from around the polished metal of the dagger blade. Susanne turned to search for the other part of her mission to be fulfilled.

* * * * * * * * * * *

Nathaniel stood by watching as Logan and Emries pushed each other to the limits of mortal comprehension. The powers at their disposal defied anything that Nathaniel could have imagined, and all he could see was the flashes of power as the two blades connected. There were points when the two moved so fast that they blurred into streaks of green and white light, only becoming visible for a matter of seconds when their blades collided in their dance of death. Logan had been cut early into the confrontation, a long slash across his chest, but Emries too had seen his blood drawn, and his perfect face had been scarred across the left cheek by a strike that passed a little too close for comfort. Rachel and Galen were close to Nathaniel, doing as Lord Rhuiden had commanded before the duel with Duncan had started. They were to protect Nathaniel at all costs. While Rachel did not like the idea that she was taking orders from the lying bastard that she had once dedicated her life to, she knew that her place was at the side of the *Coromor*. She would make sure that the petty feuds, like the one that had consumed her former lord, would not be the end of the savior of the human race. Though Galen could not see the breathtaking spectacle that was unfolding before him, he could sense the power as it flowed from one man to the other. The importance of the battle was without measure, as that neither man could truly be victorious over the other. Even if Emries were to be struck down, he still lived within the boy Nathaniel and would continue to live so long as the prophecies existed. Logan also would continue should he be struck down, as the words and deeds of the man known as the Lord Dragon had given the world hope that could never be taken away by even the darkest of shadows. Finally the blur of motion slowed and the two men stood apart from one another again. Logan was panting hard, his chest rising and falling faster than it should. He was physically exhausted and Nathaniel wondered if he had enough left for another round with the god. But to his credit, Logan had taken a lot out of Emries as well. The two were a bloody mess, hundreds of minute wounds littering their bodies where a dodge and parry had come at the last second to prevent death. While both men had the power and ability to heal the wounds that riddled their bodies, to use such power would give them less reserves to use against their opponent, and even the smallest trickle could mean the difference between life and death. Emries drew himself up and held his shoulders pulled back proudly as he looked down at his opponent.

"You are beaten, Ranthall," Emries prodded. "Even with your blasphemous powers you are no match for the champion of the Creator. But you have fought valiantly and I will end your life quickly for it. I have won the day Logan, your little rebellion is over."

"Strike me down if you can, Emries," Logan answered in a weakened voice, "but don't think you've won. The truth about you is spreading, and as long as there are people who call themselves the People of the Dragon, then you will find your road to god-hood littered with brambles and thorns. And though we may only prick at your feet and be an annoyance for you, one day we will cause you to trip and fall."

Emries laughed loudly.

"Don't worry about your little friends, Logan," Emries responded holding his sword aloft, "I shall dispatch them as quickly and joyfully as I did that pathetic wife of yours. You don't know how satisfied it is going to make me knowing that I got to kill you twice. Once in the Light reality where I strangled you in your sleep, and then now."

Logan felt his blood boil.

"I don't know which will be better, carving you up right here in the wood that was named in your honor, or staring down at you as you gasped for breath and died like the tiny worm that you are."

Logan charged the next moment, but Emries was ready. He parried the strike from the Dragon Sword and continued through with a long slash that struck Logan in the stomach and continued across the abdomen. Pain wrenched the former *Coromor's* body, and he hunched forward reflexively reacting to the pain. Emries then lifted his blade high and held it poised to drive the tip through Logan's back through his monotonously beating heart.

"Remember, Nathaniel," Logan said with a raspy voice, "this is the price for following your heart."

The strike came a moment later, the pure clear crystalline blade thrusting downward, shattering ribs and spine as it ripped through Logan's body, impaling his heart, and then erupting from his chest with a spray of cold Blaze-laced blood. A last gasp escaped Logan's mouth, and then his body went limp, hanging lifeless on the blade of Emries' sword. The god drove the body to the ground and then stamped on Logan's back, pulling the blood-soaked crystalline blade free, looking around for his next target only to find a surprise waiting for him.

CHAPTER 41

* * * * * * * * * * *

Lissa and Sabrina looked at one another as they ducked down behind a large rock as another stream of ice passed over. They could both see that this battle was going nowhere and dealing with Aldridge and Erdric was keeping them from protecting Nathaniel and Lord Rhuiden. Lissa though had seen a pattern. It was obvious that Aldridge was the more arrogant of the two and wanted to see if his attacks bore fruit and were able to pick off either of the two women.

"Aldridge keeps his head up after his attacks. I'll go up and wait for him, create a small shield of fire and let his attack hit me. He'll think he got me and stay up and gloat. When he does you have to get him. Just keep in mind that you won't have much time, so make the shot count."

Sabrina nodded and waited. Lissa stood quickly, launched an attack of fire and lingered. Sabrina could see her friend weave the flows of fire around herself forming a makeshift and nearly undetectable shield. A moment later both Aldridge and Erdric emerged from their hiding places and sent streams of tiny ice daggers at the large rock. Dozens of the tiny projectiles struck Lissa in the chest, and while most of them disappeared in tiny wisps of steam, Lissa had underestimated the power of the attack and some of the daggers had pierced her defenses and ripped through her body. However, Sabrina had to follow the plan. Quickly Sabrina ducked around the rock and took quick, careful aim. Aldridge had indeed remained in the open, obviously proud of his supposed kill, but his eyes widened in shock the next moment as a stream of chaos energy enveloped him and reduced him to base elements. When the cloud of blackness disappeared, nothing remained of the phase. However, Sabrina was more worried about her friend than she was about the kill. Moments later Sabrina was sending flows of Water and Wind into the fallen form, trying to mend the wounds that perforated her body. Sabrina then sensed another power and a moment later the woman whom she knew only through legend and story, Eldar Merin, crouched down beside Lissa.

"I'll take her out of here, and make sure that she is well cared for. You be careful and stick close to Nathaniel and you'll be alright."

"Go," Sabrina said understanding immediately, "get Lissa and Wolf out of here, don't worry about me."

It was then that they both heard Wolf's scream.

* * * * * * * * * * *

Again and again Duncan found himself sprawling to the ground under the force of the powerful blows of the man he had once called father, the impetuous Lord Rhuiden. After being cast to the ground yet again, Duncan looked up and watched as Lord Rhuiden motioned for him to get back to his feet and waited. It was obvious to Duncan that the older man was enjoying this. However, the longer the fight wore on, the less Duncan could remember why they were fighting. In the beginning there had been the anger in the back of his mind that had fueled him, the loud paranoia and the knowledge that his father was trying to kill him and would not rest until he was dead. Now though, the thoughts were leaving his mind. As he was cast to the ground again, he saw that Michael had been struck down by the older blond woman who had called herself his mother. Some of the voices of paranoia and hatred in the back of Duncan's mind were immediately silenced. Most of the rage had vanished, but as he looked in his father's eyes, he knew there would be no talking and no backing out. One of them would end up dead. The mistakes of the past were etched in Duncan's mind as he locked blades with his father once again. Words of fear and hatred were whispered in his ear and planted in his mind from the very beginning. The phasia had simply been using him to sow the seeds of discord in the most powerful kingdoms in the world, and they had succeed. Once Duncan had supplanted his father, the phasia would have quickly dispatched him and taken Marcwell for themselves. The truth and horror of it all struck Duncan suddenly, and though he fought, part of him longed to drop his guard and let his life become forfeit to the man that he had betrayed so completely. Then Duncan saw Lissa fall followed by Aldridge, and all control over his mind was snapped. Every emotion came flooding back. He remember vaguely the sensation of loving Lissa and spending nights with her in quiet and seclusion, back before his mind was poisoned.

A hard slash of his father's axe shook him back to reality, and Duncan fought with every part of his being. He had to live, at least long enough to make good on all of the things that he had done so badly. It was then that

Wolf's shout echoed through the battlefield. The woman's name shocked Lord Rhuiden and the gentle parry that would have come in answer to Duncan's amateur thrust never came and Duncan found the blade of his sword buried deep in Lord Rhuiden's gut. The wound not have been fatal had it not caught the old wound from the last great war, reopening it once again. Blood flowed freely, but the shock ignited the famous fury of Lord Rhuiden, bringing a hard slash of the great ax raining down on the dumbstruck boy, splintering his shoulder and killing him instantly. The two men fell together, one dead as he hit the ground, the other not far behind.

"So no one gets Marcwell," Lord Rhuiden said pulling the blade from his stomach.

Darkness then fell over his vision.

* * * * * * * * * * *

Aryx spun out of the way of two slashes and thrust the point of his blade toward Nightwing's chest, however, the feline grace of the creature was far too quick for the man who was now mostly mortal. Blades found one another once again and the two traded strikes, one after the other, but it was clear that the winged beast had the advantage. Another of Aryx's strikes was parried quickly away and a quick strike embedded the tip of one of Nightwing's bladed feathers into Aryx's left shoulder. The older man shrank back, his sword arm hanging limp and useless at his side. The beast had known exactly where to strike him in order to sever the tendon and render his only means of attack totally worthless. Aryx knew that the battle was over, and he fell to his knees, waiting for the blow that would end his life.

"YOU ARE A FOOL TO THINK THAT YOU COULD BEAT ME ARYX TERIAN," Nightwing chided in the cool metallic voice. "I KNOW EVERY STRENGTH THAT YOU HAVE, AS WELL AS EVERY WEAKNESS. I ALSO KNOW OF THE WEAKNESS OF YOUR LEFT SHOULDER THAT YOU DID SO WELL TO KEEP SHIELDED IN YOUR MIND."

Aryx remained silent.

"SHOULD I REMIND YOU ARYX? AFTER YOUR ILL FATED DUEL WITH ARATHORN GEOFFRY, YOU GOT DRUNK, GOT INTO A BAR BRAWL, AND WERE THROWN THROUGH A WINDOW WHERE YOUR SHOULDER WAS BADLY INJURED. THE TENDON WAS PARTIALLTY TORN, AND NOW IF YOU ARE SO MUCH AS GRAZED WITH A BLADE, YOUR SWORD ARM BECOMES WORTHLESS."

Aryx raised his head, shocked. No one knew of his injury. He had kept it buried in the back of his mind during his time as Nightwing for this very reason. He did not want the knowledge being used against him were another Nightwing to ever be created.

"NO ARYX, YOUR BLOCKADE AGAINST THE FLOWS OF THE BLAZE WAS PERFECT. IT IS NOT STORED IN THE MEMORIES THERE, AND IT WILL NOT BE AFTER THIS CONVERSATION FOR I TOO HAVE BLOCKED IT AWAY."

A moment later Nightwing took a step forward and Aryx watched the armor retract. The beautiful feminine form that was revealed brought a warmth to Aryx's heart but more confusion to his mind. The blond hair was the same as the last day he had seen his lovely wife Diana, and leaving her was the hardest thing he had ever had to do.

"I guess I needed part of you with me forever," Diana Terian answered slowly, "and so Shau-ling's offer was not something I could refuse. I felt drawn to him after Lissa was born, and I know now that it was because Cedric touched the Blaze. Shau-ling told me the truth about you and offered me Nightwing. I accepted. But I promised Shau-ling that if I came in contact with you that I would make you listen by any means necessary and tell you that he is ready to forgive you."

Aryx's expression was blank.

"He wanted me to tell you that you were right. The war got out of hand and he was fighting for the wrong reasons. A stubborn father wants his stubborn son back."

Aryx was about to speak with he saw Midarin fall.

CHAPTER 41

* * * * * * * * * * *

Gwydeon's blade came raining down on Draven, but thanks to the phase's increased reflexes, Draven was able to spin out of the way of the strike. However, rather than retaliating directly, Draven channeled the powers of the Blaze into his chaos sword and hurled it like a spear at the unsuspecting form of Midarin Rice. The scream from the boy Wolf did not give Midarin enough time to do anything, and the sickening black blade pierced the woman in the chest, but did not pierce her heart. Midarin fell immediately. Gwydeon, shocked by the turn of events flew across the short distance and scooped the wounded woman up in his arms. Draven also sped across the battlefield, but he had another target in mind. Sabrina was shocked to find herself wrapped in the arms of the evil phase moments after helping Eldar Merin pull her wounded friend away. Though she tried to struggle, the blade of pure Blaze flame at her throat ended any resistance. The entire battlefield froze at the act, and even Emries took a step back when Sabrina's life was threatened.

"I warned you that I would be the winner of this little game," Draven taunted, "but you all wanted to play anyway. Well, fine, but now we are playing by my rules. It was a very good fight Gwydeon, but I'm afraid I'm not quite ready to die yet. So, I sacrificed your little Midarin. Don't worry, you still have another one in the other reality that you can play with, that is if I don't get to her first."

Draven laughed loudly, and Gwydeon tensed.

"Don't get any ideas," Draven chided. "Remember, I hold the *Chosen One* of the prophecies here in my hands, and if I kill her, the prophecies are as good as done. Oh, and Gwydeon, that wound in Midarin's perfect chest is infected with Blaze flame. If you touch it, you know what happens. The same goes for the rest of you."

Emries tensed and raised his hand slowly.

"Don't even think about it Emries," Draven said not even looking in the robed man's direction. "I'm willing to bet that I can kill her long before your bolt of power got here. And again, this is a Blaze knife, totally untouchable by the likes of you."

"You don't honestly believe that we are going to let you walk away do you?" Gwydeon asked, holding back all the emotion he could manage.

Draven smiled.

"About as much as you expect me to let this little toy go."

The knife of Blaze energy slashed Sabrina's throat the next second, bringing gasps of disbelief from the assemblage, but no one was in any position to stop Draven from falling through the portal that had opened under his feet only milliseconds later.

CHAPTER 41

Chapter XLII

Aftermath

Creator's Calendar Year 1205; Light Reality

The tumult of confrontation left a wake of regret and pain resounding through Logan's Wood, most noticeable by the quiet agony of Gwydeon Sandar, and the awe and disbelief of Wolf Ranthall and Lissa Terian. But while sorrow takes many shapes, some of the sorrow had begun to turn to anger in the little girl Liette Forer. As soon as Midarin fell, her eyes locked on Wolf Ranthall and the hatred began to boil. However, something told her to wait, and she did, her hands clutching tightly to the hilt of her sword. Wolf also had rage within him, but while he could have taken such rage out on Emries for murdering his father, the opportunity was short-lived as the robed man disappeared without a word. Though for those last few seconds, Wolf thought he saw Emries smile. So much had already gone terribly wrong for both realities in the span of a few heartbeats, and now the future of the light reality could well be decided in a few more seconds. Wolf's examination of Sabrina was quick and painful. He knew that she was dead from the moment the dagger touched her skin and no amount of healing would bring her back. However, Lissa would not let go.

"Nathaniel," she cried out, trying desperately to hold back the tears, "you brought her back once, you can do it again."

"He can't Lissa," Wolf said finally. "Emries was guiding his actions before, but even Emries knows that this wound can't be healed."

Lissa looked up at Wolf tears filling her eyes.

"But you and Jerrard can remove the Blaze and fix the wound so Nathaniel can heal her."

Wolf put his hand on her shoulder.

"Even if Jerrard and Wolf cleanse the wound," Evan interjected, "Nathaniel cannot use his powers to heal her. Emries will not allow it."

Lissa looked at the man she knew well as a member of the Enforcers.

"Emries is forbidden to interfere in events surrounding the Dark Mirror reality. Since this wound was inflicted by the phase Draven, who hails from that reality, Emries will not extend his power to return Sabrina's life. I'm sorry."

The young red-haired girl could not hold back any longer and broke down. Tears flowed freely, and there was nothing that Wolf could do to console her. But there was another woman who was wounded, and when Jared looked at the wound, he winced. He could see the Blaze fire eating its way through her body, and even using all of the power within himself, he could only halt its progress.

"Wolf," Jared said quickly, "you need to help me with Midarin."

It took only a moment for Wolf to shake himself back to reality, and after a quick squeeze of Lissa's shoulder, Wolf ran across the clearing to where Midarin lay clutched in Gwydeon's arms. The infection within the older woman's body had stopped advancing, but it was fighting against Jared's intervention. It would only be a matter of time before the infection spread to her heart where it would slowly burn the delicate organ until it was unable to pump blood to the rest of the body and Midarin would simply die. Softly, Wolf pushed his powers into the limp form and exercised his power in an attempt to fight off the infiltrating powers of the Blaze. Piece by piece, Wolf was able to extricate pieces of the infection, but for every piece he removed, another piece grew. Between Jared and himself there was just not enough power.

"There's nothing more we can do, Gwydeon," Wolf said softly. "Even if we could get all of the Blaze out of the wound, she would likely bleed to death before we could knit the rest of the wound, or she would simply die from the shock and pain of the removal of the infection. We can numb the pain and make it easier, but that's all."

Gwydeon nodded.

Wolf exercised a little of the power he had and numbed all of the nerves in Midarin's body, making all the pain go away. As he looked around, Wolf noticed that Rachel, Nathaniel, Galen and Susanne had cornered Erdric and were keeping him quiet. Shaking his head, Wolf tapped Jared on the shoulder and left Gwydeon to say whatever needed to be said in private.

Midarin looked up at Gwydeon and smiled a weak smile.

"The wings are very handsome," she said softly. "I knew Emries would keep his promise."

Gwydeon's mouth was dry, and the cold emotionless mask began to crack at the woman's sweet words. Though this was not the woman that he had spent so many years with, he still felt the strings of love being pulled in his heart, and the pain of her passing was hitting her very hard.

"I'll get Draven for this…" Gwydeon started.

Midarin raised her left hand and covered his mouth to stop his words. When he had stopped talking, the arm fell back to the ground, all strength gone from it. She only had a few moments left, Gwydeon was sure, and he wanted to make sure he heard every word, so he leaned in closer.

"When Elwyne told me you died protecting everyone from Jeroch, I was so proud of you. I only wish you could have been there when Nathaniel was born. He's a lot like you, always worried about duty and responsibility. I'm sorry about Pike and Aryx, but I know you'll understand my loneliness. Besides, I owed you for Leane."

Gwydeon smiled.

"Yes I know you were with her before me, but that was a mistake anyway."

A single tear rolled down Gwydeon's cheek.

"It's time, Gwydeon," she said slowly.

Gwydeon nodded.

"Hold me and tell me you love me."

Gwydeon pulled Midarin's limp body up into his arms and held her tightly against his chest. He whispered the words 'I love you' into her ear as the last bindings of life fled from her body. For several long moments Gwydeon held her there, too shocked and in too much agony to move. It was the angry words of Liette that shook Gwydeon from his morose stupor.

Liette had walked over to Wolf with her sword ready. When her mouth opened, Wolf found himself assaulted by violent and hate-filled words.

"It your fault," Liette said coldly, "if you hadn't been born with Basille's powers, none of this would have ever happened. There wouldn't be two worlds, Draven wouldn't have come here to cause trouble, and my mother wouldn't be dead!"

Wolf took a step back from the little girl, but Evan Sinn was quick to interject.

"He didn't choose to have Basille's powers, Liette," Evan countered. "Wolf is as much a victim in this as anyone else. This war has cost him the lives of his mother, father, and many of his friends. You heard Emries say himself that he killed Logan with his own two hands. Emries is not the patron that everyone wants him to be, and he is as much to blame for Midarin's death as Wolf is. Every part of this war is not what we thought it was, every person is guilty only of playing the role that gods willed for them. Now though our eyes our open and we are beginning to walk our own paths."

Gwillim helped Gwydeon to his feet, and after a very quick and emotion-filled embrace, Gwydeon turned his attention to the confrontation between Liette and Wolf. He knew that what Evan was saying was true, and everyone else knew it too. However, for some reason, the little girl was either not willing or not able to change her mode of thinking.

"Evan is right, Liette," Gwydeon said calmly, sheathing his sword. "Emries is the evil in this world, and is as much to blame for the suffering of the people in both our realities as the phasia are. Aryx will gladly tell you that Emries has killed as many innocent people as all of the phasia combined and he will not stop doing it, even after Shau-ling has been destroyed. Every time a human asks a question or does not follow Emries' plan, Emries will strike him down rather than risk another rebellion."

Aryx, by this time, had made it to his feet and was cradling his useless sword arm. Diana walked close to him, still on guard for any retaliation to her appearance as Nightwing.

"Gwydeon speaks the truth, Liette. Emries is wrong. Just as Shau-ling was all those generations ago for killing the innocent men and women that Emries sent to defend his honor and his name. Emries is wrong for letting powerless mortals fight in his stead. This is not a war about lives, it is a war about ideology. As long as both Halicon and Emries exist to battle over their views, the battle will continue. This world will burn, coated in blood, and their lust to be right will not be sated."

The girl dropped her sword and everyone in the clearing could feel power welling up inside of her. As the moments passed, the girl grew to full womanly stature, and her red hair flowed like fire in the light breeze. Slowly her features dissolved into a blurry light and her entire body was bathed in an angelic glow. When Liette finally spoke again, it was in an other-worldly tone, the same words spoken in several pitches all at the same time with a faint echo that followed. Gwydeon immediately recognized the power as divine, an extension of the Creator's might on the physical plane.

"My purpose here has been fulfilled," the formerly mortal creature said. "I am the being known as the *Redaar*. I was dispatched by the Creator to gather information and find the true nature of this war between rebellious children. You mortals have proven that though you can easily be misled by those with power, you will walk the true path once you find it. However, it is not the actions of your group that will dictate whether or not the Creator will sentence this world to fire. The mandate is clear, one force must succeed. For Emries to be defeated, you must work with Shau-ling and kill the *Coromor*. However, doing so will kill one of your own in Nathaniel. Perhaps the Creator has been right from the beginning of this conflict. Perhaps there is no way to win the game, at least not in its current form."

Evan stood face to face with the *Redaar* for a moment and smiled.

"The Creator did not count on the fact that there are not just two sides to this war Liette," he said calmly. "There was always a third side represented by Aerith Seth. This is the side that was used for the purposes of both the Light and the Shadow, but it always had the same goal."

"And what was that goal?" Liette asked.

"To know the truth and do what was right," Meredith answered joining Evan.

"It's not about following the Light or the Shadow anymore," Pike chimed in, "that much Shau-ling taught me. He can't control the phasia anymore because they are the Shadow. Emries is the Light. They are both wrong."

"But it is up to the mortals to make their choice and no longer be used," Galen said quickly. "The Moridon once believed that, and because they were deemed too dangerous, Emries put them to work for his own purposes, and naturally that led to their extinction."

"A task he was trying to duplicate with the Torch," Susanne added.

Liette listened silently.

"I know we may not have saved our world," Evan concluded, "but we can try to save the rest of the innocents who are just pawns in Emries' little game.

The girl nodded.

"I shall take my report to the Creator. In the end, only the Creator can resolve this conflict, though the resolution may not be found in this or a thousand human lifetimes. Though this may have no meaning any longer, I cannot help but wish you good luck."

After a bright flash of light, the *Redaar* was gone. For a moment, no one said or did anything until finally Wolf broke the silence.

"So what do we do now?"

Suddenly a new power filled the woods. Jared, Wolf, Nathaniel, Gwydeon, Eldar, and Diana all commented at once.

"Portal."

It took only a moment for the swirling blue portal to appear in the center of the clearing, and when the originator of the portal stepped through, she was greeted with drawn weapons and charged powers. Though Bryn was shocked at the amount of power that was waiting for her, she softly smiled and held her hands up innocently.

"My, my, all of this for me?" her coy voice called out. "I'm flattered."

Evan balked at the comment, but it was Wolf who spoke first.

"It's good to see you, Bryn," the boy said slowly. "I at least get to thank you for bailing us out in Marcwell."

Bryn smiled.

"I was doing a favor for an old friend. But you'll all be happy to know that Marcwell has been secured and is waiting for its ruler to return from whatever crusade he has gone traipsing off on."

It was then that Bryn's eyes fell on Lord Rhuiden and Duncan's fallen forms as well as the body of Sabrina.

"Or maybe not."

There was a rustling from behind several bushes, and a proud red-headed woman dressed in the battle uniform of the Creator's Torch Society emerged from hiding. Wolf remember her from the throne room of Marcwell. Duncan had introduced her as his wife Bridgette, and while Wolf remembered seeing her when Duncan, Michael, Aldridge, and Erdric appeared, he did not remember seeing her actually fight during the battle.

"My son Feyd is the rightful heir to the throne of Marcwell, and I will hold it in trust until he is of age. Marcwell is mine now."

"No!" Erdric screamed. "That kingdom is mine! I have been plotting and scheming for generations and now finally it is within my grasp."

"You aren't going to make it out of this forest alive," Susanne countered, "and corpses make lousy kings."

The comment quieted Erdric but gave Wolf an idea.

"Sorry, Bridgette," Wolf said smiling, "but the last I checked, Pike Rhuiden is the Lord of Marcwell."

Bridgette's eyes went wide, and color rushed to her face.

"Lord Rhuiden is dead," Bridgette countered, but then suddenly realized the younger Pike was standing there in front of her.

"That Lord Rhuiden may be dead," Eldar continued, "but this Lord Rhuiden is alive and well. And so this Lord Rhuiden will keep the Kingdom of Marcwell under his protection until such time as your son is old and responsible enough to take care of the kingdom."

Bridgette fumed and reached for the sword that was at her hip. A moment later, Rachel stood beside her and held her blade at the other woman's throat.

"While I may have had issues with the other Lord Rhuiden, I would be willing to give this one the benefit of the doubt. I would suggest that you do the same."

Bridgette removed her hand from the hilt of her sword and smiled weakly before turning and starting the slow walk through Logan's Wood back toward the wilds in the southlands. Wolf watched her go for a moment and then turned toward Gwydeon.

"With Logan gone, I suppose we look to you now for direction," he said softly.

"Now is the time that we have to go our own separate ways, Wolf," Gwydeon replied. "You and Lissa should go with Pike and Eldar to try and fix this disaster that Basille got us into. I have to go after Draven. I know he is still in this reality somewhere, at least for the time being."

"And while Wolf is trying to solve the bigger problems," Nathaniel added, "we can solve the more immediate problems by going to Scalla and helping Jerrard with Jeroch and the army that is descending upon them."

Bryn smiled.

"From what my spies have been telling me, Jeroch is leading Caris' army with Ellis and her brood in tow. But from the latest reports, the battle is not going to take place in Scalla, but rather in Lakestone. So if you want to join this little fray, you need to go there."

Nathaniel nodded.

"Any of you who wish to go with me are more than welcome to, but I will understand if you resist considering the fact that my powers come from Emries."

"I'm with you little brother," Gwillim replied. "And now that we all know what the real fight is, we don't need to worry about Emries. He can't trick us again."

"We'll take Wolf and Lissa now," Eldar said quickly, "because the more time we delay, the closer the Creator gets to destroying our world."

Wolf nodded, and after helping Lissa up, followed Pike and Eldar over to where Evan stood patiently waiting. Evan quickly reached into his pocket and pulled out a white stone. It took only a matter of moments for him to kneed and pull the stone into the shape of a portal, and as soon as he released the edges of the stone, it sparked to life.

"Have a good trip, and be careful," Evan said with a slight hint of comedy in his voice, "I'm not very good at aiming these things yet.

Wolf smiled and then the four of them stepped through. Aryx walked over to where Midarin lay and looked down at her briefly before turning his attention to Gwydeon. If there was any discomfort or bruised feelings between the two men, it did not pass between them, either in words or posture.

"I hope that the Midarin in your world is as loving and caring as ours was."

Gwydeon nodded.

"She is. Would you like me to heal that?" he asked pointing at the wound in Aryx's left shoulder.

"No," the older man responded. "I need a little of a reminder of my stupidity and my pride. Besides, my fighting days are over. I think after all these years, all these generations, and all of these wars, I've earned myself a little bit of a rest."

Gwydeon nodded and watched as Diana created a portal and ushered Aryx and herself through. After the two older warriors departed, Gwydeon turned to the remaining members of the group.

"I wish you all the best of luck on the road that lies ahead, and I hope that when the final battle occurs between Shau-ling and Emries, you are all on the right side of the line."

With that, Gwydeon extended his wings and then let them curl around him and then the wings began to glow. The light suddenly intensified and when it faded, Gwydeon was gone. Evan heard the words, but knew that they didn't come from the hero, but from the Creator Himself.

Bryn turned to Evan the next moment.

"So, you are the one that has been using Aerith's powers."

It was more of a statement than a question, and Evan silently nodded.

"I knew Aerith was up to something when he came to Barer to ask me for a favor. He was the reason that the Army of the Fox marched on Marcwell, and he is also the reason that I am being nice enough to not take the kingdom for myself. But I know that he would want to know that everything he asked for has been done. So when you report to him, and you know where, let him know that everything is well. Grawn and I will secure the kingdom and stay out of the rest of this. We all have our promises to keep, and I made mine long before Aerith came along. This war is not ours any longer. Aryx is right. We are too old, have seen too much, and I think it is far past time for us to follow our brother's lead."

Evan nodded and watched as Bryn turned her attention to Meredith.

"Be careful with this one, young lady. They are wonderful, charming, powerful, handsome, and are complete devils. Just make sure you don't lose sight of the fact that his powers will always pull him in a different direction from where you are going. And in the end, you will have to learn to be as in love with not having them, as you are with having them."

Meredith took the advice for what it was and then watched as Bryn created a portal and silently stepped through.

"Well, I guess you will have to find alternate means of travel," Evan said after a moment. "I need to report in with Aerith, and I don't think he would appreciate it if I brought a lot of company. He is a very solitary person."

Gwillim smiled.

"It's no problem, Evan. I think between Jared and Nathaniel, we can get where we are going."

"Good enough," Evan replied and then pulled another stone out of his pocket and formed it into a portal. Meredith waived to everyone and the two lovers quickly stepped through.

Gwillim turned his attention to Erdric next.

"So, what do we do with him?"

Susanne was quick to pull her dagger and press it to the flesh of Erdric's throat. The phase did not even have a moment to gasp before the cold hard steel of the blade sliced deeply into the weak flesh, sending the cold red blood flooding from the open wound, ending the phase's life in a matter of moment.

"It was more merciful than I wanted," the blond woman added, cleaning her blade on the fallen phase's clothing. "But you did say we were in a hurry."

Nathaniel nodded, trying not to give in to the part of him that wanted to be serious and draw fully on the powers that were at his disposal as the *Coromor* of the prophecies. There was a long fight ahead, and if he allowed himself to fall to the power of the man who had called himself the patron of humanity, the Nathaniel would find himself as the enemy of all of the people that he cared about.

"We need to bury the fallen," Gwillim said looking down at the bodies of Logan, Midarin, and Lissa.

"Yes," Rachel agreed. "Even Pike deserves a proper burial."

It only took a few minutes to bury the fallen heroes there in the clearing outside of Logan's Wood, as Gwillim's power over the Earth, while not originally for grave digging, seemed to be useful enough in that capacity. Each grave was marked with a headstone, also courtesy of Gwillim's power, and names were carefully carved into each headstone. After the quiet few moments of prayer for the fallen, Jared and Nathaniel created a portal, and as the small group stepped through, each wondered what was waiting on the other side.

Tempting Fate

Creator's Calendar Year 1205; Dark Mirror

Gideon sat by his mother watching her closely for any movement. Fear had been the first emotion to run through his heart when he watched Bryn gasp for breath and suddenly collapse, seemingly dead. That emotion was quickly followed by sadness and confusion. Silently holding Bryn's hand, Gideon looked up at Taya, who was standing vigil over Caris' motionless form. Taya shook her head glumly, and then focused her eyes back on the fallen phase's perfect face. Suddenly, Gideon felt the hand in his twitch. A matter of moments later, Bryn's body began to slowly move until she forced her way to a sitting position. Her free hand went immediately to her temple, rubbing the location of where the pain had been the most severe. Caris too was showing signs of life, opening and closing her eyes slowly, adjusting to the patchwork light in the ruined throne room. As Bryn opened her eyes, a strong sense of vertigo still held her, and she shut her eyes again tightly to keep some sense of balance and equilibrium. Gideon was squeezing Bryn's hand tightly, relieved that his mother was still alive, but puzzled as to the mysterious ailment that had struck down two of the most resilient members of the phasia. Caris had just begun to sit up when Bryn tried to get to her feet, but the proud and stubborn woman immediately fell back to the ground, in a sitting position. The pain in her head had begun to ease, but for every bit of pain that was gone, that much more confusion had set in. All Bryn remembered was the searing pain that held her mind, and the sensation of fire burning through her brain. It was only when she tried to open herself to the regenerative and healing properties of the Blaze that she realized the eternal green fire was no longer there in the blackness of her mind. The primal string that had been granted to her from the moment of her birth as a member of the phasia, even through her lifetimes of exile, had been ripped away from her, rendering her powerless.

Caris too had felt a change within her, but it was not in the aspect of missing powers, it was more of a physical and emotional change. Caris had always had the reputation of being the coldest and most unfeeling member of the Brotherhood, and it was only due to her recent contact with Logan Ranthall that she had begun to feel that stigma being lifted. After whatever had happened to her had finally released her mind, new feelings began to flood through her body that were unlike any that she had ever felt in her lifetimes of existence. Her heart beat strong and proud, a complete change from the slow and cold methodical beat that it had always been. Though she had often used her powers to simulate a rapid heartbeat to help maintain the ego of her many lovers, such a manipulation was not necessary now. Sitting up slowly, Caris felt the uneven rhythm of her heart and a nagging sadness in the back of her mind. She vaguely knew the name of the emotion from her many years of playing as a real woman, and the name was longing. Love had finally found Caris, and something had happened to her in those last few moments that was allowing her to feel the way that she did. Seeing the dismay on Bryn's face was what prompted her to reach for the strings of power in the back of her mind. When Caris found that they were not there, a mix of both joy and sorrow filled her. Every emotion was like a gift, and even the negative ones seemed like a blessing. For Caris there had only been hate and vengeance in her life, nothing more. She had never been capable of love, as Bryn had been, and that was part of the reason that Caris had always despised her older sisters. Bryn had found love in the arms of Aerith Seth, and even the cold and calculating Ellis had a taste of the sweet emotion with Arin Ranthall. Caris had always used her body as a weapon and a means to get what she wanted, and in order to do that, she had shut off the pieces of her heart that would have gotten in the way of her goals. Because of her sacrifice, she had become the perfect seductress. It was only after the powers give to her by Shau-ling had been ripped away that Caris began to realize the amount she had sacrificed.

"Are you alright, mother?" Gideon asked in his natural voice.

Bryn struggled to her feet again, this time able to keep her balance and not surrender to the sickening and unstable sensations that held her mind. There were gaps in her memory now, a fact that dismayed her more than the loss of her powers. For so many years Bryn had dedicated herself to learning everything she could. For the lifetimes that she had been exiled from the Council, reading and researching was all there was to do to fill the largely empty years. There was no better way to avoid Grawn then to strike up a deep philosophical conversation with Ellis or to bury her nose in a book in her private library, surrounded by remembrances of her time with Aerith Seth. Knowledge and the search for it kept the boredom at bay. Now that her powers had been taken away, many of the memories from previous lifetimes had begun to fade. Only the memories of the nights with Aerith Seth seemed unaffected by the fog that had descended over her mind, and while the loss of so much dismayed Bryn, the fact that the most powerful and important of the memories remained warmed her heart.

"I don't know, Gideon," Bryn replied. "Something has happened to us, and we don't have our powers anymore."

Gideon was shocked by the news, even more when he remembered that they were waiting for the *Coromor* to show up and were planning to have a battle with him. Now they were down two people with powers. Even though Bryn and Caris had never been the most adept with their powers in combat, every little bit would have helped to keep Nathan off-balance when he came calling. Caris had finally made her way back to her feet, and she seemed very dizzy and disoriented as well. More than once, Caris reached out to use Taya to keep from falling flat on her face.

"How?" was all Taya could ask.

Bryn scanned the remaining part of her memory to find some answer to the obvious question. In all of her time as a member of the Council, she could not remember a phase ever being robbed of their primal string. No, that wasn't true. When Aryx had been exiled from the Council, Shau-ling had taken away his ability to draw on the Blaze and purged of the gift of the innate string of power. However, Shau-ling had said later something about the Blaze and his nature as a member of the phasia, but no matter how hard she pushed at the fog on her thoughts, the answer would not come to her. Aryx was the key, and the more she tried to remember, the more the memory seemed to shrink away.

"Shau-ling had taken our strings of power away," Bryn said finally.

Gideon shuddered. It was obvious that Rael and Trece's plan had not worked, and Shau-ling had seen through the deception. However, Gideon could not believe that this had been the punishment that Shau-ling had chosen to enforce for not answering a summons to the Council. If that had been within Shau-ling's province and had been his preferred method for disciplining his phasia, then Saurn would have been robbed of his powers long ago. No, this was something else, something that had much farther reaching implications.

"So this is your punishment for not going to the Council?" Taya asked, obviously on the same page as her father.

Bryn shook her head.

"No, this was not a punishment. This is something else. I can't remember everything, but when Aryx left the Council, Shau-ling said that he could no long have the primal string that marked him as a member of the phasia, so Shau-ling removed it. But there was more, there had to be. There is something I'm missing, some thing that made Aryx's removal from the Council special."

Bryn closed her eyes and rubbed her temples furiously.

"Why can't I remember?"

Caris smiled and laid her hand on her sister's shoulder.

"We're mortal now," Caris said calmly. "Mortals only live one life, and so we should only have the memories from this generation since our rebirth. Frankly I am relieved not to be burdened with the memory of all of the slobs and malcontents that I had to coddle and cater to in order to get what I wanted from them. That of course doesn't even begin to describe my relief from the laundry list of bastards who found their way into my bed."

One corner of Midarin's mouth cocked up at the description, and even Bryn through her confusion found humor in the description.

"I am glad you're relieved Caris, but lest you remember that Nathan Sandar is on his way here, and if he challenges us in this condition, you will lose your precious humanity shortly after gaining it, so help me think."

Caris scowled and realized the gravity of the situation. Bryn was right. Without their powers she and Bryn were no match for the *Coromor* and would only be a hindrance to Gideon, Taya, Midarin and Sabrina in the battle that would occur. It was the little girl Sabrina though that shocked everyone by putting the pieces together first.

"Bryn, something you said when you were explaining the whole thing about Aryx doesn't make sense," the little girl said quickly.

It took Bryn a moment to acknowledge the younger girl.

"What is that young one?"

Sabrina, still carrying the Sword of the Ram, slowly crossed the throne room until she stood in the middle of her five new companions. Through she did not feel comfortable away from Pike and Gwydeon, the fact that she was among friends helped to ease her fragile psyche. Ever since her torture under the watchful eye of the fiend Draven, she had been jumping at shadows wherever they lurked and spent most of her time curled up and hiding. But now she felt the familiar strength returning to her. There was something important that she had to do, and no matter the pain and discomfort that were in her mind, she would do everything that she could. But there was more. Being close to Bryn had unlocked something in her mind, and a new power began to flow through her, a strength and confidence too massive to be held down by pain and trepidation.

"You said that even though Aryx had been banished from the Council, he still did not age and retained the phase quality of being moderately eternal."

"Yes," Bryn said trying to follow the little girl's logic.

"Then he was still a phase, but he did not still have the ability to draw on a primal string of power or access to the Blaze through the bond with Shau-ling. He's not human, because he was never human."

"That's right," Caris answered. "So he was just like we are now, totally powerless and helpless against the forces of the Light. It was only because Emries played a trick on Shau-ling by giving Aryx the powers of a member of the *Erieal* in the first generation of the prophecies that he was able to survive as long as he has."

Gideon scratched his chin and looked back and forth between Sabrina and Bryn. There was a quiet dialogue that was being exchanged between the two even while Caris was speaking. Gideon was hoping that between the two, they would come up with something that would help to get them out of the deep trouble they would be in should Nathan Sandar show up unannounced. Gideon had never trusted Emries or his agenda, but in the previous generation it was strength of the Ranthall family that helped allay all of the terrible fears that the teachings of Basille had planted within him. Now though it seemed that Emries had gotten exactly what he had intended the *Coromor* to always be. A weapon.

"But he still did not age, which means he retained all of his gifts that were a birthright as a member of the phasia," Sabrina continued.

"Except the powers," Caris countered.

"Wrong," Bryn said, the thoughts suddenly coming to her.

Caris looked at her sister confused but was met with Bryn's wide genius-filled smile.

"The primal string was given to each of the phasia by Shau-ling as a permanent bond to his powers and his control over the Blaze. When any member of the phasia touches the Blaze, it is funneled through the primal string back to Shau-ling, that is why we were told only to draw on it when absolutely necessary."

"Circular logic," Caris said shaking her head. "The methodology is different, but we are still powerless."

Bryn scowled.

"Think Caris," she said roughly, "in all of our times watching Shau-ling fight or punish one of our own kind, do you remember him ever drawing on the Blaze?"

Caris thought back as hard as she could, and only found the fog of forgetfulness waiting for her. However, there were a few memories that she was able to draw on. One of them was Shau-ling's long duel with Zarsi. For seven days Caris watched the two titans battle, but Zarsi was never able to gain an advantage and it was clear that Shau-ling was just toying with him. When Shau-ling would lash out, he did not pull on the Blaze and grab for it like the phasia did. He would open his mind and let the power fill him, surrendering to it. Bryn could see the light in her sister's eyes, and knew that she too had begun to put the pieces together.

"Shau-ling lets the Blaze fill him," Bryn continued, finishing the thoughts for Caris, "he lets it come into him and grant him the power to do what he wishes. Because of the primal string, Shau-ling could control how much we were allowed to use through him and was able to keep us on a tight leash."

"He was afraid you would use the Blaze against him?" Taya asked.

"Kamen was dangerous," Bryn answered, "because his power was unfettered by such restrictions as the primal strings. The leash got a little shorter with each new breed of phase created, but the original six had the most flexibility. Jeroch had two primal strings after Aryx's expulsion, but they were not leashes. Neither is mine nor were Grawn's or Ellis's. The six of us were parts of Shau-ling, a part of a greater whole, and we wielded his powers just as the *Erieal* wielded the powers of the *Coromor* as extensions of himself. Later phasia were just tools."

Caris scowled.

"No offense intended sister," Bryn conceded, "but that is what they were. Disposable tools to help stave off the growing masses who mindlessly followed Emries."

"So does that mean you still have powers?" Midarin questioned.

"No," Bryn said shaking her head, "but it does mean that we have the potential for power."

Gideon's blank look prompted a reply, but instead of hearing Bryn's voice, it was Sabrina that spoke. However, the young woman's voice was no longer shy and reserved. It was as though she were gaining strength from some other source, and Gideon surmised it was because she was the *Chosen One* of the third generation, and Aerith Seth had decided to make his presence felt.

"Didn't you wonder why it was that Logan could touch the Blaze? Or maybe why it is that people like Eldar can draw on it even though she is just a mortal? It's simple. The Blaze is all around us and it is in everything in this world. As much as it has become the life-force of Shau-ling, it is also the essence of every plant and animal on this world. Man is the only one who does not come from the Blaze or touch the Blaze, and that is because the Creator has punished us for Emries' arrogance. But if anyone ever makes a conscious effort to get back to where it was the Creator always intended us to be, living in harmony with nature and being just a creation and not the paragon of animals, then the Blaze will come to them. The Blaze is a force on this world, and beyond this world. It is an extension of the Creator."

"You mean like the Moridon and their magic?" Midarin asked, trying to understand.

"Something like that," Sabrina answered smiling.

Bryn's stare was blank, and it was directed at the little girl. While the memories of hers that were still anchored in the Blaze allowed her to know that Sabrina was the *Chosen One* of the prophecies, there was no way that the little girl should have had the knowledge that she had. It was only when a new set of footsteps echoed in the hall and Bryn looked up to see a familiar handsome face that she guessed the truth.

With every step more of the man named Aerith Seth began to appear, and while Bryn was elated at his appearance, she knew that what was about to happen must have been of such grave importance that would pull the man of neutral birth out of hiding.

"Good to see you again Bryn, only I was hoping it would be under much better circumstances."

The former phase smiled weakly and waited.

"Sabrina has become very astute in the few days that she has had to come to grips with all that has occurred to her. I wish I could take credit for all of it, but being in the presence of Pike Rhuiden, Gwydeon Sandar, and Logan Ranthall has had a lot to do with it as well."

Gideon looked at the man who stood before him in awe. Hearing the voice and seeing Bryn's reaction were enough to tip him to the identity of the man who stood before him, but there were no words to express what was going through his mind or his heart at that moment.

"Well Gideon," Aerith said after a moment, "I have to say that you have certainly made me proud. I only wish that I would have been able to be a father to you, but then I wish I could have been a father to my other children Cedric and Anabel as well. But, thanks to Emries, I was not allowed to have a normal or happy life, and it has taken me a hundred years of searching before I finally found the truth."

Aerith then turned his attention to Taya.

"You look so much like your mother, but you definitely have your grandmother's eyes."

Taya blushed and smiled.

"Your husband is a wonderful man," Aerith said moving next to Midarin. "I just wish I could have been there to fight alongside him, it would have been an honor."

"Is he alright?" Midarin asked slowly.

"Don't worry Midarin," Aerith said coyly, "men like Gwydeon only die once."

The cryptic answer somehow soothed Midarin's heart.

"And now to you, Caris," Aerith said, his tone suddenly somber. "I'm afraid that Logan isn't coming back."

The pain that rippled through Caris' heart was unlike any she had felt in her life. All of the emotions that had been so new and enjoyable were suddenly a painful and terrible burden. Every beat of the raging heart in her chest sent more stinging pains through her, and her mind rebelled against the sensations causing more grief. Suddenly Caris felt something cold and moist streak down her cheek from the corner of her eye. In life she had created false tears on many occasions to help seduce her would-be conquests, but this was the first time in her generation spanning existence that she had ever really cried.

"I'm sorry," was all that Aerith could say.

Midarin tried her best to console Caris, but even with the tears that had begun to stream from her eyes, Caris choked out a question.

"How?"

"Emries," Aerith responded. "The two dueled, and even with all of his powers, Logan was no match. However, all is not lost. It was because of Logan's intervention that the *Coromor* in the Light reality has a chance to resist the pull of Emries' wicked power. If all goes as planned, everyone will be making their way to the Council for the final confrontation."

Caris suddenly stood firm, wiping the tears from her eyes.

"Then we need the rest of the answer to this riddle about our powers so that we can help Shau-ling defeat Emries."

Aerith smiled.

"And that is why I am here, my dear Lady Wolf. As Sabrina so eloquently put it, everyone has the ability to touch the Blaze so long as they are following the path laid down by the Creator. However, just as man vied to control nature, so too would he try to control the Blaze, and it is because of this attempt to control that he would die."

"That was why Shau-ling always told the phasia to never draw too deeply," Gideon added.

"Correct," Aerith nodded. "If you surrender yourself to the power of the Blaze, it will come to you and allow you to work whatever miracles you see fit. However, if you pull for that power, it will resent you and attempt to destroy you. Bryn, you and Caris know well the seductive voice of the Blaze as it begs you to draw deeper and deeper upon the sweet and incredible power."

"Of course," Bryn replied. "At first it is hard to resist, but thanks to the teachings of Shau-ling and the experience of actually drawing on the powers helps to teach the resistance."

"Now that your limitation has been removed however," Aerith continued, "and I stress the word limitation, you are free to open yourself up and surrender to the Blaze. It will be difficult, but you will learn to let the Blaze flow through you in the directions you wish rather than directing it through you by force."

Caris was the first to close her eyes and send peace flooding through her body. Calm thoughts of her quiet stolen seconds with Logan filled her mind, and for that brief moment she felt the burning embers of the green Blaze flame at the corners of her mind. At first she felt herself reaching for the sweet power that the Blaze would give her, and her thoughts fluttered to images of revenge and striking down Emries to somehow find peace. As soon as the thoughts came to her mind, the fires of the Blaze receded and nearly fled. Caris suppressed the thoughts as best she could, letting the peace overtake her once again. Until finally, she could feel the embers of power growing in the blackness. This time, however, she resisted the urge to reach for the power, letting it come closer to her, until the white peaked green flames completely filled her mind. Slowly, Caris could feel the familiar burning sensation fill her body until finally she felt the flows of power holding her and binding her once again. The fog in her mind slowly began to lift, and the memories from the past began to return to her mind. Filled with Blaze power once again, Caris opened her eyes, as a familiar surge of power filled the back of her mind.

"There's a portal forming in the palace. It's strong too."

Aerith drew both of his swords and waited. However, Caris had other ideas.

"I'll stay here and hold whoever it is off, the rest of you need to get to the Council and make sure you win. I should be able to delay whoever this is long enough that you'll have a good head start."

"No," Aerith said strongly. "I'm staying too."

Bryn made a move to protest, but Aerith cut her off.

"My time in this war is over Bryn, but I have to make sure that everyone is where they need to be when all is said and done. Gideon, take your mother back home, she'll tell you where. Then the rest of you get back to Sador, wait for your friends to show up, and then get to the Council as quick as you can. Your rather large friend will tell you how. Now, get out of here."

Gideon was quick to create a portal and push Bryn through. Taya, Midarin, and Sabrina lingered for only a moment before following, and before the first portal was closed, three others appeared in the room. All four closed at the same time, and Caris smiled up at Aerith as the two prepared for battle.

"A little trick I picked up from Basille."

Aerith stood firm and waited until he heard footsteps echoing through the hall outside the throne room doors. When the large oak doors creaked open, the boy Nathan Sandar stood firm in the doorway with a bright arrogant smile painted on his face. Though he looked a little worse for ware, Aerith knew the boy was more than able to defend himself if this parlay were to degenerate to a fight.

"Well," Nathan said looking around the ruined throne room, "it looks like you all started the party without me. Here I was expecting to be able to take Draven on one on one, but it looks like I'm a little too late. Where is the infamous Lord Crow?"

"Gone," Caris answered strongly. "Ran like a dog with his tail between his legs after Gwydeon Sandar showed up. The Dark Riders are dead, and Scalla is back in the hands of its rightful rulers."

Nathan laughed.

"And what are you doing here Caris? Tagging along?"

Caris scowled.

"Well, it's no matter. After single-handedly dispatching both Zarsi and Farax, I doubt that your limited combat prowess will give me much difficulty. After all, most of your skills require you to be horizontal, not vertical."

Caris released the anger and hatred and let the Blaze fill her to the brim. The sweet seductive call to draw deeper was gone, and was replaced with an inner peace and a feeling that she could do anything that she set her mind to.

"You'll find I'm full of surprises." Caris retorted.

"I'm sure you are," Nathan said, "but the savior of the world has little time to consort with whores."

Caris wanted to lash out, but restrained, knowing the longer Nathan chose to talk, the more time the others would have to get to the Council.

"And what is your story, old man?" Nathan mocked. "Had your fill with Bryn and decided to move to the younger sisters? Before long you'll be bedding down with Trece. Or maybe Rael is more to your taste."

Aerith let the insult pass by him and smiled.

"For the son of an angel, you certainly have a devilish tongue."

The comment stopped Nathan in his tracks, and the proud smile was gone from his lips in a moment.

"I wanted to avoid a confrontation with you old man, but if I must, I will gladly test my skill against you. Considering the fact I have beaten

Logan Ranthall as well as two members of the phasia, the first *Chosen One* shouldn't be much of a challenge."

Aerith grinned slyly.

"Oh, if you want to fight, I'll be glad to. See, I'm a neutral being and that means for every good thing I do, I have to do something bad. Well, earlier today, I killed Saurn. Now, in my mind that was a very good thing for humanity. So now, if I kill you, I will be doing a very bad thing for humanity. Makes everything nice and neat."

Nathan froze.

"Oh, you weren't expecting that, were you?" Aerith teased. "You thought you could just insult me and I wouldn't do anything to stop you. Then you could just gut poor Caris here and go on about your merry way. Well sunshine, things don't work like that anymore."

Nathan channeled some of his powers and let twin blades of Order and Chaos form in his hands.

"You will not live to regret this."

Aerith laughed and stuck one sword in the ground long enough to unfasten his cloak and pull the shirt quickly over his head.

"I've lived to regret everything I've done little pup, and I can assure you that when all is said and done, I'll be the one still standing."

The cocky smile returned to Nathan's face, and he motioned for Aerith to make the first move.

"Age before beauty of course."

Aerith took a step forward, but Caris put her hand on his shoulder.

"Are you sure this is a good idea?"

Aerith smiled wider.

"Of course. This should be fun."

Back to the Beginning

Creator's Calendar Year 1205; Light Reality

Jerrard and Erika emerged from the portal that led from Basille's study in time to see another portal opening in the courtyard. Jerrard had enough time to trace the line of power back to its point of origin, and upon seeing that the portal came from the kingdom of Marcwell, the burden on his heart lifted a little. The four men that stepped out made Jerrard feel even more secure, for in a fight if any of the members of the People of the Dragon were not available, Jerrard would have gladly substituted any of the members of the Enforcers. Turok was quick to make his way over to Jerrard, snap a salute and then give his report.

"Marcwell has been sieged by the Creator's Torch Society, but then was assaulted again by the Army of the Fox under the command of the phase Bryn Aplee. Duncan and his phasia cohorts were able to escape and headed off to Aradon where Lord Pike and the rest of the group intend to catch up with them and put an end to their treachery. We came here because I felt we would be more useful to you and the Raven's Wing in a fight against Jeroch and his army."

"I most assuredly welcome your assistance, Turok," Jerrard replied, "and the rest of you as well. The Enforcers have truly proven themselves as stalwart warriors in the past."

Turok shook his head.

"The Enforcers no longer exist my lord," his tone was a mix of disappointment and anger. "From now on we fight against the phasia as we were trained to do, but answer to no lord and no kingdom."

"It's about time you got your head on straight."

The proud woman's voice caused Turok to smile immediately. Jerrard turned and watched as Celina Veshaw and Jerrard's daughter Taya emerged from the palace. Celina was still walking with a slight limp, but she seemed more than capable to make the march with the rest of the army. When Celina and Turok were face to face, the two kissed for only a moment and then embraced one another for what seemed like forever. When they finally separated, Turok smiled.

"What can we do to help, Lord Jerrard?"

Jerrard pointed toward the motion in the courtyard.

"The Raven's wing is mobilizing toward Lakestone. I instructed the scouts and the vanguard to move first so that Jeroch would know we were heading there. I want him in those flooded streets, and I want him to bring the fight to us. Because we are outnumbered, the tight corners and narrow alleys should at least give us a fighting chance. In an open field the Jeresei can eat up men pretty quickly when the odds are six or seven to one, but I figure the waters and the buildings should help us cut that to at worse three to one at any time."

"A sound plan my lord," Ren added. "Hopefully the move will also confuse Jeroch enough for him to hesitate and give us enough time to prepare for his charge."

"My thoughts exactly," Jerrard said smiling. "Now, Storm is mobilizing the archers, but that is not where his strength lies. Zak, I want you to get the scouts and the archers in position. Turok, Celina, Valin, it's going to be your responsibility to get my ranks in order and keep them steady for the first charge. Ren, I'm putting you in control of the support troop. Make sure we don't get flanked and protect the archers and scouts at all costs."

All saluted and gave an affirmative before heading off. When Taya looked at her father, she could see the discomfort and trepidation in his eyes. Her mother too seemed as though she was worried.

"What's wrong father?"

Jerrard sighed hard.

"The war isn't simple anymore Taya," Jerrard answered. "But things are starting to come full circle. The last time I fought against Jeroch's army, I was a raw cadet in Lord Cedric Binosear's army, and we marched on Lakestone. Lord Cedric always thought there was something more to that place than just the one palace that he destroyed, but after half of the city collapsed, he never got a chance to go back. Though we know now that it is where every single generation has seen the rebirth of the war between Light and Shadow, and the invasions have started from there. I guess it's just a matter of fate that we are all going back there."

Taya took the explanation at face value but could sense that there was more to it than that. She nodded and went off to help Zak with his preparations for the archers and the scouts and inwardly prayed that the cost of the war would not be to high should they be victorious.

* * * * * * * * * * *

Jeroch shifted impatiently in his saddle, trying not to listen to Ellis' nearly monotonous voice as it droned on about battle plans and effective combat strategies. For as long as Jeroch could remember, there was only one member of the phasia that he hated dealing with more than Ellis. Like all female members of the Brotherhood of Phasia Ellis was beautiful, but in a different way from her sisters. Ellis' features were flawless to be sure, and her white hair gave her a very exotic look, but the real allure to Ellis was the unapproachable quality that she exuded. It was this quality that had earned her the title the Ice Queen from her fellow phasia, but while each member of the Brotherhood had their own reasons for loathing her, each secretly wanted her. Jeroch too had felt the desire to entrap his dear sister, but there were too many negatives in her personality and Jeroch was not about to brave the hours of tedious conversation to fulfill a desire within him that he did not understand. Perhaps if Ellis had been more shy and reserved, it would have been possible. But, as Jeroch thought about it, Ellis was one of the most conceited and pompous members of the phasia, but unlike Taron, Ellis had cause and justification for her arrogance.

The most impressive aspect of Ellis had always been her mind, and her ability to figure out schemes. While not the trickster or the planner that Saurn was, Ellis' fancies were always tilted to the more obscure. If there was something in the world that did not make sense, Ellis used all of the resources at her disposal to seek that mystery out and put a resolution to it. Naturally, the problem of the prophecies was a downfall to that inquisitive nature, but as far as Ellis was concerned, the only bad outcome to a mystery was to leave it unsolved. Jeroch found that Ellis' council was very valuable at times, but to be with it for several days, and having it given to you without asking was nearly unbearable.

"And so if we deploy the Jeresei here at the western walls, the Kalbraks should . . ."

Jeroch tuned out the voice again, not wanting to hear the same argument hashed out again. For the past three days, Ellis had been debating the deployment of all of the units in the army; the problem was however that she was debating with herself. Jeroch already had a plan in mind, and despite all of Ellis' hard thinking and pondering, he was in command of the army, and Jeroch would do as he saw fit. But, it was hard to ignore both Ellis and her daughter Jessica.

Jessica was as eccentric as her mother, but it seemed that her tilt was much darker. The penchant for bats aside, Jessica shared her mother's interest in everything that was unusual, going so far as to study her own powers as an offspring of the phasia and deepening her connection with the Blaze. The thing that had disturbed Jeroch the most was that Jessica had the ability to speak to the Jeresei and the Kalbraks in their own language. All of the phasia had the same ability, but it was normally beneath them to speak to the lowly creatures in their own language. Jessica on the other hand took great pride in her linguistic achievement, even going so far as to learn the dialects of each of the clans.

"But mother," Jeroch heard Jessica interject, "Clan Gernal is much better in close combat because of their origins in the high mountains where conditions require great strength and endurance. So if you deploy them on the flank those qualities will be useless. In my opinion . . ."

Jeroch rolled his eyes and tuned out the other voice. Ellis was bad enough alone, now Jeroch found himself cursed with two of them. The only relief Jeroch had was the fact that his grandson, Rand Merin, did not speak or seem to pay much attention to the bickering of his wife and mother in law. From the brief few days that Jeroch had spent with Rand during the march, he was reminded of another quiet and reserved young man. Jeroch hoped that Rand had half the potential of Gwydeon Sandar.

Out of the corner of his eye, Jeroch saw several bushes move, and so he pulled up on the reins of his horse and waited. Mere seconds later, two Jeresei scouts emerged from the brush and bowed to their commander.

"Lord Jeroch," the lead Jeresei grumbled with a guttural tone, "scouts reporting back the activities of the Raven's Wing."

Jeroch waived his hand.

"Make it quick lowborn."

The Jeresei did his best to ignore insult.

"The Raven's Wing has mobilized, but they do not appear as though they are going to make an effort to defend Scalla. Their archers and scouts are making great haste toward the city of Lakestone, so much so that they are not making efforts to cover their tracks. From the look of the mobilization of the infantry within the walls of the city, the rest of the army sill soon be marching as well."

"Very well," Jeroch replied, trying not to let his thoughts show, "return to your posts and report if anything changes.

Both Jeresei bowed quickly and returned to the brush. Jeroch sat for a moment, gathering his thoughts before the torrent of suggestions flooded him. Ellis and Jessica were sure to have their own opinions about the maneuver, which Jeroch found extremely clever.

"It's a trick," Ellis said almost as soon as the Jeresei had disappeared into the undergrowth. "They want us to turn toward Lakestone so they can flank us. It's a classic feint. They let us see their scouts and archers moving to trick us."

"While your theory is not off base mother, I don't believe that a force that small would dare attack our flank," Jessica countered. "Jerrard Mystic knows well enough the capability of our troops, and his plan is merely to make us second-guess ourselves. Charge now while they are still moving and we will not only catch them unawares but they will also be at a disadvantage without their archers and scouts."

Jeroch finally took the opportunity to chime in.

"We are still too far away for an acceptable charge, and by the time our troops are able to engage, we will not catch them as flat-footed as you believe. Jerrard is a tenacious foe, and I am sure that he has instilled some of that into his troops. If our troops make the charge all the way to the palace walls, they will not have enough energy for the kind of fight they will have in front of them."

For the first time, Rand interjected himself into the conversation.

"I agree with Lord Jeroch."

Jeroch was impressed with the boy. Even in the face of his wife and mother in law, he was still obeying courtly courtesy and showing Jeroch the respect that he was due.

"But," the young man continued, "if we wait until the Raven's Wing has entered Lakestone before striking, then our chances of victory decrease by an incredible amount."

Ellis stared coldly at the boy.

"A force of Jeresei and Kalbraks this size should have no trouble with a mob of humans, no matter the battlefield."

Rand shook his head.

"You of all people mother should understand that Lakestone favors a smaller army. I had a long time to study the maps of the city, and since the War of the Lion, half of the city is flooded, and the other half is dominated by ruined buildings, tight streets, and even smaller alleyways. In that environment, the Raven's Wing will fight as though it were five or six times bigger, and it has been proven that one on one, the Jeresei are no match for a trained human warrior. The strength of the Jeresei is in numbers."

Jessica frowned.

"And what about the Kalbraks?"

"The Kalbraks will be hampered by the flood waters," Rand replied. "Because of their slow foot speed, they are a liability in any function other than shock troops to compliment the Jeresei's speed. However, this will become even more of a hindrance in Lakestone because of the knee deep waters that have risen through most of the streets. While this will hamper the Jeresei and mortals as well, the Kalbraks will be sitting ducks ripe to be picked off by the archers."

Jeroch smiled and nodded.

"Which is why they are moving the archers and scouts there at utmost haste. They can set up in the ruined buildings and on the rooftops and pick off our troops one by one without any danger of retribution. It's such a pity that Jerrard ignored the call of his blood. He would have been a formidable ally like his father."

Ellis' scowl ran deeper.

"So this is a hopeless battle?"

Jeroch smiled and shook his head.

"No dear sister, not hopeless. While it would turn more in our favor if I had a flight of Shadowwalkers at my disposal, I shall have to make due with the troops that Caris saw fit to provide. The men of the Army of the Wolf shall lead the charge into the streets of Lakestone with the Jeresei supporting them. This will give the Kalbraks time to wade in and be more than moving targets. The primary goal will be to eliminate the archers and scouts. We need them blind with no distance attacks. Then it will come down to numbers and tenacity. We may have the numbers, but I have a hunch that the Raven's Wing will not die easily."

Ellis scoffed at the plan.

"Sometimes your stupidity amazes me, Jeroch. You and I together have the power to level that city."

"Yes dear sister," Jeroch replied, "we do. And as much as I would love to sink Lakestone to the bottom of Exeter Lake with the entire Raven's Wing in it, there is part of me that wants to fight this battle. It was here that the forces of the Shadow made their final stand against the army of Cedric Binosear in the War of the Lion. It's like I'm getting a second chance to make things right. This time though, I won't slip on a rock."

* * * * * * * * * *

Several hours had passed and the deployment of the Raven's Wing had gone almost perfectly to plan. Jerrard proudly looked over the ranks of his troops and for the first time felt a ray of hope creep into his heart. Thanks to the Enforcers, the Raven's Wing had enough tactical information to deploy properly and take the most advantage of the nearly sunken ruins of Lakestone. Taya and Zak had made quick work of getting all of the archers into their proper positions and setting up relay lines for the scouts to get information back to the leadership in the least amount of time. Information was going to make all the difference in the battle that was about to begin. With still a hint of a smile on his lips, Jerrard turned toward his friends from the Enforcers and his family.

"We've done well friends, and whether we win or lose the day, no one can say that we did not give it our best."

"The Army of the Wolf will be upon us soon Lord Jerrard," Turok said holding his sword at the ready. "We should get in position."

"Very well," Jerrard answered. "What is the latest from the scouts, Zak?"

Zak looked over the scraps of paper in his hand for a moment.

"No change sir. The Army of the Wolf is still advancing with the Jeresei and Kalbraks at their vanguard. They should be in range any time."

Jerrard nodded.

"You all know what to do, good luck."

* * * * * * * * * * *

Nearly an hour after occupying Lakestone, the Raven's Wing could see the object of their torment. The Army of the Wolf's banners were clearly visible at the top of the ridge, and it would only be a matter of moments before the primal screams of the Jeresei would hit the air, and the sea of red skinned demons would be loosed upon them. Several of the archers were just finishing restringing their bows when the first chorus of screams went up, but they were quick to draw an arrow from their quiver and nock it on the fresh bowstring. Seconds later the arrow would be guided by the soft currents of the air toward the mass of demonic flesh, and hopefully it would keep one of the monsters from making it to the front ranks of the Wing. Zak let a low whistle escape his lips. From his position on one of the highest remaining buildings in Lakestone, the charge of the Army of the Wolf looked very impressive. It took only a few moments until the red skinned beasts were within range, and Zak let his hand rise into the air, bringing a quick series of motions from the massed archers. Steadily each one took aim and waited, bowstrings drawn back with lethal grace. As Zak's hand dropped, dozens of bowstrings snapped into action, sending a hail of black streaks soaring into the sky. When finally the deadly rain fell on the advancing troops, several cries of pain mixed with the feral screams and Zak watched as many of the Jeresei fell. The second flight of arrows hit the air, and Zak made his way down to the rest of the troops and stood with his brethren of the Enforcers and waited.

When the first charge came, the Enforcers held the line with the front rank of the Raven's Wing, waves of Jeresei and mortal men rushing them. Suddenly, Turok's voice hit the air.

"Split!"

With incredible precision and speed, every member of the front rank of the Raven's Wing broke to the sides of the street, leaving a huge gap as they filtered into the tight alleys. The Jeresei were confused for a moment but quickly recovered, dividing the mass charge so that it ran laterally though the winding and narrow streets of the city. The Enforcers worked quickly enough, but the planning of the brain trust in charge of the Shadow army was keeping in step. Turok split from his group of soldiers and cut back toward the main street to meet up with Celina where she hid in one of the ruined buildings. They had hoped to catch some of the Jeresei from behind, draw a line in the sand, and fight back to back taking everything that came at them. As members of the Lion's Mane, the two lovers had fought in Lakestone before, in the dark days of the first generation of the prophecies. They knew the layout of the city better than anyone, and they intended to use every bit of that knowledge to their fullest advantage. The first group of Jeresei flooded past Turok and Celina, and after a quick glance to one another, the staunch warriors appeared from their hiding place. Turok found himself face to face with a line of advancing Jeresei, while Celina had an unobstructed view at the flanks of another set. Lashing out together, Turok and Celina were quick to draw Jeresei blood, downing the first two in only a matter of seconds. A howl of pain from Celina's kill alerted the other, bringing them back on the limping woman and forcing her to work for her next series of kills. One by one the Jeresei came down the choked alleyway, unable to utilize their speed or numbers to their advantage. Fighting back to back, the two humans had all the advantage, immobile and in complete control of the surroundings they killed twenty or thirty Jeresei without a scratch. However, they could not hold out indefinitely. The Jeresei were intelligent creatures and were adapting their fighting style to the cramped quarters by using more quick and precise strikes rather than the wild slashes that could be easily covered up by numbers. Each kill brought a Jeresei who was learning from the mistakes of his predecessor, and Celina and Turok both found themselves tiring. Suddenly, a sharp pain ripped through Turok and as he looked down he realized that the long talons of a Kalbrak had reached through one of the cracks in the ruined wall to his left and impaled his side. The distraction was enough for the Jeresei before him to rip the sword out of Turok's hand and bring its claws ripping though the weakened flesh of Turok's chest. Turok's cry of agony also distracted Celina, but while she was able to block the blows that came at her front, the Jeresei that stepped over Turok's fallen body was able to rip at her back with its long claws, sending her crashing to the ground as well. The Jeresei laughed as they stepped over the fallen bodies, leaving the two lovers to bleed to death in each other's arms.

* * * * * * * * * * *

Ren Dalin brandished his lightning blade and led the first counter charge toward the ranks of Jeresei and Kalbraks. The battle had not gone well for the Raven's Wing, and the losses had been high thus far. Had the battle taken place on an open field, they probably would have been much worse. However, Ren charged in anyway, his supernatural blade cutting down everything in his path. But as Ren looked around after every kill, he saw dozens of mortal bodies littering the ground along with those of the Jeresei. More and more of the red skinned beasts came, but each in turn were dispatched by Ren and his reserves. However, the ranks were beginning to be depleted, with no end to the threat in sight. It was as though the demons kept multiplying as the battle went on. Then Ren saw the dark form walking with the ranks of Jeresei. The man held twin blades that hummed with power, one a bright white, the other a sickening black color, a congealing mass of motion and chaos. When Ren caught sight of the man's eyes, the description fit none other than the First of the Shadow, Jeroch Yetre.

"You handle the blade of a member of the phasia well, mortal," Jeroch said when he was finally face to face with Ren. "Let's see how well you fight against one."

Ren was embroiled in the challenge before he knew it as Jeroch slashed quickly with the blade of Order and followed with a broad slash from the Chaos blade. Ren's parry gave him only a few seconds to dodge the second attack, and for all of his skill and training, Ren knew he was greatly overmatched. Slashes flowed into thrusts which Ren helpless parried and dodged, fully on the defensive. Jeroch stopped mid-thrust and looked down at his foe.

"Too slow for you? Perhaps I should speed up then."

Ren then found himself in the path of a deluge of blades. Jeroch's two swords had suddenly become twenty as the phase move faster than it should have been possible to move. The surgical precision of the strikes left Ren riddled with small cuts and gashes, each of which poured forth a stream of blood. When the blur of motion finally ended, Ren did not have the power to stand, and his sword had long since fallen from his grip and clattered to the ground. An amateur strike could have ended his life at this point, and even if Jeroch had walked away, Ren probably would have bled to death before help arrived.

"You have good skill for a mortal," Jeroch send in the most complimentary voice that he could manage. "But you are no Gwydeon Sandar."

The strike from the blade of Order was quick and lethal, thrusting through Ren's chest, burying the point deep into the raggedly beating heart.

* * * * * * * * * * *

Jerrard and Storm had been holding their own for some time until Valin appeared and began to help turn the tide. Between the three and with generous use of power from both Jerrard and Storm, many of the Jeresei and Kalbraks fell. The heart of Lakestone was the final line between victory and defeat, and with every retreat came a new low for morale. Jerrard had finally drawn the line. They would hold or they would all be killed. For the better part of three hours the war had raged through the streets of Lakestone, and while the Army of the Wolf had taken significant losses, the Raven's Wing had been nearly totally decimated. The plan of Jeroch's army had been sound, even with the mortal's tactical advantage. The beasts had hunted the archers down, and even with the loss of several hundred careless Jeresei, every one of the bow carrying warriors had been flushed out of his hiding place and quickly slaughtered. Once it was down to a simple numbers game, Jerrard knew the battle was lost. But he would not go down without a fight, and if Jerrard had his way, he would keep fighting, even after the fatal blow was struck just so he could get his hands on Jeroch.

"My lord," Zak called as he sprinted through several of the ruined buildings toward the final line.

Zak was an absolute mess. His shirt had been ripped and torn in dozens of places, each of which revealed a shallow slash that marked an incursion too close to enemy line. The Jeresei were very precise with their strikes, and it was a credit to Zak's skills that he was able to escape at all.

"Report," Jerrard grunted as his blade ripped free from the dying body of a Jeresei.

"The line is breaking sir. There are just too many of the Jeresei. Turok and Celina fell almost immediately into the foray, and Ren was cut down by Jeroch."

Jerrard's blood boiled. Not only did he want to take revenge for Ren, but the memory of Arin Domae and the battle between Gwydeon Sandar and Jeroch was still very fresh in his mind. While he may not have had the skill of Gwydeon, Jerrard wanted to try, to uphold the Mystic name and make his father proud wherever his soul lay.

"Find Jeroch, Zak," Jerrard replied coldly, "whatever the cost."

Zak was about to sprint away when a voice called from the enemy ranks.

"Looking for me, Mystic?"

Jerrard watched as the Jeresei retreated back from the line and parted to make way for a small group. Jerrard recognized Jeroch and Ellis immediately, and from the posture of the woman that walked with Ellis, she was a child of the phasia. The young man that walked with a calm gait, shoulders reared back and sword held at the ready could have been merely a general of the army, but something told Jerrard that there was more to the boy.

"Well, Jerrard," Jeroch said when the two finally stood eye to eye, "it looks like you are beaten. Now, we could go back to fighting this battle the old fashioned way, and you can all end up as a late night meal for the Jeresei, or we can do this the way of the phasia, the way of your blood, with honor."

"Honor," Taya scoffed, "I'm surprised you know what that word means."

It was Jerrard that answered the challenge.

"The phasia may be a group of cowards and braggarts, but they do have honor, Taya. I accept Jeroch. You and I will duel as is the custom of the phasia, and whoever shall win that duel shall be the victor of this battle and will dictate the fate of the loser's army."

Jeroch smiled.

"Agreed."

CHAPTER 42

Chapter XLIII

Salvation

Creator's Calendar Year 1205; Dark Mirror

Aerith Seth and Nathan Sandar stood eye to eye, swords ready for a fight, but neither made a move for the first few moments. Watching the two powerful warriors, Caris stood by, Blaze energy still filling her to the brim. She too wanted a piece of the upstart boy Nathan Sandar, partially for what Emries had done to the only man that Caris had ever really loved, Logan Ranthall, and partially because the boy was the third generation's *Coromor*. Every part of her being wanted to strike him down, and while the sensation had never been that strong while she had a primal string and called herself a member of the Brotherhood of Phasia, since she had embraced the Blaze the feelings had taken on a new intensity. Finally Caris had begun to understand the true nature of the war. The fog in her mind had been totally lifted allowing her to see not only things as they were in her many lifetimes, but also how they were on both sides of the world, both Light and Shadow. It was as though the Caris was looking down on the war, seeing all of the pointless and self-defeating schemes that led both the Light and the Shadow down a spiral of destruction and ultimate defeat.

Aerith smiled as he looked over the boy. Even though most of his power was gone, Aerith knew that there was enough left in his tired old body to delay the boy long enough for the others to get to the Council chambers and start the final act of the war. There were only three people in all of creation who knew how things would turn out, and to his credit,

Aerith owed most of the fact finding to Evan Sinn and his woman Meredith. Halicon had begun to see the truth, and of course the Creator knew how all would end up. It was not that the Creator wanted to destroy the world, but it was the only way that he could set his errant flock back on the right path. Inwardly Aerith hoped that there would be a small place for him in the world that would be created after this war had ended.

Still drifting in his own thoughts, Aerith nearly did not feel the familiar twinge of intuition in the back of his mind that told him danger was coming. The boy Nathan struck first, lashing out with both of his blades at the same time. Even caught flat-footed, Aerith was able to bring his blades up and parry both strikes. When the younger man withdrew his blades, Aerith smiled again and began to round his younger opponent. The two men rounded each other slowly, looking for some weakness that they could exploit. From the knowledge that Nathan had inherited as the third *Coromor* of the prophecies, he knew that Aerith Seth was a master of the sword, even without his powers as the first *Chosen One*. The part that concerned Nathan the most was the fact that even though Aerith had handed off his mantle as was demanded by the Creator, he still had powers left. He could travel between the different realities, as well as wield the powers that should have only been reserved for the forces of the Light or the forces of the Shadow. In Nathan's mind, a person who stood middle ground in a war between Light and Darkness was the enemy. Not taking sides was almost as bad as choosing the wrong one. Aerith on the other hand was quite impressed with the boy who stood opposite him. It was obvious that the skill he was displaying was a mix of what his father Gwydeon taught him and an amalgamation of everything the previous men who wore the title *Coromor* knew. Cedric, while not a blade master, was a powerful swordsman, and Korrd Ranthall was yet another student of the infamous Gwydeon Sandar. Aerith reminded himself at that moment that he wanted to meet the winged man before time was over.

Nathan saw a bit of hesitation in Aerith's movements and lashed out again, but the older man was able to parry and counter into a slow slash. Caris watched the smile grow on the boy's face, as he saw the opening in Aerith's defenses. Pivoting in, Nathan shifted his weight into a thrust with his sword of Order whose target was Aerith's heart. Caris watched in horror, her mind not able to envision even Aerith Seth surviving the strike.

But then, at the last possible moment, Seth's weight shifted, turning his body roughly to the side so the blade of Order barely grazed his shoulder leaving a small incision. Aerith continued the moved into a full spin, bringing his swords back to bear with an even wider smile on his face.

"Not bad pup," Aerith taunted. "But my heart is right here. This is a shoulder," he said pointing at the small wound, "and you're not going to get anywhere aiming here."

Nathan growled and launched forward again, slashing and thrusting in a reckless manner. Aerith dodged and parried each of the blows until he brought the flat of his blade thundering down on the back of Nathan's head after an errant pass. When Nathan turned, Aerith was standing with his guard down, one blade stuck in the ground, the other perched on his uninjured shoulder.

"I had such high hopes for you young pup. After all, your father is probably the greatest swordsman in the world after me, and only a little bit above Korrd Ranthall and Arathorn Geoffry. With that kind of lineage boy, you shouldn't be making mistakes like this. Come on, try harder this time."

The comment infuriated the boy even further, but Caris could tell a difference. The fury was controlled and being used as fuel for the skill that existed deep in the boy. As Aerith recovered his sword and stood firm, Nathan attacked again, two quick hard thrusts followed by a long slash. Aerith parried each of the thrusts and sidestepped the slash before finally taking a defensive position. The two rounded each other once again, and Caris could feel the tenseness in the two fighters. As much as Aerith was playing at being arrogant and superior, he knew what was riding on the duel. The longer they could keep Nathan out of the loop the better it was for everyone involved. However, it was only a matter of time before Nathan tired of the game and used more of the powers at his disposal. Swords were fine for dealing with matters of honor or testing your skills against another, but when it came down to removing problems from your path, the kind of power that the *Coromor* possessed was very effective. If Aerith was not mindful of the situation, he could find himself burned to a cinder before he felt a bit of heat.

SALVATION

As Nathan charged in again, Aerith went totally on the defense, no longer parrying blows but simply dodging and sidestepping them one right after the other. Some of the slashes came closer than others, but Caris could see a gradual increase in speed between the two men, until finally the strikes were coming dangerously close to Aerith's flesh. Finally what Caris feared happened. After stepping clear of one slash, the sword of Chaos swept across the distance. Aerith saw the attack too late and threw his upper body backward, trying to increase the distance enough to save his life. The tip of the sword of Chaos barely grazed the older man's chest, leaving a thin trail of blood. When Aerith emerged from the attack, he smiled again and began laughing.

"Not bad at all. I would have expected nothing less from someone like you," Aerith mocked. "I guess I'm going to have to get serious now."

What Caris saw in the next few moments was a complete change come over the man Aerith Seth. The brightness of his eyes dimmed to nearly nothing, and the coy smile was replaced by a firmly set jaw and determined stare. Even his body posture changed as he crouched from a standing position into a defensive stance, one blade held parallel with his body while the other was held over his head, blade outward. For the next few moments, Aerith waited, totally motionless, until finally Nathan lashed out again. This time, instead of going on the defensive and simply parrying away or dodging the strike, Aerith countered, knocking the slash to one side and then stepping into the boy. Turning quickly, Aerith jabbed his elbow into Nathan's chest, knocking the wind out of him, and then dropped to one knee and smashed the younger man's knee with the hilt of his sword. Caught totally by surprise, the *Coromor* stumbled and ended up sprawled face first on the ground. Aerith walked over the fallen youth and buried the tip of his blade beside Nathan's face before stepping away.

"Not bad, but I wouldn't recommend doing that every time. It's rather difficult to defend yourself while laying down. Or is that one of Emries' special techniques?"

Nathan was back on his feet in a heartbeat, growling deeply and striking with all of the fury and intensity within him. To Aerith's credit, he parried and countered every single blow without breaking a sweat, and then proceeded to launch an attack of his own. In only a matter of moments,

Nathan was totally on the defensive. One of Aerith's thrusts stopped short, an obvious feint, but Nathan moved to block the blow anyway, leaving his defenses wide open. Aerith's second blade pierced the opening the next second, the tip of the blade barely breaking the skin of Nathan's chest right above the heart. The two men stood frozen, Aerith's sword poised for the killing strike and the boy with no defense.

"I could kill you now, Nathan, and the world will be a much better place for it. But it's not your time yet. If I were you, I would be portaling off to the Council chambers to meet up with your patron. I think that what you will find there will give you plenty to worry about."

Nathan stepped back from the point of Aerith's blade and scowled.

"And if I refuse?"

Aerith's tone was suddenly cold.

"Then you'll die right here and now."

There was something in the tone of Aerith's voice that made Caris believe that Aerith could strike the boy down with a thought if he truly wanted to. But as if conceding defeat, the boy lowered his blades and bowed his head. A moment later a portal appeared and Nathan turned toward it. What happened next was the last thing that Caris would have ever expected. A huge gust of wind penetrated the room, slamming hard into Aerith's back and sending him tumbling through the open portal. After Aerith disappeared, the portal slammed shut, and Nathan turned to face a suddenly very scared Caris.

"Much better," Nathan said smiling, "now we can have a much more intimate time together."

Caris took several steps backward and tried to keep peace filling her. Her only chance of survival was to keep connected with the Blaze. There was no way that Nathan could have known that the limitation had been lifted on her powers, and Caris was going to try to keep that advantage as long as possible.

"So," Nathan said calmly, "here we are, just the two of us. Once I dispatch you, I'm going to take care of the rest of your pathetic little Council and then I'll make quick work of Shau-ling. Oh, and don't think that your white knight Aerith is going to show up, he's going to be quite busy for a while."

An evil laugh escaped Nathan's lips.

* * * * * * * * * * *

A portal opened above the ruined city of Sarmeel, and a form shot from the opening and tumbled to the ground in a heap. Aerith lay motionless for a few moments, pain rocketing through every part of his body. Nathan had been able to catch him by surprise, and the shock of the landing on the hard ground did not help matters any. It wasn't until Aerith looked up that he began to grow concerned. Before Aerith stood a very lifelike representation of the phase Farax, complete with shocked expression. Though part of the former *Chosen One* wanted to laugh at the irony, the small balls of fur that surrounded the statue prevented any levity. Aerith's thunderous appearance in the quiet city had been enough to alert the little beasts, and they had already begun their slow rhythmic bouncing motion toward him. Very carefully Aerith gathered his feet under him and started to stand. Though he made no threatening motions, every slight movement of his body seemed to aggravate the small creatures, as their bouncing gained speed. The small white and brown balls of fur had surrounded him in a matter of moments, and Aerith found himself getting lost in the odd patterns. When the purring started, Aerith shook himself back to reality and brought his guard up. Unlike most in the world, Aerith knew about the Snags, thanks in part to Logan Ranthall's run in with the horrid little beasts in the second generation of the prophecies. However, when Aerith saw six black Snags appear, true fear struck his heart. The black creatures' low purring was driving the rest of the Snags, setting the pattern for attack. While Aerith knew he could have used a portal to escape, he didn't know if there would be enough time to get out unscathed. Going back to Scalla was certainly an option, but by the time he got back, Caris would probably already be dead.

The purring stopped, and flashes of light could be seen through the mass of fur as the Blaze-hued tails came into clear view. The charge would begin any moment, and Aerith felt himself tense. There was very little power left for him to draw on, and while a focused attack would give him breathing room to get out of the battle alive, it would only leave enough left for two or three more portals, but not nearly enough to cross between the worlds. That was another reason for not going back to Scalla. While in a duel with no powers being utilized, Aerith could have battled Nathan for the rest of eternity that would certainly not be the case for the next act of the duel. The problem with facing the *Coromor* was that he could exercise his enormous powers at any time. Aerith too had power, but there was nowhere near enough left in him for the kind of battle that was probably raging between Nathan and Caris. It would be like a fly sitting on the battlefield while two giants clubbed away at one another. There was enough for one focused burst of energy, and then a portal to somewhere safe, but after that, any use of power could bring an end to Aerith's existence.

"Looks like I'll be walking for a while," Aerith said to himself, waiting for the inevitable charge from the bouncing balls of fur.

Suddenly one of the balls launched forward, tail spinning with deadly speed. Aerith was able to duck the blow and accidentally moved into the path of several more of the creatures. Reflex took over at that point, bringing the blades of his swords to bear, slicing two of the vile creature wide open. While Aerith knew about the acidic blood, there was nothing he could do to avoid the smoking viscous liquid. Several drops landed on his skin and began to burn. But there were other things to worry about as more of the balls of fur leapt toward Aerith all at once, trying to swarm him. The time for retaliation was at hand, and Aerith reached deep into himself and drew forth the power of the *Chosen One*. From under the mass of biting and purring fur, a haze of power began to grow around Aerith, protecting him from the gnashing teeth and stabbing tails. The haze grew in intensity until it suddenly flashed. A shockwave of heat and power erupted from Aerith, vaporizing any Snag in its path. When the release was over, Aerith fell to his hands and knees, bleeding from several wounds. Bite marks littered his shoulders and back, while his sides and chest were covered with long slashes from the impossibly sharp tails. Aerith had never felt more drained in his life. It was as though he had lifted the entire city of

Sarmeel, hefted it on his back and carried it around the world several times. But then a sound found his ear, a familiar sound. Something was purring.

When Aerith looked up, he saw a single black Snag sitting before him, teeth bared and tail wagging behind it. If Aerith didn't know any better he would say that the thing was smiling. It was then that Aerith felt a twinge in the back of his mind in the most primal core of his thoughts. Suddenly Aerith realized that the creature was trying to communicate with him on the most basic of levels. There were no words or true communication, just a feeling. If there was anything that the feeling translated to, it was respect. Aerith laughed to himself.

"I just killed a couple hundred of your kind and now you're sitting here trying to tell me that I've earned your respect?"

There was a kind of an answer in the evil smile of razor sharp teeth that stared back at Aerith. Laughing to himself again, Aerith shook his head and started walking toward the edge of Sarmeel, the faintest bit of power starting to flow through him again. For every step, the Snag was right there by his side, bouncing in time.

"Well one thing's for sure," Aerith said as the two forms began to fade into nothingness, "I'm glad Shau-ling chose the Jeresei over the Snags, otherwise the humans would have never stood a chance."

* * * * * * * * * * *

Caris stood firm watching the eyes of her true enemy, trying to predict how he would attack. Power for power, Caris knew she had no chance of taking the *Coromor* on and winning, but she had no choice now. Nathan would attack any time, but unlike the battle with Aerith, he would not simply confine himself to blades of energy. With the command of his powers and the interference of Emries, Nathan had been powerful enough to destroy Zarsi, and Zarsi had the best command of the powers granted by Shau-ling. It was then that Caris suddenly remembered that she was no longer an ordinary phase. Aerith had been right, the primal string of power had been a limitation. It had held back the true nature of the powers of the Blaze. Now that Caris had been opened up fully to the sweet fires, there was nothing that she could not do.

"Are you ready to die, Caris? Or are you going to make a pathetic attempt to seduce me in an effort to save your life?"

Caris spat at Nathan's feet.

"I have slept with some toads in my time boy, but I would never degrade myself as to share the same bed with you."

Nathan laughed.

"No one accused you of having taste Caris, after all, you had two children with Jeroch."

A bit of anger fluttered through the peace in Caris' mind, making the Blaze retreat a bit from her grasp. But the longer Caris tried, the more she was able to control her emotions and let the Blaze fill her to the utmost capacity. Channeling a little of that power, Caris bathed her body in the cleansing fires of the Blaze, creating a kind of armor. The sly grin on Nathan's face faded, and was replaced by a more serious and determined look.

"No more games, Nathan." Caris said coldly. "You may have been able to kill Zarsi and Farax, but you will have a much harder time with me."

Nathan cocked one corner of his mouth.

"We shall see."

Seconds later a burst of fire erupted from Nathan's fingertips. Caris did not move, letting the Blaze fill her and bind her. The bolt of flame struck the aura, and was quickly dissipated. Not believing what had just occurred, Nathan fired bolt after bolt at the motionless woman, but watched in horror as each stream of fire was simply negated by the bright green aura. Nathan was beginning to rethink his strategy when the aura around Caris suddenly intensified until it was like a shroud. The green glow mimicked every feature and every curve of the woman that it covered, and when Caris opened her eyes a fiendish grin came to her face.

"I learned a few tricks from my brothers, Nathan, but I never got a chance to try them out. I think this is a golden opportunity. First, let me show you what Rael and Trece taught me."

Caris let the Blaze fill her again, but this time channeled it throughout her body, modifying her muscles and her speed. Slowly Caris began to move, but each motion was faster than the human mind could perceive. As Nathan stood and watched, Caris suddenly disappeared, and the next thing he knew, she was on the other side of the throne room. But then she disappeared again and was immediately standing right in front of him. Shocked, Nathan took a step back, but instead of being in front of him, Caris was suddenly behind him. Caris shoved Nathan hard in the back and then sped across the room again, back to the position she was when the game started. Nathan righted himself from the strong shove and when he looked up Caris stood in her original position, grinning.

"Rael and Trece are very fast, and they showed me how to use the Blaze to speed myself up. After throwing in a little improvement that Basille accidentally showed me, I think it's quite an impressive little tactic, don't you?"

Nathan frowned.

"Now, let me combine that with a little technique that I learned from Taron."

In the blink of an eye Caris disappeared again, only this time when she appeared in front of Nathan, she struck. All Nathan saw were two hands wrapped in the green aura speeding toward him. The first struck his jaw, shattering it on impact, while the other became a quick palm strike that shattered his sternum. Nathan collapsed to the ground, blood pouring from his mouth. Caris sped back across the room and looked down at the fallen boy, admiring her handiwork.

"I may not have the strength of Taron," Caris said firmly, "but its quality, not quantity."

It took only a matter of seconds for Nathan to channel the flows of Wind and Water to the wounds, and then the flows of Earth into his bones. When finally the boy stood, there was a fury in his eyes unlike any that Caris had seen before. It was possible that her playfulness had backfired on her. In a moment, Nathan was bathed in the angelic glow of the powers of the *Coromor* and he flooded himself with the power drawing from sources that Caris could neither see nor comprehend. Reaching out with the Blaze, Caris could feel the different powers that inhabited Nathan, as he was drawing power from at least two of the *Erieal* and the *Chosen One*. There seemed to be another power at work as well, a more complete and potent power. It was almost as though Emries himself where shadowing the boy's movements, pushing him along the path.

"Your speedy tricks are nothing to me now phase. I can match whatever speed you choose to run, but after I am finished toying with you, I will overtake you and strike you down."

There was a new power in Nathan's voice as well. It was a haunting and eerie tone that filled Caris with fear and wonder all at the same time. There were no more words spoken as Nathan charged forward, his fists coated in different layers of power. Caris, keeping up her high rate of speed, was able to dodge most of the attacks, sending her fists and feet into dazzling combinations of attacks and counters. The two remained locked in a totally drawn competition of who would miss first. Each strike with elbow, fist, knee, or foot flowed into the next, each taking only a moment to block and counter. It was Caris that scored first, a knee strike to Nathan's ribs. While any other mortal would have been floored by the impact, Nathan continued in his series of strikes, but was only met with empty air. Again and again the two flew at each other, trading blow and counters until finally Nathan struck true. His fist hit home in Caris' stomach, driving the wind out of her and forcing her to the ground. Nathan stood over the fallen phase, channeling his powers into his fists, making the energy more complete and lethal. However, Caris was not beaten. She kicked her legs hard and struck Nathan's knee, driving him off balance and crashing to the floor. Caris then wrapped herself in the powers of the Blaze and quickly transformed into her guise as a Wolf.

Nathan never saw what happened and then suddenly a hot breath was on his ankle. Pain struck him the next moment as sharp teeth sank into the tender flesh of his right calf, slicing through into the taught cord of his tendons. Tendon and muscle were severed with a single bite. His mobility nearly robbed from him, all Nathan could do was roll toward the Wolf and lash out. The beam of power that emerged singed a little of the Wolf's hair but forced it to release the hold on his leg. Blood dripped from the mouth of the Wolf, and Nathan waited, his eyes locked on the beast. It would go for his throat soon enough. The monstrous wolf glowed with Blaze fire, and slowly began to round its prey. Fighting the pain, Nathan had fought to a sitting position and was turning with the Wolf to keep it in plain view. The wound in his leg was healing slowly, but it was healing. In just a few more seconds he would be back to his feet and fighting. Nathan blinked and then suddenly there were two wolves. Nathan was struck dumb by the occurrence and that shock allowed both to leap at him at the same time. The jaws of one locked around his shoulder while the other went straight for his throat. Suddenly a beam of light shot across the throne room claiming the wolf in the chest. It yelped and fell to the ground. The other wolf disappeared, and when finally Nathan made it to his feet, he was looking down on Caris rather than the wounded wolf. Her dress was tattered and a huge burn dominated her chest. The blow had struck her in the heart, killing her instantly. Nathan turned to see his patron Emries looking at him.

"The time for these petty games is over. The forces of the Shadow have gathered for a final battle in the Council chambers and they have merely delayed you in an attempt to muster enough force to try to stop you. They must not succeed. You must kill Shau-ling and force the next generation of the prophecies to occur. You own family may stand in your way, but you must not lose sight of your goal."

Nathan nodded and stared coldly at Emries.

"I have no family. I am the Ram, the third *Coromor* of the prophecies, and I shall destroy Shau-ling and all who serve him."

Emries watched smiling as the boy created a portal and stepped through into the final battle that awaited him. Soon enough Emries would face his arch nemesis Shau-ling and once and for all he would prove that it was he and not the Creator that was the one true power on this world and every other in the Cosmos.

The Source

Creator's Calendar Year 1205; Light Reality

Jerrard pulled the polished black metal blade from the scabbard at his side and let the powers of the Blaze fill him. His father Basille had taught him well the meaning of the birthright that he had inherited. Though part of him despised the fact that he had an intimate link to people like Jeroch and Saurn, it also filled him with hope that the kinds of power that he had could be used for good rather than for evil. The sword was a constant reminder of that. Basille's sword was a symbol of power and respect in the Kingdom of Scalla, but also a reminder that with power comes responsibility to use that power in the best interests of the weak and the defenseless, not in the interests of the strong. For many years after the war between the Light and the Shadow ended, the world would remember the cruel and twisted nature of the phasia, how they ruled with an iron fist through fear and manipulation. They would always remember the Jeresei striking down the most defenseless people to cook on their spits late at night when they sang and screeched in those demonic voices, sending chills down even the bravest man's spine. So many images ran through Jerrard's mind as he prepared to cross swords with Jeroch, but none was more prominent than the execution of his father at the hands of Nightwing and Shau-ling. Basille had done what was right. He had been fighting for the right side, but just going about it the wrong way. Had he only had those last pieces of information before he interfered in the schemes of Saurn and spited Shau-ling. But all of that was the past, and the future would rest on the outcome of the battle that was about to be fought.

"I give you one final chance," Jeroch said drawing a blade from his scabbard, "if you surrender, I'll let your family go free. Then you and I will meet Shau-ling and you will swear your allegiance and beg forgiveness for your crimes against your family."

Jerrard's answer was to take hold of the green string in the back on his mind and fill himself with the sickeningly sweet power of the Blaze. Rather than keeping the power within him, Jerrard channeled the power into the polished blade, as his father had done so many times before, until it glowed with an eerie fury. Jeroch smiled to himself, inwardly taking pleasure in the skill of his adversary. For several moments, the two combatants stood motionless, staring at one another. Each knew that with the skill and tenacity of the other, this combat could be ended in a single pass. Jerrard, sensing hesitation in Jeroch charged forward. Though confident in his abilities, Jerrard did not know if he would be powerful enough to stand toe to toe with a full member of the phasia and survive. However, Jeroch was not just any member of the Brotherhood, he was the First of the Shadow, Shau-ling's personal champion. Jerrard's first strike came as a hard downward blow. The parry was quick and tight, and at the contact of the two blades, sparks of green fire erupted from the metal. The two, now in close proximity to one another, continued the duel at a slower pace, Jeroch thrusting and parrying while Jerrard countered and slashed with his blade. Now blows found their way through the defenses to the soft skin underneath, but the showers of sparks continued. After parrying another long slash from Jeroch, Jerrard spun through and lunged forward, the tip of his black sword speeding toward his adversary. However, Jeroch was a step faster, and Jerrard's blade found only the cloth of Jeroch's shirt. The ripping sound caused everyone in the vicinity to hold their breath, and as Jerrard stepped back he waited. When no blood fell from the area of the ripped shirt, Jerrard's heart sank. Jeroch on the other hand smiled widely.

"That was a very well timed strike, Jerrard," the much older man taunted. "Unfortunately you were not fast enough."

Jerrard smiled at the suggestion.

"Fast? Oh, I'll show you fast."

That instant Jerrard pulled harder on the sting of the Blaze in the back of his mind, filling his body. The cold fires penetrated his muscles, augmenting their strength, until Jerrard was capable of moving with speed and grace that would make a cheetah envious. Jeroch was not ready for Jerrard's next attack and was caught flat-footed as the child of his former enemy charged. While Jeroch was able to get his blade up in time to block any strike that would have come at him, no strike ever came. Jerrard instead leapt into the air, continuing through a full flip and twist until he landed behind Jeroch. Upon descent, Jerrard's blade arched downward slashing through the tender flesh of Jeroch's back, sending blood splattering in all directions. The First of the Shadow cried out in pain, but did not lose his footing. Jerrard had not thought Jeroch would have had enough strength for a counter attack, but the phase pivoted, bringing his blade around with great speed. With Jerrard's altered physiology, he was able to jump backwards, but the move only served to keep him from being cut in half by the blow. When he landed, he felt the blood gushing from the huge open wound in his stomach. The wound was not deep, but it would continue to bleed as though it were. Each stared at the other as their blood collected on the ground at their feet. Because of the speed that each had at their disposal, neither would take the few seconds to channel healing forces into the wounds. Even a second could mean the end of one of their lives. Suddenly a new power filled the area, one that both men knew all too well. It was the feeling of a portal forming very close to their location. The two men nodded to one another, silently agreeing to a break in the duel to attend to the intruder. It also gave each man a few moments to heal their wounds.

The portal opened near where Ellis and Jessica sat silently critiquing the duel between the two men. While both had felt the portal forming, neither viewed such a creation as a threat considering the forces gathered around them. When the female form stepped through however, a wide smile came to Ellis' face. While Caris was not her favorite member of the Brotherhood, the fact that she was still alive boded well for the forces of the Shadow. Caris looked around for a few moments and then shook her head and sighed.

"I knew you would be the ruination of my army, Jeroch," she said glaring at her former ally. "Of all places to fight a war. I thought you learned your lesson with Cedric Binosear."

Jeroch's blood boiled at the mention of the man's name. It had taken Jeroch nearly the entire second generation to make peace with the humiliation that he suffered at the hands of the Lion, and it was complicated by the fact that none of the other phasia would let him forget his mistake. The battle against the Lion was well in hand, and Jeroch was deeply embroiled in a duel with the so-called savior. The Lion had suffered several wounds, while Jeroch was unscathed. The end looked to be in sight. However, while circling one another, Jeroch's foot hit a small rock that caused him to lose his balance. Always the opportunistic fighter, Cedric launched his attack at that moment, severing Jeroch's head from his body and squashing the last visage of defense for Shau-ling.

"I would remind you, dear sister," Jeroch responded with venom, "that had it not been for your meddling, Cedric would have never stumbled on his destiny and we could have quietly exterminated him. But your greed and Basille's conscious ended up costing us all dearly."

Caris glared at Jeroch.

"My plan was working perfectly Jeroch, and you know it. I could have destroyed Cedric at any time, but I wanted to control him. You knew my plans, and you knew that I would take every opportunity to make sure that he was well in our control. Or had you forgotten that we planned the little coup together so that you could get your hands on your precious Marcwell?"

Jeroch frowned. He had forgotten. During the time that he was allied with Caris in their faux marriage, Caris had indeed mentioned her intentions to seduce and control Cedric Binosear. Jeroch of course wanted to turn the arrangement into an advantage for himself and so promised to help his ally in exchange for the throne of Marcwell. Once the agreement was struck, Jeroch used the Erdric to get information from the palace and then found the way to get Caris into Marcwell. While it was ultimately Basille who assisted Caris in the infiltration, it was Jeroch's plan.

CHAPTER 43

"Why are you here?" Jeroch retorted coldly. He had no time for Caris' game of trading blame. There were more important things to be tended to.

"I am resuming control of my army, Jeroch," she answered. "The Ranthall boy and his little group must be destroyed."

Jeroch fumed.

"This rabble who call themselves the Raven's Wing will be eliminated soon enough Caris. After I have dispatched Mystic here, you can pursue whatever personal vendettas you may have against the young Ranthall. But until I say otherwise, you gave your army to me to use as I see fit, remember?"

Caris' frown was all Jeroch needed in answer. Jeroch turned to face Jerrard but felt the familiar twinge of another portal forming.

"These interruptions will only save you for so long, Mystic."

Jerrard answered with a smirk and turned to face the new portal that was opening near his family. The two men that stepped out first brought a smile to Jerrard's face. It seemed as though fate was evening up the sides. Nathaniel and Gwillim Sandar were the best reinforcements that Jerrard could think of, short of the original People of the Dragon walking through that portal. Rachel, the only remaining female member of the Enforcers, and the woman named Susanne Praen emerged next. Last through the portal was Jared Vale. However, there was no time for words to be spoken, as all hell broke loose as soon as Jared set eyes on Caris. In Jared's mind there was no way that his mother could still be alive, and he would make sure that he rectified the problem immediately. Though Gwillim tried to hold the younger man back, he was not quick enough.

Jared darted forward, sword and scepter in hand, channeling the flows of the Blaze into a potent strike. Caris was not caught completely by surprise and she too filled herself with Blaze energy. The honorable duel to end the war had been shattered, and a cry went up from the ranks of the Jeresei. Jared's rash movement had incited the war to begin again, only this time there would be no simple end. The bolt of power launched from the end of Jared's scepter, speeding toward Caris. The woman dressed in green was quick, sidestepping the bolt of power, which streaked past her and claimed an unsuspecting Jeresei in the chest. After dodging, Caris extended both of her hands to the ground, causing the entire island to shake. Jared was momentarily knocked off-balance by the attack, and the delay was long enough for two large stone fists to form out of the ground to defend Caris. One of the hands reached out for Jared, but he was quick to step by the assault. Another bolt of power erupted from the scepter and sped toward the phase. The bolt struck Caris in the chest, but seemed to have no effect. Jared, angered by the turn of events lashed out with several more bolts of power. Each blow hit home, but not a single strike seemed to stun the phase. It was as though she were being protected somehow. One of the stone hands swatted at Jared again, but the young man ducked the blow and barreled into his mother, with the tip of his sword poised to strike her heart. The blow struck, however the tip shattered as soon as it had struck, and the release of power was enough to send Jared flying backwards. Caris had somehow coated herself with a diamond hard shell of earth that made her totally untouchable. However, Jared had other worries as he struggled back to his feet. The stone hands continued to swat at him, trying in vain to catch him in their fatal grip. Jared ducked and dodged through the assaults, but another rumble from the ground beneath him threw Jared off-balance and right into the firm grip of one of the hands. The grip tightened and squeezed, driving the life out of the boy. There was very little time left, as Jared could see sparkles of light in front of his eyes. It would only take a few more moments as the force of the grip squeezed the air out of his lungs and forced him to black out.

Caris took a step forward gloating over the kill. All it took was for her to contract her fist, and the boy that she had sired with Cedric Binosear would be destroyed once and for all. Jared had other ideas. Instead of lashing out at the hand, he was drawing Caris in, channeling all of the power that he had at his disposal into the scepter that was still clutched in his hand. The amount of power was dangerous, and if he blacked out before the process was completed, it would most likely kill him and not have the desired effect. All he needed was for Caris to come a little close. In the next seconds, Jared got his wish, but he was only barely holding on to consciousness. He had already lost his vision to the blackness, but his consciousness was not letting him fall into the slumber of death. He owed it to himself to do what needed to be done. When he heard his mother's voice so near to him, he smiled.

CHAPTER 43

"Say hello to your father for me," Caris remarked coldly.

"Tell him yourself."

Jared's reply preceded the release of power from his scepter. A shockwave of power erupted from the stone hand, shattering it instantly. The wave continued outward, ripping through Caris like a scythe through ripened wheat. When Jared hit the ground, his sight returned for a moment, long enough to see the dead, broken body of his mother lying before him. Pain hit the next moment, forcing a hard cough from his tortured lungs. Blood splattered from Jared's mouth, sending more waves of pain through his tortured body. It wasn't hard to imagine that several of his ribs were broken, and from the trouble he was having with drawing even the smallest breaths, he assumed that one if not both of his lungs had been punctured. Though he fought hard to stay awake, his eyes slowly closed, and the slowly over the next few seconds, all of the pain vanished as eternal slumber took hold.

* * * * * * * * * *

Valin and Zak surged forward with the remaining ranks of the Raven's Wing to try to fight off the hundreds of remaining Kalbraks and Jeresei. Both knew that it was a hopeless battle, but it was what they signed on for when they joined the Enforcers. They were merely mortal men, and while they did not stand a chance against full members of the phasia, they could buy time for the people meant to fight the Brotherhood. Rachel had wanted to join them in the fight, but in the last seconds before the charge, Zak had convinced Rachel to stay with Erika Mystic and protect her. As the two men leapt into the fray, they saw the flashes of power from Jared's staff as he fought with Caris. Valin was the first to make contact with the enemy line. His two axes hefted high, he waded into the enemy striking down anything that got in his path. One after another of the red skinned beasts fell under the might of his heavy blows, but the ranks around him were beginning to thin, and he was having to take on enemies from too many directions. As he turned to strike down a Jeresei that was threatening his flank, a clawed hand darted in from his left, opening five large cuts on his side. Valin did his best to ignore the pain, and turned to strike down the creature that had wounded him. However, when he turned, two Jeresei and a Kalbrak were waiting for him. One axe found the skull of one of the

Jeresei, while the other severed the head of the Kalbrak. Valin was not quick enough to take on the remaining Jeresei, and the beast darted forward, its long claws slashing at the exposed flesh of the large man's throat. His last breaths gurgled in the blood that rushed from the wounds, and Valin fell to the ground, his body another in the growing pile of corpses.

Zak was faring little better than the men in his unit. After watching Valin and Jared fall, Zak had circled his men and were fighting back to back against the growing tumult of opposition. However, every strike from the monsters created a scream of agony from one in the ranks. It would only be a matter of time before they were all killed. Zak was not one to give up easily. With a dagger in each hand, Zak climbed up a piece of a ruined building and starting hurling his daggers at any creature that was within striking distance. The accurate offence felled several of the beasts, but before long, Zak found himself surrounded on all sides. His last two daggers were clutched firmly in his hands when he leapt into the mass of red, slashing and striking at anything within range, trying his best to shut out the pain as nail after razor-sharp nail sliced through his body. Finally strength fled from him, and he fell to the ground, dead before his body stopped falling.

* * * * * * * * * * *

Storm saw the opportunity for glory and charged forward toward Ellis and the man and woman at her side. Taya knew that her brother stood little chance alone against the group and followed him. Gwillim had his own reasons for charging forward, but they had come from Nathaniel's realization that the boy at Ellis' side was the Wind *Erieal* of the third generation. However, Jared's rash action had made this unnecessary battle a reality. Ellis took her opportunity to strike at the threat she knew the best. Gwillim Sandar was a hero from the War of the Dragon, and she would use all of the powers at her disposal to make sure that he would not be remembered as a hero from the War of the Ram as well. A pure white beam of energy sped toward Gwillim, but he was quick enough to drop to the ground and let it pass over him. Drawing on the string of Earth in the back of his mind, Gwillim smashed his fist on the ground, sending a tremor toward Ellis. The rocking of the foundation beneath her caused the phase to stumble and gave Gwillim the opportunity to get back to his feet and continue his charge. Ellis continued her assault, throwing spikes of ice and crystals of Order in Gwillim's direction, but each was dodged in turn. Finally Gwillim was in range of the woman, and he wrapped his fists in diamond hard energy and swung as hard as he could at Ellis's jaw. The phase was quicker, a sword of ice appearing in her hand and slicing at Gwillim's throat. The blow didn't connect, and Gwillim stepped back away from the phase, a new respect for the power at her disposal. But, Ellis's strength was never in the arena of combat, and the next errant slash from the woman was more than proof of that. Gwillim on the other hand was well schooled, though the brutal tactics that he employed in the next moment were not technical by any means. Ellis' attack sailed wide, and Gwillim took the opportunity to step into the phase and strike with his fists to her midsection. The blow from the diamond enhanced fists forced Ellis to release her hold of the powers of the Blaze, thus causing the sword of ice to vanish. Gwillim could feel bones break under his fist, and as he struck again, the breaking sound was louder and deeper. Most of Ellis' ribs had been cracked with the two punches, and Gwillim reached up and took the phase by the throat and squeezed. The shock in her eyes seemed to quell something deep inside of Gwillim as he shattered her neck in a single squeeze. But as he looked over, he saw two more dead bodies, and a duel that could very well end in a third.

* * * * * * * * * * *

Nathaniel saw everything happening around him, and he knew that it was all wrong. Instead of fighting one another, they should have been pooling their resources and taking the fight to Emries who was the true enemy of everyone on the world. It was because of Emries that this fighting in Lakestone would eventually be pointless. There would be no more world to fight over. Something though was holding him back. He could feel the voice of Emries in the back of his mind telling him to not interfere in the battle that was taking place before him. All would be well if he would just leave everything alone. He looked around and watched as Jared and Caris both died in a single explosion of power. Valin and Zak had already been killed in the fight against the animalistic Jeresei. Ellis had been killed by Gwillim's brutal tactics, and now Storm and the man who was obviously the Wind *Erieal* were locked in a duel that would leave one of them dead if it were not stopped. Even Jerrard and Jeroch were fighting as though the entire war were going to be decided by this small battle, and still Nathaniel resisted the urge to make it all stop. It was only when he saw Taya fall that something within him snapped, and he knew it all had to end before there was no strength left to avert the fate that waited for all of them.

* * * * * * * * * * *

Taya found herself standing against a lean woman who stood calm even in the tumult of the battle around her. Storm had locked himself in a duel with the man who had ridden with Ellis, leaving this woman for Taya to handle. Though Taya had no reason to attack this young woman, something told her that there was more to her then met the eye.

"So," the young woman said looking at Taya, "they send a girl to deal with a child of the phasia?"

Taya's blood ran cold. If the girl was telling the truth, and she was a child of the phasia, Taya stood no chance against her. But she had to do what she could. Taya charged forward with sword ready, but a single flick of the girl's wrist sent Taya tumbling to the ground. It was then that Taya felt an anger well up in her like she had never felt before. Suddenly there was a fire in the back of her mind. A bright green glowing fire that her father had told her about so many times. It was the Blaze. The tie to Shau-ling's power was still very strong in the Mystic family, and though Taya was two generations removed from the man who she could have called grandfather, Basille, the ability to touch the Blaze was still hidden within her. She had never shown the aptitude before, but Jerrard has always said that it was only a matter of time before the need for her to touch such powers would present itself. Her father had always taught her that the basest emotions were what allowed people to draw on the powers within them, whether they were phasia, *Erieal*, the *Coromor* or just an ordinary person. It was one of the lessons that Pike had taught Jerrard long ago. Pike was a strong fighter, but it wasn't until he embraced hatred that he was truly powerful. Now Taya knew the truth of the lesson as well, and as soon as she clutched the fires of the Blaze within her mind, her body began to glow with power.

CHAPTER 43

Jessica saw the change come over the girl immediately and began to take the battle more seriously. Drawing on the limited teachings of her mother Ellis, Jessica began to fire bolt after bolt of ice at the fallen girl, only to watch in horror as they were turned away by unseen forces. The attacks were greeted with retaliation from Taya, as a stream of Blaze fire erupted from the girl's outstretched fingers. The attack was an obvious one from someone who had no experience with powers, as it was poorly aimed and poorly executed. Jessica laughed to herself as she got back to her feet, thinking she could pick off the girl in due time. Taya had other ideas. The attack with the full force of the Blaze had been an involuntary release. Taya had drawn too deeply, and as soon as the words of her father echoed in her mind about the dangers of the Blaze, she released the power. Now, she held a much smaller quantity, letting it fill her and sooth her with its seductive voice always begging for more to be drawn in. However, Taya would not listen, she knew the dangers and exhibited all the control she could.

Jessica shot another series of ice daggers at the girl, and watched as each was consumed by a shield of Blaze energy that appeared around her. The girl was simply using the Blaze, unable to break the green fires down into their primal elements, but Jessica was surprised at how effective the tactic was. Feeling she needed a greater advantage, Jessica opened herself up to the full forces of the Blaze, drawing deeply on the fires and letting them permeate every part of her being. The sweet voice sang in the back of her mind, begging her to draw deeper, to take all of the power at her disposal within her to smite her enemies. Jessica continued to draw, and did not hear the quiet warnings mentioned by her mother Ellis in passing. The mystery and sweetness of the Blaze was too much to resist. Taya watched as the girl drew more into her with every moment. Her body glowed with the power of the Blaze, but she was still drawing deeper. The very air around Jessica began to hum with the force of the Blaze, and a small breeze wrapped around her, lifting her hair up over her head. A moment later, Jessica's hair ignited, the white peaked flames of the Blaze consuming the strands and wreathing her head in a halo of power.

"Now," Jessica said in an inhuman voice, "you shall witness the true power of a child of the phasia."

Jessica pulled one last time on the Blaze, but suddenly the sweet voice changed. A horrible wail filled her mind, driving her senses crazy. More and more of the fires filled her, but the sweet sensation eroded, and a pain filled her unlike any she had ever felt before. Every fiber of Jessica's being sang with pain and the smell of burning flesh began to hit the air. Taya watched in horror as the woman was consumed from the inside out by the power of the Blaze until nothing was left but her ashes.

* * * * * * * * * * *

Out of the corner of his eye, Rand watched as his wife burned to a cinder. His duel with Storm had been escalating slowly, the stocky boy no match for his true skill, but good enough to avoid most of his strike thus far. But now rage filled Rand, and he slashed hard at Storm knocking the blade out of his hands and sending him sprawling to the ground. While Rand had no knowledge of the seductive nature of the Blaze, he was observant enough to know that it was the green fires that had claimed the life of the woman he loved. Only moments ago, he had seen the blond woman wielding that fire and using it as a weapon. It took only a moment for Rand to reach into the blackness of his mind and take hold of the string of Air. There was no defense from the attack, and in a heartbeat, all of the breath was ripped from Taya's lungs, and she fell to the ground, her eyes wide with shock. The death was more painless than Rand believed the murderer deserved, but it was fitting at least. Storm watched in horror as his sister fell silently into the waters that still flooded the streets of Lakestone. Storm felt the fury rise up within him, and he charged the young man who had just killed his sister.

* * * * * * * * * * *

Nathaniel watched Taya fall and finally the restraint snapped. Emries' voice faded away in his mind, and Nathaniel reached into the back of his mind and took hold of the primal string of Order and let it fill him to the fullest extent. A single bolt of power streaked from Nathaniel's hand the next moment and struck between Storm and Rand forcing them apart. The amount of power being employed by the boy also caused Jeroch to move away from Jerrard. Though he was a full member of the phasia and the First of the Shadow, Jeroch knew that he was no match for the *Coromor* at the height of his powers, especially with the amount of allies that were around him.

"That is enough, all of you. Jeroch, call off your army. You are completely outnumbered, and while I do not want to kill you, I will if you make me."

Jeroch could tell that there was something different about the boy. He could have struck Jeroch down in a heartbeat if he wanted to, instead of using that bolt of power to separate Storm and Rand, he could have just as easily have struck down Jeroch. With a thought, Jeroch ordered the Jeresei to stand down. Begrudgingly the creatures obeyed.

"I'm listening, *Coromor*," Jeroch said coldly.

Nathaniel let some of the power ease from his body and then locked his eyes back on the phase.

"You have no reason to believe me Jeroch, but I am on your side. Emries is the enemy and he needs to be destroyed. Great forces are gathering, and a battle for the fate of the world is about to be fought. It is critical that we get to Shau-ling in time to stop Emries from carrying out his plan."

Jeroch laughed.

"You expect me to take you before Shau-ling with that story?"

Jerrard lowered his sword and returned it to the scabbard.

"He's telling the truth, Jeroch," Jerrard said firmly. "There are things that have come to light that make this situation unavoidable. We know about Emries' manipulation of the bloodlines to bring about his own rebirth."

"We also know about the prophecies and why they came about," Nathaniel added. "And about Aryx."

Jeroch scowled. Some of the best guarded secrets of the phasia had fallen into the hands of the forces of the Light. Jeroch had an uneasy feeling in the pit of his stomach.

"I don't trust you," he said finally. "But some of the things you know you could not know if Shau-ling had not allowed it. I will take you to the Council. If this battle that you speak of does not happen, I assure you that you will meet the same fate as Aerith Seth when he was brought before my master."

Nathaniel nodded.

"You have my word, Jeroch. If there is no battle, I will be glad to lay down my life."

Jeroch frowned and created a portal.

Worlds Collide

Creator's Calendar Year 1205

Scalla stood quietly in the distance as Evan and Meredith sat watching the sun go down over the western expanse that held Lakestone and the battle that was no doubt being fought between the Army of the Wolf and the Raven's Wing. As Evan paced and found his eyes drawn to the colorful hues of the sky in the distance he wondered if Nathaniel and the others had been in time to stop any of the bloodshed or if they had stepped into another bloody slaughter. Meredith too seemed a bit on edge, but then she had never liked waiting for anything. Patience was not a virtue that any former member of the Enforcers had in any great abundance. There were other nagging thoughts that bothered Evan, the most prominent of which had been the death of the man that he had trusted and admired for so long. Pike Rhuiden had been a valued ally and a trusted friend from the moment Evan had met him, but after his passing, there was no remorse or sorrow. Something deep inside of him had told him it was for the best. Pike was a hero that had fallen to the darker natures that lurked inside of him, consumed by the guilt he could never admit to. It was as though the lines of fate had determined who would live and die, and now that the final grains were flowing through the hourglass on this world's life, it seemed all the more fitting that fate should start to reveal the truth.

As he looked up at the sky, Evan felt a strange power running through him. It was as though he could feel again the separation between the realities weakening, and then as his eyes moved even higher in the sky he witnessed an explosion of power unlike any he had ever seen in his life. A wave of brilliant and blinding light erupted from the center of the setting sun, sending ripples of red, orange and yellow through the sky. The entire sky was on fire with color and motion, explosions as bright as suns suddenly flaring and then extinguishing themselves in a matter of seconds. Thousands of stars burned through the haze of red and yellow, their bright white and blue shapes shining like beacons through the confused sky. The moon glowed impossibly bright with a greenish hue, and then the entire sky erupted again in a burst of red. When it all fell away, back into the blackness of night, not even the stars shown. The moon and sun were gone, and not even the far away stars could pierce the shroud of blackness that veiled the world. For the next few moments Evan stared at the sky bewildered, not understanding what he was feeling or seeing, and then being shocked back to reality by the rumbling beneath his feet.

The ground groaned as though it were being tormented by some powerful force. The groan grew in intensity until the land beneath Evan's feet began to quake and rumble. Thunderous explosions erupted from somewhere in the area, and Meredith pointed off to the east, and when Evan turned awe filled him. A pillar of fire had erupted into the sky, a fountain of hot magma from deep beneath the mines of Quea, Evan guessed.

"It's begun," a voice said from behind Evan.

When Evan turned, he saw the saddened face of the man who had given him everything, Aerith Seth. There were several wounds on the man's body, and it looked as though he had seen much combat in the few hours since their meeting. He had also picked up a companion in that time, a small black ball of fur that sat perched on his shoulder. As Evan looked at the strange little ball, he saw a small tail whipping around behind it, and then the memories of his predecessor filled in the details. The creature was a Snag, and Evan's shocked look prompted a smile from the older man.

"It would take too long to explain my little friend here, but I will say that we have learned to respect one another's abilities."

Evan nodded.

"But there is no time for any of that now. I know why you have come here, and what you have to report. The two realities have started to merge, and a final battle is shaping up in the Council chambers of the Brotherhood of Phasia. You will go there now. You are allowed to fight in this battle friends, but remember, the actions in that battle will determine if anyone will win this battle, or if we will all be consumed in the Creator's fires."

Evan nodded again and watched as Aerith turned to walk away.

"What about you?" Meredith asked. "Aren't you going to go with us, to see the final truth for yourself? That's what this was all about, wasn't it? Knowing the truth?"

Aerith turned back to face his very capable and loyal team. They had come so far in a short time, and it was a pity that he would not be able to see them reach the end of the story.

"I have done too much in this war as it is dear lady," Aerith answered smiling. "My powers are diminished to the point of non-existence, and I figure I have one more portal left in me before any use of power would be fatal. I'm just going to go somewhere and let the world fall down around me. And maybe, just maybe, I've earned a place in the Creator's new world if everything turns out the way it should."

Evan took a step forward.

"Bryn said . . ."

Aerith smiled and shook his head.

"I know, Evan, I know. Bryn is a good woman, but even her love for me could not break her loyalty to Grawn. As much as she hates him and as much as he does not appreciate her, the two of them are meant to be together. It's the bond bred into them as phasia."

Aerith could see Meredith frown.

"Don't worry my dear lady," Aerith said smiling. "There are always alternatives."

With that, Aerith turned and created a portal. Evan looked on for the last few seconds as Aerith stepped through and then disappeared. The empty portal hung in the air for a few seconds before collapsing in on itself, and ending Aerith's role in the war. Evan turned back to Meredith and tried his best to smile. He knew the grim work ahead and the bloody battle that would await them in the Council Chambers.

"Well," Evan said trying to smile, "I guess we should get going."

Meredith nodded and watched as Evan pulled a stone from his pocket. The forming process had become easy at this point, and seconds later, a portal swirled before them. Evan held Meredith's hand for a moment before reaching into his cloak and withdrawing a long golden sword. If there was any time for a sword named Justice, it was now. A deep breath later, the two entered the portal that would take them to their fate.

* * * * * * * * * * *

Sador bristled with a mix of excitement and fear as the members of the Order of the Sword welcomed their allies from the rogue army, the Swords of Alimidar. As per Midarin's instructions, Stone had helped the Order of the Sword to defend the palace, and though a few straggling Jeresei had returned from their hunting parties and put up a bit of a fight, there had been no invasions or significant losses. With the Swords in the city, there was no chance for anything but a fully outfitted army of Jeresei, Shadowwalkers, Stone, and Kalbraks to breach the defenses. However, when Stone alerted the one-armed Evan Sinn that there was a portal forming in the courtyard, everyone became a little nervous. As the swirling blue mass appeared on the ground, a huge explosion rocked the palace. Every soldier that did not have his eyes locked on the portal had turned to look skyward, as a fireworks display of godly proportions was taking place above. Most of the fears were allayed when Midarin stepped through the portal first, followed by Gideon and Taya. But there were more than a few anxious looks when the phase Bryn Aplee appeared. Sabrina was the last through the portal. Bryn looked up immediately and shook her head.

"It's time," she said coldly. "Even without my powers, I know that the two worlds have begun to merge and all of the players in this little game are being called in for the final battle. Every phase that still exists in this world and in the other will be making their way to the Council. They won't know why, but that is where they will feel they need to be. Even I feel that way, even without my string of power."

Midarin nodded and looked at the towering Stone who sat closely by.

"Stone," she said quickly, "I need you to tell Gideon how to get to the Council."

Stone shook his head.

"Stone, please."

Stone shook its head again.

"There's another way, Midarin," Bryn said softly.

Bryn walked over to the large creature and put her hand softly on its outstretched foot. There was a rumbling deep inside of the Stone, as though it recognized the touch.

"Open a portal back to the Source, Stone, it is time."

The massive creature nodded and raised its huge hand. After a moment a large blue portal sparked into existence.

"There are very few things that the Stone know for themselves, but one of those things is the command of the Breakage," Bryn said answering Midarin's puzzled look. "Every Stone is used in the creation of others like him, and when the time comes, he is to return to the location his making and be broken by Shau-ling. When this time has come, the Stone will use the little bit of power that it is gifted with to create a portal directly to the Council where it will await its death and rebirth. Since I do not have the power to open a portal myself, and since the location of the Council is not something that can be told to anyone, this was the only way."

Sabrina looked up at Bryn.

"Why can't the location be told?"

250 – EPHEMERAL TOMORROWS

"Because dear child," Bryn said smiling, "the Council is not a place that can be gotten to by walking or flying or swimming. It is not a physical place at all. It exists outside all realms of reality and time in the dimension where thought is the only medium."

The answer puzzled the young girl, but somehow she still understood.

"Let's go," Taya said as she turned toward the portal.

"Not you Taya," Gideon said firmly. "You have another errand to run."

Taya turned and looked at her father. The look was one of disbelief.

"Take your grandmother home to Barer."

Taya shook her head.

"Why don't you have Evan or Shim or one of the other's do it?"

Gideon walked over to his daughter and put his hands on her shoulders.

"This is battle is not yours to fight, Taya. All of us feel a pull to be there for the final battle, to try and save whatever we can. But you, you have another future ahead of you, one that I can't even begin to imagine. You have to feel it too."

Taya shook her head hard. Something inside of her was telling her that Gideon was right, that she was not supposed to be at the final battle, but she did not want to believe the voice. She had lost so much in the stupid war between the Light and the Shadow, her mother, her life, her home, her security. Now that it was all coming to an end, she wanted to see it though. However, that voice in the back of her head would not relent. It kept telling her that there was something greater waiting for her.

"Taya," Gideon insisted in his old accent, "ye know it's true."

Taya tried her best to stifle a laugh at the sound of the accented voice, but finally a smile cracked her lips and she nodded her head in accent. There was more to the war than just the battle that lay ahead, but no one was sure what that was. Bryn took a moment to hug Gideon and even shook hands with Midarin. Taya also hugged her father and then watched as Midarin, Gideon, and Sabrina stepped through the sparking portal into the great battle that lay ahead.

"I'm never going to see him again," Taya said as the portal closed.

"Don't worry my sweet child," Bryn said smiling, "never is a very long time."

Taya nodded and then reached deep into herself for the fires of the Blaze that lay buried behind the primal string of Air. She was still the granddaughter of a member of the phasia, and though the blood was tainted by the power of Emries, it was still hot within her veins. With a little coaching from Bryn, Taya was able to open a portal that led to a clearing just outside the palace of Sador, where a little farmhouse stood by a cliff.

* * * * * * * * * * *

Jeroch stood looking at the portal he created, inwardly cursing himself for making a deal with the *Coromor* and his band of travelers. The boy Rand was still alive though, giving Jeroch at least one ally on the other side of the portal. As Jeroch looked over the faces of the group, he felt a power well up inside of him. It was unlike any he had ever felt before, and it was almost as though part of himself was being pulled away. He reached for the two primal strings in the back of his mind and held onto them firmly, but it was no use. Over the next few painful seconds, the primal string of Order was ripped from his mind.

Jerrard stood watching as Jeroch fell to his knees and cried out in pain. Almost at the same time, an explosion rocketed through the ground beneath them, sending the island of Lakestone shifting and settling deeper under the cold waters of Exeter Lake. The sound of rushing waters filled his ears, and over the next seconds, waves of turbulent water crashed through the streets, claiming some of the Jeresei who were not smart enough to get out of the way. Storm was not one to watch while the waters flooded over his family, so he reached into the back of his mind, and took hold of the string of Water and channeled all of the power at his disposal. The flows of water started to divert away from the clustered group, but the untrained powers of the young man was not enough. Feeling the use of power, Nathaniel took hold of the strings of power in his mind and drew on the two members of the *Erieal* and on Jerrard to help Storm to divert the waters. Gwillim also lent a hand in the endeavor, creating large outcroppings of rock as a shield against the flowing waters. When the rumbling from the ground, and the shifting of the island finally ceased, Jeroch fought his way back to his feet, feeling incomplete and nearly powerless.

"By the light," Erika said looking up, "look at the sky."

When Jerrard turned his eyes skyward, he was not ready for the sight that would greet him. Every inch of the firmament above was littered with small explosions of color, all in the hues of the evening sunset. But the strange greenish glow of the moon and the bright white of the stars was what attracted the most of Jerrard's attention. There was an evil feeling from the moon, but after a flash of light and another explosion of color, all of the light and fire in the sky was gone. Not even the stars shone through the black sky. Jeroch was quick to channel some of his remaining power into a stack of ruined wood that lay by, making a small fire.

"The Breech has grown," Jeroch said absently.

"The time is getting close for the battle," Nathaniel added.

Jerrard turned to Erika and kissed her softly on the cheek.

"Go back to Scalla and make sure everyone is alright. Storm and I will go with the others to make sure that this battle ends it once and for all."

Erika smiled and nodded, knowing in her heart that her place was elsewhere.

"I shall accompany her to help in whatever way I can," the blind Galen said proudly. "The traditions of the Moridon must live on past this battle, and between Kaylea and myself, I believe that one day the Creator's will can be served by common men."

Jerrard shook the blind man's hand and then opened a portal back to the palace. Erika and Galen stepped through, but Jerrard let the portal linger in the air for a few moments, and turned back to the rest of the group.

"This is the last chance for anyone who does not want to fight in the battle that is ahead. Everything that we have ever fought for will be on the other side of this portal. My son and I have to go, as do Nathaniel and Gwillim. No one else here has any reason to fight."

Rachel looked up at Nathaniel and frowned.

"The Enforcers are dead, Lord Rhuiden is dead, Elizabeth is dead, and I have no home to go back to. The only way for me is forward, and if I die in the Council chambers, I will be doing it for what I believe in."

Susanne was the next to speak.

"Being with all of you taught me that revenge is never the right motivation for any action. Even though I was able to right the wrongs that were performed against me, I learned that there was an even greater injustice. The Torch was used, just as the Moridon was by Emries. I want a chance to make sure that it never happens to anyone ever again."

Rand moved over to Jeroch's side and helped to support some of his weight.

"I stand with Jeroch, and I will see this battle through as I have been taught to since my birth."

Jerrard nodded and let the portal behind him close. He then locked his eyes on Jeroch.

"Are you still able to fight old man?"

Jeroch scowled at the comment.

"Something has happened to this world. Perhaps you were telling the truth about your battle between the Light and the Shadow, but for some reason, I do not think you will be siding with Emries this time."

Gwillim crossed the distance and stood before Jeroch. The phase drew himself up to full height and pulled away from Rand's grasp. The two men stood eye to eye for a moment and then Gwillim spoke.

"The man who should have been my father was the one that ended your life in the last generation Jeroch, and while he was doing what he thought was right, he was fighting for the wrong side. I fight now to protect Shau-ling from Emries and the forces that would call him their patron. I have a feeling though that when the rest of your brothers show up in the Council, their petty jealousies and desires will side them with Emries rather than with you."

Jeroch nodded.

"I offer myself to you as a brother, friend, and comrade."

Gwillim extended his hand and waited. Jeroch looked down and then placed his hand firmly in Gwillim's.

"We'll fight and die together Sandar," Jeroch said coldly, "and protect Shau-ling at all costs."

Jeroch turned and stepped through the portal with Gwillim and Rand only a few paces behind him. Rachel and Susanne stepped through nearly together and Storm went through next leaving Nathaniel and Jerrard in the wasteland that had once been the rich city of Lakestone.

"How do you think it will end, Jerrard?"

Jerrard looked back up at the black sky and then shifted his gaze off to the distance, and watched as a pillar of flame shot into the sky near the mines of Quea.

"If any of us survive, I will be pleasantly surprised."

Jerrard considered the words he had spoken for a moment and then stepped through the portal. Nathaniel too considered the words. Through he was trying hard to ignore the thoughts and words of Emries that still echoed in the back of his mind, the boy wondered too if it was too late for anything to be done to prevent the total and final destruction of the entire human race. With a heavy heart, Nathaniel stepped through the portal, into the Council Chambers and into the future of man.

* * * * * * * * * * *

Gwydeon Sandar looked up at the dark sky and inwardly wondered how it was that things had gotten so far out of control. It had all been so simple those years ago when it was just him and his sword, training and working toward a destiny that he would have never dreamed possible. It had all started so innocently enough with a simple quest to find a treasure and return it to the great hero Cedric Binosear. But along the way there were phasia, Jeresei, Shadowwalkers, and Snags. There were the bar brawls and the Twin Towns, and the different lovers and loves lost. Gwydeon could still remember the stark whiteness of his room in Sador, and the horrific test of the gods on Mount Tantis. Everything seemed so clear in his mind. Once he was joined partially with the powers of the Creator, Gwydeon had been given the ability to see his life in the Light Reality as well, and became fascinated with the final moments of his life on that world. In all of his memories, he had lived through the battle with Jeroch and had been with Logan and Korrd when the final battle against Shau-ling took place. However, in the light reality, Rael had ended his life long before the duel with Jeroch, and though Gwydeon was responsible for getting the People of the Dragon in to fight Shau-ling, he died there in the center of the Hall of Terrors.

As another explosion rocked the earth, Gwydeon shook himself away from the thoughts of distant pasts. The time had come for the final confrontation with Emries and those that chose to fight with him. Part of Gwydeon did not care about the battle between Light and Shadow. All that he had left to do before he returned to the realm of the Creator was to finish his score with Draven. When Draven was dead, the rest would be in the hands of those who could still call themselves mortals. Softly, Gwydeon let his wings extend and catch the strong breeze that had begun to blow. It only took a few bats of his wings to lift him into the air. The feeling of exhilaration filled Gwydeon for those few moments of unfettered flight, but it was short-lived. Letting the powers of the Creator fill him, Gwydeon's wings glowed a bright white light, and then the Brother of Angels disappeared.

* * * * * * * * * * *

The lights in the Council chambers of the Brotherhood of Phasia sparked to life. The symbol on the floor of the chamber glowed with the powers of the Blaze, and the forms of the animals that represented each of the members of the phasia also glowed with the same powerful light. Halicon and Jeroch stood stoically in the chamber, feeling the power beginning to surge all around them. The two realities were beginning to merge, and before long the world would be devastated by all manner of disasters. Halicon sighed and shook his head, knowing there was nothing left he could do to prevent what was to come. Jeroch too felt the surges of power, but because he was not used to feeling the depth of power from the intimate connection with the Blaze, he could not have felt the pain and anguish from the world that was slowly tearing itself apart. What Jeroch did feel however was the forming of a portal near the very center of the chamber. Jeroch's first reaction was to fill himself with the force of the Blaze, but it was Halicon's steady gaze that kept Jeroch from lashing out at the mysterious visitors. When the portal opened, Jeroch tensed, and when the four mortals appeared, it did not calm his nerves.

"Welcome children." Halicon said warmly addressing the four new arrivals.

Wolf looked at the man who stood before them and did not know what to feel. Basille's voice in the back of his mind told him that the man he was looking at was indeed Shau-ling, but something was different about the man. He was more man than monster. Jeroch too seemed different, and his power was more complete and seated deeply in the Blaze.

"We brought Wolf as you asked," Eldar said drawing her sword.

Halicon nodded and smiled at the boy and the red-haired woman who stood beside him.

"I wished I could have spoken to you long before this point young Ranthall," Halicon said shaking his head, "then perhaps this would not have gotten this far down the path. I am afraid at this point that there is nothing else that can be done except to fight against the forces of Emries."

Pike reached down and pulled *Fury* from the loop in his belt.

"Then I guess we fight."

A small arrogant laugh came from the far side of the Council chambers. Everyone turned and watched as Emries stepped from the shadows.

"What an interesting scene we have here," Emries said stepping into full view. "You think that you stand a chance against me? You pitiful deluded fools. Right now everyone that remains in either world who has been blessed with power is on their way here. I assure you that after that battle is all said and done, the clear victor will be apparent. And that, I assure you, will be me."

Pike took a step forward.

"I say we take him out now."

Wolf took hold of Pike's axe and looked him in the eye.

"That won't solve anything Pike. It's not about him and it's not about Halicon. It's about the choices that the phasia and the mortals make now that everyone knows the truth. They are not this war anymore, we are."

Emries laughed as he watched Pike lower his axe.

"We shall see young Ranthall. Though I think I shall enjoy crushing the life out of you as I did you mother and father."

Wolf tensed, but found his attention drawn to the huge number of portals that were about to form in the Council Chambers.

"It's time," Halicon said looking at his brother and mortal enemy.

Emries could only smile, sensing victory well within his grasp.

Chapter XLIV

Ending Times

Creator's Calendar Year 1205

Wolf stood looking at Emries, a new rage building within him, but the time for settling grudges had not come yet, and he had to stand and watch patiently as portals opened throughout the room. All of the players had to be in attendance before any spark of conflict could bloom. This was not another skirmish, another act in the play that had stretched out over countless generations. This was the end of the story, the end of the conflict between Light and Shadow. In the end, there could be no loose ends, no forces retreating for battle another day. There had to be a clear victor, no matter the cost. The first few portals that opened spewed forth members of the phasia that still existed in the light reality. The first to step through was the short but still extremely powerful Warron. He took hold of the powers of the Blaze as soon as he saw Emries standing in the Council chambers, but as he looked across the room and saw the heroes Pike and Eldar and two other young people standing with his master Shau-ling, confusion set in. The feeling of confusion spread when Farax and Zarsi appeared. The three stood motionless for several moments, not knowing whether to attack or simply watch. However, as the seconds passed, the old hatreds and grudges began to build. Without knowing what was happening, the weight was descending upon the minds of the phasia, and they equally wanted to see both Emries and Shau-ling fall. Next into the room was the group of Gideon Viruci, Midarin Rice, and Sabrina Binosear from the Dark

Mirror reality. From where he stood, Zarsi could feel the power from the little girl and Warron knew the two heroes that stood before him rather well, but from every indication that he had ever had in the present lifetime, Gideon Viruci should have been long dead. The phasia knew about the two realities, but had not believed that the existence of this dystopian quagmire impacted them or their need to conquer the reality that they knew to be the true one.

Warron had been sitting peacefully in his kingdom, working on his plots and plans trying to figure out what steps to take next in order to stop the prophecies and take his revenge on all that had wronged him in the past. There were many old grudges, and the first of which was with the creature Nightwing, or more to the point with the man that had once been called White Lightning, Aryx Terian. Aryx was responsible for Warron's death in the previous generation, and he was also one of the instruments of Basille's banishment. Basille was the only member of the phasia that Warron had ever trusted, and the loss of his friend and comrade was a personal blow that would not heal for a very long time. That vendetta would have extended to Shau-ling as well, but there was something more, there was a reasoning that was not fully understood. Shau-ling had to have a reason for the banishment. But pulling the threads of greater hidden plans had never been Warron's strength. He had always chosen to rip through plots through force of arms or strength of will rather than manipulate around the edges like some of his contemporaries. He had been in the middle of dinner when Warron had seen the sky explode with fire, and he felt the burning sensation in the back of his mind where the primal string of power lay. Every fiber of his being was telling him to return to the Council, but he did not understand why. However, he could not disobey the instinct, one that was more powerful and compelling than the Call. As Warron looked at the faces of the other members of the Brotherhood in the room, he could see the same confusion.

More portals opened to reveal more of the remaining members of the phasia. Rael and Trece stepped through a portal together followed quickly by Saurn, Cash, Grimm, and the young and impetuous Rane. As soon as Rane's eyes found the face of the red-haired girl Lissa, she started to charge. Grimm however caught his ally in his arms holding her back. Though he was one of the newly born members of the Brotherhood, Grimm understood that there was more to what was about to come than simply another chance to settle old scores. The force that had driven all three of them together, Grimm, Cash, and Rane, to abandon their plans and return to the Council had to have some explanation. That explanation would not come if a battle started. Halicon smiled as he felt the thoughts of his youngest son, a pride filling him. It had been many generations, but perhaps he had finally started to get things right with his phasia. It was too bad that all of the advancement was about to be a moot point. But Halicon would never have chosen this conflict, not in any form, but his rebellious brother had made any type of peace impossible. It had to be war from the moment Emries set foot on this world, and the more Emries' machinations drove Onea to the brink of extermination, the more reckless the being that was Shau-ling was in the application of his power. His children had become monsters through his own complacency and his need to win. But now it seemed that winning was impossible, and only through that realization could his children find the redemption that had been denied to them by Halicon's pride.

The next portal to open revealed a large group, and one member in particular caused waves of concern and anger to pass through the members of the phasia that had already entered the Council Chambers. First to emerge was the Mystic family that everyone knew so well. Jerrard Mystic had been a thorn in the side of the phasia since his birth. However, the pattern of behavior that Basille had exhibited in his disobeying of Shau-ling's commandments would not end with his son, and would continue through each generation until it finally culminated with the creation of the mirror realities. Jerrard and Storm moved quickly across the chamber to stand with their old allies, the silent questions about the return of Pike Rhuiden and Eldar Merin left for another time. If they all survived there would be plenty of time for questions. Other questions filled both Storm and Jerrard when they saw a young woman who looked like Taya standing with another dead man Gideon Viruci. It was a family reunion of sorts, and though Jerrard knew better than most the ramifications of the merging of the two realities, the shock of the return of his old friend and the daughter that he saw fall only moments before was almost too much for his fragile psyche. Perhaps Storm had the better of things not knowing the secrets that his grandfather had been keeping for so long.

The next two into the room were Rachel Core and Susanne Praen. As the two mortals stepped into the tumult, they immediately felt completely out of place. It was as though they were two grains of sand in a hurricane. But Rachel took solace in the fact that mortals had stood against the kinds of forces that were arrayed before them in the past, and if they could survive and even triumph, perhaps all was not lost. Susanne Praen on the other hand could do nothing but tremble. Her need for revenge had been sated, and all that was left to her was duty, but fear was quickly winning out over it. Gwillim Sandar and his half-brother Nathaniel Rice were the next into the room, and the boy's appearance was almost enough to ignite the powder keg of conflict that was building. Warron in particular had to hold himself back from lashing out at the boy, knowing his powers as the third *Coromor* of the prophecies were dangerous to say the least. Gwillim's glance found Grimm quickly, and the desire to test his strength against the large man and renew their conflict was very strong within him. Nathaniel on the other had did not look for combat but rather fixed his gaze on Emries and tried hard to fight the conflicting voices in the back of his mind that told him to strike at Shau-ling and end the battle quickly. However, there were so many distractions in the room, Nathaniel's control was being tested. If he slipped, everything could have been lost.

When the Light reality Jeroch and Rand appeared in the room, there were more than just a few shocked gasps. While every member of the phasia, and most of the forces of the Light had some understanding of the Breech and the two realities, very few of them had actually seen anyone from the other reality until this point. However, none of them, save those who were in the clearing and watched the different Pikes face off against one another, had ever seen the same person from different realities at the same time. Warron in particular felt his heart in his throat as he watched the two Jerochs eye one another. One of them had been bad enough for generations of war, but two was more than Warron could stand. The mirror images stood staring at one another, each taking an inner pleasure in the sight. Few doppelgangers had lived long enough to face one another, and it should be fitting that the one member of the Brotherhood of phasia that held two of the primal strings should meet. However, while the Dark Mirror Jeroch knew the truth about the conflict and the intentions of those he had once called enemies, the Light reality Jeroch was still only the loyal son of a mad god. If that loyal son could not be made to see the truth, would he betray his father and his duplicate and stand behind Emries in the battle to come?

Taron and Stryfe were the next phasia into the room. As Taron looked across the room he locked his eyes on Pike Rhuiden. The smile came to Taron's face for only a moment, and then was wiped away when he realized that he was not looking at the same man he had fought only days earlier in the city of Lakestone. This Pike was younger, looking almost as he had in the previous lifetime when they had battled in both Taren and Dreamscape. Perhaps this Pike would put up more of a challenge than the old and broken man who had been so easily manipulated into a trap. Stryfe eyed the girl Rachel, remembering her from the battle in Lakestone as one of Pike's Enforcers. He smiled to himself knowing that he would get a chance when all was said and done to avenge the humiliation that he suffered at the hands of the pathetic mortals who had stupidly chosen to follow Lord Rhuiden.

Four portals opened simultaneously in the room, and when the five people stepped through at nearly the same time, only the barest shreds of self-control kept them from flying across the room and attempting to destroy one another. Evan Sinn and Meredith Heron were the first to have their feet hit the floor of the Council Chambers, and since Aerith had taken off the restriction to fight, Evan wanted his shot at Emries more than he could imagine possible. But when Gwydeon Sandar, the phase Draven, and Nathan Sandar appeared at the same time, the tension could be felt through everyone in the room. Warron knew the face of the man who had once worn the name Gwydeon Sandar, and so did Jeroch. The Jeroch from the Light reality fumed when he saw the winged man, but somehow he realized that it was not the same man who had killed him over twenty years prior. This Gwydeon was different; stronger, and singularly focused, and there was a bloodlust that Jeroch didn't think was possible for the gentle man to possess. The wings and power were secondary in Jeroch's estimation. He knew where that power came from, but it was the change in Gwydeon's nature that was most remarkable. Gwydeon did not pay attention to anyone except his black clad prey, Draven Batoe. The thin newcomer was a complete mystery to everyone in the room who was not native to the Dark Mirror reality. Warron could feel the power of the Blaze flowing through the man, but the attachment was much like that in a member of the phasia.

However, there were no other new phasia. When Warron probed deeper, he could feel differences in him. It was as though this new creature was not from their world. But deeper at the core there was something familiar about the root powers. The primal string of power within the man was identical to the one that Basille had held. That was when Warron guess the truth. In the Dark Mirror reality, Shau-ling had been able to use Basille's primal string of power to create another phasia, and that phase was the man that stood staring back at the winged Gwydeon Sandar. However, it was Nathan Sandar that drew the most attention. Now there were two *Coromors* besides Emries in the room, an incredible danger for all involved. As the last portal closed in the room, Emries looked quickly around the room and then spoke.

"It is good that all of the pieces have finally been assembled. The game can begin. Now we shall see who is truly the stronger."

Warron turned to face Emries and his cold hard stare pierced the man.

"I am not a pawn in some game Emries," Warron grumbled. "There are more than enough phasia left to strike you down and all of your little puppets here."

"And by my count Pig," Nathan countered, "there is one of each of the *Erieal*, a *Chosen One*, a *Coromor*, and more than enough of the phasia. The forces of the Light now have the ability to banish Shau-ling forever."

Evan sighed and shook his head. Everything had been brought to balance. Each force, the Light and the Shadow, had the ability to destroy the other once and for all. However, should either of them succeed, the Creator would destroy everything. The only way for the truth to be known and the Creator's will to be done was for neither to succeed in ultimate victory. This is what Aerith had been trying to discover, this was what his influence was pushing both of the Sabrinas as well as the Dark Mirror's Logan Ranthall too. Logan had been the first, he had broken the wall between Light and Shadow, had found a path to the truth and led several of the phasia along with him. But Emries was smart, that was why he had targeted Logan for extinction in the Light Reality, and why Nathan Sandar had turned on him in the Dark Mirror. When Wolf had started to open Sabrina's eyes in the Light reality, she had been destroyed, and it was only through a great deal of fortune and misfortune that the other Sabrina still stood. Evan would be fighting an uphill battle to find allies in the coming conflict, as the armies of Light and Shadow seemed intent to throw themselves at one another until there was nothing left of either of them.

"Stand with me champions of the Light," Nathan continued, "and strike down the forces of darkness."

Nathaniel stepped forward and stood face to face with his mirror image from the alternate reality. As Gwydeon and Midarin looked on at the two young men who were by all rights their children, for a moment neither could tell them apart. It was only when the cruel smile appeared on Nathan's lips that Midarin knew for sure.

"You follow a false god," Nathaniel said in a clear voice. "Emries has lied from the first moment that he set foot on this world. He has manipulated and schemed so that he could take hold of the Blaze and save his precious human race. The Creator knows his sins, and if you continue to use the powers that Emries granted you, then you will stricken down just as surely as he will be. This battle is not about some ancient slight, it's about greed and pride. Emries must fail, or there will be nothing left of us."

"Harsh words, *Coromor*," Emries said smiling, "but do you not feel it within you that the world will end if the evil of Shau-ling is not ended forever. Even his own children wish to strike him down. Isn't that right Saurn? You phasia have been plotting for generations to overthrow your master and take the war down your own road. Did not your own siblings give the world the tools necessary to end your servitude? Did you not yourself stand with the *Coromor* of the last generation and intend to end the life of your master? You need do nothing now to make that a reality. Simply stand aside and let the forces of the Light do what they came to do, and then you can go on squabbling amongst yourselves for eternity."

Saurn stepped forward and drew his sword. The viper etched in the blade glowed in the white light for a moment as Saurn pointed the tip at Emries.

"Do you think we are stupid, Emries?" Saurn asked. "If you succeed in killing Shau-ling, then all of our lives are forfeit. We must destroy him for our fates to be protected. We must be the masters of our own destiny. Would you hesitate to strike us down when the opportunity afforded itself? Once you dispatch Shau-ling, your blade will fall to us. No, the Master of the Shadow will fall by my hand, and then I shall set my fangs upon you and rid this world of all of the false gods."

Jeroch stepped away from his master Halicon and walked toward his mirror image from the Light reality. The two men stood together and then the Dark Mirror Jeroch extended his hand. For some reason, the Light Jeroch felt compelled to do the same. Halicon could feel the power growing between the two. Each half was incomplete. Jeroch had been the only member of the phasia to be blessed with two primal strings of power, though that had not been the case at Jeroch's birth. That had been a burden placed upon him at the time of Aryx Terian's exile. Perhaps that had been predestined as well, and everything had led to this moment. Once the worlds merged, an imbalance was created in the core of power because there were two creatures who carried the title and powers of the First of the Shadow. Though the Jeroch from the Dark Mirror reality was no longer a true phase, his powers still were tied to the Blaze. As the worlds had merged the Light Jeroch had felt the emptiness inside of him as one of his strings had been pulled away, an effort by the Blaze to balance the power. However, without that second string, Jeroch was not complete. Power flared again between the two men, and a white light grew around their joined hands. As the light grew in intensity, so too did it grow in size. Finally the intense white light grew to cover both of the men, and everyone in the room had to shield their eyes, but still tried hard to watch what was going on within the barrier of light. Emries and Shau-ling could both see the forms of the two men become blurred by the light, and then when the light pulsed brightly once again, the two forms had disappeared completely. And then, just as suddenly as the brilliant and forceful illumination had appeared it was gone, and only one Jeroch stood. However, this man was filled to the brim with power, and it was a power that was finally complete.

"The Breech is no longer," Jeroch said. "The two worlds have become one. There are no more lines and no more barriers. No more Light and no more Shadow. It falls to us now to settle the grudges and vendettas that have held between us for too long. Emries and Halicon are the past, the phasia are dead, and the future looks bleak. Whosoever walks away from this battle will write the future. May the Creator have mercy on us all should Emries be the victor."

Emries smiled.

"That sounds like a challenge, Jeroch."

"Call it what you wish," Jeroch countered. "But I vow that when all is done, while I may lay dead, you shall also."

"And so it begins," Emries called and raised his crystalline blade.

Hubris Bleeds

Creator's Calendar Year 1205

Gwydeon did not wait long after Emries' challenge to charge across the room to where Draven stood waiting. The crystalline blade filled with the Creator's power sprang into Gwydeon's hands in a matter of seconds, and to the phase's credit, his sword of Chaos formed in his hand milliseconds before the first blow came raining down upon him. Had it been any other phase, the first blow would have been the last. However, Draven had anticipated the attack, but all the anticipation in the world could not have prepared him for the speed at which Gwydeon moved. The pure crystalline blade streaked in again and again, and Draven found himself dodging more of the blows than he parried. The strength of the former man was amazing, and it seemed that he had gotten stronger since the last time their blades had met. Any trepidation that came from the new powers of the Brother of Angels was gone, and Gwydeon was in full control. That meant that while Draven could not match the former man in strength, he would have to defeat him through guile and precision. Gwydeon was relying too much on his new found power, and not enough on the skill that had made the other members of the phasia quake with fear.

Explosions and streaks of power erupted around the men as others in the room began their own personal battles. Draven drew deep on the powers of the Blaze and found himself emboldened by the close proximity to the source of the Blaze. Gwydeon could feel the increase in power in his opponent, and as their blades met, there was a stalemate. The two men poured all of their strength into the cross of blades, trying to gain an advantage, but thanks to the Blaze, Draven was able to keep eye to eye with Gwydeon. However, the phase had not factored in the possibility that Gwydeon was not using his powers to their fullest potential, so when he felt the leverage battle move to his advantage, arrogance flowed through him once again. Gwydeon though was not relenting, just switching the leverage for a moment so that he could push forward with all of the strength and power at his disposal. The forward push from the Brother of Angels took Draven completely by surprise and sent him sliding across the floor of the Council chambers. Gwydeon flew across the distance, the point of the crystalline blade poised for a hard downward strike. The strike only connected with the polished white floor as Draven used his altered speed to roll out of the way. Draven continued through the roll, popping up to a knee and slashing quickly at the knees of his opponent. Reacting to the threat, Gwydeon's wings batted against the growing winds in the room, lifting him into the air and out of the way of the strike. Currents conflicted in the room, sending Gwydeon floating backwards, and when he landed, he was several feet from Draven and from where his sword was still stuck in the ground. Draven smiled at the small accomplishment, but the smile was wiped away as Gwydeon extended his hand. The sword disappeared from where it stood piercing the floor and then reappeared in Gwydeon's outstretched palm. A sly smile crept onto Gwydeon's lips as he raised the blade of his sword and prepared for another charge. That was when he heard a scream from across the room.

* * * * * * * * * * * *

Taron and Stryfe approached together, and Pike and Eldar found themselves joined by the woman they both knew as Rachel Core. Though it was not the same Rachel that Pike had bristled with during the ill-fated insurgence into the palace of Trelon in the Dark Mirror Reality, he was sure that the woman was still very tenacious and worth her own weight in a fight. There was a palpable hatred that bounded between the five people, most of which was centered between Pike and Taron. Eldar too had her own score to settle with Taron, but it was Pike's hatred of the phase that had helped to keep him alive for so long underneath the Island of Mist. Taron's aura flared almost immediately, the strong red glow coating his entire body. Pike twirled *Fury* in his hands and then launched himself forward in a charge. The blade of *Fury* streaked toward Taron's chest, but the phase caught the haft of the axe and swung with his other fist. The blow would have surely crushed Pike's skull, but Eldar was fast enough to dart in with her blade and cut the phase's side. Taron reacted to the pain, releasing the axe and then swinging wildly at Eldar. Taron was no match for the team of Pike and Eldar, and as soon as Taron shifted his attention to Eldar, Pike charged forward and buried the blade of *Fury* into Taron's chest. The red aura around Taron flared for a moment and then shattered giving Eldar the opportunity that she needed to streak through Taron's remaining defenses and slice the tender flesh of his throat. The strike was quick and painless, but Pike was not content to let the final strike be that merciful. *Fury* raised high again and then sped downward, severing skin and muscle, shattering the hard bone of the thick spinal column. When the strike was complete, Taron's head fell from his mammoth body, rolling across the floor.

Rachel's battle with Stryfe did not move as smoothly, as the phase was far too much for the mortal, no matter what her motivations. Every strike with her sword was met with a shower of sparks from Stryfe's charged armor. Lightning launched from the chest plate and flew past Rachel's head, prompting her to be more cautious with every strike. Instinct told Rachel to go for the throat, but every attempt was easily dodged. Stryfe had yet to draw his blade, but when Rachel's sword clattered against his armor once again, Stryfe began to take the battle more seriously, removing the hilt of a sword from his belt. The blade of lightning sparked to existence the next moment, flaring in the flickering light of the chamber. Rachel took several steps back and then charged forward again. When the lightning blade darted downward to parry the blow, Rachel was unprepared for the shock that flooded her body. It was like every nerve was on fire, and pain rocketed from the tips of her toes all the way to the ends of her hair. Stepping back, Rachel lifted her blade meekly. Stryfe had totally destroyed all of her defenses and all she could do was try to parry until she had regained her composure. However, Stryfe had other plans. His slash was quick and concise, and though Rachel extended her blade and tried to parry, the lightning blade passed through the cold metal, and struck true. Shock filled Rachel's body as the last bits of her life fled in a shower of sparks. Stryfe was not able to enjoy his victory long as he turned and was immediately face by both Pike and Eldar who were still fresh after dispatching Taron.

Eldar dashed in first, the point of her blade obviously seeking for the phase's throat. There was no time for Stryfe to parry the blow, and so he chose to sidestep, but his motion brought him exactly where Pike wanted him. *Fury* swung low, aiming just at the level of the knees. The blow connected, slashing though all of the tendons that connected behind the knee bringing cries of pain from the throat of the phase. Stryfe crumbled to the ground, all mobility robbed from him in a single strike. It only took a matter of moments for Eldar to thrust the point of her blade down through the throat of the fallen enemy. As Pike looked around the room he found what he wanted. Emries was still locked in combat, but Pike would be happy to interject himself. With Eldar in tow, Pike moved toward the only duel that mattered.

* * * * * * * * * * * *

Jeroch took several steps toward Emries but found his path cut off by a familiar face. Saurn's eyes glowed violet, and his intentions were clear enough in his raised sword. It took only a thought for Jeroch to form the twin blades of Order and Chaos in his hands, and though he wanted to destroy Saurn, the need to cross blades with Emries was still compelling him. This was a battle that was unnecessary. No matter what their motivations, Saurn and Jeroch should have been allies in the defeat of Emries. Whatever came after would not matter if the mad god lived. However, madness had long since shifted from Saurn's ally to his master. The wildness in his eyes was unmistakable, and the in the violent tumult of violet was only murder and need.

"You are not worth my attention, Saurn," Jeroch chided, "now stand aside."

Saurn shook his head and smiled wickedly.

"When this battle is over and Shau-ling lay dead, there will be a clear victor. I am invoking the right of challenge for the head of the Brotherhood of Phasia. You cannot deny this challenge, Jeroch. If you walk away, you must be struck down, you know that as well as I do."

Jeroch growled. Rules meant nothing here. There was no Battle for Ascension. There was not even a Brotherhood any longer. There was only life and death. But Saurn was so far gone that he was a puppet of his thwarted ambition.

"You are a fool Saurn. This battle is not about ascension, it's about the fate of the entire world. You can have the head of the Council if it matters that much to you, now stand aside!"

Jeroch pushed the man away, but Saurn lashed out with his blade. Jeroch was quick to parry and return the strike, but found himself embroiled in the battle that he did not want to fight. Saurn was too worried about something that would not come to pass if Emries and his champions were allowed to be the victors, but he was blinded by ambition and the trap that he laid for himself with hatred and plotting. Jeroch had no choice, and as the two locked blades again, Jeroch opened his mind and let the sweet powers of the Blaze fill him. Before joining with his other self, Saurn might have had a chance to defeat Jeroch, but now that he was fully open to the limitless powers of the Blaze, the battle was over long before it started. Each of Saurn's attempted strikes were blocked and countered, and when the younger phase grew frustrated, he reached for the Blaze and channeled streams of Fire at his opponent. Jeroch released the swords and extended his hand, letting a beam of pure Blaze energy erupt. The fire and Blaze struck, creating an explosion of light and color. However, Saurn could not have expected what would happen next. The stream of Blaze launched through the smoke and fire, speeding toward Saurn's chest. The mad phase could do nothing, and the fire burned through the violet robes sending a cry of pain echoing through the room. Saurn's lifeless body fell to the floor, a hole burned through its chest. Jeroch did not even watch the body fall as he turned all of his attention back to Emries. The weak would be purged, that much was clear, but none of it would matter if Jeroch failed.

* * * * * * * * * * * *

Wolf could feel Basille screaming in the back of his mind as he stood toe to toe with Emries. Everything was telling him that there was no way he stood a chance at winning, but he had to try. With sword in hand he stood before the self-proclaimed Creator and waited. Emries looked down at the boy and smiled. There was a mocking and a conceit in the smile, and something about it ignited the fires of hatred in Wolf. All that the boy could see was his father impaled on the end of Emries' sword, slowly dying for a cause that he believed in more than life itself. Logan had given up his mortal life to become a phase. He had chosen to walk the path of the Shadow. It may not have been the right path, but it was the right path for Logan. How many more innocents had Emries driven to fates that could have been avoided? How many thousands of lives were shattered by his whims? How much suffering could have been prevented if he had simply given the Creator's laws to humans as the Creator had intended? Emries' arrogance was about to sentence and entire world to death, and he was still trying to win. Emries raised the crystalline blade and smiled wider.

"I had such high hopes for you boy," the god mocked, "but now you are just another puppet that needs to have its strings cut."

Wolf raised his blade and felt the powers of the Blaze rush through him.

"And to think that you would have been reborn from my bloodline. It makes me sick."

The sly grin turned to a look of pure rage, and Emries slashed downward hard. The crystalline blade struck the flat of the blade of Wolf's sword, sending a shiver of power running through both men. The force of the blow drove Wolf down to one knee, but the god was not content with that. He kept hammering down over and over at the boy, who held his blade firmly in both hands trying hard to defend his life. One of the hard downward blows from Emries' sword was greeted with the sound of shattering metal, and Wolf dove and rolled out of the way as his blade had been broken in two. Shards of steel protruded from a wound in the boy's shoulder, but as he looked up at Emries, he knew that he should be glad to be alive. Wolf's hand shot forward, and disks of pure Chaos sped from his outstretched fingers. Emries was quick to counter, sending daggers of Order to pierce each of the disks. Wolf, beginning to get frustrated channeled all of his power into a single disk of Chaos. The disk lurched across the short distance, but Emries held his ground. When the attack was upon him, Emries swatted the disk away, sending it hurtling toward the wall of the Council chambers. When it struck, an explosion rocked the entire room, sending many of the combatants off-balance. This gave others the time to interject into the battle.

Emries barely saw the glint of steel as it sped downward toward his head. It took the merest flows of wind to redirect the strike and send Pike Rhuiden sailing past his target. Eldar helped Wolf to his feet and then the three of them stood face Emries, ready for the duel to start again.

* * * * * * * * * * * *

Nathan and Nathaniel stood looking at one another, staring into one another's eyes. Each one knew what the other was capable off, and though they originally had the same mission, they had taken different paths along the way. Nathan could feel the powers of the members of the *Erieal* and phasia all around him, and he opened himself up to those powers immediately. He could also feel the power of the patron Emries fill him to the point that he thought he would burst. Nathaniel stood looking at his counterpart, feeling all of the power flowing through him, and he also could hear the voice of Emries in the back of his mind, telling him to unite with his mirror image to vanquish Shau-ling.

"This is the way to win the war once and for all," Nathan said. "And nothing will stand in my way, not even you."

Nathaniel swallowed hard.

"I will not fight you. This is not the way to victory, it is only the way to destruction. Strike me down if you must, but you will not get me to join you in this empty battle."

Nathan smiled.

"So be it."

The young man raised his sword and prepared to strike his mirror image down, but the banished princess turned queen intervened. Midarin swooped in, blocking the blow that would have ended Nathaniel's life. Nathan's face filled with anger, and when he spoke, the hatred carried in his voice.

"I told you once before mother that I would not hesitate to kill you if you got in my way."

Midarin raised her sword again.

"You are fighting on the wrong side of this war, Nathan, and you are too far gone to be brought back. "

"Spare me the speeches, Midarin," Nathan retorted.

The slash of Nathan's blade was quick and precise. It was the move of a blade master, and it would have taken one of equal skill to block the attack. Midarin however had devoted her time and attention to the bow, and her knowledge of the sword, while better than most, was not at a good enough level to prevent the blade of her son's sword from opening a huge slash in her side. Midarin fell to the ground after a short half-stifled scream, blood pouring freely from the wound. Had it not been for the stream of fire that leapt from Nathaniel's fingers, Nathan would have finished off his mother with a hard downward slash. The searing flames were enough to cause the young man to jump backwards, but his response to the assault was brutal. Shards of ice rocketed from his palms, speeding toward Nathaniel. The *Coromor* was able to mount a defense for a moment, and then suddenly something reached into his mind and eclipsed the strings of power that dwelled there. Before all of his powers were totally removed, Nathaniel thought he could see Emries removing the mantle that he had been given. Because he would not listen to the voices in the back of his mind, Nathaniel had been betrayed by the man that had called himself the patron of all humans. With no shield to protect him, the shards of ice ripped through the tender flesh of the boy, until Nathaniel was reduced to nothing more than a bloody mess. Nathan laughed to himself and approached Midarin, ready to end her life as well. However a flash of white crossed Nathan's vision, and he found himself staring at the winged form of the Brother of Angels, Gwydeon Sandar and his crystalline blade.

* * * * * * * * * * * *

Lissa felt the hatred swell within her when Rane and Cash charged. With Susanne by her side, the two women waited patiently for their chances to make their presence felt in this pivotal battle. Rane struck quickly, streams of fire racing toward her opponent. Lissa reached for the string of Fire in her mind and sent fires of her own back toward the phase. For several moments, the two traded blows while Cash continued to charge.

Susanne darted forward with dagger drawn, and locked herself in the deadly dance with Cash. Sword and dagger struck one another time and time again as bolts of fire and lightning were traded between Lissa and Rane. Susanne was fast, almost faster than the phase Cash, and the phase's inexperience with the powers that were at her disposal were helping Susanne to stay in the fight. However, Cash was very strong. After a hard slash, Susanne found herself staggered, but Cash was not quick enough to follow up and end the battle. Susanne quickly recovered her feet and her balance and darted forward at the phase. A quick stab with her dagger struck true in the stomach of the phase, but Cash was not prepared to curl up and die. With her off hand, Cash shoved the mortal away and thrust her blade forward, impaling the woman on it. Susanne choked on her own blood as Cash pulled her blade free and left the woman to die.

Lissa and Rane continued to trade blows, but it was when Lissa caught the gleam of silver out of the corner of her eye that she dropped to the ground and drew her sword. Cash had been quick to vanquish Susanne, and now it was going to be two against one. Lissa knew that her chances were slim of getting out of the confrontation alive. Cash swung down at the prone woman, but Lissa was quick to return to her feet. The two women locked blades, but Lissa found that Rane was perfectly content to throw more streams of fire at them, not caring that she might hit her own sister. Strike after strike, Cash and Lissa felt and heard their blades collide while the searing heat and chilling cold of Rane's attacks sailed by, mere inches from their target. As the two fought, Lissa saw her opening. Even though Cash was stronger, Lissa parried a downward slash with one hand, opting to use the other to grab hold of Susanne's dagger that was still logged in the phase's stomach. Using the leverage of the dagger, Lissa steered the larger woman into the path of one of the fiery bursts that Rane was continually sending in their direction. The burst of fire struck true in Cash's back, burning through the skin, killing her instantly. As the fire burst through Cash's chest, Lissa pulled the dagger out of the woman's stomach, rolled across the ground, popped up to a knee and then sent the dagger hurtling toward Rane. The phase, though surprised, was still able to block the blow. However, Lissa had not intended the dagger to be the instrument of Rane's death, rather it was to be a distraction. Even as Rane knocked the dagger away and turned her attention back to Lissa, she was barely in time to see the bolt of white lightning cross the distance. Rane was unable to react, and the bolt struck true, electrocuting the woman. Sparks and black wisps of smoke leapt up around Rane's body and as she fell to the ground.

"That's for my father," Lissa said as she looked around for Wolf.

* * * * * * * * * * * *

Grimm smiled in spite of himself as he raised his double-bladed battle axe and waited for Gwillim to make his move. From their previous meeting in Frontier, Gwillim knew that the man was extremely powerful, and the slightest misstep would mean the end of his life. Nearby, Gideon and Warron measured each other, old grudges from a previous lifetime taking control over the moment. Gideon's daggers were drawn and he was ready for combat. In just a matter of moments, Warron began to make his body as hard as a boulder, but Gideon countered, making his knives diamond hard. Seeing all of the uses of the string of the Earth gave Gwillim an idea, and he channeled his powers into his sword, making it as hard as a diamond. Grimm smirked to himself, for he too could see the uses of the string of Earth. When Gwillim's thrust darted in at him, the taller and more powerful member of the phase slashed downward, the blade of his axe striking the flat of Gwillim's blade. The vibration resounded through the metal, briefly catching Gwillim off guard. Grimm followed up in a matter of seconds, the blades of his axe speeding toward Gwillim's exposed throat. The member of the *Erieal* raised his sword and took the brunt of the blow with his steel. The force of the impact sent Gwillim sprawling to the ground. Grimm charged after his prey, axe ready to strike the final blow, but Gwillim was quicker. Seeing the larger man coming, Gwillim rolled forward and slashed at the man's knees, cutting them out from under him. Grimm screamed in pain and fell to the ground. Gwillim followed up, burying the tip of his sword in the larger man's back, driving the point of his blade deep in the large beating heart.

Gideon was not faring as well in his battle as dagger after dagger bounced off the hardened exterior of the phase Warron. It would only be a matter of time before Warron would be on Gideon, and his speed would be no match for the incredible power that the phase could bring to bear. As another dagger bounced off Warron's chest, the phase reached into the powers of the Blaze and used his powers to make the ground beneath

Gideon's feet give way. Gideon slipped, falling to the ground, and though he tried to roll, Gideon realized that the floor had taken hold of him. After a minor use of power, Gideon found himself freed, but Warron was right there in his face. A hard punch claimed the former thief in the chest, shattered his sternum and forcing all the air out of his lungs. Gideon collapsed to the ground, all of the breath and life nearly knocked out of him. Warron smiled evilly and then bent down to take Gideon by the throat. Gwillim took the opportunity to insert himself into the fight, slashing with his diamond hard blade at the phase's exposed throat. The blow sounded like an avalanche, and when Gwillim's sword finally emerged from the other side of Warron's throat, the head rolled off the phase's shoulders and hit the ground with a loud thud. Because of the alterations made to his body however, the headless form stood still clutching Gideon's lifeless form in its hand.

* * * * * * * * * * * *

Jerrard and Storm stood back to back as the twin phasia Rael and Trece circled them. Jerrard had seen the twins fight once before, on the Island of Mist in the last generation, and he knew how dangerous they could be. Jerrard held his perfect black blade ready for any attack that would come at him, and Storm too seemed ready to fight. With perfect precision, Rael and Trece attacked, slashing and feinting at both the father and son. Jerrard found himself matched with Trece, while Storm pulled the more difficult job of handling the man Rael. Jerrard feared for his son, as that Jerrard has seen Rael fight Gwydeon Sandar to a standstill, and very nearly beat him. The black clad phase stepped forward and lowered his sword and his body into a combat stance. The next second, both of the combatants moved in unison, drawing back their blades and swinging fully at their opponent. The two swords met with a shower of sparks. Rael and Storm both leaned into one another, fighting for some kind of leverage advantage, but the two were too equal in strength. They were nearly mirror images of one another in power, but Jerrard knew that Rael was far more skillful than his son. As they disengaged the leverage duel, they circled one another with swords lowered. Rael was the first to strike, as he leapt at Storm with his sword raised high and it came down with a quick downward slash. The blow was parried as Storm fell to one knee and raised his sword above his head. He then slashed at the phase's knees, but Rael was quick enough to jump away from his prey and avoid the strike. Storm was slow to get back to his feet, but he never took his eyes off of Rael. The two warriors began to circle one another again. This time Storm charged, but as soon as he saw the strike would miss, he pulled his sword in and allowed his momentum to carry him into a roll that brought him under the path of Rael's sword. At the end of the roll, Storm popped up to a knee and brought his sword up in time to stop Rael from hurrying into another strike. However, Rael had seen this tactic before and his blade sped under the parry of the young prince and found the soft flesh of his chest. The tip of the blade pierced through and claimed Storm's heart, killing him instantly.

Jerrard stayed a safe distance from Trece as he began to circle the beautiful woman. The two circled each other at a very fast speed. Jerrard knew the kind of speed that both Rael and Trece had at their disposal, and he was hoping that Storm was distracting Rael enough to keep the twins from operating at their full capability. The respect was there, and the combatants were ready to fully test the skills of the other. Jerrard charged Trece and their swords met time and time again as the two tried to find some inch of opening that they could exploit to draw first blood. Steel flashed and sparks flew as the two swords challenged one another for superiority. The blur of motion was almost too much to keep up with as the white clad Trece and the black clad Jerrard danced around one another with deadly precision. They moved at incredible speeds, blocking slashes and thrusts that few other swordsmen could duplicate, let alone block. It was as if any moment one of the two would slip, and a strike would land that would prove to be fatal. It would only be a matter of time. The combatants broke apart again. However, Trece charged seconds later, and Jerrard was ready. As the two combatants passed one another, Jerrard channeled all of the powers at his disposal into his muscles as Basille had taught him long ago. Time slowed to a crawl in Jerrard's mind, and he could see a huge opening in Trece's defenses that he could exploit. Trece's charge ended with Jerrard's blade buried deep in her gut. The tip of the blade sped deeper into the woman's body, piercing her lung and sending blood pouring from around the dark black blade. When Jerrard withdrew his blade and turned, he found himself faced with the phase Rael, and looked down to see the body of his son Storm laying on the ground.

Rael frown when he looked down at the body of his twin sister Trece, and he felt an emptiness inside of him. Jerrard held his blood soaked blade aloft and waited for Rael to respond to the challenge. However, instead of defending himself, Rael dropped to his knees and laid his blade on the ground and gathered Trece in his arms.

"There is no point to this battle Jerrard," Rael said firmly. "Not when I cannot enjoy what life remains with my sister. Send me to meet her, Jerrard. Make it quick."

Jerrard, though puzzled, nodded silently and brought the tip of his blade up to Rael's back. After a small yet strong push, Rael's heart was impaled and within a matter of seconds he was sent to meet his sister on the Other Side.

* * * * * * * * * * * *

Rand watched as the phase Farax stalked the young timid little girl who he had heard called Sabrina, and so he moved in some effort to defend her. For some reason he felt compelled to protect the girl. However, his plan was cut off, as the phase Zarsi intercepted him.

"So, you are Jeroch's grandson. You are about as unimpressive as your father."

Rand took a moment to draw his sword and then to take hold of the string of Air that lay hidden in the back of his mind. There was no way that Zarsi could know that Rand was a member of the *Erieal* and if he was fast enough, he would be able to protect the girl before Farax had an opportunity to attack. Zarsi was quick to pull on the powers of the Blaze and send a beam of energy crashing towards Rand, but the young man drew on all of the training that he had growing up and anticipated the attack. Charging forward, Rand slashed several times at the phase, but the slashes were purposefully wide. Zarsi stepped into Rand and struck the boy with his palm directly in the center of his chest. There was an explosion of power, and Rand could feel the breath starting to be knocked from him. However, thanks to his control of the forces of the air, Rand was not incapacitated by the blow. Rather, he feigned unconsciousness, keeping enough oxygen in his lungs with his powers over the air to keep him alive without breathing. Zarsi took several steps toward the boy, all the time watching for any movement. He had not hit the boy that hard, but perhaps he was just a weakling like the rest of his family. Suddenly the boy's eyes shot open and Zarsi felt a constricting power around his throat. Rand used his powers over the air effectively, choking off the sweet oxygen from Zarsi's lungs and driving him into the sweet and permanent slumber of death. Zarsi finally fell to the floor, and Rand turned just in time to see Farax use his powers to lift into the air, ready to swoop down on the unsuspecting girl. It took only a minor use of power for Rand to knock Farax off his course, sending him tumbling through the air out of control. Sabrina showed some initiative, drawing the formerly shattered Sword of the Ram from her side and slashing at Farax as he tumbled by. The blow was enough to draw some blood, but the girl was quick to follow up with a stream of pure white flame that burned the flying phase to a crisp. Rand smiled to himself as he watched the girl take pleasure in her kill, but his distraction did not allow him to see Zarsi rise from where he had fallen. Rand had not been complete in his attack, and the phase had survived. When Rand turned to look for another enemy to strike at, Zarsi was there in his face, and a sword of pure Order jutted from his hand and pierced the boy's heart. Rand gasped in pain, a sound that alerted Sabrina to the fact that something was wrong. When she turned, Sabrina saw Rand drop to the ground, and so she channeled another blast of pure white flame. Zarsi was in no position to try and dodge the assault, and found himself dying for a second time. Sabrina clutched the Sword of the Ram hard and then looked on in horror as her savior Pike Rhuiden battled toe to toe with the power-mad patron Emries.

* * * * * * * * * * * *

Jeroch watched as the three mortals took the fight to Emries, and was about to add his sword to the battle, but he saw a form clad in black with a sword of pure Chaos streak before him. The memories from the part of Jeroch that came from the Dark Mirror reality told Jeroch that the man was named Draven, and the hatred ran deep within him.

"I've been looking forward to this, Jeroch," Draven said coldly. "Now, let's see who is the best of the phasia once and for all."

Jeroch sneered.

"With pleasure."

Draven lunged at Jeroch, but the blow was easily parried and countered. On and on the two combatants circled each other, but with each step, Draven became more cocky and predictable. Finally Draven lashed out again, catching Jeroch's right shoulder, drawing a plume of blood from the wound. Jeroch took a step back from the combat and looked at the ripped fabric of the shirt and the matted fabric that had begun to stick to the wound. But true to form, Draven continued to be cocky and overconfident in his attacks, and the slashes were wild and predictable.

"I've drawn your blood first," Draven said between attacks, "and now I shall end your life."

Jeroch dodged two or three of the strikes to get Draven's timing, and then he slashed at the arrogant phase catching his chest in a broad arching slash. Blood flowed from the wound and Draven leaped back stunned. That was a shock of reality to the phase, and he started to take his opponent more seriously. Again the combatants circled each other, but the battle was nearing its end. It was then that Draven showed his true skill. Jeroch stepped in and slashed twice, but Draven parried both blows and landed another slash to Jeroch's chest. The target for the final strike was now perfectly marked.

"Now, why does this seem familiar," Draven said scanning the memories of the Blaze as he watched Jeroch stagger back from the twin blows. "Oh yes, wasn't this how Gwydeon killed you in the last generation?"

Jeroch scowled.

"Now, after I finish with you, I will make sure that I do the same to him."

Jeroch snarled and charged forward. As the First of the Shadow came in for his final attack, Draven stepped under the arching slash and buried the point of his blade into the very center of Jeroch's chest. Jeroch gasped in shock at the impact, a shower of blood erupting from his open mouth. As Jeroch fell, Draven pulled his blade free and smiled to himself. There was only one more opponent in his way, and as the phase turned his eyes found the object of his obsession, the Brother of Angels.

* * * * * * * * * * * *

Gwydeon stood over the fallen body of his wife Midarin and stared down at Nathan with all of the fire and hatred he could muster. Every part of him was screaming to strike down the boy, and yet part of him was still trying to hold back because it was his son. However, when Nathan took the initiative and lashed out with a sword of Order, Gwydeon had no choice but to defend himself. Blow after blow the young man struck at his father, and Gwydeon stayed on the defensive, content to parry and dodge. It seemed though that the boy was tiring of the game. He pulled deeper and deeper on the powers at his disposal as the embodiment of the powers of the *Coromor* in the third generation, making himself stronger and faster. Gwydeon could feel the difference in each strike, and as the power level of the thrusts and slashes grew, Gwydeon had to employ more of his power just to keep up. Nathan then began to employ some of the lessons that his father had taught him about swordsmanship, turning one of Gwydeon's own parries against him, and stepping into the blow. Gwydeon found himself unprepared for the tactic and when Nathan darted forward and thrust the point of his blade toward his father's heart, something within Gwydeon clicked. Wings batting wildly, Gwydeon flew away from the lethal strike, and then stared hard into the eyes of the boy that he had raised. However, the boy staring back at him was not his son, but simply an empty shell. Somehow the cold stare emboldened Gwydeon, making him wish to fight and accomplish the goal that was ahead of him. So, when he and the boy crossed swords again, it was Gwydeon who took the offensive, slashing and countering everything that came his way. It was clear that the boy was no match for the power of his father, and after several counters and feints Gwydeon found his blade buried in the chest of his son. Gwydeon had been operating on pure instinct and there was too much skill and power for the young man to handle. When Gwydeon withdrew his blade, he had a clapping coming from off to his right. Looking over, hatred boiled within Gwydeon as his eyes locked on Draven.

"So," Draven said smiling, "how does it feel to kill your own son."

Gwydeon growled.

"Not as good as it will feel to kill you."

Draven laughed.

"Unfortunately that is a feeling you will never have."

Gwydeon raised his blade and took a step toward the phase.

"Let's finish this."

* * * * * * * * * * * *

Emries watched as the forces gathered around him. There was very little time left for the world, and warriors for both the Light and the Shadow had fallen in great number in the Council chamber. Wolf, Pike, and Eldar stood firm waiting for another opportunity to strike. Sabrina, Jerrard and Gwillim stood close by ready to lend their aid as well.

"Give it up Emries," Wolf said coldly, "you are outnumbered, and eventually we will get to you and take you out of this little war. We've made our choice."

Emries smiled.

"Oh have you now little Ranthall?" the god asked. "Well, perhaps then I should show you the true power of what you are facing."

Emries pointed at Gwillim.

"You are here because of me whelp, and yet you still fight. I was the one that spared your life when your so-called father Gwydeon killed your mother while you were still in her womb. Had it not been for my intervention you would have never been born, and you would have never been there to help Korrd and the rest of the pathetic People of the Dragon to vanquish Shau-ling in the last generation. Do you still renounce me?"

Gwillim took a step forward.

"I have done my part in the last war, and I am doing my part in this war as well. It doesn't matter how I got here, but I am going to do what is right. So, yes, Emries, I renounce you for what it right."

Emries snapped his fingers and Gwillim disappeared.

"He renounced me, and therefore he renounced the life that I gave him."

Pike griped *Fury* tightly.

"You bastard."

Emries laughed and extended his hand. A bolt of power flew impossibly fast across the room and claimed Eldar in the throat. The woman dropped to the ground, all life stolen out of her.

"The Blaze may have brought her back to life, but it is my spark, my power that allowed her to live in the first place. She was an abomination, and so I ended her life."

Pike growled and turned to rush Emries. However, a form stepped in front of Pike. Evan Sinn had listened to everything that had been said and could not listen to any more.

"And what about me Emries," Evan said with the golden sword Justice in his hand, "can you make me disappear just by snapping your fingers? Can you strike me down with a single blow?"

Emries' eyes widened.

"You can't can you? I not only renounce you, but I renounce Shau-ling as well. I will follow no one except for the Creator, and will follow the covenant of the Creator as long as he allows me to."

Emries laughed.

"This world has been doomed by the blind faith of the human race, and when either the Light or the Shadow are victorious, the final sentence of the Creator will be handed down and this world will cease to exist. Your precious Creator will strike you down."

Evan shook his head.

"Neither the Light nor the Shadow will be victorious, Emries. Only the humans that you have been lying to for their entire existence."

Evan raised his sword and sank back into a defensive posture.

"Now, raise your sword and meet your fate like a human."

CHAPTER 44

Epilogue

To Kill a God

Creator's Calendar Year 1205

Gwydeon and Draven stood eye to eye, waiting for the other to make a move. The war had come down to this, the last visage of pure evil against the highest champion of good. It wasn't about the war between the Light and the Shadow, and it had transcended the war between Emries and Shauling. Unlike the battle that Evan Sinn was about to fight, nothing more rode on the battle between these two men than simply life and death. Their grudge was personal, and it ran deeper than any loyalty to either side. Gwydeon's crystalline blade sang with power, and as he slowly brought the blade to bare, Draven smiled and pointed the tip of his blade at his enemy. In a moment it would begin, and for those last few seconds, there was only the silent battle of hard stares. Finally, Draven broke the standoff and charged at his opponent. The first two attacks were slightly off the mark and assisted Gwydeon in the parrying of the blows. However, Gwydeon was fighting this battle to win. Fighting the good fight for the pleasure of it was no longer an option. The only pleasure would be brought by seeing Draven's dead form lying on the floor of the Council Chambers. There were no prophecies, no obligations, only need.

Draven charged again, this time, the blade of his sword of Chaos meeting with the pure white blade of Gwydeon's sword. The phase knew that he could not stand in a strength battle with Gwydeon, so he broke the contact quickly and began to fire more rapid thrusts in the enemy's direction. Gwydeon could feel the pace of the battle beginning to pick up. Draven was channeling all of the power that he could manage into the muscles of his legs, allowing him to move at incredible speeds while retaining the cat-like agility he had always possessed. Strikes flowed into parries and counters. The two men moved at incredible speeds, neither making a mistake. Sensing an opening, Gwydeon called on some of the power that he held in reserve and boosted his strength. With a single slash, Gwydeon broke through Draven's defense. The crystalline blade ripped through the fabric of the phase's shirt and left a long bloody trail. After the strike, the two men separated and stood staring at one another.

Draven growled and charged, several strikes coming in rapid succession, but Gwydeon was able to keep pace with them all. However, Draven had another trick up his sleeve. As Gwydeon parried another of Draven's attack, the phase spun in toward Gwydeon, letting a small dagger of Chaos form in his off hand. At the end of the feint, Draven buried the tip of the dagger into Gwydeon's gut, twisting and turning the blade as deep as he could before disengaging. Gwydeon staggered back, shocked by the blow. Taking advantage of the situation, Draven charged in again, slashing with deadly precision. Reflex took over for Gwydeon as he found himself blocking blows that should have killed him. Finally Gwydeon pulled himself away from the shock and pain and launched another attack, this time though, there would be no salvation for the phase.

Faster and faster the two men pushed through the attacks, forcing the other to accelerate even faster until they moved at such a pace that the winds were changing with their every move. Flashes of light were the only clue to their true positions, but even those indicators were several seconds behind. Finally Gwydeon saw the opening that he was waiting for. The phase parried one of Gwydeon blows very low and close to his body. Pulling on all of the power that still remained open to him, Gwydeon accelerated himself one last time, penetrating Draven's defenses and slashing hard at the exposed throat of the devil. For the next few moments, time stopped. Draven and Gwydeon stared at one another, but then the phase's eyes glazed over, and the head rolled from the shoulders and the entire body of the phase crumbled to the ground, all life stolen.

"It's hard to be a king with no head upon which to set your crown," Gwydeon said walking toward the battle that still raged between the patron Emries and Evan Sinn. "And this time, you'll stay dead."

* * * * * * * * * * * *

Emries let Evan's insult pass through him before letting the pure crystalline sword the only true embodiment of his power form in his ready and waiting hand. Reaching out with his powers, Emries had seen the strength that rested within the confines of the human Evan Sinn, and while at the same time it both pleased and scared the god, it would not be enough competition. Aerith Seth had power while he was alive, and it was only Emries' own decree that had allowed Aerith's immortal life to be ended. But Aerith had passed his powers along like a good little servant to the next *Chosen One* of the prophecies. However, Aerith had kept more power hidden away, and now he had chosen to give it to this man who called himself Sinn. How fitting, Emries thought, that he would be able to crush Sinn and save his mortals from the Shadow. It had a poetic ring to it. In one fell swoop he would end the rebellion of the arrogant humans, crush Aerith Seth's remaining powers, and end any threat that his brother could have ever posed to him.

Evan stood brandishing the golden sword, his feet set firmly on the white floor of the Council Chamber. He never felt more ready for any combat in his life, and he could not shake the feeling that whether he won or lost the duel, that the human race would still be victorious. In a moment it would begin, and Emries could not feel the same confidence swell in him that had been there though every other battle in his life. The mortal should have had no chance against him, but there was doubt in Emries heart. Evan waited for Emries to make the first move, not knowing whether he would charge or send bolts of power flying toward him. Emries had shown the type of power at his command through his murder of both Gwillim and Eldar, but Evan would not allow himself to be caught off guard by anything the patron chose to send in his direction. Emries had fought against the force of the Blaze from his first day on this world, but now he was faced with a power that he had never known existed, the power of a mortal. Aerith did not owe his allegiance to anyone but himself and the neutrality that he had always subscribed to. In the final moments of the war, realization crept into Evan's mind, a realization that was far more profound than anything he had discovered during his investigations into the nature of the war between Light and Shadow. Aerith Seth's power, and his adherence to neutrality was the very ideology that Halicon had wanted all of his creations to embrace. It was the very thing that forced Aryx Terian to walk away from his master, the force that had kept the war from spinning out of control in every generation, and now Evan was going to teach that lesson to the fallen god.

Emries charged forward with his flawless crystalline blade high above his head. Evan readied for the strike, and when the crystalline blade arched down and struck the golden blade of Justice, the sound of rolling thunder resounded through the chamber. Heartbeats passed as the two combatants leaned into the cross of the perfect blades. Emries face was calm and smooth while Evan's forehead beaded with sweat as he poured every bit of his strength into the contest of wills. As the moments passed, Evan could feel the power in him begin to surge, and he opened himself up to it. When he had first been exposed to the powers, he felt as if he could move mountains with his bare hands. The feeling entered him once again, and as he leaned into the cross of blade, he felt the advantage forming. Sensing this, Emries pushed forward with all of his might, but it was to no avail. With a matter of seconds, Emries was sent sprawling to the ground where he came to rest near the far wall of the chamber. The self-proclaimed god slowly rose to his feet and renewed a firm grip on the hilt of his weapon. The stalking would continue as the two began to circle one another, looking for an opportunity to strike. Suddenly Evan lashed out with his blade, but Emries was ready, easily parrying the long diagonal slash with a block tight to his body. Sensing a weakness, Evan pressed, thrusting deep into the defenses of the white-clad Emries. However, Emries would not let his blood be shed that easily. Using barely a trickle of the power at his disposal, Emries accelerated his movements, and while the point of Justice would have pierced the heart of a lesser opponent, in this duel it found merely air. To his credit, Evan was quick to recover his senses and turn to face Emries, and but was met not with a gasp of relief, but a knowing smile.

"Too slow for you, Emries," Evan taunted, feeling the cockiness of Aerith Seth entering him. "Then let's pick up the pace a little."

The two charged at each other the next moment, their swords meeting with the violent sounds of thunder. The feeling out process was over, and each let the powers flow through them as blocks became parries that became thrusts that became repasts. Faster and faster the two moved, streaks of gold following like ghostly trails behind the movements of Justice, and trails of white hanging in the air where the crystalline blade had been only moments earlier. The former members of the People of the Dragon and others in the room watched as the men disappeared from view, leaving only flashes of light to track their movements by. Even though they could not see the battle, they knew it was a bloody one as plumes of red hit the air, and there were growing pools of blood on the floor. For some reason, Sabrina could sense the way the battle was turning, feeling the blows that Evan was landing on the god Emries, and wincing in pain when the crystalline blade ripped through the skin of the embodiment of Aerith Seth's powers. She was still the *Chosen One*, and so she made a choice. Opening herself up to the powers within her, Sabrina drew on Jerrard, Wolf, and Lissa, pulling their energies into her and mixing it with those of the *Chosen One*. With a single burst, Sabrina channeled the powers through her mind into the body of Evan Sinn that moved faster than her eyes could perceive. Evan fought for the mortals, and Sabrina had cast her lot in with his battle. Evan could feel the new power surge through him, and it was as though a hole that existed within him was suddenly filled. Aerith's mantle had been returned to mix with the rest of his power, and as Evan channeled it, he moved even faster than he moved before. But there was something more; another power that Evan had not expected. Halicon too had finally added his powers to the fray, fulfilling the debt he owed to the ancient man who had risked his very existence to save the life of one he had no reason to save. Emries could do nothing as his opponent slashed and thrust toward him, cutting into his body with a tenacity that could not be match. Rage filled Evan the next moment and he struck with all of his might at the god.

All that the heroes in the Council chamber could hear was a huge clap of thunder and then they felt the sweet rain that fell out of thin air. Evan and Emries reappeared the next moment, and when everyone saw Emries slump to the ground, all life robbed from him, they knew it was finally over. Evan nearly collapsed himself, long cuts marking his body, but Meredith and Pike were over to the man in a heartbeat, supporting his weight. The falling rain quickly healed most of the wounds of the remaining warriors, but many of Evan's wounds resisted healing. He would bear the scars for the rest of his days, badges of honor and shame worn for the whole of the human race.

"It's finally over," Evan said slowly, his breath quick and erratic.

"Not yet," Gwydeon said looking at Halicon who stood watching.

"There is no need to end my life, Gwydeon Sandar," Halicon answered. "Shau-ling and his phasia are long dead. Only Halicon remains now, his quest to destroy his rebellious brother is finally at an end. I look forward to a rest, and I pray that the Creator sees fit to give it to me."

It was then that an angelic light filled the room and a voice spoke in the back of everyone's mind. The voice was one that every creature knew from its birth. It was the voice of the Creator.

"AND SO IT ENDS HERE IN THE BIRTHPLACE OF THE WAR. YOU MORTALS HAVE DONE WELL TO FIND THE PATH THAT I HAVE LAYED FOR YOU, THOUGH I AM CONCERNED THAT THE OTHERS OF YOUR KIND MAY NOT HAVE LEARNED THE LESSON THAT THEY WERE MEANT TO LEARN. THOSE WITH POWER WILL ALWAYS LEAD AND THERE WILL ALWAYS BE THOSE THAT FOLLOW NO MATTER THE HORRIBLE PATH THAT THEY MAY WALK"

Evan stepped away from the supporting arms and spoke to the light.

"But as long as mortals have a choice, they will eventually find their way back to the path that you have set for them."

"AND FOR THAT YOU ARE TO ALL BE REWARDED WITH A NEW START AND A NEW LIFE. THE WORLD THAT YOU HAVE INHABITIED CANNOT BE SAVED, FOR THE DESTRUCTION AND DEVISTATION CAUSED BY THE MERGING OF THE TWO WORLDS CANNOT BE REVERSED, EVEN BY THE CREATOR. SO I HAVE CONSTRUCTED A NEW WORLD FOR MY CHILDREN TO LIVE UPON. PERHAPS THIS TIME THEY WILL HAVE A CHANCE TO PROSPER WITHOUT THE LURE OF MEN LIKE EMRIES. ALL

OF THE INNOCENTS WILL BE SPARED THE MEMORY OF THIS EVIL PLACE AND THE HORROR OF THE KNOWLEDGE THAT THEY HAVE SURVIVED THIS TERRIBLE WAR. BUT FOR YOU, THE HEROES, YOU WILL BEAR THE MOST BURDEN FROM ALL OF THIS. THOUGH YOU TOO WILL BE SPARED FROM THE FIRE, YOU WILL HAVE TO BEAR THE MEMORY OF ALL THAT YOU HAVE SEEN HERE. YOU MUST BE THE ONES TO LEAD IN THE NEW LIFE THAT IS TO COME, AND YOU MUST ENSURE THAT THE BATTLE BETWEEN LIGHT AND DARKNESS NEVER SPINS OUT OF CONTROL AS THEY HAVE HERE. ALWAYS REMEMBER THAT THOSE WHO DO NOT LEARN FROM THE PAST ARE DOOMED TO FIND THEIR FUTURE LITTERED WITH THE SAME PITFALLS AND FAILURES. THIS IS WHY YOU ARE TO BE SPARED."

The glow of light intensified, and when it receded, Pike, Sabrina, Wolf, Lissa, and Jerrard were gone. Gwydeon, Midarin, Evan, Meredith, and Halicon looked at one another for a moment, but found all of their questions answered when the voice returned to their minds.

"YOU HAVE ALL PROGRESSED PAST THE POINT I BELIEVED POSSIBLE FOR YOUR KIND. THE NOBILITY AND STRENGTH THAT YOU HAVE SHOWN IN THE FACE OF THIS AWESOME UNDERTAKING HAS SHOWN ME THAT THE HUMANS WERE WORTH SAVING. FOR THAT I WILL REWARD YOU ALL. GWYDEON SANDAR, I HAVE GIVEN YOU A GIFT UNLIKE ANY OTHER, AND I NOW GIVE YOU THE CHOICE. YOUR WIFE MIDARIN LIVES AND WILL LIVE FOR MANY YEARS IN THE NEW WORLD THAT I HAVE CREATED. I ALLOW YOU THE CHOICE OF WHETHER OR NOT YOU WISH TO RETURN WITH HER TO THE NEW WORLD OR IF YOU WISH TO REMAIN WITH ME AS MY EMISSARY TO THE MANY WORLDS THAT I HAVE CREATED."

Gwydeon turned to look at Midarin. Part of him wanted to go, but the love for his wife was holding him back. He wanted so much to be with her that he could not let her go.

"I am grateful for the chance you have given me," Gwydeon said looking back at the light, "but I wish to be with Midarin and raise the child that is on its way. This child will have a chance to live in the new world that is before us, and I have to be there to make sure that it knows the right path that we have fought to find."

"THOUGH I KNEW THE CHOICE YOU WOULD MAKE BEFORE THE OFFER WAS MADE, BROTHER OF ANGELS, THE NEEDS FOR YOU TO MAKE THE CHOICE WAS THE ONLY WAY YOU WOULD ACCEPT WHAT MUST HAPPEN. THE MORTAL WORLD IS NOT FOR YOU ANY LONGER, JUST AS IT IS NOT FOR YOUR FELLOW HEROES. I SHALL BRING YOU TO THE HEAVENS WHERE YOU AND YOUR CONTEMPORARIES SHALL HELP TO STEER A NEW AGE. YOUR CHILD SHALL BE THE FIRST IN A NEW ORDER OF GODS AND ANGELS, AND THE SURVIVORS OF THIS WORLD SHALL LOOK UP THE HEAVENS AND KNOW THAT THEIR FATE HAS BEEN PAID FOR WITH BLOOD AND DEVOTION UNLIKE ANY EVER SEEN."

The light flared again and Gwydeon and Midarin were gone.

"HALICON, YOU HAVE DONE ALL THAT I COULD EVER ASK OF YOU. THOUGH YOU STUMBLED ALONG THE WAY, YOU LEARNED FROM YOUR ERRORS AND FOUND THAT THE TRUE STRENGTH WAS NOT WITHIN THE BLAZE OR EVEN WITHIN YOURSELF, BUT IN FAITH. YOU HAD FAITH IN THE END THAT THE MORTALS WOULD FIND THE TRUE PATH AND THEY WOULD BE THE INSTRUMENT TO OVERTHROW EMRIES. I AM PROUD OF YOU MY SON, AND YOU ARE FREE TO RETURN TO THE HALLS OF CREATION."

The light flared one last time, and Halicon was gone. Then the light disappeared completely. Evan and Meredith stood looking at one another trying to figure out what would happen next. Evan took several steps forward.

"Did we do something wrong?" Meredith asked.

Suddenly the light returned.

"NO CHILD, YOU HAVE NOT DONE ANYTHING WRONG, IN FACT YOU HAVE DONE EVERYTHING THAT YOU WERE EVER TOLD TO DO, AND IT WAS BECAUSE OF YOU THAT I HAVE LEARNED THE TRUE NATURE OF THOSE THAT I HAVE CREATED. I CANNOT ALLOW YOU TO INHABIT THE NEW WORLD THAT I HAVE CREATED I AM AFRAID, BUT I HAVE OTHER TASKS FOR YOU TO ACCOMPLISH. THERE ARE MANY WORLDS THAT ARE UNDER MY CONTROL, AND I NEED AN ENVOY TO WALK AMONG THE PEOPLE OF THESE WORLDS AND FIND THE NATURE OF WHAT AILS THEIR WORLD. YOU WILL HELP THEM TO FIX WHAT HAS GONE WRONG, AND YOU WILL MAKE SURE THAT NO OTHER WORLD HAS TO FACE THE DESTRUCTION THAT THIS WORLD HAS. THIS GAME THAT SPUN OUT OF CONTROL BETWEEN TWO OF MY CHILDREN IS BEING REPLICATED ON OTHER WORLDS, AND IT CANNOT BE ALLOWED. THE TWO OF YOU SHALL FIND A PATH IN WHICH ALL CAN BE MADE RIGHT AGAIN, NO MATTER THE COST."

Evan smiled and nodded. He knew from the moment that he had been given Aerith Seth's powers that his life would never be the same again, and when the light flashed in the room once again, and he felt the powers flood around him, Evan felt a peace fill his heart. The last sensation Evan felt was that of Meredith's hand taking hold of his.

* * * * * * * * * * * *

In the ruins of the city of Aradon, Rael and Trece stood hand in hand looking at the book of the Creator, reading the lessons that should have been available for the mortals from the day of their birth. When they came to the passage detailing the life joining ritual, both smiled at one another and began to read the words aloud. Even with the howling wind and impending rain, the two stood together repeating the words to one another, bonding their lives together for as long as each held breath. When the final words were spoken the two embraced and then a wave of bright light passed over the two, and when the light faded, both the lovers and the book had disappeared.

* * * * * * * * * * * *

Bryn sat impatiently in the little cottage outside of the city of Frontier. Taya had left several minutes ago to find food and supplies until someone came to get them. The earthquakes and fires were beginning to get worse, and Bryn wondered how long it would be before the entire planet pulled itself apart. As Bryn was searching through her wardrobe for something more fitting to wear, she heard the door open behind her. She spun around, fully expecting to see Taya had returned with an arm full of supplies. However, the face of Aerith Seth greeted her. He stood proudly in the doorway, smiling. His sword no long hung at his side, and his cloak had been discarded. On top of his shoulder sat a ball of black fur that Bryn recognized, but she was not threatened by it. As Aerith saw Bryn's eyes move to the Snag, he laughed to himself, picked it up off his shoulder and then sat it on the ground by the door.

"Stay," he said quietly to the Snag, eliciting a purr in response.

Aerith turned back to Bryn and approached her smiling.

"I always keep my promises."

`Bryn smiled and nearly melted as Aerith took her into his arms.

"No more powers, no more responsibilities, no more wars," Aerith said stroking her hair. "Just peace together for the rest of our lives."

Bryn looked up into Aerith's eyes, and as his lips touched hers in a tender kiss, a bright white light flooded through the room.

And in the Heavens, sitting upon His golden throne, the Creator looked out upon the whole of Creation and felt the emptiness begin to fill him. The battle between two of his Children had come to an end, but there had been no resolution. Soon there would be a reckoning, a final resolution to the question that had plagued the Creator since He first looked out upon the vast nothingness of the Cosmos. As he looked down upon the new infant world He had created, plans began to whirl in His mind.

Appendicies

Dramatis Personae

Cedric Binosear
The Lord Lion
First *Coromor* of the Prophecies
Twin Brother of Anabel Binosear
Son of Aerith Seth

Anabel Binosear
Sister of Cedric Binosear
Mother of Cairyn Binosear
Murdered by Aldridge Farran
Daughter of Aerith Seth

Arathorn Geoffry
Earth *Erieal* of the First Generation of
the Prophecies
Brother of Diana Geoffry Terian

Mailock
Member of the Moridon Tribe
Water *Erieal* of the First Generation
of the Prophecies

Aryx Terian
White Lightning
Fire *Erieal* of the First Generation of
the Prophecies
Husband of Diana Geoffry Terian
Former Host of Nightwing

Diana Terian Geoffry
Wind *Erieal* of the First Generation of
the Prophecies
Sister of Arathorn Geoffry
Wife of Aryx Terian
Mother of Lissa Terian

Arin Ranthall
First *Chosen One* of the Prophecies
Husband of Victoria Rhuiden
Father of Logan Ranthall
Father of Korrd Ranthall

Victoria Rhuiden
Sister of Tam Rhuiden
Wife of Arin Ranthall
Mother of Logan Ranthall

Logan Ranthall
The Lord Dragon
Second *Chosen One* of the Prophecies
Brother of Korrd Ranthall
First Cousin of Pike Rhuiden
Husband of Elwyne Tamerlane
Ranthall
Father of Wolf Ranthall

Elwyne Tamerlane Ranthall
Sister of David Tamerlane
Wife of Logan Ranthall
Mother of Wolf Ranthall

Korrd Ranthall
Second *Coromor* of the Prophecies
Brother of Logan Ranthall
Son of Arin Ranthall and Ellis
Chandara
Father of Gwillim Sandar

Pike Rhuiden
Water *Erieal* of the Second
Generation of the Prophecies
Son of Tam Rhuiden
Best Friend of Talon Aielin
First Cousin of Logan Ranthall
Eldar Merin's Former Husband
Lord of Kandor, Marcwell, and
Trelon
Husband of Cairyn Binosear
Father of Duncan Rhuiden and
Sabrina Binosear

Gwydeon Sandar
Son of Torris Sandar
Brother of Bella Sandar
Husband of Midarin Rice Sandar
Father of Nathaniel Sandar
Killed in the Battle of the Hall of
Terrors by Jeroch Yetre

Eldar Merin
Daughter of Alfred and Ariel Merin
Best Friend of Elwyne Tamerlane
Wife of Pike Rhuiden
Killed by Taron Steen at the Battle of
Taren

Emries
The First *Coromor*

Talon Aielin
Wind *Erieal* of the Second
Generation of the Prophecies
Best Friend of Pike Rhuiden
Killed during battle with Shau-ling

Arin Domae
Fire *Erieal* of the Second Generation
of the Prophecies
Former Soldier of the Army of Brea
Killed during Battle of the Hall of
Terrors

David Tamerlane
Brother of Elwyne Tamerlane
Killed in destruction of Aradon

Lane Toridon
Apprentice Magician
Killed by Taron Steen during battle of
Taren

Tam Rhuiden
Aradon City Council Member
Brother of Victoria Rhuiden
Father of Pike Rhuiden

Torris Sandar
Aradon City Council Member
Father of Gwydeon Sandar
Father of Bella Sandar

Gideon Viruci
Earth *Erieal* of the Second Generation
of the Prophecies
Killed in Battle with Shau-ling

Midarin Rice
Queen of the Kingdom of Brea
Wife of Gwydeon Sandar
Mother of Nathaniel Sandar
Mother of Liette Forer

Aerith Seth
General of the Hand of the Light
General of the Army of the Fox
The First *Chosen One*

Cairyn Binosear
Daughter of Anabel Binosear
Niece of Cedric Binosear
Queen of the Kingdoms of Kandor,
Trelon, and Marcwell
Wife of Pike Rhuiden
Mother of Duncan Rhuiden and
Sabrina Binosear

Leane Torne
General in the Army of Rama
Former Member of the Army of Brea

Jerrard Mystic
Lord of the Kingdom of Scalla
Son of Basille Mystic
Husband of Erika Belnosian

Erika Belnosian Mystic
Wife of Jerrard Mystic

Sabrina Binosear
Third *Chosen One* of the Prophecies
Sister of Duncan Rhuiden
Daughter of Pike Rhuiden and Cairyn
Binosear

Duncan Rhuiden
Heir to the Kingdom of Marcwell
Brother of Sabrina Binosear
Son of Pike Rhuiden and Cairyn
Binosear

Lissa Terian
Fire *Erieal* of the Third Generation of
the Prophecies
Daughter of Aryx and Diana Terian
Adopted Daughter of Pike Rhuiden
and Cairyn Binosear

Liette Forer
Daughter of Midarin Rice
Sister of Nathaniel Sandar

Nathaniel Sandar
The Lord Ram
Third *Coromor* of the Prophecies
Son of Gwydeon Sandar and Midarin
Rice
Brother of Liette Forer

Gwillim Sandar
Earth *Erieal* of the Third Generation
of the Prophecies
Son of Korrd Ranthall and Gabrielle
Crill
Adopted Son of Midarin Rice

Wolf Ranthall
Son of Logan Ranthall and Elwyne
Tamerlane Ranthall

Storm Mystic
Son of Jerrard and Erika Mystic
Water *Erieal* of the Third Generation
of the Prophecies

Taya Mystic
Daughter of Jerrard and Erika Mystic

DRAMATIS PERSONAE

Taya Viruci
Daughter of Gideon Viruci and Erika
Belnosian
Dark Mirror World

Turok Korven
Member of the Enforcers

Celina Veshaw
Member of the Enforcers

Ren Dalin
Member of the Enforcers

Zak Parthan
Member of the Enforcers

Valin Kren
Member of the Enforcers

Rachel Core
Member of the Enforcers

Elizabeth Merin
Member of the Enforcers

Meredith Heron
Member of the Enforcers

Evan Sinn
Member of the Enforcers
Former Lord of Kandor
Inheritor of Aerith Seth's power

Jared Vale
Son of Caris Vale and Cedric
Binosear

Shau-ling
Master of the Shadows
Father of the Phasia

Jeroch Yetre
The Lord Shadow
First Born of the Phasia
Father of Hawk Yetre

Bryn Aplee
The Lady Fox
Member of the Brotherhood of Phasia
Former Lover of Aerith Seth
Wife of Grawn Aplee
Mother of Gideon Viruci

Ellis Chandara
The Lady Leopard
Member of the Brotherhood of Phasia
Mother of Korrd Ranthall

Grawn Aplee
The Lord Shark
Member of the Brotherhood of Phasia
Husband of Bryn Aplee

Warron Ysamaran
The Lord Boar
Member of the Brotherhood of Phasia

Basille Mystic
The Lord Raven
Member of the Brotherhood of Phasia
Father of Jerrard Mystic

Farax Soar
The Lord Vulture
Member of the Brotherhood of Phasia

The Flame
Personal Guardian of Shau-ling
Keeper of the Hall of Terrors
Originally known as Kamen, Member
of the Brotherhood of Phasia

Zarsi Aeron
The Lord Cobra
Member of the Brotherhood of Phasia

Aldridge Farran
The Lord Hawk
Member of the Brotherhood of Phasia

Saurn Macco
The Lord Viper
Member of the Brotherhood of Phasia

Caris Vale
The Lady Wolf
Member of the Brotherhood of Phasia

Erdric Yarrow
The Lord Scorpion
Member of the Brotherhood of Phasia

Taron Steen
The Lord Jackal
Member of the Brotherhood of Phasia

Draven Batoe
The Lord Crow
Member of the Brotherhood of Phasia

Rane Larion
The Lady Falcon
Member of the Brotherhood of Phasia

Stryfe Cadre
The Lord Python
Member of the Brotherhood of Phasia

Grimm Salde
The Lord Bear
Member of the Brotherhood of Phasia

Cash Griffon
The Lady Lynx
Member of the Brotherhood of Phasia

Nightwing
Member of the Dark Riders
Shau-ling's Assassin

Shadow
Member of the Dark Riders

Wrath
Member of the Dark Riders

Holocaust
Member of the Dark Riders

Vengeance
Member of the Dark Riders

Hawk Yetre
Son of Jeroch Yetre and Caris Vale

About the Author

Brian Kershner is a life-long dreamer, writer, and problem-solver. He grew up absorbing anything and everything he could get his hands on, and as a child of the Star Wars era he constantly wanted to see the worlds beyond the little Indiana town he grew up in. There was no adventure too far, and no problem too big.

Emboldened by parents who always supported his curiosity and his thoughtfulness, Brian found himself bounding from Space Camp to Laser Summer Camp to Athletic Training Camp to Piano Lessons to Football Practice to Basketball Practice to Choir Practice and back again. Despite all of the roaming and traveling, his family remained close-knit and supportive.

Though he flirted with the idea of becoming a doctor, Brian's attentions always fell back to the computer world. He got his first computer when he was six, and not long after found his way into a word processing program and began crafting his own fantastic worlds and even more fantastic characters.

As he has grown and changed and experienced life, so too have his characters. He continues to write, craft, and create; whether it is websites for his customers, or characters and worlds for his audience.